Praise for the electrifying works of
DICK COUCH

Pressure Point

"Sure to keep you on the edge of your seat."
—Clive Cussler

"A gripping insider's view of the secret world of nuclear security, counterterrorism, and post–Cold War international conflict."
—W.E.B. Griffin

Silent Descent

"Intricate plotting, exciting action, full-bodied characters and energetic dialogue. . . . Well-executed. . . . Couch maintains suspense!"
—*Publishers Weekly*

"A compelling story told by a master craftsman."
—Mark Berent, bestselling author of *Storm Flight*

Rising Wind

"Hard-as-nails adventure that will keep you riveted to your chair."
—*Stephen Coonts*

The Warrior Elite
The Forging of Seal Class 228

"Couch . . . is a well-qualified guide to this class of men."
—*The Wall Street Journal*

"Couch has written an exceptionally nuanced and insightful book."
—*The Washington Post*

The Mercenary Option

DICK COUCH

POCKET BOOKS

New York   London   Toronto   Sydney   Singapore

This book is a work of fiction. Names, characters, places and incidents are products of the author's imagination or are used fictitiously. Any resemblance to actual events or locales or persons, living or dead, is entirely coincidental.

An *Original* Publication of POCKET BOOKS

 POCKET BOOKS, a division of Simon & Schuster, Inc.
1230 Avenue of the Americas, New York, NY 10020

ISBN: 0-7434-6424-9

First Pocket Books printing November 2003

10 9 8 7 6 5 4 3 2 1

POCKET and colophon are registered trademarks of Simon & Schuster, Inc.

Cover design by Rod Hernandez
Front cover illustration by Dru Blair

Manufactured in the United States of America

For information regarding special discounts for bulk purchases, please contact Simon & Schuster Special Sales at 1-800-456-6798 or business@simonandschuster.com

For Julia,
my wife and soul mate

Acknowledgments

There are any number of people who have helped me with this book, but most work for employers who would not like to see their names in print. You know who you are, and you have my heartfelt gratitude for all your help and your patience with my persistent questions. Among those I can thank are Bob Mecoy, my agent and personal special literary operator; Mary Beth Mueller, my Arabic expert; and my editor at Pocket Books, Kevin Smith. And thanks to my loyal readers.

As you turn these pages of fiction, now and then give a thought to the real guns in the fight—the Special Forces, SEALs, Rangers, and Combat Controllers of the U.S. Special Operations Command. While I write and you read, these men stand on guard for all of us in a real and very dangerous world.

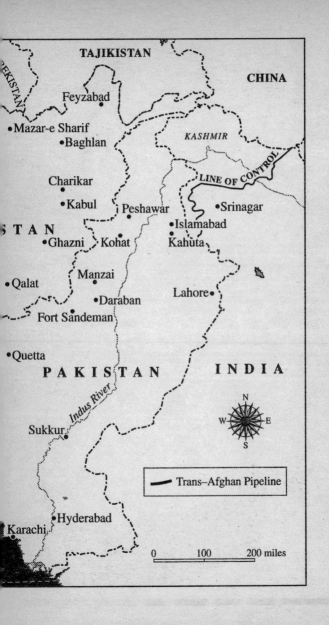

1

A tall, sparse man stepped slowly from the limousine. A blowing northeaster tugged at his thick, well-groomed hair, occasionally pulling the silver thatch away from his ample forehead. It had snowed the previous night, but much of that had melted, leaving scattered patches of soggy, wheat-colored grass pushing through the icy crust. Light rain and large flakes now slanted down from the brooding sky. A somber, well-tended man in an expensive topcoat and bowler hovered at the tall gentleman's elbow.

"This way, please, Mr. Ambassador."

He proffered a large umbrella and, walking slightly ahead, led his charge from the limousine up a shallow rise through several rows of granite markers. Another man, a clone of the one with the umbrella, quietly closed the door of the limo and followed a few steps back. Barnett & Sons had handled these affairs for the Boston Brahmins for close to two centuries. The firm was by no means an inexpensive funeral director, and had the reputation of always being discreet and thorough. Joseph Simpson, former Ambassador to Russia, now made his home on Martha's Vineyard, but he was still considered a Bostonian. Barnett & Sons had known of the death well before most in Boston; they made it their business to know when there was a death in a wealthy or important family. When the call from Simpson's office came, they asked a few polite questions and then quietly set themselves to making the arrangements.

Joseph Simpson was an impressive man in his late fifties. Normally, he exuded confidence and authority, but not today. His features were drawn, and his blue eyes, usually sharp and highly focused, were now clouded and myopic. He moved stiffly, as if with great difficulty, and he looked old and vulnerable. If Simpson seemed lost and lacking direction, the man from Barnett & Sons did not. He guided Simpson to the open grave and stepped quietly to one side. The careful distribution of artificial turf around the rectangular opening in the earth did nothing to blunt the coldness or finality of its purpose.

At Simpson's request, there had been a simple burial mass and now a small graveside ceremony at the family plot. There was no striped awning to protect close friends and business associates of the bereaved. They gathered around the grave site under a sea of umbrellas. Moments later, Simpson was joined by a stunning young woman, dressed in black. She stood near Simpson, but not too close, and clung to the arm of another man who bent to comfort her. Then six men, all but one in their mid-thirties, struggled forward with a polished walnut coffin and slid it onto a trolley at the foot of the grave. After they had joined the band of mourners, two Barnett men guided the casket smoothly over the opening. With a faint creaking, the nylon lowering straps took the strain. For several moments, the water-beaded wooden box claimed their attention. Then an elderly priest at the head of the grave cleared his throat.

"May the good Lord God bless you and keep you," he began in a thick Irish brogue. "We are gathered here to commit the worldly remains of Joseph Patrick Simpson, Jr. Please join me in prayer."

The old priest's voice strained to be heard above the wind, but true to his heritage and calling, he was most eloquent, and his words came from the heart. He asked a merciful God to receive the immortal soul of the departed and to bring comfort to the family. Joe Simpson Sr. heard almost none of it. While he stared at the box that held his firstborn, his mind flashed back to better times—his son's first communion, teaching him to drive long before he was of legal age, fishing for stripers around Buzzards Bay, shooting ducks together along the Chesapeake, his graduation from Phillips Exeter, the commencement in Harvard Yard. The images flipped through his mind like a jerky, silent black-and-white film. These reflections were punctuated by lengthy gaps of time, for Joe Simpson was a man whose business interests kept him away from home much of the time. *I'm sorry, Joey. Dear God, why couldn't it have been me instead of you? You had so much to look forward to, and I have so little. Why was it you?*

". . . dust to dust, as it was in the beginning, is now and ever shall be, world without end, amen."

"Amen," murmured the group of mourners. There was a collective motion as a number of the bundled forms crossed themselves.

"Good people, thank you for your prayers at this difficult time. And now, the family would like a few moments to themselves."

The gathered mourners moved away quickly, for the weather was every bit as bitter as the event that had brought them there. In pairs and small groups, they made their way to the line of limousines that stretched along the paved access road. The priest watched them go, then moved around to the three figures who remained. He first took Simpson's hand and squeezed it with both of his own. There was surprising strength in the old man's cold, bony fingers.

"I'll pray for him, Joe, and for you." He said no more. Experience had taught him that grieving fathers have little interest in hearing that the loss of their sons is God's will or part of His divine plan. He moved on to the young woman.

"Annie, dear, I'm so sorry," he said, also taking her hand. "I loved him, and I love you. We'll miss him." Words like these, often difficult between family members, are quite natural for an Irish priest, spoken with absolute and complete sincerity.

"Thank you, Father. Uh, Father Kelly, this is my husband, Matt."

He grasped the offered hand once again with both of his own. Father Kelly had a need to touch people. "Matthew, even at this difficult time, I'm happy to meet you." Kelly had baptized and confirmed Anne Simpson, but he had not married her. He also knew she had left the church and married away from it. Still, there was not the least hint of censure or judgment in the old cleric's voice. The priest stepped back from the three, mentally embracing them for a moment. Then he blessed them with the sign of the cross: "May Almighty God be with you and ease your burden." He raised a wide-brimmed hat, the kind worn by rural clergy in the old country, and set it firmly on the nearly bald pate, graced only with translucent wisps of white hair. Then he took his leave.

For a while, no one spoke. Then Joe turned to his daughter and son-in-law.

"I have to go, Dad," she said before he could ask her to stay. "We have to catch the next ferry if we're going to make it to Logan in time for our flight."

He started to speak, to say that if she wanted to come

back to the house for a while, his helicopter could easily get them to Logan International for their flight. Or for that matter, his private jet could take them back to St. Louis. Instead, he just nodded, knowing in his heart that nothing had changed. In most ways that counted to a father, he had lost his daughter as well as his son.

"I understand, Annie. Thank you for being here."

"Good-bye, Dad." She stepped forward, kissing him lightly on the cheek, and walked away.

Joe Simpson held himself erect with some difficulty and extended his hand. "Take care of her, Matt, please." There was a pleading in his voice, and Joseph Simpson was a man who seldom had to ask for anything.

"Yes, sir. You have my word on it." Matt looked Simpson straight in the eye as he spoke, then followed his wife to the waiting car. Strangely, amid the torrent of sympathy that had washed over Joseph Simpson during the past several days, these were the only words in which he took any measure of comfort. Simpson turned and nodded to one of the many, but seemingly invisible, attendants from Barnett & Sons.

"Now."

"Now, sir?" Family members customarily left at this time.

"Now."

Simpson watched impassively as the coffin was lowered into the ground. The spools of strapping paid out evenly so the casket remained level in its slow descent. The squeal of a single faulty roller bearing was the only sound, save for the persistent howl of the wind. This accomplished, two of the attendants returned to the waiting hearse. The others waited at a discreet distance. Joe Sr. stood there without moving, long enough for those attendants who remained to begin to lose feeling in their gloved fingers.

"Good-bye, Joey," he said, quietly enough for only the

wind and the spirit of the boy at the bottom of the grave to hear.

Simpson turned and walked a few feet to a nearby marker. He stood for a moment at the base of the small monument, then dropped to his knees. His wool trousers immediately wicked the melting snow up around his knees and shins. It was a simple granite slab with deeply-carved black lettering: "PRUDENCE SIMPSON, 1944–2000." The stone engraving continued, "Beloved Wife, Loving Mother," but the words remained blurry, no matter how much he blinked. As if he no longer had the will to remain upright, he sat back on his heels and bowed his head. Tears cut parallel tracks down his smooth cheeks, gathering briefly at the corners of his mouth before continuing down around his chin. There were no sobs or cries of anguish. He simply folded his arms across his chest and wept quietly, and as he allowed himself to cry, he finally allowed himself to grieve. Joe Simpson remained that way, kneeling at the grave of his wife, for perhaps a half hour—long enough for the day to sink into deeper shades of gray and for the wet snow to begin to collect on the shoulders of his wool topcoat.

"Joey's coming, Pru. Look after him," he said finally, realizing that if this were indeed true, Joey was probably already there. Then he added, "Please, God, in your world, let neither of them know the loneliness I now feel without them." It was the first time Joseph Simpson had asked God for anything since he prayed for the repose of his mother's soul.

With that he leaned forward and began to push himself to his feet. It was a difficult task, as he had almost no feeling below his waist. One of the attendants started forward to help, but Simpson waved him away. Then, with as much dignity as he could muster, he methodically made his way across the soggy ground toward the single waiting limousine.

On the way out of the cemetery, he glanced from the limo window at the well-known grave of John Belushi, perhaps the Vineyard's most celebrated decedent. Another time, any thought he might have had for the little cemetery's most famous resident would have been distaste for the careless manner in which he felt Belushi had lived and died. Simpson cared little for celebrities; he himself was a very private man and anything but careless. Joey and John Belushi had lived very different lives, he reflected, and yet here they were, sharing the same fate and small plot of land on a little island off Cape Cod. Just what the hell is it all about anyway? he thought. Is this all it comes down to? To be put in the ground and forgotten? I'll be damned if that's the end of it! It's not revenge I want; it's justice. There needs to be a reckoning.

Late Thursday afternoon, February 21,
Coronado, California

The tall man at the end of the bar sat hunched over his glass, staring straight ahead. He was in his late thirties, but looked much younger. There was an intensity and presence about him that suggested he might have been a trial attorney or corporate executive, but neither description really quite fit. When he leaned to one side to fish a twenty-dollar bill from his jeans, his movements were smooth and economical. He had large and powerful hands, with heavy knuckles, yet he moved with a great deal of natural grace. His thick brown hair was freshly barbered—clean, short, and neatly parted. He had handsome, open features, yet he possessed a certain aloofness that invited neither contact nor conversation.

Along the bar, an agreeable banter rose from those who had just left work and those who didn't have to work. The Brigantine was a semi-local Coronado watering hole that attracted a brisk five-o'clock crowd. Some were there for the generous shots the bar poured, and some came for the half-price fish tacos served from the bar menu during happy hour. A few of the Brig regulars made the drive over the bridge from San Diego, but most were Coronado village regulars. It was not a young person's place, and several middle-aged men scanned the growing crowd, making no attempt to be subtle. The divorcees made their way in, hoping to find an empty table so they wouldn't have to float along the edge of the bar. They came in twos and threes, some apprehensive and ill at ease, and some not. The man at the end of the bar was aware of all of this, for he had highly developed situational awareness skills, but he remained detached, isolated.

I still can't believe it. I simply can't believe I'm out. Master Chief Garrett Walker tapped the empty glass in front of him, and within seconds the bartender slid another tumbler of Johnnie Walker Black Label in front of him, neat with a splash and a twist. He nodded his thanks. Holding the base of the glass delicately between his thumb and middle finger, he began to make slow wet circles on the polished wood surface. Normally, he drank very sparingly, but this evening he was feeling anything but temperate. He smiled wryly; he had never been one to feel sorry for himself, but that was exactly what he was doing now. *In fact, it's downright ironic. All things considered, I'm better now than I was five or even ten years ago.* He smiled again. *You'd think all those years of training and time on deployment—all that experience—would count for something. Especially now—now I'm really needed.* But the doctors, the first, second, and then third opinions, had been unanimous; he was finished. Of course, there were the not-so-strenuous, nonoperational options, but the thought of riding a desk while others went off to do the real work did not sit well. For me it would be damned insulting, he thought; that's not who I am. *I'm not a goddamn cripple, and I'll not have people treating me as if I were.*

It had been ten months since it happened, nine since the last surgery. An Iraqi bullet had taken him in the side and clipped the lower portion of his right lung. The reconstruction had cost him two inches of that lung, but no more. The surgeons who had operated on him pronounced the operation a success and released him for light duty. Light duty for Garrett Walker was easy conditioning runs on the beach. Only ten days after he left the Balboa Naval Hospital, he seriously began working out—not just running and calisthenics, but a training regime carefully designed to allow his injuries to heal while he hardened other parts of his body. Then when he had fully mended internally, he began to push himself: open-ocean, cold-water swims in the cove at La Jolla, forced marches with combat load in the mountains in the La Posta Mountains, and sand runs in combat boots. He had a reputation for being hard, and he was fiercely determined to bring himself back stronger than ever. And he had done just that.

This was not the first time Garrett had pounded himself back into shape after major surgery. He had been wounded in the Gulf War, taking a round in his elbow that had sent him into a series of reconstructive surgeries. Then there was the incident three years ago with his brother. His twin brother had lost his kidneys, and Garrett had been flown back from an overseas deployment to provide his brother with one of his own organs. Apparently you could do the job with only one kidney, but not with a partial right lung.

"Jesus H. Christ," Walker said to himself. And he again thought about all those years and all those deployments. Now the real thing was here, and men like him, men with combat experience, were desperately needed. His country was at war—from the looks of it, a long war where there would be a premium on special operations. And he was out of it!

It had been real enough last year when his platoon was on a reconnaissance mission in northern Iraq, looking for evidence that Saddam was hiding weapons of mass destruction in the northern desert. The Iraqi ambush of his platoon had almost worked. Since they were in Kurdish-controlled territory, the Iraqis had taken them completely by surprise. But the rear element of his squad had immediately flanked the enemy position. So intent had the Iraqis been at shooting at the point element of his squad that they neglected to note the movement of the rest of his squad until it was too late. While he and the lead members of the squad had been pinned down, the guys bringing up the rear of the file made it look like a training exercise. When it was over, his men had killed a dozen of them. But there was a cost to the skirmish. Lieutenant Williamson had been killed in the first volley; a single AK-47 round had entered his left eye and opened the back of his head like a melon. And Garrett had also taken a bullet in his right lung. An inch or two lower, and it would have missed the lung, but it didn't. A second round had punched a perfect hole in his right ear. Involuntarily, he raised a fingertip to the ridge of his ear and felt the scar tissue. It was now a notch, as the outer portion of skin had died off and left him a U-shaped cleft instead of a circle. He smiled to himself, thinking that had the bullet been an inch or two to the left, he wouldn't be on a bar stool in the Brigantine feeling sorry for himself. But a firefight, like life

itself, is unpredictable. Their Kurdish point man, closest
to the ambush, had five bullet holes in his clothes and
equipment, but amazingly didn't get a scratch to himself. Garrett sipped his drink and permitted himself a
slight grin. But the squad, his squad—the men Garrett
Walker had personally trained—had performed flaw-
lessly, which allowed them to turn the ambush into a
killing zone for the Iraqi patrol. The engagement was
just one of the many unreported engagements in
Kurdish-controlled northern Iraq—and Garrett Walker's
last firefight. His smile quickly faded as he realized
again that he would never again lead men in harm's
way.

It's unfair, he told himself for the hundredth time;
I've never felt better or been more fit. He tried to be
philosophical about it, for Garrett Walker was a man
who knew all too well that life is not always fair.
Afghanistan had shown that special operations was now
a pivotal element in modern warfare. And now he was
about to become a civilian; he felt so frustrated.

He went back to his drink, trying to shake off the
events of the recent past he couldn't change. As he did,
two men stepped through the entrance and to either side
of the door, scanning the bar and the nearby tables. They
were dressed in blue jeans, T-shirts, and Nikes. Without
a word, the two began to work their way through the
crowd. They had the same hard, athletic look as the man
at the end of the bar, as if all three belonged to the same
professional sports team. In many ways they did; all were
members of SEAL Team Three.

"Thought we might find you hiding out in here," said
one of the new arrivals. "A few of the guys down at
Greg's would like to buy you a beer." Of the two, he was
the younger but a powerfully built man. He glanced
around at the "civilians" crowded along the bar with a

measure of disdain. "C'mon, Master Chief, you don't belong here."

Garrett swung around on his stool to face them. "Now that's where you're wrong, Lieutenant. I do belong here. You're team guys, and I'm a civilian—almost." He gave a helpless gesture that revealed an intricately tattooed dragon on his forearm.

The second man gave a quick snort and smiled. "Yeah, right, and I'm a fuckin' social worker." He was older, with a touch of gray at his temples and a hard, gravelly voice. "Look, Tag, they can put a man out of the teams, but they can't take the teams out of the man. The day you can't call yourself a SEAL, none of us can. Now are you gonna sit there like a bottle of urine and drink with these weenies, or are you gonna come have a beer with us?"

Garrett gave them both an even stare that caused the younger man to look away and smile. "You know, Master Chief, there's close to a full platoon of *your* men down at Greg's, and they'll follow just about any order I give them. Now, you can un-ass that stool and come along with us peaceably, or I'll send them in here to get you." He again glanced around the bar. "It won't be pretty, 'cause I know you can be a little recalcitrant when you want to be, but they *will* drag your sorry butt out of here."

Garrett regarded the two intruders for a moment, then knocked back his drink. He set the empty glass on the bar and slid from the stool. He waved to the bartender to keep the change. "Looks like we're all going to Greg's for a drink."

As they threaded their way out, they raised a few eyebrows, but not many. Coronado, California, was considered home base for the West Coast Navy SEAL teams. The SEAL complex occupied a stretch of Pacific beachfront less than a half mile south of Coronado on the Silver

Strand, a thread of sand that connected Coronado to Imperial Beach, just above the Mexican border. They didn't have to be in uniform to be positively identified as Navy SEALs.

McP's Irish Pub was on Orange Avenue, less than a block east of the Brigantine on the same side of the street. The owner, Greg McPartland, was a Vietnam-era SEAL, and over the years McP's had become the off-duty hangout for nondeployed Navy SEALs. Greg served good sandwiches, thick Irish stews, and plenty of beer and stout. Promotions, wakes, and even wedding receptions of team members were held at McP's. The main bar area seated thirty or more, with standing room for four times that many. Tables crowded along one wall up to a small bandstand and an even smaller dance floor along the back wall. A large SEAL insignia, an eagle clutching a trident and flintlock pistol superimposed on an anchor, hung over the bar. On most weeknights, the crowd spilled out from the main bar area onto the patio, a large walled area that was twice the size of the interior. The lieutenant led Garrett and the other SEAL around to the back entrance of the patio.

"Hooyah, Master Chief!" shouted a young SEAL standing at a bar set in an alcove to the main building. He was drawing a beer from the tap of an iced keg of Bass Ale resting on the counter.

"Yo, Tag."

"Good job, Lieutenant."

"Bong-bong; E-nine, arriving."

The three new arrivals were absorbed into the group. Someone handed Garrett a fresh schooner of beer that sent a wave of foam cascading down across his hand and fingers. There were about twelve of them, all in jeans or shorts and T-shirts. Some wore sandals, others sneakers. He quickly surveyed them with a measure of pride and sadness. This was his last platoon. He had trained these men, worked them hard, and made them into a combat team. Most of them he had taken on deployment. Soon all of them would be back in the thick of it, but he would not be with them. Navy SEALs are tough and smart, but they're also very independent. Teamwork sometimes comes hard to them. Often, getting these individuals to function as a unit requires advanced ego-management skills. Garrett did this well. He knew when to push, when to pull, and when needed, when to threaten. For the most part he had led by quiet example, but not always. As he took a long pull on the ale, he realized that was what he would miss the most: taking a bunch of rowdy, freewheeling, independent Navy SEALs and hammering them into a fighting unit—a team.

"Here, Master Chief, let me top that off for you." A young SEAL refilled his glass and quickly returned it. "Don't know what we're gonna do without you, Master Chief. Who's gonna teach us how to loot and shoot?"

Garrett smiled. Barnes was young, just out of training and new to the platoon, but already a solid performer. "How many times do I have to tell you, Barnes—first comes the shooting, then the looting."

"Oh, yeah, Master Chief." He grinned. "I always get them backward. So what are you going to do now?"

Garrett put his hand on the younger man's shoulder. "You know, Barnes, I'm going to deck the next guy who asks me that." Then, in a quieter tone, "Because I really have no fuckin' idea. And why don't you lose the 'Master Chief' and just call me Garrett, or Tag, if you like."

The young man stepped back and drew himself upright. "Oh, I don't know about that, Master Chief."

"Well, you work on it, Barnes."

Garrett moved about, taking a moment with each of his platoon mates. Gradually he worked his way to the side of the patio, where several senior enlisted SEALs were seated around a table.

"Well, look what the cat, I mean, look what the lieutenant dragged in."

"Have a seat, Tag."

"Yeah, Tag. An old guy like you shouldn't try to stand up and drink beer at the same time."

Garrett "Tag" Walker had grown up in Arkansas and had gone to the University of Michigan on a football scholarship. He was there for only two years, but gained a reputation as a vicious hitter. During his freshman year, he sidelined a star Ohio State wide receiver, knocking him unconscious. It was a clean but devastating tackle. "I only tagged him," he was heard to say as they wheeled the fallen Ohio State man from the field, and the name stuck.

Garrett kicked a chair out, spun it around, and sat down, resting his forearms across the backrest. "You know, my forced retirement does have an upside. I won't have to sit around and listen to you old ladies whine all the time."

"You know, Frank," one of them said, turning to his companion, "even though Tag here is something of a no-load and a sea lawyer, I'm gonna kind of miss him."

"I hear you, Bobby," Frank replied. Frank was one of the few black men in the teams, built like a wall but with an easy grin. "He is kind of a lightweight, but I've grown a little fond of him over the years, just a little, mind you."

The comments around the table continued at Garrett's expense, but it was a forced bonhomie. These were senior SEAL operators and all chief petty officers. They were the best of their breed, which meant they were among the elite of the world's special operations forces. Each could only imagine his own personal trauma if he were to be suddenly separated from the teams. Unlike the young SEAL, none of them asked about Garrett's plans. They all knew he would talk about his future in his own good time.

"Well it's not going to be an easy adjustment," Garrett said reflectively as he finished his beer. "No more long deployments, no more lousy Navy chow, no more weekend duty, no more night training exercises, no more long cold-water ocean swims. I'll just have to find some other way to spend my time." He signaled to a passing waitress. "Cindy, could you bring myself and these other pretenders each a double shot of tequila." A slight grin played on his lips as he surveyed the other SEAL chiefs around the table. "I don't suppose you heroes object to having a drink with a lightweight, do you? Certainly not on his last night in the teams on active duty, right?"

When Cindy arrived with a tray of double shots, Garrett immediately sent her back for another round. Two more chief petty officers joined them, along with the lieutenant who had corralled Garrett at the Brigantine. They pulled a chair up to the table before they realized what was up; all were honor-bound to drink with Master Chief Garrett Walker, USN, soon-to-be USN retired. While the younger SEALs wandered into the main bar at McP's to check out the girls who invariably appeared when the music started, the others sat with the lame-duck Master Chief and drank shot after double shot of Jose Cuervo. At closing time, about 1:00 A.M., Garrett pushed himself up from the table and surveyed his glassy-eyed companions.

"Well, gentlemen, it's about that time." He studied his wristwatch. "I see by my deep-diving, washer-proof Navy SEAL chronometer, we have quarters in about six hours. I'll be very dish-appointed if I don't see you all in formation. Good night."

With that he left the patio at McP's and walked out onto Orange Avenue. It took him no more than five minutes to cover the six blocks to his studio apartment that overlooked the Coronado Yacht Club. He let himself in, carefully set the alarm clock, and fell onto the sofa, fully clothed.

Friday morning, February 22,
Pokhara, Nepal

While it was Thursday evening on the West Coast, it was late Friday morning in Nepal. It was a clear day, but there was still a bitter chill in the air. The mountain village was now buzzing with activity as bundled women moved among the street vendors in search of daily produce. Across from the marketplace, Bijay sat at a table outside the café enjoying the morning sunshine in spite of the cold. The tea had been properly served to his specification, but it needed to steep for several more minutes before it reached the rich proportion he relished. He had not grown up in Pokhara, but several kilometers to the northwest, almost in the shadow of Annapurna. He had only been back six months, and already he was restless. *Restless* was too strong a term for Bijay; he was far too disciplined to become restless from inactivity, yet he knew that his spirit was not entirely at peace, and the inactivity did not help. Still, the sunshine and the prospect of enjoying the warm brew steaming in the pot in front of him helped to settle him.

Bijay was in much the same situation as Garrett Walker, but his circumstance could not have been more different. Garrett was rated by his peers as one of the best, but outside the small fraternity of Navy SEALs he was an unknown. In the kingdom of Nepal, Bijay Gurung was a national hero.

As the last vestiges of the British Empire were snuffed out, Britain's need for a large standing military force decreased. This was especially true for her light infantry and expeditionary forces. Perhaps the most expendable of those units, although those best loved by the British people, were the Gurkhas. The British Army and the tough little men from the hills had carried on a mutual-admiration affair for close to two centuries. The Gurkha regiments had served under the Union Jack in both world wars and numerous conflicts before and since. But when the Brits returned Hong Kong to the Chinese, the last of the British Army Gurkhas were brought home to England. At one time, more than 120,000 Gurkhas served in the British military. Today there is a single brigade of less than 6,000 men. All are now garrisoned in England, with a small contingent in Singapore and a battalion in Brunei. It was in Brunei, where Bijay served as battalion sergeant major, that the unfortunate incident had taken place—the incident that sent Bijay from that desert kingdom back to his home in the hill country.

"Mr. Gurung? Bijay Gurung?"

Bijay looked up. "Yes?"

"May I please have a moment of your time?" The speaker was dressed in a Western-style business suit, but he was clearly a man out of uniform. He had close-cropped, shiny black hair and rounded features. His complexion was smooth and dark, almost as dark as that of Bijay himself. Bijay could see that he was Hindu, and as he moved closer, could also smell that he was Hindu. The faint distinctive odor that Bijay recognized was not, however, unpleasant. Bijay felt that in some previous life, he too had been Hindu.

"Your presence is most welcome. It is a fine day, and there is room at the table for more than myself."

"Thank you," the newcomer replied, and as a show of courtesy and respect, he inclined his head with hands folded, fingers straight under his chin.

Another cup appeared immediately. The proprietor kept close watch on his most important patron and assumed that his new companion might be equally important. He also knew he could learn little from Bijay's manner, for he would treat a king or a beggar with the same polite respect.

"For my own taste, the tea has reached its proper time." He poured for the stranger. "I hope you find it pleasing."

The man murmured his thanks. Courtesy required that they first attend to the tea, each taking the next few minutes to sniff, blow, and sip at the pungent brew. After an appropriate interval, Bijay's guest cleared his throat.

"Without my having to state my business, I am sure you know who I am and why I have come to see you." For an Indian, his Gurkhali was very good. Gurkhali was not Bijay's native speech, but few outside his home village spoke his dialect of Gurungkura. "And I am sure," he continued, "that I am not the first to seek you out." Bijay inclined his head slightly in acknowledgment. "My name is Mikki Singh, Major Mikki Singh. I serve as adjutant with the 9th Indian Gurkha Rifles." He lowered his head. "My colonel sent me personally to speak with you, both as a gesture of his respect and as a tribute to the esteem with which you are held by the men in my regiment."

Bijay also lowered his head. "You have traveled far, Major Mikki Singh," he said neutrally, "and you do this humble soldier honor. But I fear you have made your journey to no avail; I will not again serve in the regiments." As a show of respect, Bijay was careful to make no distinction between the British Gurkha regiments and the Indian Army Gurkha regiments.

British Raj began the custom of hiring Gurkha mercenaries in 1814, following a bloody border war with Nepal.
They found the tough little tribesmen a formidable
enemy. After the fighting, the British quickly sought them
as retainers. Thus began the long attachment that the
British have for the doughty, reliable Gurkhas. While the
British were drastically reducing the size of their Gurkha
brigade, as well as their forward-deployed forces, the Indian Army still paid for close to a hundred thousand
Gurkha troops, a complement of eight full regiments.
India paid their Gurkhas less than the British, and the Indian Gurkha regiments were considered inferior to those
of the British brigade. Moreover, the Gurkhas genuinely
liked the British, due to the quality of the British officer
corps, while they often only tolerated the Indians. Still, the
Indians needed Gurkhas. India has a long border with
Pakistan and China, and the Gurkha regiments, even
under Indian officers, were more reliable than native
troops. America's pursuit of terrorists had done little to
quiet tensions on the Indian-Pakistani border. More than
a million men were under arms in and around the dis-
puted state of Kashmir. If fighting broke out, India
wanted as many Gurkhas under arms as possible.

"I am very sorry," Bijay concluded, "but it seems that
your visit here has been for nothing."

It violated protocol for Major Singh to continue, but
he had no alternative. "If you will permit me, may I
speak?" Bijay nodded politely; the man had, after all, traveled a great distance to see him.

"My regiment, the 9th Indian Gurkha Rifles, will offer
you a commission as a *subadar,* a captain in the Indian
Army, plus a generous signing bonus. We will also offer
you a monthly honorarium equal to what you have been
paid by your previous employer." Major Singh paused for
a moment while Bijay digested this. "We are also prepared

to honor your years of service toward an Indian Army pension."

Singh studied the man across the table. He was tall for a Gurkha, but then he was part Indian with some Persian blood—an oddity for a Gurung from the mountain tribes. Like many who served in the British Brigade of Gurkhas, Bijay's last name was the same as that of his tribe, the Gurung. Warrant Officer First Class Bijay Gurung was a famous warrior and known throughout Nepal. During the Gulf War, a small detachment of Gurkhas had been seconded to an elite force of the Special Air Service. The SAS, perhaps the best ground special operations unit in the world, is reluctant to work with outsiders, but they welcomed the Gurkhas. Since Bijay spoke flawless Arabic, he proved quite useful. One night they inserted into the western desert to pick up a downed Tornado pilot. It proved to be a Republican Guard trap. When they reached the pilot, they found themselves surrounded and badly outnumbered. Good as they are, the SAS is not infantry; Gurkhas are. Bijay led four other Gurkhas in a ferocious attack. The startled Iraqis fell back, thinking they had ambushed a company rather than a squad-sized unit. All five Gurkhas were wounded, but they broke the Iraqi line. The SAS troopers, along with the Tornado pilot, scrambled through the breach. The Gurkhas fought a rearguard action that allowed them to be rescued by an American special operations Pavehawk helicopter. On extraction, two of the Gurkhas were again hit by Iraqi fire and died of their wounds before the helicopter landed. For his bravery, then Corporal Bijay Gurung became the fourteenth Gurkha to be awarded the Victoria Cross, England's highest award for bravery.

Britain pays its retired Gurkhas who hold the V.C. the sum of one hundred pounds sterling per month. Only a few of them are alive today to collect their monthly bonus. Major Singh and the Indian Army were offering to match the hundred pounds Bijay now received, and this was in addition to his British pension. It was a very attractive offer, and Singh knew it. He also knew Bijay Gurung's enlistment in an Indian Gurkha regiment would be worth all of that and more. The Indians had experienced difficulty of late in finding good recruits from the hill tribes. In spite of the draw-down by the British Brigade, few veterans wanted to soldier with the Indians; they felt it demeaned them. That could all change if Bijay Gurung joined an Indian Gurkha regiment.

Bijay considered Singh's offer. It was more than generous. With his pension from the British, along with the Indian Army pay as a captain and the double bonus, he would make more in a month than most prosperous businessmen in Kathmandu. Bijay tried to picture himself in the uniform of an Indian Gurkha regiment with the pips of a subaltern on his epaulets. He would have smiled at the notion, but that would have been impolite.

"Major Singh, do you know why I no longer serve in the British Brigade?"

"I do," replied Singh.

"Then you must know why I can never again serve the regimental colors, any regimental colors."

Major Singh started to speak, but Bijay's features had suddenly hardened, so he remained silent.

Thursday evening, February 21, the White House

The vacuum system quietly and gently removed the cigar smoke from the room, but not quite fast enough for Armand Grummell. He sat in one of the leather chairs, polishing his glasses. That they were very fine cigars—

Dominican, not Cuban—did not alleviate his displeasure at having to deal with the acrid smell. The stewards removed the last of the place settings and returned with after-dinner drinks. The ashtrays were already in place. The pleasure of each of the four men around the table was known to the servers and quietly placed in front of him. For Grummell, it was decaf coffee; for the others, their particular brand of scotch or bourbon. It was known by a select few, which included those present, that the ferocity by which Armand Grummell buffed his spectacles was a clear indication of his level of anxiety. This evening he burnished them as if he were trying to make fire. Their work done, the servers withdrew from the room.

"Armand, why don't you tell us about it?" the President said gently. "It will make you feel a little better."

Grummell snapped the Commander in Chief a sharp look and quickly returned to his cleaning task. The President had a mild exchange of eye contact with the other two men around the table, not without a hint of amusement. But it was very guarded. All three knew too well that if Armand Grummell was apprehensive or fearful, only a fool would ignore his reasons for being so.

"Sir, I'm not so sure that this will not cause us more problems than it will solve." Grummell had been the Director of Central Intelligence for close to fourteen years. He was rapidly becoming to the CIA what Hoover had been to the FBI, although Grummell's intellect and integrity were in keeping with his tenure. He served the nation, not the administration, but that did not mean he was disloyal to his president. One of the first duties of any new Chief Executive during the last three decades was to see if he could convince Armand Grummell to stay on. He was close to seventy-five, a widower, and en-

joyed a level of trust among the political establishment of
both persuasions that rivaled Walter Cronkite.

"Go on," William St. Claire prompted. President Bill
St. Claire, or Saint Bill as his friends called him behind
his back, respected, admired, and genuinely liked his
DCI. If Grummell was troubled, then he had good reason
for concern. Bill St. Claire was well into his first term. He
had had his beefs with an opposition Congress, but by
and large, his constituents considered him a good steward of the state. He had been accused of being a caretaker
president on domestic issues, but consistently received
high marks on foreign policy. One of the reasons for his
good start was Armand Grummell.

The other two men around the table were no less appreciative of Grummell's talents, nor could they rest easy
with an issue with which he was having problems. James
Powers had been a classmate of the President's at Choate
and Cornell. He had proved a capable Secretary of State,
due more to his managerial skills than his ability at
statecraft. He was totally loyal to Bill St. Claire and a little envious of the esteem in which his president held his
DCI. But Powers could find little fault with Grummell.
He was certain Grummell knew how he felt about him,
but the older man had always treated him with dignity
and respect. But then he treated everyone that way. Anthony Barbata thought Armand Grummell was a stitch.
He treated Grummell with exaggerated deference, like a
Mafia don, but there was a twinkle in his eye as he did
so. In some ways Grummell reminded Barbata of the
butler in the movie *Arthur*—perceptive, polite to a fault,
honest, and wise. Yet he respected and genuinely admired Grummell, and they understood one another. As a
result, there was a spirit of trust and cooperation that
was seldom found between the Director of Central Intelligence and the Secretary of Defense. Barbata could ask

him anything in confidence, and Grummell would respect that confidence. All of them knew Grummell was a professional and a team player, but above all, he was a patriot.

These four men, meeting informally like this, made most of the major foreign policy decisions that affected the United States. They also passed final judgment on most national security issues. That they did so in the absence of the National Security Adviser was a testimony to the faith the President placed in these three men.

"There are too many variables. To begin with," Grummell said, grasping his left index finger with his right hand, "there are the Russians. One of the keys to stability in Central and Southwest Asia, and much of the Middle East, is Russia. Putin and his crowd stand to make a lot of money if the Caspian product goes north." He moved to grasp two left fingers. "Secondly, Iran wants the project to come across their territory. They have done little to merit our consideration, but by offending Iran, we put off any hope we may have had to advance the cause of the conservative mullahs. Thirdly, anything that benefits Pakistan will put us at odds with the Indians. And I don't have to remind you that India is the only democracy in the region. Then there is due consideration we must afford Turkey. They have stood by us in the region, and allowed us bases to stage military operations into northern Iraq. They will want to know why we do not bring this their way, to a Black Sea port and on through the Dardanelles. The Turks have been our friends; this will put that friendship at risk." Apparently satisfied with his work, he paused to hook an ear with one wire shank of his glasses and dragged the spotless lenses across his face to the other ear. Spectacles in place, he continued. "But it's the Saudis I fear the most. The Saudis cannot like the fact that a fully developed Caspian region could reach more than half their production in ten years. The House of Saud is not fully in control of their country, but so far they have been able to buy off their opposition. This Caspian venture will threaten that, which means it will threaten the royal family."

A weighty silence hung in air. President St. Claire trusted these colleagues implicitly, and he liked the dynamic by which they worked through issues. None were afraid to speak their mind, and none took a slight away from the table if their opinion ran contrary to the consensus or the decision of the President. President Bill St. Claire wanted to know how they individually *felt* about the issue.

"Jim?"

"I agree with Armand . . . up to a point. I am concerned about Russia and Turkey, but what choice do they have? And this will help both of them regarding their problems with Islamic fundamentalists—problems primarily funded by the Saudis." James Powers looked like a Secretary of State—rich silver hair, generous eyebrows, and a face that was pink, firm, and well-proportioned. He gave the impression of firmness, not rigidity, and power rather than strength. And he was a very good thinker. "I do have some reservations regarding our relations with Iran. Iran is probably the closest thing to a representative form of government in the region. They still support Hezbollah and terrorism, but that support has been waning of late. We're making progress with Iran; I'd hate to see that progress end or be reversed by all this. The Indians, well, the Indians will settle with the Paks at a time and place of their own choosing, and there will be damn little we can do to stop them. Even with my reservations about Iran, I say we do it."

"How about you, Tony?"

Anthony Barbata had brought a reputation of brilliance and perseverance from the courtroom to the defense department. The senior members of the uniformed services either loved or hated him, but few were ambivalent about the fiery SecDef. He had been a passionate and tenacious trial lawyer, and now the Department of Defense was his client. But he had always demanded total honesty from his clients. That hadn't changed. A few admirals, generals, and service secretaries had been slow to grasp this, and tried to be less than candid with him. They were now wearing suits and serving on boards of directors for defense contractors or working as lobbyists. Barbata had a degree in engineering from MIT, an MBA from Harvard, and a law degree from Columbia. He looked like an older, very fit version of Sal Mineo.

"I got special operations people all over Afghanistan, northern Iraq, and even a few in western Iran chasing these al Qaeda thugs. It's like herding squirrels. We chase 'em, we kill a few, but I'm not sure we're staying ahead of the breeding grounds in Pakistan and Saudi Arabia, let alone the smaller camps in Iran and Iraq. If we build it, we will have to guard it. And that will give us a clear reason for a strong presence there. We have a lot of technology at our disposal, but we will still have to have people on the ground. We'll be in a position to help the Paks clean their own house, and the basing to effectively move anywhere in Southwest Asia or to launch into Iran if and when we have to. It will allow us to carry a bigger stick and use it to better advantage. And it will scare the living shit out of those warlords that think they can outlast our special operations probes. I like it."

After a long pause, the President spoke. "So do I. The nation seems to be putting 9/11 behind them. We're losing popular support for preemptive measures, and we have to be in a position to respond. At this juncture, there seems to be a great deal to recommend this course of action. I am, however, sorry that you oppose the plan, Armand."

"Oh, I didn't say that I opposed the plan, Mr. President. And I agree that we may have no other alternative. I simply wanted to point out that there are many variables. And that equates to a great deal of risk." Grummell was again aggressively polishing his glasses.

The President was silent for several minutes. This was what Barbata and Powers secretly between them called the moment of truth. A decision was coming from Bill St. Claire, and they would all get behind it.

"Very well," the Chief Executive proclaimed after a heavy sigh. "I'd like to announce this in a press conference in two weeks. Jim, get me a prioritized list of the key heads of state within NATO along with the regional players, and when you feel we should let them know. Since most of these are calls I will have to make personally, I'll want the hard ones first. Tony, get your service chiefs on this as soon as possible. I'll want to know the scope of our deployed posture to begin the project, through the construction phase and when we go operational. And Armand, I want you to stay skeptical and be the devil's advocate on this. I'd like to front-run as many of the problems as possible." He paused for just a moment. "Okay then, let's make it happen."

The President rose, as did the other three men. "One more thing," James Powers interjected. "What are we going to call this project? Perhaps it should have a name of our choosing."

They paused and looked at Bill St. Claire. "How about the Trans-Afghan Pipeline?" he offered. "Or TAP for short."

There was a general murmur of agreement as they filed out of the small West Wing conference room.

Late Thursday evening, February 21,
Martha's Vineyard

The Simpson estate occupied a large tract of land near Chilmark. Considering the size of the property and quality of the grounds, the turn-of-the-century Cape Cod saltbox was modest. The house rested on a gentle knoll with an excellent view of South Beach and the Atlantic Ocean. For sheer grandeur, it was an unremarkable dwelling when compared with other estate homes on the Vineyard, but Prudence Simpson had restored it to the last detail. The home was dated, yet it had a charm and warmth that were hard to replicate with modern construction. Joe felt it was her legacy to him. After her death, he was not so sure he could bear it, seeing her empty chair by the fire—listening for her to call to him from the kitchen. But then he and Joey had spent part of that first lonely summer there together, and that had helped. It would never again be a place he could call home, but it was the place he always seemed to come back to. Now that he had just buried his only son, the familiar surroundings had become that much more distant.

Several concerned friends had tried to violate his request to be left alone that evening. He had turned them away as graciously as possible. Joe Simpson was quite used to being by himself, and now he desperately felt he needed solitude. He was not sure he could bear to again hear whispers behind his back—"That poor man, first Prudence and now Joey."

As soon as he reached the estate, he had poured himself three fingers of bourbon, then made straight for the bedroom to shed his wet clothes. He stood in the hot shower for over fifteen minutes before he stopped shaking. Now, dressed in corduroy slacks and a wool Pendleton, he sat before the fire with a second bourbon. A shudder passed through him, causing him to spill some of the amber liquid on the hand-tied rug, but he took no notice. Then the intercom to the entrance buzzed, announcing that someone was at the front gate. Simpson tried to ignore it, but the caller was rudely insistent. Finally, he pushed himself from the wingback to answer.

"Who is it?" he asked impatiently, ready to be polite but firm if it was a friend seeking to comfort him, and not so polite if it was another reporter.

"Joe, it's Frankie. Open the gate."

"Oh, hello, Frank. Listen, it's late, and now's just not a good time. I really—"

"C'mon, Joe, open the fuckin' gate. I'm freezin' my nuts off out here. Don't make me hop the fence and walk all the way up there in this weather."

Simpson smiled and shook his head. He tapped in a code and pushed a large button on the gate release panel. A half mile down the lane from the house, an electrically operated solenoid dragged back the heavy iron gate. A sensor noted the passing of a single car and automatically rolled the gate back into place. Simpson opened the door to a short, balding man who was stomping the snow from his shoes on the front mat.

"Christ, what a night. It's supposed to turn really cold and ice up." He handed Simpson a paper bag that contained a bottle. Without preamble, he shucked his overcoat and slung it on the hall tree. Then he retrieved the sack from Simpson's hand and headed for the bar in the living room. Simpson followed. There the shorter man poured two healthy measures of Wild Turkey and handed one to his host.

"*Salude,* old friend."

"*Salude,* Frank."

The two men moved to the fire and sipped at their whiskeys, neither feeling the need to speak. Simpson had met Frank Filoso in the summer of his junior year in high school. The two of them had worked as soda jerks at an ice cream parlor in Eggertown. They served up frappes and sundaes and chased after the daughters of the wealthy who summered at the Vineyard or anchored their yachts in the Eggertown harbor. It was a friendship that had endured. Frank had gone to Boston College and Simpson to Northwestern, but they roomed together at Harvard during graduate school. They had gone to Vietnam together, and after the war they began their business careers together.

Filoso quietly recharged their glasses. After another comfortable silence, he took a cautious sip and turned to his friend.

"Y'know, as I think about it, I only saw Joey maybe a half dozen times after you guys moved out here permanently." There was no hint of condolence in his voice. "Tell me about your boy, Joe. Seems like I hardly knew him."

"Well, I . . . I'm not sure where to begin." Simpson pinched the bridge of his nose, searching for a place to start.

"I do remember the first time I saw him," Filoso added. He took a careful sip and continued. "He was playing club soccer against one of my boy's teams. As I recall, he was a pretty fair midfielder, even in grade school."

"He could move the ball," Joe Simpson admitted and began to talk about his son—haltingly at first, but he did talk. Each time the conversation lagged, Filoso nudged him gently with a question. Filoso himself enjoyed a large family, but he had lost a daughter in an automobile accident. Neither man referred to it, but it was yet another tie that bound them together. They were well into the bottle and now sharing anecdotes about the outrageous things that sons do to make their fathers crazy. There were silences that would have been awkward had they not been such close friends, but they also allowed themselves to share a laugh. For Simpson, it was the first time he had done so in what seemed to him like an eternity. Occasionally the talk drifted back to their own youths, or to the attack on the United States by terrorists, but Filoso easily steered them back to Joey.

The first bottle lasted them almost two hours. Filoso inspected the liquor cabinet and wondered aloud why a man like Joe Simpson kept nothing on hand fit to drink. Then he retrieved a second bottle of whiskey from the pocket of his overcoat. Simpson slipped out to the kitchen and pulled a plate of sandwiches from the refrigerator that friends and neighbors had packed with food. The sandwiches gave them a break from the liquor, and somewhat revived them. Soon they were once again gathered by the fire with their glasses charged. They both had had a lot to drink, but the alcohol had little noticeable effect.

"You know, Frank," Simpson began, "I didn't say anything at the time, but I was against him coming to New York. I wanted him away from the corporate headquarters. I thought he might do better at a regional office where he could get a better grassroots perspective. But he wanted entry-level corporate."

"If you'd spoken up, you think Joey would have listened?"

Simpson shrugged. "Possible . . . it's hard to say. When we did talk, we always listened to each other. But would he have listened this time? Probably not, but I wish to hell now that I had at least tried." After a long pause, Simpson continued with a grim smile. "You know, Frank, he was doing pretty well. Not because he was the boss's son, but because people genuinely liked him. It was clear to everyone in the office that he had a great future with the company; everyone liked and respected him. I dunno, maybe I should have insisted that he start at a regional office."

"It was his decision, Joe. Kids don't listen to their dads. Remember when our dads tried to talk us out of going into the Marine Corps, out of going to Vietnam?"

Simpson smiled wryly. "They couldn't believe it when we threw away our deferments and joined up."

"We saw some shit over there, but that was a long time ago." Filoso hesitated a moment before he continued. "Now the shit happens here. Never thought we'd see that, Joe, I really didn't."

"But Joey wasn't a soldier, Frank, he was just another bright young man going to work in a tall building in the city. One minute it was there, the next it was just a pile of ashes."

Filoso wanted to say, At least they found him, but he demurred. Joey's remains had been discovered only ten days ago, among the last that were pulled from World Trade Center wreckage. "Wrong place, wrong time," he offered, "and bad luck."

Simpson looked at him sharply. "Just what is the right place and the right time for the United States these days? 'Pay any price, bear any burden,' that's what Jack Kennedy said. Hell, Frank, we're not the sole remaining superpower; we're just a super eunuch. Somalia, Bosnia, the Gulf War, Kosovo, and now this al Qaeda group that has become an international infestation. We simply don't have the wherewithal to deal with these problems effectively—and with finality. So we cleaned out the Taliban; now what? When it comes to major states that sponsor terrorism, there will always be too much debate followed by too little resolve. We'll always be kissing ass at the UN. Our nation has the resources, but we don't have the killer instinct. We have to take the gloves off. I tell you, Frank, somehow this has just got to stop. We can't let these people do this to us."

Simpson rose and made his way to the side bar for the bottle. He returned and recharged their glasses, then slumped back into his chair.

"Sorry to go on like this, old friend, but this is not just about Joey's death. Sometimes the folly of our nation's affairs gets to me. How many other fathers will be made to grieve over their sons because our country has lacked a coherent foreign policy for most of a decade? For too many years we did nothing. After the Soviet Union died, we just stood around gloating over the corpse and watching our stock portfolios. Bill St. Claire's not a bad man, but he was left with too many years of bad decisions. Now they've brought their war to our doorstep, and we seem incapable of running them to ground. Now bin Laden and most of his senior aides have slipped away. Saddam's still thumbing his nose at us. We put on a good show in responding to terror and aggression, but we have no plan to preempt it. We just respond, and that's not enough."

Filoso spread his hands in agreement. Who was he to argue? Joe Simpson had served as the U.S. Ambassador to Russia for close to four years. He was widely regarded as an expert on foreign affairs. Senior career foreign service officers still called him for advice, although he had left his ambassadorial post over a decade ago.

"How's Annie?" Filoso ventured. "I saw her only briefly at the service."

"About the same, as near as I can tell. Joey's death has changed little between us. This morning I found myself thinking it might, but I was wrong. She wants her own life now, and very little to do with me." Simpson pulled his hand across his face and sighed. "She still blames me for Pru's death, and I'm not going to change that. It's like

I don't have a daughter, Frank. God help me, but it's like both of my kids are dead. But I think she's got a pretty good man. There's something to be said for that."

Filoso nodded in a knowing way. He too had daughters, and they were often a mystery to him. Sons and sons-in-law were much easier to understand and deal with. Filoso also knew that no price could be put on a good son-in-law, one that loved and cared for your daughter.

Prudence Simpson had been horseback riding alone while Joe was out of town. It was late fall, and the weather had been much like it was today, only colder. She and her mount had taken a bad fall, and the horse had rolled on top of her. Her injuries were serious, but she had died of exposure trying to crawl back to the house. Annie had been out late with friends and thought her mother had gone to bed early, as she usually did when Joe was gone. It was Annie who found her mother the following morning, near one of the barns.

Filoso knocked back the last of his drink, drawing his lips tightly across his teeth and savoring the warmth of the whiskey.

"How's the business?"

Simpson shrugged indifferently. "Doing well. Very well, as a matter of fact. I expect our earnings to be up twenty percent from last year." He sighed and drained his glass. He didn't really want to talk business; he was just going through the motions. "How many stock options are you still sitting on?"

Filoso shrugged and feigned a bewildered look. "I'm not sure. The share prices keep going up, and you keep declaring stock splits. I can't keep up with 'em."

Joe Simpson was one of the wealthiest men in America, and Frank Filoso had had a hand in it. Simpson was to beef what Boeing was to commercial aviation. At

Northwestern, he had taken a degree in business, but he often visited the stockyards in Chicago. He studied the ranching and meatpacking business, and quickly learned that the United States raised the highest quality beef in the world but was not terribly efficient at it. Simpson thought he knew how it could be done better. But there were severe export limitations on American beef, and the dynamics of the cattle business was changing rapidly. Government subsidies were soon to be a thing of the past, and the government was becoming more mercenary about grazing rights on federal land. With a keen understanding of the cattle business, capital markets, joint ventures with multinational corporations, and sound business instincts, he'd built a meatpacking empire. Iowa beef was now on the tables in Kobe and Stuttgart, and Joe Simpson collected a small fee on nearly every steak and hamburger that came from America. The dominant players, Conagra and Archer Daniels Midland, never took Simpson and his Ameribeef enterprise seriously until it was too late. Demand quickly began to exceed what he could supply. In the beginning, he and Frank Filoso had been partners, the first two employees of Ameribeef. Years later, after their first public offering, Frank wanted to take more time off with his family, and Joe wanted to take the business to the next level. So they parted ways, financially; Joe got the company, but Frank, so as not to take cash from the business, had taken out-of-the-money stock options. He believed in Joe Simpson. His holdings were now valued in the tens of millions. Joe often thought that Frank had made the better decision. Tonight he was sure of it.

With Frank's departure, Joe reorganized the company using advanced production and distribution technologies and the principles of total quality management. He quickly began to attract some of the best young management talent available. Ameribeef now ran smoothly and efficiently with little direction from Joe Simpson. He still held the title of CEO and Chairman of the Board, but the capable managers he had trained over the years saw to the day-to-day operations of the company and made high-level management decisions. It had been the crowning achievement of his business career—the development of a bright and talented corps of managers to continue what he and Frank had started. Some achievement, Simpson thought bitterly. A number of those fine young managers had been lost last week, along with Joey, but others in the regional offices could step up; they already had. The Ameribeef New York corporate office had been up and running at an alternate location two days after the disaster.

Suddenly he flung his glass into the fireplace, sending shards off the firebrick and into the dying embers. Filoso raised an eyebrow and regarded him thoughtfully.

"What's it all about, Frank? I mean, what's it fucking all about, anyway?"

"Life and death, my friend, life and death. You've just had more than your share of death." The smaller man opened his hands in resignation. There was nothing more to say. Filoso glanced at his watch; it was 11:45. "I gotta get on the road."

"And go where?" Simpson said. "The roads are ice, and you're probably still driving that ridiculous Italian sports car, right?"

Filoso shrugged. "Angie'll be waitin' up for me."

"So call her. You know where the guest room is. If the roads are still bad in the morning, I'll take you back in the Jeep."

Filoso shrugged again. The two men slowly made their way up the stairs, clipping lights off as they went.

• • •

For the next week or so, Joe Simpson stayed very close to home. Each morning he checked in with his corporate offices, but the business was running quite well without him, as he knew it would. The reconstituted management team had done wonders in the wake of the disaster. So he stayed on the Vineyard.

Simpson was a man who relished a harsh climate and was more comfortable during the off season in a resort town. In the evenings he would drive into Eggertown or over to Ipswich for a quiet dinner. About half of the establishments on Martha's Vineyard were closed for the season, but those that did remain open seemed to accrue a measure of warmth in their perseverance. Most days he simply wandered over the estate or along the cold, deserted beaches. There is something very sober and candid about a New England winter beach, something that urges a lone trespasser to be honest with himself and about his place in the world. Joe Simpson did a lot of thinking while he walked on those beaches. He visited the graves of his wife and his son one more time before he caught the ferry for Woods Hole. It would have been more convenient to call for the corporate helicopter, but he decided against it. He was a different man from the one that had buried his only son ten days ago. Joe Simpson was once again a very focused man, one who moved with a great deal of assurance and sense of purpose.

Friday morning, February 22,
Coronado

At 6:45 A.M., Garrett Walker wheeled up to the front of the imposing three-story building just off the Strand

Highway. The sun was not quite up, but there was a pink glow behind the skyline of San Diego. Lights still twinkled through the clear morning along the sweeping arch of the Coronado Bridge, and it promised to be another gorgeous southern California day. There was a series of parking slots with "E-9" painted on the curb—slots reserved for cars belonging to the command's master chief petty officers, enlisted pay grade nine, the most senior enlisted rank. Normally he would have simply ridden his bike through the chain-link gate near the door and placed it in the bike rack just inside the compound. But today he parked it in one of the reserved spaces out front. He didn't bother locking it; no one in his right mind would steal a bicycle from in front of the SEAL Team Three compound. Garrett replaced his helmet with a khaki garrison cap, set at a rakish angle down on his forehead, and walked through the entryway to the quarterdeck.

A young petty officer behind a counter that guarded the front door got to his feet. "Good morning, Master Chief."

"Morning, Mantalas. How're you today?"

"Not bad, Master Chief. The skipper was asking for you; said for you to go right on up to his office."

"Thanks, Manny."

"Uh, Master Chief, I got one of the guys from Team One coming over to relieve me. I'll see you out back with the others."

Garrett nodded. He punched the key to the cyber lock and slipped through the security door that led up to the second deck. He paused at the entrance marked "Commanding Officer." Garrett rapped twice on the doorjamb and stepped inside. He was dressed in a fresh set of summer khakis with six rows of colored ribbons neatly arranged under his SEAL pin. Two stars and a fouled anchor, the insignia of a master chief petty officer, rested on each collar point. His belt buckle was buffed to a high gloss, the shoes spit-shined. The garrison cap, now neatly folded, hung flat from his belt. He was scrubbed and shaved, and if the large amounts of tequila he had consumed the night before had any effect on him, he didn't let it show. Garrett Walker was the very picture of a squared-away chief petty officer in the United States Navy.

"You wanted to see me, sir."

Behind the desk, Commander Gary Stennis looked up at Garrett. He was an impressive man, even in his canvas swim trunks, faded blue T-shirt, and desert boots. Stennis was a Naval Academy graduate and relatively new to Team Three. At one time he had been a nationally ranked triathlete, and he still placed well in local events. He was tough, demanding, and fair, which was what SEALs expected of their commanding officers. Stennis also tended to let his junior officers and senior petty officers handle the day-to-day running of the team, which made him a respected leader. He rose from the desk and walked around to face Garrett.

"Master Chief, it's a sad day in this man's Navy when we lose an operator like you." He paused, trying to find the right words. His features were firm, but there was genuine compassion in his eyes. "You don't need to again hear how much we'll all miss you here at Team Three." He looked away from Garrett and pursed his lips. "I'm just sorry, that's all. If there's something you need or anything I can do, you call me, here or at home, understood?"

"Understood, Skipper. And thanks for your endorsement on my request for a medical waiver. You did what you could, sir. It just wasn't in the cards."

Stennis nodded. There wasn't anything more to say, and he knew it. He reached back to the desk and retrieved a starched desert-cammie fatigue cap, pulling the bill within a few inches of his nose.

"SEAL Team Three will be standing by at zero seven hundred. At your pleasure, Master Chief." He stepped past Garrett and left the office.

Garrett slowly made his way to the adjoining building and up to his platoon's bay of lockers. This wasn't a fancy athletic club, but the Navy recognized the importance of an adequate locker facility for their SEALs. Each SEAL had his own wire-mesh storage bay. The floor was tiled, and there was ample room to house swim gear, wetsuits, and personal field equipment. Garrett had cleaned out his storage bay earlier that week; all that remained were his PT gear and a change of civilian clothes in one of the wall lockers. He had not looked forward to this day, but he had planned for it.

This was the painful part, and Garrett knew it—the ritual of doing, for the last time, some of the things he had done by rote for so many years. His only comfort was that he was a man who seldom took the routines of a Navy SEAL for granted, and he certainly didn't on this day. He didn't rush, nor did he let the empty feeling that occasionally surged through his bowels slow his movements. Carefully, he removed his uniform, hung it on the front of the locker, and donned his blue-and-gold T-shirt, blue side out. He pulled on the standard-issue canvas UDT trunks. Then he laced on his tan jungle boots and carefully rolled the socks down over the top, wrapping the lace ends in the folds. They were well broken-in and as comfortable as moccasins. All the other SEAL teams wore green jungle-pattern camouflage fatigues and green and black boots. Since most of their recent deployments had been to the Middle East, the men assigned to SEAL Team Three wore desert-pattern fatigues and tan boots. Finally he stepped to a full-length mirror and pulled on a freshly starched fatigue cap. A blackened master chief petty officer emblem was pinned to the front panel, just above the bill. Garrett quickly inspected himself. He was just as lean and muscular as the day he walked onto the campus of the University of Michigan in Ann Arbor to play football for the Wolverines. And that was twenty years ago. The waist was the same, the stomach perhaps harder, and if anything, he had added bulk to his chest, shoulders, and thighs. Except for a few scars and the lines at the corners of his green eyes, he still had the physique of a college athlete.

"Well, fuck it," he said aloud. "Just fuck it."

The sun was up but had not reached the blacktop in back of the SEAL Team Three grinder, a large open area lined on either side by Connex boxes, trucks, Humvees, and equipment trailers. Only a tall chain-link fence segregated the compound from the beach and the Pacific Ocean.

"SEAL Team Three, a-ten-HUT!"

Close to ninety men, all dressed like Master Chief Garrett Walker, came from a parade rest to attention. Full strength, Team Three numbered close to 120 men, but some of the SEALs were on training away from the team area. Already, the prospect of accelerated deployments to the Middle East expedited the platoon training cycle. Garrett walked across the compound and faced Commander Stennis. Behind Stennis and to either side were Team Three's Executive Officer and the Command Master Chief. The Exec was small and wiry, as were many SEALs, but the Command Master Chief was a very large black man.

Stennis saluted Garrett. "Sir, Team Three is standing by for inspection and instruction."

"Thank you, Skipper," Garrett replied as he returned the salute. He glanced from the Exec to the CMC. "You going to be okay, Frank?"

"Hooyah, short-timer," he said in a game, gravelly

voice, but he was obviously feeling the effects of the previous night at McP's and far too many tequila shooters.

"Well, let's see if we can do something about that." Then to Stennis. "Skipper, would you and the others please fall in."

"Aye aye, sir."

Stennis again saluted and led the other two men to the rear of the formation. Garrett took a step forward and regarded the men arrayed before him. Tradition held that a SEAL who retired after a full career, or retired early for medical reasons, be allowed to inspect the team and lead them in PT on his last day. More than one maimed SEAL, even an amputee, had bravely put his teammates through their paces on his final day. But Garrett Walker was neither maimed nor visibly disfigured; he simply couldn't pass a SEAL diving physical. With his damaged lung, he could handle just about anything except the Navy treatment tables for recompression sickness. Since he couldn't dive, he could no longer be an operational Navy SEAL.

"Good morning, gentlemen!"

"HOOYAH, MASTER CHIEF!"

"We'll dispense with the inspection today, gentlemen. Otherwise, half of you would be out doing push-ups in the surf with the BUD/S trainees for improper haircuts or poorly starched caps." An amused murmur passed through the ranks. "But since we're all out here on this fine morning, why don't we do a little light PT?" Another murmur swelled into a collective grumble. "Okay, girls, circle up!"

The formation broke, and the men melded into two large concentric circles. An undercurrent of quiet joking and easy banter accompanied the SEALs as they moved to the perimeter. More than a few rolled their eyes at the thought of what lay ahead of them. Fortunately, they were men who could endure and sometimes even enjoy pain. Garrett moved to the center, rubbing his hands together as he turned to watch the SEALs settle into the expanded rings. They shifted and moved, raising their arms until they touched the fingertips of the man to either side, expanding the large circles. Garrett stood with his feet apart, hands on his hips, and the other SEALs did the same.

"Ready!"

"HOOYAH!"

"Push-ups!"

"HOOYAH, PUSH-UPS!"

Garrett dropped to the leaning rest position, and the rings of men followed him down.

"A-down!"

"ONE!"

"A-down!"

"TWO!"

"A-down!"

"THREE!"

Garrett took them through a hundred push-ups, and more than a few of the SEALs had difficulty with the last dozen or more. Then he took them methodically through a series of squat thrusts, leg levers, stomach crunchers, and a few sadistic exercises that only SEALs visit on one another.

"A-one, two, three, ONE!"

"A-one, two, three, TWO!"

"A-one, two, three, THREE!"

Every five exercises, he took them back for fifty push-ups. He punished them. When he sensed that some of the less able were at the breaking point, he would say, "C'mon, girls. It's only a few push-ups," then drop them for another fifty. Many of the SEALs lagged the count, but none of them stopped. About the time even some of the better-conditioned men were starting to falter, he took them to a soothing routine of neck rotations, trunk benders, and stretches. The push-up count went down to twenty-five, then to ten.

"All right, ladies, let's hit the bars."

By the rear entrance to the compound was a long, well-supported horizontal metal bar with room enough for twelve SEALs at a time to do pull-ups. They lined up in eleven files, eight deep.

"Ready, up!"

Garrett and eleven other SEALs leaped up to the bar and hung by their arms, like a line of bats in a sleeping cave.

"Up!"

"ONE!"

"Up!"

"TWO!"

"Up!"

"THREE!"

After fifteen reps, "Re-cover!"

"HOOYAH!"

"Next group!"

"HOOYAH!"

The team moved through the bars, each man doing his fifteen pull-ups. To the amazement of even those who knew Garrett Walker well, he led each group through their fifteen reps.

"Okay, girls, let's fall in and go for a little stroll on the beach."

The team assembled outside the chain link in running formation of six across, fifteen rows deep. Garrett led them at a comfortable pace across the berm to the hard sand near the water's edge. There he turned north. The tide was dead low, so an expanse of flat wet sand provided excellent footing. A gentle surf pooled and receded at the edge of the wide smooth beach. It was an easy run to the rocks just seaward of the Hotel del Coronado. Normally, they ran through a break in the rocks to cross the del Coronado beach. Today, Garrett took them seaward around the rocks. The water was only knee deep at best, but wet boots and socks make for a different kind of run. Then he took them up to the soft sand as the formation continued north up the beach. Garrett never changed the pace, but every hundred yards or so he took them back into the water and back up into the soft sand. He led them past the North Island fence and out to the North Island jetty, a man-made extension of boulders that marked the entrance to San Diego Bay. In the elbow where the beach gave way to the rocks, the wave action had created a treacherous mudflat. Again, the pace never increased or slackened, but SEALs sloshed in close formation through four inches of black silt. Save for Garrett at the head of the pack, each SEAL was spattered with mud from head to foot.

They made the trip back to the team compound entirely in the soft sand. The beachcombers in Coronado are used to formations of SEALs and SEAL trainees running along the public beaches between the del Coronado and North Island. Those few out this early morning stared openmouthed at the obviously fit but very dirty group of men who struggled south just above the high-water mark. A hundred yards north of the team complex, less than two dozen men were still in formation. The others were strung out behind, but none had quit. Two men stopped briefly to throw up, but they kept running.

"Quick-time, march!"

Garrett brought the lead ranks to a walk. The formation began to swell as stragglers caught up and rejoined the group. Many of the SEALs walked on rubber legs, but they carried themselves as well as they could. Garrett timed their pace so the formation was intact when they reached the team area.

"Team Three, halt!" The formation lurched to a stop. A collective mist of steam rose from the blue-shirted mass. Each man did his best to stand tall.

"Right . . . face!"

Garrett walked slowly around to face his teammates. He pushed the billed fatigue cap a few inches back and surveyed the formation. The sun was full up now, illuminating his face and the gentle Pacific swells behind him. He stood at rigid attention. The SEALs in the front ranks could see that he was sweating, but not breathing heavily.

"Gentlemen, thank you for joining me this morning. I will always consider it an honor that I once counted myself as one of your number. It has been a privilege to serve with you." He saluted, and the SEALs collectively drew themselves up and returned his salute.

Garrett dropped his hand. "You are secured."

"HOOYAH, MASTER CHIEF WALKER!" It was a throaty, exhausted bellow, but one charged with emotion.

They surged around him, and tired, strong arms lifted him up over their heads. They carried him out to the surf line as if he were a fallen Viking in funeral procession, and on the count of three, tossed him facedown into an oncoming wave.

Thirty minutes later, Garrett Walker was performing yet another ritual. With this one, there was closure. He had cleaned out his personal locker many times before, but only to move on to another SEAL assignment, another team, or an overseas deployment. This time he would not return. He put the wet boots and PT gear into a plastic bag and pushed the bag to the bottom of a light backpack. Then he rolled his dress shoes in his uniform and crammed them in. The few remaining toiletries rounded out the load. He knew he would not be coming back, nor did he want to, not as a civilian. Garrett made his way from the locker room to the quarterdeck, pausing only for a quick checkout at the team supply and administration offices. He nodded a greeting to the SEALs he passed. Several wished him well, but few could meet his eye. Suddenly Garrett began to feel confined, almost claustrophobic; he just wanted to be out of the building. It was a long journey from the locker room to the entrance of SEAL Team Three. As he stepped onto the quarterdeck, he was met by the shrill cry of a boatswain's pipe.

"Attention on deck! Master Chief Petty Officer, arriving!"

The two remaining SEAL Team Three master chiefs and four senior chief petty officers were dressed in choker whites and posted by the door. They were arranged on either side of the entrance in columns of threes. Garrett could see that some of them were still sweating, having only had time to towel off, dress quickly, and be down here to meet him. Commander Stennis, also in a starched white collar, stood at the head of one column. Behind him, in a white jumper and bell bottoms, a first-class boatswain's mate waited with his pipe at the ready. Stennis glanced at the others and stepped forward.

"Master Chief, I know you specifically requested no formal ceremony, but this was the doing of your fellow chief petty officers." He hesitated as he surveyed Garrett. He was dressed in jeans, sneakers with no socks, and a faded aloha shirt. "I was honored that they asked me to take part. No long speeches, but we want you to know that this door is always open to Navy SEALs, and that means it's always open to you. Oh, and here's a little token from your teammates. God forbid that you ever become a nine-to-fiver, but if you do, we wouldn't want you to be late."

Stennis handed Garrett a small case. Garrett let his pack slip from his shoulder to the floor and opened the case. It was a Rolex oyster-shell diving watch. Many SEALs conveniently "lose" their team-issue diving watch when they leave the teams, but Garrett Walker was not one of those. Only a few minutes ago, he had unstrapped his own and dropped it by the Team Three supply department. He looked up at the two files of chiefs in their dress whites; they stood at attention, but each looked at him, grinning broadly.

Garrett took the watch and carefully strapped it to his wrist, then dropped to one knee to slide the case into his pack. As he rose, he swung the pack across one shoulder. He paused for a long moment to regard the SEALs in white on the Team Three quarterdeck.

"Thanks, guys," he said to his former shipmates. "This means a great deal to me." He would have said more, but there was a lump building in his throat. Then to Stennis, "Thank you too, sir." He held out his hand, and Stennis took it. "Good luck to you and this fine SEAL team."

As Garrett took a step for the door, Stennis nodded to the quarterdeck watchstander, who stood holding the handset to the team public address. The boatswain began a long two-toned trill on his pipe. As the uniformed chief petty officers and their commander saluted, loudspeakers echoed throughout the Team Three spaces.

"Master Chief Petty Officer, U.S. Navy, retired . . . Departing."

Garrett walked across the quarterdeck between the two files of chief petty officers and out the door. He reclaimed his bicycle and pedaled away without looking back. About halfway along the strand toward Coronado, a wry smile crossed his face as he glanced down at his new watch. *They retire me from the Navy because I can't pass a diving physical. And the guys give me a diving watch as a retirement present. Go figure.*

2

Watson sat at his desk at the massive CIA headquarters
building and read another scathing article about his
agency in the *Washington Post*. It was E. J. Dionne this
time. What a complete asshole, he thought. After three
decades of declining budgets and ACLU oversight, now
everyone wants us to do something, and they're label-
ing the attacks on New York and Washington as an intelligence failure. It had all started with the Church
Commission in the mid-1970s and had slowly gone
downhill from there. Of course, mused Watson, we
didn't exactly cover ourselves with glory during the
Ames affair. True, Aldridge Ames was not the only in-
glorious incident at CIA, yet the press seldom cut the
intelligence community any slack, and they never mentioned the overwhelming numbers of hardworking,
dedicated intelligence professionals who risked their
lives on a daily basis. When you were overseas on a field
assignment, you could ignore the Washington chatter,
but it was much more difficult when you were at headquarters. And Jim Watson was a field man, or at least
he used to be. A career intelligence officer, he had spent
twenty-four of the last thirty years of his life outside
the United States. That was all behind him now. He'd

now become one of *them*, what he and his fellow CIA
case officers in the field had called a headquarters puke.
But it was time to come in, and he knew it. The office
was very plush—it went with the title, Assistant Deputy
Director for Operations—and Patty, his fourth wife,
liked the Washington scene, even if he did not. The life
of an intelligence officer made married life a difficult
proposition, but Watson, like many of his breed, kept
trying. A fellow case officer had once advised him just
to find a woman he couldn't get along with and buy her
a house.

Watson was also a tired man who looked much older
than his fifty-five years. His skin was mottled, and he had
bags under his eyes, in large part due to several decades
of embassy cocktail parties. CIA staffers in the DDO
were, for the most part, fairly well used up by the time
they were called back to Langley. "Rode hard and soaked
in alcohol" was the phrase frequently used. And when
they went on the retired list, they didn't last long. Retired
military officers seemed to go on forever, drawing their
pensions well into their eighties. Foreign intelligence case
officers like Watson, on the other hand, lasted just over
three years in retirement on average. It was commonly
thought that they drank themselves to death, and that
was certainly a factor. The reality was that after so many
years on the "inside," they simply withered on the outside. There was no American Legion or VFW for old case
officers to go and reminisce, and their spouses, if they
still had them, didn't want to hear about it anymore.
Watson tossed the *Post* on the desk just as the intercom
buzzed.

"Sir, I have an Ambassador Simpson for you on line
one."

Watson smiled. "Thanks, Holly." He paused a moment
and raised his eyebrows. Then he sat up in his chair and

straightened his tie as he took the receiver. "Good morning, Ambassador. It's certainly been a while; how are you, sir?"

"Doing well, thank you. I see they finally have you tied down to a desk. How're you holding up?"

Watson chuckled. "As well as can be expected, I suppose. The world has changed a great deal since we were last together, sir. A whole new set of bad guys, and these are not so civilized as our Russian friends."

"I'm afraid our nation will always have enemies, and sometimes old enemies can become friends. One thing is certain, there will always be a need for good information, about friends and enemies alike. I happened to be in town, so I thought I'd give you a call. I hope it's not an inconvenience."

Simpson's not a Washington regular, Watson thought. I wonder what he's doing here—and why he's calling me? "Not at all, sir; I'm pleased that you did. Ah, Ambassador, I read about your loss during 9/11. I was very sorry to hear about it."

"Thank you, Jim. I was wondering if you would have time for lunch sometime this week."

Watson glanced at his desk calendar, but there was very little he couldn't reschedule to have lunch with the former ambassador to Russia. "What day did you have in mind, sir?"

"Would this Thursday be all right, say twelve o'clock?"

"That would be fine. Did you want to come out here?" The CIA had an executive dining room with exceptional food and a passable wine list.

"I'd rather not, if you don't mind. Could you meet me at the Army-Navy Club at Farragut Square on Seventeenth?"

"Of course. I'll see you there at noon on Thursday."

"Thanks, Jim. I'll look forward to it."

"So will I, sir. Good-bye."

Watson replaced the phone and sat for a long while staring out the window. The cold rain had let up for a while, and the sun had just broken through. The well-tended grounds of the CIA headquarters seemed so tranquil and serene compared with the ups and downs at Langley over the past several years. *Just what does the former ambassador to Russia want? Does he want something from me?* He pondered on this for a moment. *And why doesn't he want to come out here?*

Watson had been the Chief of Station, or COS, in Moscow. As the senior spook during Simpson's tenure as ambassador, he knew the man well—professionally, very well. Watson smiled as he recalled when he and the other CIA station personnel learned that a rich industrialist with no diplomatic or foreign relations experience had been appointed as the ambassador to Russia. He had been a strong financial backer of the President, and this was his reward—or punishment, as some found out just how severe the Russian winter could be. Simpson had moved carefully when he first arrived in Moscow, deferring to the professionals on his country team. But then, gradually, he began to manage them, something few ambassadorial appointees tried to do and even fewer succeeded. Most either micromanaged the legation, making everyone's life miserable, or handed over all but the ceremonial duties to the senior State Department staffer and quietly became alcoholics. CIA Station Chief in Moscow was the top field job at the agency. For Jim Watson, or any professional intelligence officer, it was the highlight of a career—and the end of the line, operationally. The COS, for all his power, still worked under the direction of the ambassador, which could make the job a rewarding experience or a nightmare. Joe Simpson hadn't rolled over like his predecessor, who wanted to

"know nothing so he could deny everything." Simpson
had been cooperative, supportive, and even helpful, but
there had been no question that Ambassador Joseph
Simpson was in charge. He had made Watson's tour as
COS a good one—productive and professionally satisfy-
ing. Watson owed him. He thought about telling his
boss, the Deputy Director for Operations, of his lunch
with the former ambassador, but decided to wait and see
what Simpson wanted.

Thursday, March 7,
Washington, D.C.

Simpson was waiting for him at a table in the corner of
the ornate dining room precisely at noon. The Army-
Navy Club was an old facility that had been extensively
remodeled during Ronald Reagan's second term. It
retained the stuffy atmosphere of an exclusive men's
club, even though it was no longer that. The club provided a meeting place for Washington's chowder and
marching society, mostly retired career officers, and
Watson recognized at least one former military attaché
as he passed through the lobby. Watson himself, however, went unnoticed. Like most experienced CIA case
officers, he seemed to have a cloak of anonymity, the result of his years in the trade. He was a smooth article,
and when it suited him, he could move unnoticed in
public. As soon as he entered the dining room, Simpson
rose to meet him.

"Thanks for coming, Jim. It's very good to see you again."

"Good to see you too, sir. What's it been, six years or
more?"

"You've a good memory. It was at a reception for Hel-
mut Kohl at the German Embassy, the week before Easter.
I left the legation shortly after that. Please, sit."

Watson took a seat across from him, noting that Simpson's memory was also very good. He did remember the reception, a black-tie affair that Watson had attended at the invitation of the Bundesnachrichtendienst, or BND, resident. That was the last time he saw Simpson in person; he left his post soon after that. Watson had, however, seen his ambassador on television after the death of his wife. He looked at the man across the table and was able to detect only a hint of the reserved, sad nobility he recalled from the TV coverage. Watson was a trained observer. He could not put his finger on it, but Joe Simpson seemed very different from the man he remembered from those last days of his ambassadorial tour. They talked a while about the old times—compared the Washington, D.C., winter to that in Russia, where old colleagues were now posted. It was all very pleasant, but they were circling, like a pair of sparring partners.

While the waiter delivered water glasses and reviewed the luncheon specials, Watson watched his host carefully. It's the eyes, he finally concluded. Joseph Simpson was at a point in his life where he aged very little physically. He was a man with good bone structure and one who took care of himself. His rich white hair was as thick as ever, and while his face was lined, the complexion was richly tanned. But the royal blue eyes that had always made him look younger than his years now had a special intensity, almost the look of a bird of prey. Watson somehow found this faintly disturbing. Simpson selected the poached salmon and Watson the chicken Florentine. Both ordered iced tea, which suggested that Simpson might have something serious on his mind and that Watson would be prepared, if necessary, to act in an official capacity.

"I understand that things have been a little strained at Langley the past few years," Simpson began over coffee, "notwithstanding the finger-pointing in the aftermath of the 9/11 attacks?"

Watson shrugged. "The world and our business have been changing since the wall went down. Not all of the cold warriors have chosen to go quietly. There's always been work to do, and a lot of the old hands had a hard time making the transition. Now, of course, there is a new urgency and a new focus. We've known about al Qaeda and many of the splinter terrorist groups for a long time, and we've reported extensively on the prospect of a domestic terrorist attack. I think we've always done well with our reporting on the terrorist target in general. But I don't mind saying, we certainly didn't expect what happened on 9/11. Trouble is, they're street fighters, often beyond the control of governments. They don't play by the old rules, and there is resistance in this country, or at least there was, to playing by theirs." Watson pursed his lips. "It won't get any easier if that's what you mean."

"How is it with you, Jim? Having trouble adjusting to Langley?"

"I don't think so," Watson replied honestly. "I've had my day in the sun—I was Moscow COS. I'll play the hand out and go quietly; I've no complaints."

"Any chance at the DDO?"

Watson sipped his coffee carefully. "I don't really think so. Armand will be looking for younger men for the key jobs, and well he should. Only Armand is exempt from being too old or too dated for the task. The Agency's not had an easy time of it—the Ames thing, the reporting and policy failures that came to light in Kosovo and the Middle East. There's no hiding the fact that we could have done better with the likes of bin Laden and al Qaeda. And there have been some other things that can only be viewed as breaches of trust. Maybe I had nothing to do with them, but my generation of spies did. We let the country down. I think we even let Armand down. Maybe it's time for a lot of us to go." He smiled ruefully. "And contrary to what some of the old hands may think, there are some damn fine young intelligence officers coming up through the ranks. It's their turn to keep the wolves away from the door. I, for one, think they'll do just fine." Watson set his cup down. He was not one to make speeches and realized that he just had.

"It would appear that these current wolves could turn out to be just as nasty as the old ones, maybe more so," Simpson replied as he held Watson with his intense blue eyes.

"You just may be right about that, Ambassador," Watson replied evenly. "There are a lot of people out there doing things clearly not in our national interest, some with state sponsorship and some acting on their own. Sadly, we know far too little about them and how they operate. With the Soviet Union and the Russians there were rules. For the most part, they played by them, and so did we. It's a lot different today."

They both sipped at their coffee, and neither spoke for a while. Finally Simpson wiped his hands with his napkin and folded them in front of him, elbows on the table.

"Jim, I need to ask a favor. If you think you can help me, fine. If not, then it'll not be a problem, and we'll just call it a lunch. But I'll have to ask that you keep my asking and the favor, whether you do decide to help me or not, strictly confidential." He paused a moment before continuing. "I can assure you that my request does not violate your charter, nor will it embarrass you or the agency."

"Moscow rules?"

Simpson flashed a smile and replied, "Moscow rules."

There was really no such thing in the CIA, but Watson

remembered that Ambassador Simpson had been an avid
fan of David Cornwall, alias John Le Carré. Le Carré's tattered spymaster, George Smiley, often played by what he
termed as Moscow Rules—assume that your own organization is penetrated, so tell no one, not even those on
your own side, about your next move.

"Very well, Ambassador. How do you think I might be
of service?"

"From what I understand, a large number of highly capable intelligence officers have been let go in the last several years—many of them in the prime of their operational careers."

"That's correct."

"I would expect that among those pensioned off there
may have been one or two highly capable covert-action
specialists."

That was certainly not a secret. Watson knew, as he assumed Simpson did, that among the congressional oversight committees, covert action had been as popular as a
special federal prosecutor. The agency had been all but
gutted of its covert-action capability. This was an issue
that was sure to be revisited in the wake of the events of
the September 11 attacks, but there was little current capacity for offensive covert operations. It took years to
build that kind of capability.

"Perhaps one or two, sir."

"Jim, I need the name of one, a good one. One with
personal and operational integrity, who would not . . . say,
take on a project unless he felt he could bring it to a successful conclusion."

"No matter what the job paid?" Watson added.

"Exactly," Simpson replied.

Watson did not move or say anything for several moments. "Can I get back to you on this, Ambassador?"

"By all means." He handed Watson a card. "I have a

suite at the Watergate, and I'll be there through the end of the week. If I'm not in, leave word that you called, and my service will find me."

Watson slipped the card into his shirt pocket and smiled. They sipped at their coffee, chatting amiably about old colleagues and times gone by, but the business of the luncheon was over.

"Thank you for lunch, sir," Watson said as he laid his refolded napkin back on the table. "We'll speak again soon."

They rose and shook hands. Watson left, and Simpson reclaimed his chair to finish his coffee. This certainly was not an agent meeting, but Simpson remained out of courtesy to Jim Watson. Leaving together would have been a flagrant violation of tradecraft.

Friday afternoon, March 8,
Langley

Armand Grummell's misgivings about the venture had not been groundless. Neither Turkey, Russia, nor India supported the measure. As he predicted, the Indians were furious because it benefited Pakistan. The Russians would extract concessions, like a freer hand in Chechnya, for while it was a unilateral action on the part of the United States, they would need at least Russian compliance if not assistance. They had decided to consult no one else. Had they done so, someone would have told the French, and the French would have told the world. The only favorable support had come when the ISI, the Turkish security service, had quietly suggested it might not be a bad idea. An American military presence in the area might make their job of controlling fundamentalists just a little easier. And if Istanbul felt the need to take a heavier hand with their Kurdish minority, well, the United

States would be reminded that the Turks were owed one. The old spymaster was in his study when the President appeared on television. Grummell's study, which was small and richly appointed, adjoined his office at the CIA headquarters at Langley. This extravagance in a government building had raised a congressional eyebrow or two over the years, but then it was pointed out that Grummell often spent sixteen hours a day at the office and drew a salary of one dollar a year. The news conference was carried live. The impact of the Trans-Afghan Pipeline was considered of such import that the announcement was scheduled after the New York Stock Exchange closed for the weekend to allow international markets to adjust to the news.

"Ladies and gentlemen, the President of the United States."

They rose from their seats amid a gentle murmur that suggested this was going to be just another press conference. Bill St. Claire waved them to their seats in a gesture that, though it stopped short of being condescending, was slightly dismissive. The polite, perfunctory applause quickly subsided.

"Thank you. It's good to see you all again," the President lied. "I have a statement to read, and then I will take questions." He made a show of leafing through his briefing papers. "An agreement has been reached between a group of Central Asian oil and natural gas producers and a consortium of American and British oil companies to build an oil pipeline from the Caspian Sea region, beginning in Turkmenistan, across Afghanistan to a deepwater port in Pakistan. Along with the governments of Azerbaijan, Turkmenistan, Kazakhstan, Afghanistan, and Pakistan, the United States will also enter an agreement to provide certain safeguards during the construction and operation of this pipeline."

The President turned to an easel off to the side of his podium. An aide lifted back the cover sheet to reveal a map of the area. It showed a black line representing the proposed pipeline, trekking south from the Turkmen border across Afghanistan to the port of Pasni in Pakistan. The oil terminal that would service the supertankers would be well offshore.

"As many of you are aware, preliminary studies and surveys for a Trans-Afghan Pipeline, or TAP, have been in place for some time. We expect construction to begin in Afghanistan in a matter of weeks just west of Herat, and proceed northward toward the Turkmen border and south toward Pakistan simultaneously. The work on the deepwater port in Pakistan will begin approximately six months after the work on the pipeline begins. It will be an engineering project on a scale with the Alaskan Pipeline, and will open up the reserves of the Caspian to world markets. Needless to say, the TAP will also be of substantial benefit to those nations whose production is restricted by existing pipeline capacity and for those nations across whose territory the pipeline will travel. Obviously there will be engineering and political challenges to this undertaking, but the ultimate good to the world economy and the economies of those nations affected is undeniable." The President returned to the podium. "And now I will take your questions."

Hands shot into the air, and the President nodded to an older woman in the front row.

"Helen?" Helen Thomas was as perennial as Armand Grummell.

"How many barrels a day will this pipeline be able to carry?"

Bill St. Claire did not flinch. "About three million barrels a day—just under half the production of the Persian Gulf region."

There were shouts of colleagues all around, but she would not yield. "And will this lead to a buildup of American military forces in the region?"

Here, the President backed off a little. "We will do what is necessary to protect our interests in the area, and the interests of our friends, business partners, and allies associated with this project."

Armand Grummell clipped off the TV and turned on one of his computers. He preferred to read the news rather than listen to the attack dogs in the presidential press gallery. This also applied to the talking-head analysis that would follow the President's remarks. Grummell's computer screen brought up a list of names, journalists around the world that he respected and sometimes trusted. When any of these published or broadcasted something, it was rapidly translated and placed in a queue on his machine. He selected a highly regarded reporter in Ankara and brought up his latest remarks, which were still being translated. He scanned the piece quickly and shifted to a Russian journalist. As he waited for the computer to bring up the new piece, Grummell quickly passed his handkerchief across the already spotless lenses of his reading glasses.

Saturday morning, March 9,
Al Kharj, Saudi Arabia

Amir Sahabi sat in the study of his expansive home. The house was the largest structure in the walled family compound, located near the city, some ninety miles southeast of Riyadh. The study of Amir Sahabi was larger and far more grandiose than that of Armand Grummell, but the three monitors recessed in the mahogany wall paneling delivered the same message. William St. Claire's announcement was flashed around the world, arriving live in Saudi Arabia just after 8:00 A.M. The Americans were going to tap the Caspian reserves and bring them out across Afghanistan to a deepwater port on the Indian Ocean. If this happened, there would be three regional competitors in the world oil market plus the rogue producers, as Sahabi called them—the Venezuelans and the Nigerians. Russia had just passed Saudi Arabia as the largest single-nation oil exporter. The Caspian could some day rival Saudi production. All of this spelled trouble for the house of Saud. And if the Saudis had trouble, then he had trouble. Those fools in Riyadh had made a mess of it, and now the Americans would provide the means for their final demise.

Sahabi called for tea. He must take time to carefully review his options, which were not good. He was a man who had little time for religion, yet he was on the verge of asking Allah to intervene and save them all from this madness. But only Christians ask God for intervention. *"Insha'allah,"* he murmured; "if God wills it." This turn of events was not unlike what had caused his father to be exiled from Iraq. And Iraq, still in the clutches of Saddam and his Sunni elites, was still a land where his family was not welcome. Sahabi and his family had exiled themselves to Saudi Arabia. Saudi Arabia had once been a stable monarchy, but that was changing. The royal family could not have handled the affairs of state worse. At one time, oil and gas revenues were more than adequate to buy off the loyalty of the population. That seemed no longer possible. Barely fifteen years ago, the population of the kingdom was 7 million; now it was 22 million. In 1986, domestic debt was zero; today it was just under 200 billion, a figure that rivaled their gross domestic product. The Sunni Muslim leaders now openly challenged the royal family. If oil revenues dropped further, which they certainly would when the American pipeline is completed, then the house of Saud would fall. If that happened, he would again have to go into exile, this time with the royal family, and that was something he did not want to do.

Amir Sahabi's father was a man who knew how to collect information, and that was the legacy he passed on to his son. The Sahabi family, which Amir now headed, had dealt in that commodity for the last twenty years and had made their fortune with it. His knowledge and files of the House of Saud would make those kept by the famed J. Edgar Hoover on American presidents look like credit-card applications. Ostensibly, he was paid for his counsel and advice to the royal family, but though it was never spoken of, the Saudi princes also paid for his discretion. The Saudis did not like this Iranian in their presence, but his knowledge and his secret files protected him. If Saudi Arabia became the next Iran, and the royals were thrown out, he would not be far behind them. Like his robber-benefactors, he had millions in Swiss banks, but where would he go? Paris, London, Cairo? He was safe here—for now, his information kept him safe. That would not be the case outside the Arabian Peninsula. If the House of Saud were to fall, and they were forced out of Saudi Arabia, they would then have nothing to lose. The exiled princes would then have him killed; they had the money to do it. Sahabi tried to think of alternatives, but there seemed to be only one. The pipeline from the Caspian must never be built. It was the only chance for the House of Saud—and for him. The Americans must be stopped, but that was no easy task. Bin Laden had greatly underestimated them. His tactical victories in New York and Washington proved to be strategic blunders. The Americans will fight if they are attacked or threatened, and they can be very dangerous when provoked.

He sipped his tea and carefully thought through the problem. Sahabi was a large man with a magnificent mustache. His cheeks were heavily bearded, but he had himself shaved twice a day to keep it in check. At fifty-eight, he was a fit and handsome man, and spent no less than two hours a day in the hands of his personal trainer—a Western personal trainer. Those who served in his household remarked in private that Sahabi bore a striking resemblance to Saddam Hussein. But these remarks were made in whispers, for such talk was dangerous. Sahabi and Saddam were quite similar—up to a point. Both prized devotion; both were quick to kill if there was any hint of disloyalty in their inner circle. But where Saddam often purged those around him who were competent, Sahabi rewarded them. Within his organization and his family, he was part businessman, part charismatic leader, and part despot. Like Saddam, he loved the grand power game, yet he was smarter than Saddam. At least, he took fewer chances.

One thing is certain, he thought; if I am to deal with Americans and their pipeline, I will need money and I will need expertise. And I cannot afford to underestimate them like Saddam. After a moment's reflection he pushed himself from the leather armchair and walked to his desk. He picked up one of the phones, a secure line. I may as well satisfy the easy requirement first—the money. He hit a button on the speed dialer. It was answered after the first ring.

"Yes?"

"This is Amir Sahabi. I would like to speak to His Excellency."

"One moment, and I will see if he is available to the telephone."

The voice at the other end of the line was dripping with contempt. Sahabi knew this; it was to be expected.

When and if the time came, he would have the man killed, but it was no more than a passing thought.

"Amir, my friend, how are you? When are you coming to Riyadh?"

"Perhaps soon, Excellency. Have you heard what the Americans are proposing?"

"I have. We were just talking about this new turn of events. Can the Americans do this?"

Sahabi sighed inwardly at the naïveté, no—the stupidity—of the man. "They can and they will, Excellency. Would it please the royal family if a way can be found to dissuade the Americans from this course of action?"

What Sahabi was saying, and what His Excellency, a first cousin of Crown Prince Abdullah, clearly understood, was, "If I can make the problem go away, are you willing to pay?"

"I think it would be very pleasing. Can you tell me about it?"

"I'd rather not discuss it on the phone. I will be in the capital late next week. I will telephone for an appointment at that time, Excellency. You may, however, tell the Crown Prince that there may yet be a way to avert all this."

"I'll look forward to our meeting, Amir. Just call my personal representative, and he will arrange for the meeting."

"As you wish, Excellency. Good-bye."

He put the phone to its cradle, but did not take his hand away. *Your personal representative, indeed, you rump-wrangling twit.* Sahabi's father had sent him to Harvard for his undergraduate work. He often found American idioms most appropriate for behavior he deemed amoral or deviant. The next call would be a little more difficult. Sahabi had no idea how to stop the Americans, but he knew who might be able to bring this about. This was dangerous business, and he paused again to turn the matter over again in his mind. There seemed to be no other way. The man was good—the best; there was no question of that. Very few knew that this was the person who had been the brain behind bin Laden's ability to orchestrate the 9/11 attacks. Fewer still knew that this same man had counseled against the attacks. But Amir Sahabi knew; he was in the business of information. It took the overseas operator five minutes to put through his call, and another five for the scramblers on either end to engage. Then another several minutes for his party to come on the line. The call itself lasted less than two minutes. His request was brief. The man on the other end of the line simply said he understood and that he would be in touch.

Sahabi wandered out through the heavy portal to the veranda to enjoy the dry, warm late afternoon. The family would not gather for dinner for another hour and a half. After such weighty considerations, he felt himself in the need of a diversion. Slowly, he made his way across a columned portico to one of the servants' quarters—one that was away from the other compound buildings and off limits to all but himself. He let himself inside and stood just inside the door, allowing his eyes to adjust to the dim light. Then he moved forward into the room. He smelled the scented olive oil before he felt the soft hands from behind ease off his robe. Another pair of gentle hands held his forearm, her firm young breast pressed lightly against it. She guided him to a large sunken tub in the middle of the room that had been prepared for his pleasure.

Saturday morning, March 9, Villefranche, France

Pavel Zelinkow stood on the large veranda, silent and imposing like the nearby marble sculptures, and basked in the spectacular view from his villa. Shifting his gaze slowly, he took in the full 180-degree panorama that embraced layered shades of emerald green and royal blue stretching as far as the eye could see. Closer to shore, the sweeping arc that was the Bay of Villefranche was dotted with yachts riding at anchor. Each morning, while Dominique busied herself with the espresso machine, he admired the view from this corner of the veranda and had his first cigar, a mild H. Uppman robusto made to his specifications. Since they had been out the night before, they had slept late. His bathrobe hung open, revealing that he wore nothing but a Speedo and a gold chain. The chain cut an oval in the small, dense mat of gray hair on his chest, making it almost invisible. The rest of his body was clean and tanned to a healthy olive glow. Zelinkow, himself totally immodest, could see nothing of the Speedo due to his ample belly.

He had lived in the villa for close to four years, and he loved it dearly. The previous owner lived in Paris and had been reluctant to sell it. Only recently had Zelinkow found the means to make the owner an offer he couldn't refuse. But it had taken nearly all of his cash reserves.

"Your coffee, darling."

"Ah, you are a dear. Thank you," he replied in fluent French. "And how are you on this beautiful morning?"

She smiled pleasantly and set about visiting the potted plants with her watering can. Zelinkow parked his cigar on the stone railing of the veranda and sipped cautiously at his steaming espresso. After a companionable silence, he again turned to her. She was busy arranging a massive display of bougainvillea that erupted from a large clay urn.

"And what did you think of the opera?"

She paused and considered the question. "In truth, I was a little disappointed. Luciano was all I hoped he would be, and more, but they could have supported him better. The female lead was simply not up to it, and the orchestra, well . . ." She shrugged and went back to the plants.

Zelinkow considered this. "I agree," he said. "But the orchestra is improving. I think we may be two, perhaps three, woodwinds and a French horn away from a very decent ensemble. As for the soprano, well, perhaps she was simply intimated by the maestro. He can do that, you know."

Zelinkow cared about two things in the world, privacy and culture. He kept a small flat in Paris so that he could attend the theater and opera. From the airport in Nice, he was only a short flight from Paris or Rome. He occasionally returned to Moscow for the Bolshoi, but it was not what it had once been. *But then what is?* He took up his cigar and took a final draw before returning it to the railing. He never snubbed out a good cigar, but parked them down in a safe place, allowing them to die in their own fashion. Dominique would be along later in the day to take care of it, just as he took care of her.

He again turned from the Mediterranean and watched Dominique while he finished his coffee. She moved from plant to plant like a honeybee working a flowering bush, smooth and economical in her movements from one to another. They had been together for close to a year now, and it was proving to be a good arrangement. It *was* an arrangement, no more and no less. She understood this, or at least he felt she did, and he was seldom wrong in his assessment of people and circumstances. He had met her at an art exhibition in Toulon. She was on holiday, and at the time had been a contralto and engaged in a performance of *Carmen* with the Malaga philharmonic. They had begun their relationship over a series of dinner dates when he visited the Costa del Sol, and they began attending plays together. She was younger than he, but she was not young. They eventually became lovers, and soon after that, he asked that she share the villa with him. The invitation came with a proposal—a proposal that they have a highly defined arrangement. After he explained it, she thought about it a long moment, gave him one of her wan, delicious smiles, and nodded slowly. They would live together and share the villa. The domestic demands they would place on each other would be in keeping with those of any two educated, cultured adults who were together because they did not want to be alone. He would deposit fifteen hundred Euros each month to an account registered in her name. The arrangement would end when either of them decided that it should.

Physically, the relationship had cooled over time, but on occasion, and usually in the afternoon after a bottle of amarone while enjoying a selection of Italian arias, they felt a physical need for each other. Both were experienced and warm-blooded, making love like a pair of breeding lions on the Serengeti. Intellectually, they had grown closer, and they shared much in the art world. They occasionally disagreed, but they never quarreled. Most importantly, they gave each other space. All of this made for an acceptable arrangement, Zelinkow felt. He was satisfied, content, and at peace. And he drew a measure of satisfaction that Dominique was happy. He felt she was a woman of character, one that deserved to be taken care of and made happy. If and when it ended, well, then so be it. It was an understanding that suited him, and he sensed that it was not disagreeable to her.

A soft purring from a speaker under the eave of the house broke his reverie. Dominique did not look up; it was not the house phone. He sighed and made his way through the open double doors that led to a single door with a security alarm. His fingers flew over the keypad, and he pushed open the metal door to his office. It was a small room, and the only place in the villa that Zelinkow had ordered strictly off limits to Dominique. She would no more have violated their understanding that this space was his alone than he would have rummaged about in her lingerie drawer. But this room was dangerous as well. To turn on one of the computers or open a file cabinet without certain protocols would create a thermite event that would consume the entire room and anyone in it. Once inside, he studied the ID screen a moment, then picked up the telephone.

"Yes?" he replied neutrally in Farsi.

Moments later, he returned to the veranda, deep in thought. Dominique demurely lifted an eyebrow when he said that he needed to cancel their afternoon luncheon. Preoccupied as he was, he could tell she was disappointed. The fields above Villefranche grew the flowers for much of France's perfume industry, and they were in riotous bloom. They had planned to take a picnic basket to a favorite, secluded spot on a hill overlooking the aromatic color. There, with a blanket, a plate of cucumber sandwiches and deviled eggs, and perhaps a bottle of superb amarone . . . well, it was something she had been looking forward to. Actually, so had he.

"I need a few hours to attend to some matters, *chérie*," he told her in a soothing voice. "The day is warm, so why don't we take in an early dinner and drive into the country afterward? Perhaps take along a bottle of cognac and some cheese, and we can enjoy the sunset from one of the roadside vista overlooks."

She smiled and went back to her flowers. He returned to his office and sat, lost in thought, for close to an hour. After he hung up the telephone, he had instantly known what his next move would be. But like the accomplished chess player he was, he needed time to plan several moves ahead—to think through the consequence of each successive move.

Then he took out a legal pad and a fountain pen and began to write. For several hours the office resonated with the scratching of his pen point across the paper, punctuated by the tearing of a finished sheet as begin the next. He wrote in a beautiful Cyrillic hand, line after neat line, page after page. Occasionally he would pause and neatly line out a word or two, then continue without hesitation. When he was finished, he assembled the loose pages in order and quickly began to read them. There was a gentle tapping at the door, and he paused. When he opened the door, there was a plate of sausages and toast points, and a glass of red wine resting on the stone floor by the jamb. He retrieved them and continued to read. By early afternoon he had finished. He leaned back in the high-backed office chair and closed his eyes for fifteen minutes. Finally he nodded slowly and picked up one of the several phones on his desk. The small stack of handwritten pages sat neatly in front of him. He made six phone calls, pausing after each call to make notes in the margins of his text. Then he locked the manuscript in his desk safe, set the alarm, and stepped into the private shower that adjoined the office. The prospect of a meal and a drive into the country was suddenly very appealing to him.

Tuesday, April 16,
Lahore, Pakistan

Moshe tried to contain himself as he walked along Peshawar Boulevard and turned north along Songhai Street. He was on fire, his mind racing. All the planning, carefully building the cell, creating the trust among the others—it had consumed him for the last two years. And now it was all on the line—everything. *Finally, they have sent for me. We can do so much for the cause, but not without their help. And what took them so long?*

Halfway down the block, he turned abruptly to look in
a shop window. As he pretended to look at the cheap jew-
elry and beadwork, he caught his own reflection. Moshe
was tall for a Pakistani, but he had an agreeable academic
slouch. He was ethnic Pashtun with a high forehead and
delicate bone structure. His fine, black hair was short and
pushed into an indifferent middle part. There were already signs that he would be bald by middle age, as were
all the men in his family. He wore a tattered wool topcoat
over an open-collared white shirt, baggy cotton trousers,
and heavy leather sandals with wool socks. His careless
dress was in keeping with what he was, or at least what he
had been for most of his life, a student. There were a
number of fine universities in Lahore, and this section of
town saw its share of itinerant students looking for bar-
gains. Lahore was Pakistan's most culturally progressive
city. Due to its central location in the Punjab, it was also a
hotbed of intrigue.

Moshe would have blended totally with the other men
on this street full of heavily robed and partially veiled
women but for his eyes. They burned with the passion
and intensity of total commitment. His smooth, light-
brown skin and narrow, prominent nose served to make
those fierce dark eyes appear as smoldering holes in his
skull. Since Lahore was a cultural center, those who
passed him and sensed his passion would probably have
taken him for an artist. He had taken the train down
from Islamabad the previous day and found lodging in
the Old City near Aserkais. Earlier that morning, per his
instructions, he made his way along the Mail Road to Peshawar Boulevard and now walked through the shopping
district.

Moshe was an engineer by training, an anarchist by av-
ocation—and a most passionate Muslim. He had trained
in the United States, taking a degree in physics, with hon-

ors, from MIT. In Islamabad he might have been recognized, for in some circles he was quite well known. There was little chance of that in Lahore. His colleagues were scientists and engineers, and seldom left the capital. Moshe continued walking until he eventually turned onto a street crammed with open-air stalls. As he threaded his way through the crowded bazaar, he reflected on his time at Cambridge and his four-year stay in America. He could not think of America and Americans without bitterness and disdain—their arrogance, their consumptive lifestyle, their horrible manners! They were almost as offensive as Indians, Moshe thought, and Hindus as well were an abomination. *If they will help us, we can change all that. If they will allow us to help them!* Moshe walked onto the appointed corner, paused momentarily at a storefront, then retraced his steps for perhaps fifty meters. Abruptly, he proceeded back along his original track and turned down an alleyway. So anxious was he about the meeting that he almost failed to turn left into the rear entrance to the market. He pushed his way through the throng of housewives who were busy fingering the produce and back out onto a main thoroughfare. There he turned right and walked another two blocks to a small café. He ducked quickly through the door and into the dimly lit interior. Once inside, he went to an empty table, took a seat, and waited.

The café furnishings were shabby and dusty, as were most of the patrons. The rich, sweet smell of coffee competed with harsh, acrid smoke from Turkish tobacco. For a while, no one seemed to notice him. Moshe was beginning to panic, thinking he had not properly followed the detailed instructions given him by his contact. He had been given the directions only once, and he had not written them down. He didn't have to; he had a photographic memory and could repeat the instructions word for

word—a set of directives whispered to him by a man
whose face he never saw.

For some time Moshe had tried to contact them, but
since he was in the employ of the government, he could
understand their reluctance to speak with him. Initially he
thought he would have to travel into Afghanistan or perhaps to Iran. Then suddenly, six days ago, he had been
contacted by phone and told to go to a mosque in central
Islamabad. There he took his place along the lines of the
faithful for evening prayers. The man beside him said in a
low voice, barely audible to his ears, "Moshe Abramin, listen closely, for I will say this only once," and Moshe received the directions that brought him to Lahore and this
café. He knew he must be dealing with al Qaeda. Only al
Qaeda, or what was left of them in the area, could operate
on the streets of a major Pakistani city.

Or perhaps it is a trap! he thought as he waited; perhaps agents of the Mossad, or the Indian Suritam, or the
ISI of his own country had penetrated this group, and this
was a setup. His anxiety was such that he could hardly sit
still. Then a man in clerics' robes sat down across from
him.

"God is great, Moshe Abramin," he said pleasantly in
the Muslim way of greeting. His smile was open, almost
naive, but his eyes were hard and measured Moshe carefully. Moshe felt a cold chill when he looked into them.

"As is his Prophet," Moshe replied, inclining his head
but only taking his eyes from the man for a brief second.
"Praise be to God and his Prophet."

"You have been trying to contact us for some time
now. We understand that you wish to serve the cause. Tell
me why you want to do this."

"I serve God, and what I have to say is only for his
ears."

The man measured Moshe coldly across the table. "And

who is 'he,' Moshe Abramin? Unless I am convinced that what you have to say is of value, there will be no audience."

Moshe considered this, knowing it might be his only opportunity. "You know who I am, my background, and my commitment?" The man nodded in a neutral manner. "I am prepared to place my knowledge and the fruits of my labor at your disposal. It is important that I be granted an audience and place this matter before him. And if he is not still with us, then with someone who is in a position of authority." Like many who lived for Islamic revolution, he clung to the belief that bin Laden was still alive—still lived for the chance to touch the hem of his garment.

The man in the guise of a mullah studied this American-educated scholar. He was nervous, but that was natural. Still, one must be very careful of a trap, however frightened or nonthreatening this educated man seemed. Since the attack on America and subsequent events in Southwest Asia, their very survival depended on security measures that bordered on the paranoid. Because of his clan organization and his ability to move relatively freely in Lahore, he had agreed to make contact with Moshe Abramin. It was known that this scientist-engineer might prove useful, but they had long avoided him for security reasons. He was also known to have a reputation for being something of a genius. And one thing was certain; the fire of Islam burned deep within him. Is that not true of all of us, he thought—we, the true believers? The man in the clerical robes continued to regard Moshe in silence, seeking to confirm his judgment while allowing the surveillance teams, who had watched his every move on the street, to reposition themselves.

"Very well. I will leave in a few minutes, and I want you to follow me but at an interval of thirty meters, no closer.

If you truly believe that God is great, then do as you are instructed."

"I understand," Moshe replied quietly, anxiety showing in his voice.

The cleric rose, bowed to the proprietor who hovered near the door, and then slowly walked out. Moshe followed. He was careful to maintain the proper interval, as the dark robe ahead of him wandered casually through the marketplace for several blocks. On occasion, he paused to offer a blessing or to drop a coin into the bowl of a street beggar. After several turns, he disappeared into a storefront. Moshe had started to pick up the pace to reach the entrance when a hand reached out to grab him from an alleyway and drew him in.

"God is great," a gruff, bearded face whispered, his hand clamping Moshe's arm in a vicelike grip.

"As is his Prophet. Praise b-be to God and his Prophet."

The man drew him farther into the alley. "Raise your hands over your head," he commanded. Moshe did as he was told, and a pair of rough hands searched him thoroughly and professionally. "Walk ahead of me and do exactly as I say. If you do one thing that is not at my command, I will kill you."

Moshe believed him and did as he was told. There was just enough light for him to see his way. He was directed through a series of doorways, up two flights of stairs and down one. At the end of a dimly lit hallway, they came to a closed door. A half dozen shoes were neatly lined up by the doorway.

"You may enter," said the voice behind him. "Close the door quietly when you are inside. You may approach, but you may not look at him—under penalty of death."

Moshe removed his sandals and stepped inside. He was greeted by shadows and a layer of cigarette smoke. There were no windows. The room was not large, and it was un-

lighted except for one corner, where a man in robes sat at
a table with a lamp beside his chair. The shade was shoulder height so light spilled across his torso but revealed
none of his features. Moshe slowly crossed the room and
stood in front of the table. He was aware of others in the
room, in the shadows. He could not see them, and he dare
not look around. Moshe knelt on the floor across the table
from the seated man and lowered his head looking at the
floor.

"May Allah guard and protect you, effendi."

"May Allah watch over you, Moshe Abramin." The
man's Arabic was precise, well schooled, but not stilted.
On hearing his voice, Moshe was stunned. He had hoped
that Osama, if he were still alive, might receive him. *But
this man?* The man spoke with a Lebanese accent, and
Moshe knew instantly it could be only one man. His
heart began to beat so fast he feared it would jump from
his chest. *Could he have traveled so far just to meet with
me?*

"I have been given to understand," the man in the
shadows continued, "that you are willing to serve the
cause. Now I must hear it from you. Are you willing to
help us?"

"Yes, effendi."

For a long moment, Imad Mugniyah—the faceless one;
the one they reverently called Abu Dokhan—watched the
sweat pour from the man before him. Mugniyah was not
an imposing man, perhaps five-seven, 150 pounds. He
was in his late forties and had regular if undistinguished
features. His rich, dark beard was cut, not trimmed, and
his hair short and unruly. He had none of the charisma or
stature of Osama bin Laden, and one would be hard
pressed to pick him from a crowd. There had not been a
reliable photo taken of him in ten years. Yet if Western
counterterrorist chiefs had to choose which of these two

men they would take into custody and which was to remain at large, they would most certainly allow bin Laden to go free. Imad Mugniyah was simply the most wanted, the most successful, and the most dangerous terrorist alive.

"Very well. Listen closely, for this is what you must do."

Moshe Abramin listened carefully, memorizing every word. Occasionally he nodded his head, and not once did he look up.

Wednesday morning, April 24, Larkspur, California

Steven Fagan never liked to think of himself as predictable, but most others had that impression of him. He was simply a very ordered person. He took comfort in routine. And while his personal tastes and interests were quite varied, there were daily rituals in which he took a great deal of pleasure.

"Good morning, Mr. Fagan. How are you this morning?" He always came into the coffee shop about nine, right after the early-morning crowd had thinned out.

"Very well, thank you, and yourself, Mrs. Capella?"

He listened patiently to a short litany of complaints about state and local politicians from the elderly woman behind the counter.

"Still, it could be worse, I suppose," she concluded.

"Indeed it could. How is your family doing?"

The question brought another stream of information to which Fagan listened pleasantly. He was a man who asked a great many inoffensive personal questions—inquiries that prompted people to talk about themselves. For the most part, he was interested in what they had to say. He had lived in the little community of Larkspur, a few miles past Sausalito over the Golden Gate, for only

eighteen months, but most people seemed to think it had
been much longer. When others asked about him, he said
that he'd been with the federal government and had taken
early retirement—that he'd come to Larkspur to be as far
away from Washington, D.C., as possible. On the rare occasion when he was pressed about his government service,
he said that he had spent most of his time in Washington
with the Interstate Commerce Commission, an unimportant junior functionary with an agency that had ceased to
exist over a decade ago. He took his double Americano
espresso to the condiment bar, where he added a small
measure of cream and just a touch of vanilla. Then, as was
his custom, he took his newspapers to a small table by the
wall with a clear view of the door and began to read. He
began with the *New York Times,* then moved on to the
Washington Post, the *San Francisco Chronicle,* and the
Spanish edition of the *Miami Herald.* The papers took
him about an hour and a half-cup refill on the espresso.
He then carefully culled from the stack those sections of
the *Times* and the *Chronicle* he knew Lon would enjoy.
Steven Fagan always bussed his table and wiped any
splotches from the polished Formica before quietly slipping out the door.

He walked slowly along Magnolia Avenue and turned
north up Myrtle Street toward the residential homes
stacked on the side of the hill. The road itself was a paved
series of switchbacks that climbed well above the level of
town. Their home rested on a lot near the top, well populated with eucalyptus trees. He paused, as he did most
days, to appreciate the cantilevered placement of the small
house on the hillside, and the well-tended, terraced gar-
dens that cascaded down from the home. Most of the
homes were large, multilevel affairs that crowded a small
piece of ground. His and Lon's was just the opposite. He
started to continue, then stopped again, a smile cutting

his tan, regular features. A lithe figure squatted by one of the flower beds in a sunny patch near the garage. Only someone who grew up in Asia could squat comfortably with their buttocks on their heels, arms between their thighs. It was an awkward and undignified position for a westerner, yet for an oriental it seemed effortless and natural—even graceful. Steven had always felt that Lon was his reward for the wasted and difficult years he'd spent in Southeast Asia. Perhaps *wasted* was too strong a word, but they had been difficult. He remained to watch her for almost five minutes before continuing on. Steven was a patient man and a careful observer. He did this often—observed his wife when she didn't know he was watching. Every once in a while she would catch him and scold him for it, but in a way that let him know she approved. He made his way up the hill and turned into the drive, approaching her as quietly as he could.

"Were you spying on me again, *chérie?*"

"Of course not. And since when is a man looking at his wife spying?"

She looked up at him slyly and smiled. "I felt someone watching me. I wondered if it was you."

"It was probably Billy keeping an eye on you." An elderly widower lived next door. He was a private man, almost reclusive, but they had often found him staring over the fence at their property.

"I think it was you," she replied as she shifted to search a well-tended herb plot for some hapless weed that dared to set its roots in one of her beds.

Steven dropped to one knee beside her. "Would you like some help?"

"No. You don't know the difference between a thistle and a sprig of watercress." It was true, Steven reflected, he didn't have a clue. "But I would be grateful for the company," she said sweetly.

He rose and walked a few steps to find a seat with his back to a pine tree. Then he set the papers aside and watched Lon continue her weeding. Neither felt the need to talk. He picked up a pine cone and began to dissect it, thinking back to the first time he saw Lon.

He and his Hmong irregulars had been moving for several hours at a jog-trot across the Plaine des Jarres in northern Laos. They were crossing a burned-out rubber plantation with a North Vietnamese Army battalion close behind them. It was late in the war, and NVA had become very aggressive. This particular NVA battalion was well led. They moved quickly and were relentless. He had already lost five men that day fighting rearguard actions to slow his pursuers. There were close to a hundred Hmong tribesmen with him, and he was desperately trying to put enough distance between himself and the North Vietnamese to call for an extraction—if they could find a landing zone. Steven Fagan was then a twenty-three-year-old Special Forces sergeant on loan to the CIA and serving as a paramilitary adviser. All one hundred of those tribesmen looked to him for direction—and salvation. If he couldn't find an LZ and get an aircraft there soon, it was going to be a long, bloody night. The NVA had to know what he was trying to do, and Steven was sure they had skirmishers moving in on his flanks. He was scared, yet he had to be careful not to let his Hmong see fear in him.

Then a spindly teenage girl appeared from behind a wrecked outbuilding. She looked like a figure in a Goya painting—dirty oval face, tattered dress, tangled hair, and immense dark eyes. She spoke in a dialect that his tribesmen understood, but he didn't. She then turned to him and spoke in flawless French.

"Where do you wish to go?"

"A landing area . . . an open field . . . room for a helicopter," he replied, as much with his hands as his school-boy French.

"Follow me, but we must hurry."

She led them on a dead run to a clearing in the rubber trees. Moments later, an Air America CH-47 landed and they scrambled aboard, abandoning their weapons and ammunition to save weight and space. The big Chinook took ground fire as it struggled from the clearing with his tribesmen and the girl that had just led them to safety. After they landed at Savannakhet, she disappeared as soon as the ramp went down. He never saw her again—in Laos.

Almost three years later, then a civilian and a contract agent with the CIA, he was walking down Monoran Boulevard in Phnom Penh. A girl who was a little tall for a Cambodian was selling flowers from a wheeled wooden cart in the central market near Quatre Bras. She was Eurasian, French-Lao mix he rightly guessed, with that wide-shouldered, regal bearing that reflected the best of both races. He would not have recognized her but for the eyes. She was quite simply the most beautiful woman he had ever seen.

"What are you doing here?" he stammered. Thanks to his Agency training, his French had improved.

She recognized him instantly. "Waiting for you to come back," she replied simply.

They were married in a Buddhist ceremony a few months later. The CIA didn't particularly care for their paramilitary officers, even contract agents, marrying locals, but there was little they could do about it. That Lon's father had been an expatriate French planter murdered by the Pathet Lao made no difference. They left for the States just ahead of the fall of Phnom Penh. Vientiane was gone, and Saigon would soon follow. Very shortly all the Americans would come home, at least the ones that could be accounted for.

"What are you thinking, my husband?" She continued to work, but turned to glance at him.

Steven stared at her with open admiration. That marvelous, honey-colored skin still stretched firmly across her high cheekbones. And those eyes! Why doesn't she age like the rest of us? he thought. Then he smiled and answered truthfully; too often, she knew what he was thinking, so he seldom withheld anything from her.

"I was thinking about the skinny little girl I met in Laos."

"Ha!" she laughed, patting her bottom. "Not skinny now. Now fat American."

No, he thought, just right, but he said nothing. He'd often wondered what would have happened had she not been there to help him that day. He would have been killed or worse. The NVA made a practice of turning captured American advisers over to the Pathet Lao guerrillas. Sometimes it took days for them to die. Lon too had been a prisoner of the Pathet Lao at one time, which was why they had no children. That day in Phnom Penh, just after he'd found her with her flower cart, he swore he would spend the rest of his life making things better for her, a vow he'd never regretted. In many ways, they had both been refugees from Southeast Asia and had helped to repatriate each other.

After he and Lon returned from Cambodia, Steven had been granted permanent staff status at the Agency. During the extensive year-long training program for all DDO case officers, he displayed an exceptional aptitude for covert operations. As soon as this became apparent, Steven Fagan's days as a paramilitary officer were, for the most part, over.

Covert action had long been a unique and controversial faculty of the Central Intelligence Agency. The job of the CIA is to gather information using open sources, technical collectors, and clandestine methods. Their customer is the U.S. government. While the intelligence product, both the raw data and the information generated through analysis and deduction, is provided to a long list of consumers throughout the government, the Agency operates under the direction of the executive branch with oversight from Congress. In the past, the president had sometimes wanted more from the CIA than just reporting. Covert action is not intelligence collection; it is a means of changing the course of events in a foreign country to produce an outcome favorable to the interests of the United States or one of its allies. Basically, covert action was the illegal meddling in the affairs of another sovereign nation.

In its crudest form, covert action becomes a not-so-secret activity, as the toppling of Salvador Allende and his communist government in Chile or the support of the Contras in Nicaragua. Both were expensive, bloody affairs that attracted the Western press like tramps to a muffin and made enemies for the Agency in Congress. When done properly, it was cheap, effective, and left no fingerprints. The objective could simply be to influence an election or to bring to light damaging information on some dictator. Fagan had been particularly skilled with the use of information, or disinformation, often by coopting a foreign politician or an influential journalist to work under his direction. On occasion, covert action might call for some heavy-handed activity like a kidnaping or a beating, or worse, with the responsibility laid at the doorstep of an opposition service. In the old days, the Eastern European intelligence services were good scapegoats for this activity, because they were operationally quite brutish. Normally, this thuggery, or wet work as it was called, was to be avoided if at all possible. It increased the risk of disclosure and, if brought to light, was usually disastrous for those behind it. And contrary to what their detractors in Congress and the press might think, this kind of brutality was morally objectionable to most who worked at the CIA. While terrorism, extortion, bribery, physical threats, and violence were all a part of the covert operator's world, he generally looked on them as crude and dangerous tools. The mark of a true professional was to accomplish the objective cleanly, with neither "side" aware that the course of events had been manipulated, unless of course, the strategy called for one side or the other to be so informed. Basically, covert action was the stuff of the old television series *Mission Impossible* or *MacGyver*, but without much of the derring-do.

Covert operations were usually preceded by a great deal of research and target analysis. A safe and effective covert undertaking began with a detailed picture of the people and local environment. Because Steven was particularly good at this tedious aspect of covert action, he had earned a reputation as one of the best at his trade. Since his retirement, he had been hired as a consultant by several corporations who did business overseas on a regular basis. He undertook no action but presented a range of options, most of them legal and aboveboard, to help the corporation in its business dealings or to enhance its image in its host country. Since the terrorists had struck New York and Washington, the calls were invariably about corporate and personal security. But for the most part the work had been modestly interesting and fairly lucrative, and had it kept his hand in the game.

The last eighteen months in Larkspur had been far different from what Steven could have imagined—and far better. Though the handwriting had been on the wall for more than a year, he was still a little shocked when the early retirement notice was circulated to "selected personnel" at Langley's CIA headquarters. He had been a covert-actions specialist for the better part of the last twenty years, living and operating under shifting U.S. government and commercial cover arrangements. He had been based at Langley, but his work took him overseas, usually two to four months at a time—occasionally longer. The nature of his work meant finding related employment in the private sector was all but impossible. Anything meaningful he could put on a resume was top secret. And the Agency didn't really fire him; they just offered him an additional five years of seniority if he'd take retirement now and go quietly. The alternative was to be subject to a reduction in force, or RIF, notice, which he could expect probably sooner than later. Then he would be put on the street with less credit for retirement. He had bought the home in Larkspur ten years ago when he worked for two years out of a San Francisco–based notional corporation in support of operations in Asia. This had meant that he and Lon had to live in a small rented condo in Washington, but the sacrifice paid off. They now owned their Larkspur home free and clear. And after a few weeks of life as a retiree, he was astonished to learn that there was plenty of consulting work for a man of his considerable skill—work that was, for the most part, completely legal. The jobs seldom kept him on the road for longer than a week at a time, and usually came with first-class airline tickets.

Steven was shaken free of his daydream by a muffled purring. He pulled the cell phone from the pocket of his windbreaker and unfolded the transceiver.

"Hello."

"Hello. This is Joseph Simpson calling. May I speak with Mr. Steven Fagan, please?"

"This is Steven Fagan speaking. How can I help you, Ambassador?" Fagan had no advance warning of Simpson's call, and while Simpson was not a conspicuous public figure, Fagan was well read and made it a point to stay informed.

"Mr. Fagan, I understand that you're retired, but a number of your former colleagues still speak very highly of you. I have a project I'm entertaining, and I was calling to inquire if you might be interested in serving as a consultant."

Steven didn't answer for a moment. Lon had stopped weeding and was now watching him carefully. "It would be something to consider, sir, but obviously I'd have to know a great deal more before I could give you an answer."

"I understand. My plans call for me to be on the West Coast next week, so I'll be in the Bay Area this coming Monday and Tuesday. Would sometime either of those days be convenient?"

"Monday would be fine. What did you have in mind?"

"I was hoping we could meet for lunch, if that's satisfactory."

"Not a problem, sir. Would you like me to meet you in San Francisco, or would you like to come across the Golden Gate to Marin County?"

"I'll have a car, so something away from the city in Marin County would be most satisfactory. Perhaps you could recommend a convenient restaurant."

Steven did, giving him the address and directions, and they agreed to meet at noon on Monday. He collapsed the phone and absentmindedly pushed it back into his pocket. *Now why the hell would Ambassador Joe Simpson be calling me?* He considered the call for a moment, quickly concluding that he would just have to wait until they met for lunch. While he had been lost in thought, Lon quietly approached and now sat beside him.

"You look puzzled, my husband. Is something wrong?"

"I don't think so. That was Joseph Simpson; he was the U.S. ambassador to Russia a few years ago."

"Another mysterious phone call?"

He smiled at her. "It could be. You never know about these things."

Unsolicited offers of employment often began like this, with a polite phone call from someone important he had never met. He again smiled. Those who called had usually never met, let alone dealt with, someone in the CIA. They often spoke in a stilted, cautious manner, as if in some James Bond film. Simpson had seemed comfortable and very straightforward on the phone, but then Joe Simpson was no stranger to dealing with intelligence officers.

Steven put his arm around Lon. "I'll tell you what, why don't you hurry and finish your weeding. I'll put on some soup and make up some avocado sandwiches. We'll have lunch on the deck." The house was wrapped with an expansive redwood deck that enjoyed a distant view of the Golden Gate, Alcatraz, and the city.

She blew him a kiss and returned to her chores. After enjoying a leisurely meal with Lon, Steven slipped into his library office and clipped on the computer. It was a state-of-the-art, high-speed processor with a large, high-resolution screen and served by a high-speed DSL phone line. He quickly entered the Web and instructed the Google browser to search for information about Joseph Simpson. There were a number of documents, and Steven read them all in chronological order. Occasionally he tapped the keyboard, and a nearby machine began to hiss as it issued a hard copy of text. He then searched the Web for information about Ameribeef, which provided a great deal more information. Again, he read and copied documents. He paused from the scope to do a few calculations, then whistled softly in appreciation. "I knew he was a wealthy man," he murmured, "but I had no idea he was *that* wealthy!"

He finished late that afternoon, placed the documents

neatly in a labeled file, and turned off the equipment. He closed and locked the door, as much from habit as anything, and found Lon reading in the living room.

"So what now, Mr. Retired Ex-Spy?" she said, laying the book aside.

"I say we grab a bottle of wine and drive over to Stinson Beach and watch the sunset, then maybe stop for an early dinner on the way home—or maybe not." Five minutes later they were snaking down the hill in Steven's old BMW.

The following Monday, Steven arrived well before noon. The Pelican Inn restaurant, just up from the beach at Mill Valley, was as close to an English country inn as there was on the West Coast. An unruly bed of wildflowers segregated a cobbled walk from the white stucco of the main building. Sweeping gables, weathered cedar shakes, and shutter-flanked windows completed the image. A small single-room pub just off the entrance seemed a little contrived. The darts were plastic fletched and the beer was cold—but it had rigid wooden chairs and a damp atmosphere that lent authenticity. Steven and Lon had been there on several occasions, but not enough to be recognized by the inn staff regulars. He parked in a corner of the lot with a good view of the entrance and waited. Simpson arrived precisely at twelve. Steven waited five minutes, then followed him inside. The previous day, he had made the reservation in the name of a Mr. Simpson rather than his own. Old habits were sometimes hard to break.

The hostess showed him to a private table by a dark stone walk-in fireplace. A small fire burned between a set of massive andirons. Stout cooking arms and pot hooks suggested that the structure had once done more than provide atmosphere. Rough oak flooring and heavy exposed post-and-beam construction contributed to the dim interior. Joseph Simpson smiled up at him, then rose and extended his hand. He was dressed casually in a soft tweed sports coat and tan slacks, but he was a tall man, and his bearing was impressive. Several heads turned when he rose. No one recognized him, but he was the kind of man people seemed to think that they should know. Steven noted this as he accepted Simpson's firm handshake.

"Mr. Fagan?"

"That's right, sir. It's an honor to meet you."

They took their seats. "Thank you for agreeing to meet with me. Lovely spot. You live nearby, do you not?"

That's really no concern of yours, Ambassador. "In Larkspur. It's the next town, just over the mountain north of here." There was an edge in his voice that he had not intended. Spies had a phobia about mixing their personal life with their business life, even when they were technically no longer in the business of spying. But it told Steven that Simpson too had done his homework, which Steven fully expected.

The Pelican Inn served a modest fare, English in origin, but with continental seasoning and a superb house chardonnay. They made casual conversation as they began to eat. Halfway through the meal, Simpson rested his fork and regarded the man across from him.

"A few weeks ago I had lunch with Jim Watson in Washington. I told him I was considering an undertaking that might require someone with your background and experience. Shortly after our meeting, he called and suggested that I contact you. Am I correct in assuming that you may be available for some consulting work?"

"There's that possibility, sir. Obviously, that would depend on your requirements and the nature of the work."

Simpson toyed with his food for a moment before continuing. "Mr. Fagan . . . Steven?" Fagan nodded. "Thank you. Steven, I think the only way to do this is for me to be totally candid with you so that you can fairly evaluate what it is that I have in mind. Then you can decide if you can help me. Fair enough?" Fagan nodded. "In Moscow, my relations with Jim Watson and the other members of the station were first rate, so I know the premium you place on security and confidentiality. But I still have to ask you for your word that what I am about to tell you remains strictly between us, for you may find what I'm about to say rather startling."

Steven considered this. The deadly blue eyes of the man across from him said that he was about to hear something quite dramatic, but he regarded Simpson with an even gaze. These were certainly dramatic times, and Steven could only assume that this might be related to terrorism. Fagan knew Ameribeef had a first-rate corporate security department, so he could only conclude that what Simpson wanted was of a highly personal nature or involved an issue well beyond the capabilities of his corporate staff.

"You hardly know me, sir. Are you sure you want to do this? Isn't this something of a risk for you?"

"Of course it is. But then, if I could do this myself—if I didn't need your help—I wouldn't be here in the first place. I'm certainly not a foolish man, Steven, but I understand the risk and am prepared to take it. May I have your word?"

Curiosity was not the issue. Information, this knowledge that Simpson was about to share with him, brought involvement and responsibility and, Steven sensed, even danger.

"Very well," he replied, "you have my word."

Simpson extended his hand across the table, and Fagan

took it. Ordinarily, he might have been offended by the need for shaking hands after he'd just given his word. But for the last twenty years, Steven had been in the business of reading people and understanding why they acted as they did. He knew Simpson had made this gesture for his own benefit.

"I'll need to fill you in on a few things about myself, Steven, so to save time, tell me what you know about me personally. I would assume by now that you've made a few inquiries."

"Yes, sir, but only what is of record or has been made public," Steven said simply. "You're chairman of the board and chief executive officer of Ameribeef as well as the major stockholder. You have a number of other business interests, most of them quite successful. After what is considered a very successful tour as ambassador to Russia, you returned from Moscow to your business in early 1997. You are a widower, and you're a very wealthy man. Perhaps not quite in the same league as Bill Gates or Warren Buffett, but what's a couple of billion, one way or another? Unless you're into bragging rights, which I understand you are not. The terrorist attack on the World Trade Center Towers destroyed your corporate headquarters, and cost the lives of a dozen or so of your top managers. You also lost your only son. The events of 9/11 were a personal loss for you but not a financial one; your stock made up the ground it lost in the wake of the terrorist attacks and them some. You have bipartisan respect within the highest circles of the government and in the financial community—not an easy feat. With all due respect, sir, I'm also aware that your relationship with your daughter is not what a father might hope it to be. How am I doing so far?"

"Pretty well, I'd say. Just how familiar are you with my business affairs?"

Steven shrugged. "Only what is of record or what's been reported in the press."

Simpson paused while the waitress cleared the table and they ordered coffee. "Then let me bring you up to date. I will continue to function in an official capacity on certain corporate boards and in an advisory capacity when invited, but I've just resigned as chairman and CEO of Ameribeef. I have just notified the SEC, as I'm required to do, that I will be selling my interest in the company. I've also notified my attorneys to proceed with the sale of my interests in a wide range of my other holdings. It'll take a while to do this, of course, but in six months at the outside, I expect to be in a fully liquid position." Simpson sighed. "The new capital gains laws will soften the blow to some degree, but my tax bill will still be well into twelve figures.

"With a portion of the proceeds, I plan to establish and supervise the Joseph Simpson Junior Foundation. This enterprise will be dedicated to fighting poverty and hunger on a global basis, and provide humanitarian relief following disasters, natural and otherwise. Candidly, I expect the resources I can bring to bear on this project to be four times that of the federal government or any existing NGO, or nongovernmental organization. And since I will be directing the implementation of the foundation programs, I believe the efficiencies of the organization to be superior to current philanthropics and NGOs. I'm quite good at building an organization and running an efficient and effective operation, if I do say so myself." Steven inclined his head to acknowledge this. "And this enterprise may, in some cases, come to serve as a notional or cover organization for another project I have in mind."

Steven started to speak, but the waitress intervened with the coffee. "Thank you," he replied with a soft smile.

After she moved away, he returned to Simpson. "You were speaking of another project, sir. And this project is one that might need a frontal organization?"

Simpson smiled and carefully added a ration of cream into his cup. When he looked up, his blue eyes were positively burning. "It is my intention to set aside a portion of my available liquid funds to carry out a different fight.

"Steven," Simpson continued after a moment, "it's obvious that the threats to our national security have multiplied since the end of the cold war. Today it is terrorism and rogue states with weapons of mass destruction; tomorrow it could be Korea, a military exchange across the Strait of Formosa, or further turmoil in Africa. I fear this terrorist business may be with us like the drug problem; we can fight it, but it may never go away. Our government's ability to carry on this fight is limited, but there are certain inefficiencies in our military and intelligence services. If they get too far outside the box, there are political ramifications. It's a tough problem and may be very difficult to extinguish or eliminate. And it's always a problem trying to get the international community to take action on a timely basis. We end up with a protracted debate in the UN or with the NATO allies, so there is little prospect of nipping a small problem before it becomes a big one."

Steven paused to consider this. What Simpson said rang true. When our focus was on the Soviets, considerations of ethnic differences, political repression, and human rights were minor considerations to a pro-Communist/anti-Communist agenda. Steven had seen it firsthand; we had pumped large amounts of money into the coffers of some brutal dictators because they had taken an anti-Communist stance—or convinced us that they were anti-Communist. Any pro-democracy leanings were a bonus. And Simpson was right, Steven conceded, about the perspective. When he was working at the agency, he was usually involved in a project, and the work was consuming. He seldom had time to step back and give some thought to the larger picture. Over the last year, Steven had had time to read and reflect. He had become increasingly aware that the seeds of a great deal of misery had been sown during the cold war. And a great deal of ethnic anger and religious fundamentalism had been held in check by the two superpowers as well.

"I think I understand what you're saying," Steven replied. "The Communist system was our ideological enemy. Nuclear confrontation was unthinkable, so we made client states our battleground. Nations like Afghanistan."

"I think most of us agree," Simpson continued, his eyes still blazing, "that the passing of the Cold War has left us with some very ugly residue. Instead of one big burning building, we are faced with a number of brush fires around the globe, some blazing openly, some smoldering but ready to ignite. In many ways this is a more difficult problem." He looked away, releasing Steven from his iron gaze. "But until recently, we never thought that our national security was really at stake. We have a capable military, but we're reluctant to use it. After the Gulf War and Bosnia, we thought we could solve our problems with airpower. Until 9/11, we were very reluctant to shed blood; it was too easy to send in the cruise missiles and the smart bombs rather than the Marines." A look of disgust briefly passed over his features. "Even after 9/11 our national military response has been measured, proportional. Look how long it took us to face down Saddam Hussein. We still move too slowly."

Simpson sipped cautiously at his coffee. Steven sensed that Ambassador Joe Simpson was struggling to keep his emotions under control.

"You see, Steven, at Ameribeef we retained a number

of private intelligence services. For the most part their work had to do with the personal security of our people overseas, but not entirely. We kept an eye on terrorist activity because it affects where we do business and how we do business. Half of those twenty individuals on the FBI's most-wanted list were terrorists we tracked on a regular basis. When bin Laden was expelled from the Sudan, we tracked him from Khartoum across North Africa and onto a freighter bound for Karachi. We passed this information through channels to the government, but no action was taken." He pursed his lips. "I'm not saying this was a missed opportunity or that 9/11 could have been prevented if we'd moved on bin Laden; I understand nations have to make decisions based on politics, both domestic and international. But the gloves should have come off with the terrorist attacks on New York and Washington. They haven't. We're still playing the coalition games and letting world opinion unduly influence our decisions. Well, maybe it's time to wean ourselves from these restrictions. Tell me, Steven, what do you know about the work of multinational nongovernmental organizations—excluding those sponsored by the United Nations?"

"Not really that much," Steven admitted. "There's Amnesty International, Doctors without Borders, the Catholic relief organizations, and of course the International Red Cross. I'm far from any authority, but they seem to be effective when they are free to operate, but all too often the men with the guns restrict their effectiveness. When I worked at Langley, they were strictly off limits to us."

Simpson nodded. "Have you ever heard of an NGO that distributed armed force rather than food or medicine?"

Steven hesitated. "No, sir, I don't believe that I have."

"I see. Then tell me, if such an organization existed, are

there not perhaps a number of situations around the world where this kind of NGO might be quite effective? Perhaps more effective than even our special operations forces or intelligence operatives, who are still subject to domestic and coalition politics?"

Steven was now leaning on the table with both elbows. He felt the hair on the back of his neck bristle, because he now knew precisely what Joseph Simpson wanted. Still, he wanted to hear him say it.

"So exactly what do you want me to do, Ambassador?"

"I want you to do a study for me. There are sovereign nations playing cat-and-mouse with terrorists and providing them sanctuary. They support them financially; Iran gives money to Hezbollah, Saudi Arabia to Hamas. You tell me; how effective could such an organization, or force if you will, be in addressing those problems? We are talking about a small, secretly armed NGO. What should be its size; what would be its charter, its composition, its scope of involvement?" Simpson again paused as if to consider his words, but Steven was quite sure he was very sure of his agenda. "I'd also like you to consider the operational aspects—command and control, logistics, communications, training requirements. Just what would it take to organize, stand up, and deploy this kind of a force?"

Steven stared at him for a long moment. He started to ask, but Simpson answered before he could.

"We'll have four billion dollars to devote to the project. More if we need it."

Steven Fagan did not go straight home from the Pelican Inn. Instead, he drove over to Muir Woods and took a long walk among the redwoods. He did this on occasion when he wanted to think or to sort things out. Usually he brought Lon. Long ago she understood when he needed to talk, and even when he didn't, her quiet presence was a comfort. Had she been with him today, she would have said nothing.

The sheer enormity of what Simpson had proposed overwhelmed him—operationally and morally—and he'd told Simpson as much. They did not use the *M* word, but the use of a mercenary force by any national or international entity could become a political nightmare. The United States had done this in Africa and in Laos, and neither achieved a satisfactory result. When the mercenary force left the field, as all mercenary forces must, the bloodshed that followed was usually unforeseen and catastrophic. The covert employment of an armed or paramilitary force is a serious piece of business; Steven Fagan had learned this from bitter experience.

The planning for such an undertaking was staggering, let alone the operational considerations. It would be a massive and far-reaching undertaking. While the availability of near-unlimited funds was an asset, the handling of those funds in itself would present problems. There was the basic question of whether such a venture were feasible on the scale Simpson had in mind. If so, could it be effective—could it make a difference? Security considerations alone would be formidable. And if it were feasible, could he do it—would he be asked to do it? For his previous employer he had rigged elections, funded political movements, raised small armies, bribed politicians, coopted government officials, and recruited foreign agents. He had done all of this. Sometimes he had acted in the name of his own government, but more often than not in the name of foreign governments, real corporations, fictitious corporations, wealthy individuals, and in a few rare occasions, other unwitting U.S. government agencies. His was an art that required the talents of an accountant, a corporate executive, a military field commander, a choreographer, and a city planner. But always he had acted as an agent of his government; he had the moral authority of a soldier.

Well into the main part of the woods and off on a side trail, he hoisted himself atop a huge downed redwood. Steven Fagan was not a large man, perhaps five ten, but he was very fit. He had been a college wrestler and retained a slight slope to his shoulders that came from a well-muscled back and neck. His wiry brown hair was just thinning in front, yet there was no hint of gray. Lon had encouraged him to let it grow longer, but he kept it near military length. Soft hazel eyes and a pleasant, regular face suggested that he might have been an actuary rather than a man of action. Americans often place much emphasis on appearances; Steven Fagan was a man people seldom looked at twice. But there was a particular intensity about him, and the hazel eyes seemed to darken when he was aroused or focused. He was also a man people seldom forgot once they had met him.

Muir Woods was a well-visited tourist attraction, but if you kept to the side trails, it was not hard to find some privacy to enjoy the unique serenity of the old-growth redwood forest. The immense, silent trees, some of which had been there since the birth of Christ, seemed to mock men and their problems. Much of Marin County was arid with grass and scrub for vegetation, but the redwoods seemed to gather a cloak of damp air about them and press the moisture to the forest floor. It was a world of moss and ferns and thick, massive trunks. Steven closed his eyes and let the spirituality of the big trees settle over him. Then he smiled to himself and relaxed.

Just as he had always done with a prospective assignment, he had mentally moved ahead to the operational aspects of the problem—the mechanics of doing the job.

Perhaps it was his military training coming to the surface. But no course of action could be considered until he had studied the problem. Analysis and feasibility—that came first. No workable plan could be developed until the research was done. The key to successful covert operations was a careful examination of the situation. *Forget the operational planning; study the problem.* Only after he had thoroughly examined the problem could he begin to answer three key questions: was it doable, how could it be done, and what were the risks? Then, like a threatening storm cloud on the horizon, there was a fourth question. Was this something that he, or someone like him, would do—even want to do? And he had not been asked that last question. It was really that simple. Because it was a difficult and very complex problem, it would require a great deal of study. That was what he had promised Joseph Simpson he would do—study the problem and make recommendations. He smiled again and wished that Lon were with him to enjoy the last of the mid-afternoon sunlight that slanted in through the mist to the forest floor.

Steven arrived back home late that afternoon and found Lon in her studio. She sat on a stool at her easel in a paint-smeared white smock. A vase of fresh-cut flowers perched on a fern stand in the center of the well-lighted room. Her watercolors had recently begun selling quite briskly in the galleries around Marin County.

"That was a long lunch."

He stood behind her, leaning forward with his hands on his knees and looking over her shoulder to admire the canvas. "I stopped on the way back for a walk in the woods."

"Ah. Then would you like some tea?" Over the years, an invitation to tea meant, "Let's spend some time together, and should you want to talk about it, I'll be there to listen."

"That would be terrific," Steven replied.

The day had been warmer than usual, but it cooled quickly once the sun had ducked behind Mount Tamalpais. She brought tea and a couple of sweaters out onto the deck.

"So how was your lunch with the ambassador?"

"Interesting. He has a rather large project in mind, something that could ultimately turn into a very large operation—that is, if he decides to go ahead with it. For now, it's a feasibility study." Steven's work since leaving the Agency had been a series of lucrative consulting jobs, although he had seldom done real work on these assignments—at least, not what a covert-action specialist would consider real work.

"Are you going to do it?"

"I've agreed to study the problem and make some recommendations."

She raised an eyebrow. "Just a study?" It was not an accusation. She had spent three decades married to a spy, and if her husband declined to go into detail about what he was doing, she was never offended.

"For now. But he did pay in advance." He handed her a check. "I told him it would take about three months. Two months to gather the data, and the balance of the time to work up a rough operational plan. There will be some travel involved, but I doubt if I'll be away for more than three or four weeks in all—mostly short trips."

She lifted both eyebrows. "Fifty thousand dollars! Ambassadors must get paid very well."

"Well, he really hasn't been in the ambassador business for some time. He has, or at least he used to have, another job."

"I see." She set the check aside and poured him more tea, then refilled her own cup.

Monday afternoon, May 6,
San Diego, California

A file of black-clad figures moved silently across the metal decking and flattened against the bulkhead. Some were armed with light, collapsible-stock weapons, others with pistols. The leader made a few hand signals, and the squad members positioned themselves around the door. One of them stepped back and kicked the door before dropping to a shooter's crouch. Two men entered quickly, crossing in front of the shooter, sweeping the room with their aimed weapons.

"Clear left," one said in an audible voice just above a whisper.

"Clear right," his companion replied.

The other men poured through the door and quickly crossed the room, setting up on a second door on the far side of the room. In much the same fashion, they entered the next room.

A third door took them back outside to a large sheltered area that led to an open interior passageway. The leader and one other man moved ahead along one wall, pausing periodically as a second pair leapfrogged along the far wall. Cautiously, they worked their way along the passageway, moving and covering, moving and covering, and always in a shooting stance. When they came to another open area, the leader raised a clenched fist, signaling a halt. He wore a long-sleeved jacket, helmet, goggles, and gloves. Cautiously, he peered around the corner.

Across the open area, Garrett Walker and a second man waited behind a pair of fifty-five-gallon drums. Carefully, he aimed where the face briefly appeared.

"Okay, turkey," he said just loud enough for his companion to hear, "one more time."

A few seconds later, as if on cue, the face reappeared in

the same place as before, and Garrett shot him twice in the head. Then all hell broke loose.

Two of the squad members leaped forward and began to lay down a barrage of covering fire, while another man pulled the fallen man to safety.

"Compromised," yelled one of the dark figures. "Rear security out!" Dragging their leader by the collar across the deck, they retreated in semi-organized confusion. Two men at the rear of the file tried to leapfrog back down the dim passageway, but they spent most of their time looking behind them.

Garrett left his barrel and jogged down the side of the ship to a thwart-ships passageway. He took cover behind a lifeboat davit and waited; he didn't have to wait long. Two men in black backed out of the passageway, casting only an occasional glance over their shoulder. Garrett shot one of them in the back, two rounds between his shoulder blades. He sighted on the second man, but held his fire. After his opponent fired and missed, Garrett center-punched him twice in the chest. Then he rose and walked toward the confusion in the passageway, pumping rounds into the black forms crouched along the metal. A dark silhouette leaped forward, but before he could raise his weapon, Garrett put three rounds in him.

"Aw, for Christ's sake!" the man said and took a seat on the deck.

Meanwhile, Garrett's companion had left the oil drums and attacked from the other end of the passageway. Within seconds, the slaughter was complete. Garrett stepped to the head of the passageway and surveyed the damage.

"Time!" he called and raised the goggles to his forehead. Except for some isolated grumbling, there was order. "Okay, heroes, let's get back to the classroom."

The men began to pour from the shadows. They were spattered with red paint splotches. Their leader pulled a rag from his pocket and began to wipe the goo from his goggles. Red paint across the front of his helmet seeped into his hairline. He also had a small welt on his forehead. The 9mm Simunitions were close to the real thing; though the bullet was paint instead of lead, it still hurt when you got hit. The SEAL officer led his men slowly down the port side of the vessel toward the stern and into an interior space that had been converted into a well-lighted classroom. The squad slumped into the chairs in the front of the room. They looked like a high school basketball team down thirty points at halftime.

A few moments later, Garrett entered. There was not a mark on him. He paused to confer with a small group of instructors who congregated at the door before walking to the front of the room.

"All right, everybody's dead. How does it feel?" Those seated exchanged sheepish grins. "Gentlemen, this is a course designed to teach you the proper procedures for close-quarter battle. Just because you're SEALs doesn't mean you're experts at CQB—not yet, anyway. It's a learned skill, and it's a team skill. Now, there were only two of us out there opposing you today." A groan went through the group. "I know you thought there was a whole platoon of us, and there could have been. And we only initiated fire when you did something wrong." He gave them a broad smile. "But we've done this a time or two, and we know what to expect. After all, this is our home ground. Remember, most of your fighting will be done on your enemy's home ground."

Garrett let this sink in, then continued. "Okay, let's take a look at what happened." He pulled down a screen that had a simplified floor plan of the training area. He took a pointer and tapped the end of the passageway. "Here's where you made your first mistake." Garrett's focus fell on the group's officer. "Sir, try to never look twice. If for some reason you feel you need a second peek, get on your hands and knees—find a different location, and do it very quickly. Next, your withdrawal sucked. When you have to retreat, maintain your discipline and group integrity. In a hostile environment, you have to move with care and trust your shipmates. You guys in the rear, when you become the lead element, you have to look where you're going, not behind you, where you thought the threat was. Again, trust your teammates. You all know about 360-degree security; use it." He regarded the group, quickly making eye contact with each man. "Now, let's talk about what you did right."

For the next several minutes, Garrett talked about their patrol order and room-clearing procedures. He complimented them where possible, and the whole attitude of the group changed. He kidded with them, encouraged them.

"Remember, this is only Monday. We have nine more days of this. It takes practice and it takes discipline; you have to remain focused. Think about what happened and think about what you learned." He glanced at his watch. "That's it for today. Let's get the weapons cleaned up and the training areas policed. Sir, have your men back here at zero eight hundred tomorrow, and we'll move on to the next problem." As the trainees filed out, the young SEAL who had fired at Garrett and missed paused at the door.

"Master Chief?"

"Yes, Dyer," Garrett said with a sigh. He was tired of asking Navy SEALs to not address him by a title he felt he no longer rated.

"When we were backing out of that passageway, you let me shoot first."

"That's right, I did."

"How come? You could have tapped me just like you did Charlie and the lieutenant."

"Tell me, Dyer, are you a qualified expert on the range?"

He nodded. "Rifle and pistol, just like the rest of the guys."

Garrett put a hand on his shoulder. "Those expert ribbons you wear on your dress blues don't mean shit. Good shooting only counts when the other guy is shooting back. Getting your rounds on target when you're under fire is what it's all about. Remember, you cannot aim; you must hit." Garrett watched him carefully; he was a good kid— serious about the training. "You see, we can preach good shooting technique, sight picture and trigger squeeze, until we're blue in the face. We can put you through live fire drills and the pop-up range, but that only does so much. To be a good combat shooter, you must train while you yourself are under fire. And that's one of the things we teach here." Garrett gave him a grin. "I doubt you would have missed a pop-up target like you missed me today."

He returned Garrett's grin. "Anybody ever hit you when you give them a free shot?"

"Oh yeah." Garrett laughed. "A few classes ago, some snap shooter from Team Five put a couple in my ten ring." He touched his nose. "I forgot that he had been through the course before. Combat shooting is a learned skill. With a little practice, Dyer, you can do the same. But I may not give you another free pass. I don't think you'll miss next time."

"Thanks, Master Chief," Dyer replied as he turned to leave. "See you tomorrow."

"Fair enough, and 'Garrett' or 'Instructor' will do just fine."

"Whatever you say, Master Chief." He grinned, and he was gone.

• • •

Later that evening, Garrett walked up from his apartment to the Hotel Del Coronado. It was one of those soft, temperate evenings that are rare treasures for most Americans but regular fare for those who live along the coast in San Diego. He was dressed in a crisp blue oxford-cloth shirt, chino slacks, and polished loafers. His hair was longer now, just on the edge of what might be called a military cut but with an extra curl in the thick brown wave.

The Navy SEALs had always had a close training relationship with the Federal Bureau of Investigation, especially the FBI Hostage Rescue Team. There were a number of former SEALs on the HRT. Since 9/11, the FBI had asked the military for more combat shooting training for their street agents, including the course Garrett taught for the Navy SEALs. One of those FBI agents Garrett had trained was a rookie agent named Judy Burks. She was a software engineer by training, but a cop at heart. Garrett had never seen anyone with more natural shooting talent than Judy Burks. She was with an FBI team that took down a gang of Russian mafiosi who were smuggling illegal firearms through the Port of Oakland. There had been a shootout, and Judy Burks had been in the thick of it. She had taken out two armed men at short range. Those who witnessed the action said it happened so fast that it was like a scene from a *Die Hard* movie. Garrett did not see the action; he had arrived at the scene after it happened.

Judy's work now periodically brought her to San Diego, and when it did, she gave Garrett a call. Garrett Walker found Judy Burks interesting and unsettling; he never knew quite what to expect from her. He found her seated at a table on the courtyard patio of the del Coronado, a lipstick in one hand and a cigarette in the other. He approached from her blind side.

"Hello, gorgeous. Is that a pistol you're packing or one of those new pushup bras?"

"Hi, sailor," she replied, turning her head and smiling broadly. There was a smudge of a beauty mark under her left eye. "Wanna buy a lady a drink?"

Garrett kissed her on the cheek warmly and slid into the seat across from her. She smelled like a lilac bush in full bloom. She wore an orange cotton blazer over a low-cut white blouse with a short black skirt and heels. Everything was tight. Her makeup was heavy and exaggerated, with dark blue eye shadow and bright red Marilyn Monroe lipstick. Judy was normally a honey blond, but now her hair was so heavily moussed that it had a tangerine cast.

"Well, how do I look?"

"Like the bad fairy."

"No fooling? I was going for a kind of an upscale barrio look—stepping up and stepping out. Does that mean you won't buy me a drink?"

A waiter appeared and frowned at her. He was clearly unhappy with her presence and was about to ask her to leave when Garrett turned and gave him a cold smile. "Give the *lady* whatever the *lady* would like."

The waiter hesitated, then bobbed his head. "As you say, sir."

Judy grinned. "I think what I'd like is a cup of coffee."

"Make that two," Garrett replied. Then after they were alone, "So what gives? You doing surveillance on hookers, or is this just the after-six Judy Burks?"

"Nope, nothing like that. The Customs guys called us in. They think the drug money down south is buying too many border patrol agents, so they wanted us to look into it. I've got a short list of bars to prowl down in Imperial Beach. See if some of the off-duty border cops are spending a little too freely for what the government pays them. How about you?" She gave him a careful appraisal. "You look like you're on your way to a fraternity party."

"No need to get defensive, Agent Burks. I'm just a natty dresser. And when did you take up smoking?"

"I didn't. It's just a prop. It makes me look cool and sexy."

She took a puff and exhaled immediately, holding the cigarette high and to one side with her elbow just off the table—very continental. But a wisp of smoke from the burning tip drifted back across her face and caused her to begin coughing.

"Hey, don't go and hurt yourself," he said, handing her a napkin from the table.

She took it without comment and loudly cleared her throat. "It takes a while to get the hang of it." She coughed again and blew her nose. "By the way, I like your hair longer. And you don't have to stop there; keep it up." She paused while the coffee service was delivered. "So how's my favorite shooting instructor?"

Garrett made a neutral gesture. "It's a job, and I have no complaints, but it's boring. Same thing every day with a new cast of characters every few weeks. I find myself wishing I could be a student. The students get to move on."

Judy Burks had come to know Garrett well enough to understand his frustration and disappointment at being retired from the Navy. She sensed he was still bitter about it, though he never said so. She also knew he was a man who would not allow himself to dwell on the past for any length of time.

"Well, you just hang in there," she said seriously. "You're a great instructor, and a lot of those guys are going to live to fight again because of what you're teaching them. I'm one who knows."

He blew across the top of his coffee. "Like I said, no complaints, but I'm a doer, not a teacher. How'd you like to be on the range at Quantico teaching shooting? You've had a taste of field work; would you give it up to be a range instructor?"

She smiled. That's what she and Garrett had in common. They were direct-action people. He was a rugged article—lean, angular, talented—an aggressive leader. She was a wisp of a girl with soft edges, but in her own way, she was just as tough. When the FBI raided the Oakland warehouse that served as headquarters for the smuggling ring run by the Russians, she had come in through the side entrance. There she had killed two men in a wild shootout. When it was over, she was consumed with panic and revulsion at what she had done. It happened so fast, she had no time to think, only to react— kill or be killed. At that instant, when the smoke had cleared, they were no longer Mafia scum who deserved to die; they were human beings, and she had ended their lives.

Following the shooting, he had been there for her. He had taken her home and stayed with her the entire night, holding her and talking her through the nightmare. He soothed her and helped her to purge the terrible, blood-soaked visions that appeared whenever she closed her eyes. He calmed her, reasoned with her, even made her laugh. Killing was something he knew a great deal about; he comforted her and put the taking of life in perspective. He was both strong and tender, and she had never forgotten it. Since that time, they met frequently for dinner or for daytime outings. They had not become lovers, although the prospect hung heavily between them. Garrett Walker was a wild thing, at times warm and giving and at others isolated and emotionally closed. If they were ever to sleep together, it would have to happen in the natural course of events. More than that, she knew he was still in transition, and she understood that this passage might take some time. Judy Burks was content to bide her time and remain his friend. Still, the image of having sex with this man was a fantasy that often surged through her consciousness in exciting detail.

She shook off her reverie. "I'd like to think that I'd be a damn good shooting coach. But I know what you're saying, or at least I think I do. It's a high. Most of the girls I grew up with are home with children or doing the nine-to-five commuter thing. I'm off to a redneck cop bar with an FBI shield and a snub-nosed .38 in my purse." She grinned. "Are we nuts or what?"

When she smiled like that, Garrett thought, she looked like a teenager, makeup and all. It was a radiant smile.

"How's Ray?"

Ray Stannick was Judy's boss and the special agent in charge of an FBI unit called the Special Investigation Team. Stannick and his team were a mobile unit, but for the past six months they had worked out of the San Francisco field office. They worked primarily against organized crime and the terrorist target. Occasionally the two were the same.

"You know, he asks about you every time I'm down here."

"Maybe he thinks I'm trying to lead you astray."

"Well, sailor," she replied, awkwardly recrossing her legs in the tight skirt, "are you trying to lead me astray?"

"Possibly. You free for dinner tomorrow night, or will you still be pub-crawling with the border Mounties?" He gave her a wolfish smile, and his green eyes danced.

"That depends. Could you be one of those lowlifes bringing hash across the border?"

"You'll never know, Agent Burks, until you investigate."

"Well, that settles it then. Duty calls. I'm staying over at the Hyatt on Shelter Island. Why don't you pick me up about six-thirty?"

3

Initially, Steven wondered if the fifty thousand dollars Simpson had given him was too extravagant. That was three months ago, and now he wasn't so sure. While the pay was generous for the time, the work had consumed him. He had worked seven days a week, almost twelve hours a day—an effort that tried even Lon's inexhaustible patience. Neatly filed in the locked briefcase on his lap were the results of his labor. He had begun his work with little idea of quite where it would lead. The idea of an NGO that would employ armed force and intervene directly in the affairs of a foreign nation was a serious and compelling venture. This intervention could come in a number of ways and in all probability would not have the knowledge or blessing of the "invaded" nation. This was an undertaking that required him to draw on his experience as a paramilitary officer and as a covert-actions specialist. Few men in the world were as capable or as experienced in either of these unique callings as Steven Fagan. That he was an expert in both was rare indeed.

The project had fascinated Steven from the beginning. He knew himself well enough to guard against allowing a project or a cause to become personal. He was a professional and hadn't the luxury of allowing his emotions to influence his work. Creating the organization that Ambassador Simpson had in mind wouldn't be an easy task, nor would the work of this organization be terribly pretty. But he did feel it was feasible—organizationally and operationally. And he found the prospect of continuing to work with this project strangely exciting. Perhaps I have let it become personal, he thought; perhaps professionally personal, he admitted, is a better term. That, or I was put out to pasture too early, and I still want to be part of the action. Or had he simply allowed it to become a challenge—the ultimate covert undertaking with a real chance to make a difference?

The objective was a worthy one; cool global flash points early and quickly, and avoid allowing a situation to deteriorate to the point where U.S. special operations or conventional forces had to be called in—or too many innocent people died. In some cases, he knew the force he had in mind would have capabilities that exceeded conventional military means, even those of America's special operations forces. Al Qaeda had gone to ground, but any number of terrorist cells were operating around the world. What better organization than this to root them out? Done properly, it could save tens of thousands of lives. It was anybody's guess just what technologies had leaked out of Iraq or Iran, or Pakistan for that matter. Steven's abilities and special talents had certainly been employed in lesser causes. He could name several leftist political leaders whose careers he had ended. On a rare occasion, he had also ended their lives, leaving only vague suspicions that the act had been sanctioned by the leader of the free world. Some of these men had been duly elected officials. Because he analyzed each mission carefully, Fagan usually knew his targets well. In many cases they were patriots—nationalists who had embraced communism out of convenience. It had been their undoing.

The United States, because of the Central Intelligence Agency and men like Steven Fagan, had the ability to make changes, often in ways that the average American would consider most un-American. To the powerful men in Washington, covert action was a way to exert influence. It was not a course of action to be taken imprudently, of course, but an extension of foreign policy that was stronger than a diplomatic protest but well short of landing the Marines. Marines, and even the special operations forces, he thought, were unable to successfully intervene in a great many global problems. In still others, their response, physically or bureaucratically, was simply too slow. Perhaps, just perhaps, this was a chance to repair some of the damage he and his country had done during the Cold War and its aftermath. For some time now, he felt that his career as a covert operator had done more harm than good. Just maybe, this was a chance to redeem himself—personally. But, he reminded himself, I have not been asked to do this; it is only a feasibility study.

At the Agency, Steven had always practiced his trade from a strong moral fortress; he acted on instructions from his government—he was a soldier. A man could do some cruel and inhumane things in the name of his country, he reflected, and be officially absolved of all sin. That's the way it was in America. But Fagan knew this would not be the case if he remained in the employment of Joseph Simpson. This was a whole different game. Hell, he thought, it became a different game when those bastards took down the World Trade Center.

"Sir, we'll be landing at Kennedy Airport in just a few minutes. Would you like me to place that in the overhead compartment for you?"

"No, thanks," he replied. "I'll just keep it with me."

He slid the case under the seat in front of him without difficulty. First-class seating was quite spacious, and no one was seated next to him. During the last few months he had done a great deal of traveling for short meetings and sight surveys—a day here, two days there, occasionally out of the country. Simpson had authorized a generous travel budget, but Steven normally traveled in coach class; it was less conspicuous. Today, however, he wanted to relax and think about the work he had just completed and what, if anything, might lie ahead. He had spent a great deal of time on airplanes over the years. Yet, even an experienced traveler sometimes feels a little vulnerable at thirty-seven thousand feet, and Steven had found this vague uneasiness often helped him to think.

Steven Fagan honestly believed there was evil in the world. He had formed this opinion well before 9/11. He could not have done the things he had done at the CIA if he didn't. *But was covert action suited to the work of an NGO? Or was this just a sophisticated, do-gooder version of the Mafia's Murder Incorporated?* The evil that Steven thought this organization could effectively target could be a movement, an individual, a government, or a fanatical religious faction. If this business could be conducted with no attribution to the U.S. government, then the range of targets and methods were virtually unlimited. And if the action taken were skillful, his nation just might avoid responsibility or retaliation. The possibilities were endless.

The flight attendant came back up the aisle and tonged him a damp, warm terry-cloth towel. He wiped his face and hands, then relaxed into the headrest and stared across a layer of unbroken clouds. Fagan knew there were situations in the world that, if not directly in opposition to U.S. interests, adversely affected our allies. Some posed threats to fledgling democracies. In the Muslim world,

they were a threat to secular governments. Still others, if
left unchecked, would cause immense humanitarian suffering. In short, there was still evil. *How many thousands
could have been saved if we had been effective in Somalia, or
had moved early and quickly in the Balkans? And how
many American lives are too many to put a tyrant in his
place or to disband a small army of thugs preying on a de-
fenseless population?* Steven had always felt that if a cause
was worth fighting for, it was worth dying for. Cruise missiles and smart bombs could only do so much. The
Marines and Special Forces could do only so much.
*Maybe this way was a better answer all around; an idea
whose time has come.*

Perhaps, he concluded, the old ways of conflict resolution are outdated. Economic sanctions and conventional
armed intervention are just archaic, ineffective solutions
to rogue states and rogue organizations. And consensus in
the UN sometimes comes too late or not at all. Our nation is often bound by international organization, but I
am not, he thought. Some very real problems could be
better dealt with by someone like him. And, Steven reflected, not for the first time, maybe only by someone like
him. Like all good covert operators, he was an excellent
chess player; he could see several moves ahead. Politicians
did not always do this. Sometimes a crisis cannot wait for
a debate in Congress or the building of a coalition. If he
had the funds to build the infrastructure and a free hand
in the operational planning, a great deal of good could be
accomplished by a very small number of people. He also
knew there could be some terrible side effects along the
way.

The long, comfortable flight had afforded him little
new insight. Perhaps that would come when he again met
with his employer. They were out of the overcast just long
enough for Fagan to glimpse the bland, rain-soaked

Queens landscape before the wheels thumped onto the tarmac at JFK.

Simpson was waiting for him at the table that evening. The dining room at the New York Athletic Club was not a place Steven would have chosen, but perhaps it didn't matter. This was, after all, the final day of his assignment. Simpson rose and shook his hand warmly, and they settled into the booth.

"Steven, thank you for coming. It's good to see you again."

Fagan immediately noticed subtle changes in Simpson. He was dressed well, as he had been at their first meeting, but there was a certain crispness to him that had previously been absent. He looked less drawn, perhaps more confident than before, and there was a sense of purpose and well-being about him. While Steven had carried out his assignment, there had been a series of articles in the national papers about the Joseph Simpson Jr. Foundation. An unprecedented amount of food had just been delivered to refugees in the Sudan, Mozambique, and northern Iraq, and there were indications that relief efforts for victims of the recent flooding in Bangladesh had arrived in record time. What the public didn't see were the millions of dollars quietly being pumped into secular education in Islamic nations. Some of these funds supported madrasas, or Islamic schools, but if they were found to be teaching violent anti-Western doctrine, the money stopped. Joseph Simpson, heretofore the private, publicity-shy man, was now photographed in the company of celebrities and industry leaders. He had been successful in attracting corporate gifts to add to his own resources. But the smiling, handsome face Steven had seen at fund-raisers in the paper differed from the one seated across from him. This man was cordial, but he was also deadly serious.

Over dinner, Simpson told him of the work of the foundation. Fagan felt the older man's controlled passion for the project. From Simpson's description, Fagan could see that he employed the same expertise and organizational skills that had built his business empire. He had hired top people and had structured the foundation to work with existing, successful relief organizations. Steven knew from his own research that Simpson's approach was sound. He was doing everything right—taking the best from established programs and building on them. Fagan also knew that such programs, even an effort skillfully managed by a man as capable as Joseph Simpson, could only work at the margins of the problem. Too often men with an ethnic or religious agenda controlled things. Too often the opposition had guns and lived beyond the reach of a central government.

After the coffee was served, Simpson turned to him. "So what have you learned, Steven? Is there a way we can effectively attack this problem in, shall we say, an unconventional manner?"

"Yes, sir, I believe there is. It's not a course of action that can be taken without risks, but I believe it is possible. As you can perhaps imagine, there would always be the potential for attribution and political fallout. Not like when U.S. forces are involved, but there is always that risk." He withdrew two thick, bound portfolios and handed them to Simpson. "The first document is a compilation of my research on the most recent flash points and the action, if any, taken by the international community to resolve them. Frankly, it's not a very impressive track record. Then I took each scenario and applied the force structure that I believe is possible to create within the established parameters." He met Simpson's eye. "With a few exceptions, we could have positively influenced these situations, or at least provided a measure of stability until more permanent solutions could be found. In two of them we could have brought about a total resolution. As far as dealing with terrorists, well, in many cases not as many would have escaped. And we probably would have gotten bin Laden."

"The second document is basically an operational plan to stand up such a force, maintain it in an operational posture and ready to deploy on short notice. And since we must have the internal ability to support these operations in the field, the cost is substantial. I recommend an ethnic bias to the force structure. There are still some unknowns, not the least of which is the command and control structure." Steven hesitated before continuing. "It's not a course of action for the squeamish. We're dealing with small units who must achieve a force multiplier through decisive, lethal, and often vicious action. Candidly, I think you may find my cure philosophically worse than the kind of thing we want to prevent."

Simpson set the two documents to one side and fingered his dessert fork. "Perhaps, but I doubt it." Then he looked up at Fagan. "Naturally, I'll want to spend some time with these. I have a feeling that your assessment of the problem may not be dissimilar to my own. Right now, I'd like you to tell me about your proposal. And more specifically, what some of the things you, or someone like you, could do if you had the funding and a mandate to act."

Steven anticipated this, but it was still difficult to know where to begin. "First of all, most of these problems are diverse, and their origins often rooted in generations of ethnic or religious hatred. Often it's about religion, but mostly it's about power. What would work in one situation may not be effective in another. And the effect may only be temporary, perhaps some breathing room until more substantial, multinational forces are brought into play."

"Or until some coalition can be formed?" Simpson almost spat the words.

"You should also know, Ambassador, that some of these methods are not only illegal, they may in some cases be quite brutal, perhaps indiscriminately so."

Simpson seemed lost in thought, then again focused on Fagan. "Just how brutal, Steven?"

"The use of force may not always be warranted. If it is, we must be prepared to do three things—three things that any unilateral or multinational force is usually unwilling to do. We have to take sides, take casualties, and shoot preemptively, perhaps even indiscriminately." He paused, carefully framing his words. "For example, take the UN force currently in Bosnia and Kosovo. It is made up of Americans, British, and French servicemen who operate under very strict rules of engagement—a document the size of a phone book. Under an arrangement like we're discussing, one that is to be effective, there will be rules, but only our rules." He cautiously sipped at his coffee. "Occasionally, we may be able to use misdirection or camouflage in our work with *Mission: Impossible* tactics, but not often. Quite often these situations require the direct, straightforward application of force. And sometimes the best way to kill the snake is to cut his head off."

"Assassination?"

Steven nodded.

"Tell me something of how you would go about putting this organization together."

Again, Steven was ready for this. "Ambassador—"

"Please, if I may, I would appreciate it if you would call me Joe."

With a conscious effort, Steven continued, "Ah, Joe, I

understand that you retained some of your real estate holdings—that you still own a few selected ranch lands and are now leasing them to Ameribeef."

"That is correct."

Steven talked for close to a half hour, and Simpson listened intently, interrupting only to clarify a point. When he finished, the older man sat forward, lost in thought. He remained like that for several minutes, then slowly shook his head and looked at Steven.

"It's brilliant, Steven—bold and brilliant." Steven smiled tightly to acknowledge the compliment. Simpson continued, "And to do this right, to be effective, there will have to be a commitment of this size?"

"That is my assessment. Our current foreign policy is a trail of failures because we hesitated, then acted indecisively and hoped for the best. No, Ambass—I mean, Joe— there are no guarantees, and most certainly there are situations that defy resolution. On the other hand, I firmly believe there are some very nasty, isolated problems we can address, but only if we are prepared to move quickly and with resolve. I think we can be particularly effective against the secret terrorist networks acting with tacit, if not overt, state sponsorship. And we have one decided advantage. Our decision making can be driven by operational considerations—clear assessments of the risk versus the chance for success. And how grave is the danger. No political considerations, no congressional debate, no UN resolutions, no public opinion polls, and no CNN. And another thing, Joe, the success of the mission may override the welfare of the men we send to do the job. That's not always the case when we send 'our boys' in."

Neither man spoke for several moments. Steven reflected on how for the last half hour, he had talked of "we" doing this and "we" doing that. *Have I come under the spell of this powerful and charismatic man?*

"How did we get here, Steven?" Simpson said quietly. "In a world that's so exciting and full of possibilities, how can there be such inhumanity and suffering? How is it that two men like us are brought to contemplate such an undertaking?"

Steven studied Simpson. The confidence he saw earlier was now sincerity and sadness. Steven made a helpless gesture.

"I don't know, but I've given it some thought. I think it may be related to the times we live in. It may be simply a matter of modern technology and dated cultures; them and us. Before 9/11, the evil and suffering were largely confined to other parts of the world. Now we know it can happen anywhere. Much of what is good in the world is related to technology, but it's leaving a growing number of people behind. Technology is also empowering some small but very deadly and evil forces. Some cultures resist what the modern world offers because they are locked in the past and semiliterate. Tribal and ethnic rivalries dictate everything. Technology and secularism threaten their control."

Simpson considered this and agreed silently. Then he straightened up and measured Fagan.

"Let me study this, and I'll get back to you. I'm sure I'll have some questions."

"That'll be fine, sir."

He slipped the two documents into his briefcase and locked it, then handed Steven an envelope. "I want to thank you for what you've done so far. This is a bonus to show my appreciation for your professionalism and your work." Fagan started to protest, but Simpson held up his hand. "I also have a few more questions, if I may?" Fagan held his gaze. "How do you feel about all this? More specifically, how will you respond if I ask you to carry out this plan—to be my CEO, if you will?"

"I'm not sure, sir. During the past few weeks, I've thought a great deal about it—little else, as a matter of fact. To be truthful, I still don't know." He glanced at the envelope that still lay on the table. "It's not the money; you've been more than generous. This is a big step, a life-altering step."

Simpson nodded. "I think we've both taken the time to learn something of each other in the last few months, Steven. I'm sure you know why I may be considering this. But what about you? It's more than a big step for you; you have a great deal to lose. Why would you even contemplate this?"

Steven gave the older man a twisted smile. "I can't answer that one either. The whole business scares the hell out of me, but maybe it's something that needs to be done. Our political process, and the American people, don't seem to deal with this very well. Evil can attack at will without warning. We, on the other hand, must have a lengthy public debate. The attack by al Qaeda shocked us profoundly, but already America is drifting back into complacency. It is economically and psychologically very costly to respond to terror and evil. Politically as well. If we don't have a preemptive strategy, we stand at risk for another strike, perhaps one far more devastating than the World Trade Center. I'm sure of one thing, though. If we don't do it, no one else will. No one else can."

There was a heavy silence between them until Simpson spoke. "I'll read what you've done. Then we'll talk again."

Fagan slipped the envelope into his suit pocket, and they shook hands. Simpson sat alone at the table, deep in thought, for quite some time after Fagan left.

Saturday morning, August 31,
Coronado

Judy Burks, lying on her stomach, moaned softly as she slowly awoke from a very sound sleep. Like a little bear, she was groggy and burrowed among the sheets, a pillow across the top of her head and shoulders. Gradually she became aware that she was not in her own bed—not in her San Francisco apartment. A faint notion of apprehension began to grip her. *Where am I?* Then she remembered exactly where she was, and a faint smile crept across her face. She moved a hand to the other side of the bed, and the smile faded.

Garrett Walker stepped from the closet and dropped silently to the carpet. Quickly, he laced his running shoes. Then he began a precise, deliberate routine of stretching exercises. She watched him through slitted eyes as he moved smoothly from one position to the next. He was long-muscled and well-proportioned. His wide shoulders and heavy thighs seemed to accent his slim waist and hips. There was not an ounce of fat on him. His face was tranquil and relaxed, as if he were preparing for holy communion. Judy knew that this stretching routine and his morning run were a daily ritual with Garrett—a solitary, semireligious thing from which she was totally excluded. She also knew that he would be relaxed and very easy to be with when he returned. He adjusted the bezel on his watch and moved to the side of the bed. Gently he lifted the pillow from her head.

"You awake, or are you playing possum?"

She flapped an eye open. "I'm sound asleep and wish not to be disturbed."

"I see." He leaned over and kissed her on the cheek; she

was soft and warm and looked about twelve. "See you in a bit."

"That's it," she managed. "Going to just kiss and run?"

"Uh-huh," he replied with a broad smile and was out the door.

Judy rolled over and pulled the sheets up protectively around her chin. She was not unhappy to have a few moments to herself; the night before had been one full of passion, and she was now feeling the uncomfortable aftereffects. She and Garrett had become lovers about two months ago. Even though they were lucky to see each other every other weekend, she now considered them an item. The first time had been an evening not unlike last night. They had dinner at La Contessa and walked slowly back along Glorietta Bay to Garrett's studio apartment. It was in an older building with a comfortable, spacious balcony that looked out across the Coronado Yacht Club and south along the Silver Strand. On a clear night, as most tended to be in Coronado, you could see the city lights that ringed San Diego Bay as far south as Imperial Beach. In the past, they had their coffee on the balcony, and then they would talk for an hour or so before she left. Last night, as he had that first time two months ago, Garrett asked if she would like some scotch. He brought her a tumbler with only a splash of Glenlivet. She was normally not a scotch drinker, but in the clear night air of the balcony with the bay lights sparkling, it was like sipping liquid gold. The combination of a warm, balmy evening and the liquor seemed to weave a seductive spell over them. As they kissed, Garrett pulled her up to him, and she followed him inside.

She had tried to prepare herself, for she sensed that he would be passionate and physically demanding. He was that and more, but she was totally unprepared for his tenderness. He made love like he stretched—slowly and with a deliberate patience. There was an undercurrent of desire and urgency in his passion, but he managed it well, allowing her a full measure of pleasure before giving himself over. They made love more than once, and each time it was as if she was astride a volcano that could control its time and place, but not always its fury.

Not wanting to fall back asleep, she rose and walked to the closet. There she slipped into one of Garrett's long-sleeved rugby shirts. It dropped to just above her knees. She retrieved a glass of juice from the fridge and stepped out onto the balcony to survey the morning. Gulls wheeled overhead and dived through a light mist rising off Glorietta Bay. The sun was not yet up and the Coronado Bay Bridge arched against the growing light like a cardboard cutout. She caught a glimpse of Garrett as he trotted south along the Strand bicycle path. Like everything else, he ran smoothly and with a great deal of control. She watched until he passed from view behind the Naval Amphibious Base, then returned to the apartment.

It was large for a studio, with good storage closets, and incredibly neat and clean. Neat and clean not because of a good housekeeper or some special effort for her visit; Garrett Walker was simply a very well-ordered person. He took care of his space and his personal effects much as he had taken care of his military equipment and his men. Judy had never thought of herself as a slob, but when Garrett visited her in San Francisco, she spent several evenings preparing for his arrival. Still, there was a notable difference between a good cleaning and living clean. Sometimes she felt she was spending the night in a model home.

The furnishings were spartan but comfortable. A stereo system along one wall of the living area was com-

pact and expensive, and there was no TV. He kept a ceremonial uniform in his closet, pressed and in a garment
bag, and there were two gray canvas bags of field gear
nestled on the floor of a small storage bay. Otherwise,
there was no evidence that he had been a Navy SEAL—
no plaques, no photos, no display cases with colorful, rib-
boned decorations. In her own apartment, she had
mounted her diplomas from Cal Tech and her graduation
certificate from the FBI Academy. There were scattered
framed photos of her parents, one of her receiving an
award from the Director and several candid photos with
her and other members of the Special Investigations
Team. Garrett had nothing like that. She had once asked
him why there were no memorabilia about. "It was a hard
door to close," he told her, "and I need to focus on the future." Judy also sensed that he was not the kind of man
who needed reminders to tell him who he was or where
he had been. She knew being a Navy SEAL meant a great
deal to him. She also felt he was a man who could open
doors as well as close them, no matter how difficult they
were.

Garrett returned in less than an hour, time enough for
her to fold the bedding and put away the futon. Judy had
already showered and was curled up on the sofa with the
Sunday edition of the *San Diego Union*. She was dressed
in shorts, sneakers, and a striped blouse. She had thought
of timing her shower for when he arrived, but decided
against it. It was not that she didn't want more of him, but
she had learned that he was not one to lie about making
love after the sun was up. For Garrett Walker, sex was part
of a romantic evening—the intimacy that follows a nice
dinner, a good wine, and soft conversation. He had surprised her one afternoon, but for the most part they were
evening lovers. He was out of the shower, shaved, and
dressed in less than ten minutes. She pulled the front

page, editorial, sports, and travel sections and rose to meet him.

"Ready?"

"You bet."

It took them close to a half hour to walk the length of Pomona Avenue, east across the island. Garrett favored a small coffee shop, an older, locally owned establishment. He refused to defect to the local Starbucks. Judy found a table out front by the sidewalk while Garrett went inside for coffee and scones. When he returned, the sun had just peeked over the row of condos along the east side of Bayview Avenue and chased away the light morning chill. They positioned the chairs to take best advantage of the warmth and camped around their warm mugs.

"Life is good."

He returned her smile and reached over and squeezed her shoulder. "Life is good."

Coronado is a delightful pancake of an island, or near island, that forms the western arm of San Diego Bay and keeps downtown San Diego from becoming an ocean-front city without a harbor. A thin strand of sand, at places just wide enough for Highway 75, connects Coronado to the border community of Imperial Beach. The huge North Island Naval Air Base anchors one end of the community, and the Naval Amphibious Base the other. Coronado is a wealthy community, but unlike La Jolla and Del Mar, people don't show their wealth. Any flash seen on the streets of Coronado usually suggests a guest at the Hotel del Coronado.

Coronado is a Navy town and home to a great number of sailors and military retirees. The population can jump dramatically when all three aircraft carriers are tied up at North Island. This morning, the outside tables were occupied by locals, most of them older couples. Judy easily caught Garrett's reaction as three very fit, tanned young men in shorts and T-shirts jogged passed them on the sidewalk, noting the brief, dark cloud that passed over his rugged features.

"Still hurts a little, doesn't it?" She had learned that straight talk never offended him.

He gave her a lopsided grin. "Yeah, it does. Teaching combat shooting to others only goes so far."

"It's really important for you to be in the middle of the action, isn't it—to be in the field and carry a rifle." He raised his eyebrows and gave her a neutral stare. "I know what it means to be a field agent and to do field work," she continued. "Most of it is routine gumshoe work, but there's always the prospect of some action. I suppose it's not like SEAL work, where you're always in the action."

Garrett was silent a moment before he replied. "It is important—the action part—but it's not just the action. Quite a few SEALs spend their whole career training for a fight and never fire a shot in anger. I've been lucky, or depending on how you look at it, unlucky. If I were still in and never saw action again, I'd have seen more of it than most." He measured her, carefully framing his words. "It's not the prospect of combat I miss, although I admit that it is a rush; it's the team thing. I really miss being with a team—showing the new men the way things are done, challenging the older guys to take their game to the next level. It's taking the best of a bunch of good men and making it collectively better. That's what it's about; that's what it's always been about." He sipped thoughtfully on his coffee, then gave her a generous smile. "Y'know, I never saw it as clearly as I do now, but that's how it is."

"So the shooting training just won't do?" She seldom got this far under the surface with him and wanted to keep him talking.

"I don't think so. It's been a good transition, but I need something more. I've already started to look around."

"Oh?"

"It's not the easiest thing in the world." He now looked a little puzzled, unsure of himself. It made her want to touch him. "I mean, my résumé is not terribly inviting—college dropout, medically retired from the Navy, proficient with an automatic weapon. There's not a lot in the want ads for a guy like me."

"You said that you've been looking around. Found anything?"

He rolled a corner of a scone into his mouth. "Every once in a while I get a call from one of those corporate security consultants—typically guys responsible for the safety of U.S. citizens working in the Middle East, Russia, or South America. Some say they have contracts with third-world countries for special military training. But so far, nothing's come along that seems very interesting."

"You mean, nothing where you could be on your own or where you could be in charge."

He looked at her and smiled warmly. She was getting to know him, what he was thinking, and he found that pleasantly disturbing.

"Yeah, I guess you could say that."

Sunday afternoon, September 1, San Francisco

Steven Fagan had only carry-on luggage, so he went directly from the gate to the passenger pickup area. Lon came slashing across two lanes of traffic, oblivious to the drivers who had to slam on their brakes to keep from hitting her. She bounced the right front wheel up onto the curb, then back into the street, bringing the car to a halt.

Steven stood well back until the BMW came to a complete stop before the terminal. His wife was the most caring, understanding person he knew, but she drove like a maniac. Not unlike many Asian-born Americans, she didn't really drive a car; she aimed it. Sometimes he would ask to drive when she met him, even though he knew it offended her. She was very proud of her driving skills. He tossed his overnight bag in back and got in.

"Hello, *chérie,* welcome home."

"Hi, honey." He leaned over and kissed her on the cheek, quickly fumbling for his seat belt. She shot forward into the traffic, fighting her way onto the freeway and heading north from San Francisco International on Highway 101.

"So how did it go? Was Ambassador Simpson pleased with your efforts?"

"I think so. It'll take him some time to get through the material, but he seemed satisfied with what I had to tell him." He started to show her the bonus check but refrained, not wanting her to take her eyes from the road. "He gave me a bonus of twenty-five thousand dollars."

"Twenty-five big ones!" Lon watched a lot of gangster movies on TV. "He must have really liked your work."

"Perhaps," he replied. "But I'm not so sure that was the reason for the bonus. In any case, he's a very wealthy man."

"Does he have another job for you?" she asked cautiously. Sensing that he was concerned, she slowed the car to just over the legal limit and eased into the right-hand lane. Cars on the freeway shot past them. Lon knew only that he had been doing research on establishing some kind of an illegal, international force. He had not directly told her about any future involvement, but she knew in general terms what he did at the CIA. She also knew when he was troubled, and he *was* troubled.

Perhaps *reflective* was a better word than *troubled*. She had sensed an anxiety building in him for several months but assumed that it would end with the completion of the project. That did not seem to now be the case.

"I'm not sure. He may not have anything more for me, and if he does, I'm not entirely sure it's something I want to do—we want to do," he quickly added.

"So, he may offer you another contract, but if he does, you are not sure if you want to take it?"

Steven nodded but said nothing. They headed north for Marin County while Lon talked about her garden and about a bond issue that would extend the jogging trails along the canal through Larkspur. All the while, she drove quite sensibly. After they crossed the Golden Gate, she turned off the freeway before they reached the Larkspur exit.

"We're not going home?"

She smiled. "It's early yet. Let's take a walk in the woods."

Muir Woods is always crowded in the summer, but less so during the weekdays. Lon took his arm, and they strolled along the paved walkway with the rest of the tourists, then took one of the side trails that branched off along a small stream. Steven had shed his coat and tie, but the slacks and loafers precluded any serious trekking. They found a crude log bench, one strategically placed a few steps from the trail to allow visitors a quiet place to enjoy the forest. Once seated, he picked up a twig and began to section it, flipping pieces into the feeder stream that gurgled just below them. They sat for some time before he spoke.

"When all this began, I thought it would be only a consulting contract," he began, "a study for dealing directly with isolated problem spots in the world. But the proposal, in many ways, has become an extension or evolution of the work I was doing at Langley. Ambassador Simpson—it's Joe now—asked me for a plan to develop a small, mobile force that could be used as an intervention force in problem spots around the world. This . . . this intervention force would be privately funded and have a charter to operate freely and use whatever means possible. Some of the work would be paramilitary in nature and some of it pure direct action. Much of it would involve covert activity. There could also be a measure of disinformation and subversion." Steven spoke of this with no distaste; these were the tools of his trade.

"A mercenary force?" she said, raising her eyebrows.

"That's right."

"Wow! You mean a small army where the good guys can be just as bad as the bad guys?" Lon also liked the old westerns. "Like in *The Magnificent Seven?*"

Steven smiled. "Well, sort of. A great deal of the work I did for Simpson was to study the issues; I examined why our foreign policy has been so ineffective in dealing with these ethnic and religious flash points around the globe. And why the terrorist cells always seem to elude us." He paused and tossed the rest of the twig into the current. "Two things have become clear to me during the last few months. First, there is no end to these problems in the world. There is no end to thuggish dictators who will support terrorists like al Qaeda to protect their corrupt regimes. Or to keep democratic reforms out. If left unchecked, they will continue to cause instability and suffering, abroad and occasionally here at home. The second is that America usually lacks the will to intervene in a timely and efficient manner. If our past efforts are any indication, we only exacerbate the problem."

"Exacerbate?"

"We get involved and make things worse."

"Oh. So this Mr. Simpson may ask you to form a posse of good guys and go about the world to make bad things right? Like the Seven Samurai?"

Fagan nodded.

"Can you do this?"

"Yes. At least I think so. And that's part of what troubles me," he said sadly. "Over the past few months, I've come to believe that I may be one of the only people who can."

After a while, Lon spoke quietly. "Can it be so bad a thing, that there is this evil in the world and that you can do something about it?" Steven shrugged. Lon was silent for a moment, then continued. "In Laos, our people lived for centuries under the old ways, and we followed the teaching of Lord Buddha. When the French came, they brought change, but it was gentle change. They brought their religion, but Catholics and Buddhists can live in harmony, as did my father and mother. After Dien Bien Phu, things changed. The Viet Minh came and murdered all who opposed them. Three or four of them with guns could subject a whole village of peasants." She lowered her head. "In my village they came at night. They murdered our village chief, my father, and my mother. They hung them in the village center for all to see—for me to see. After that, they were feared and obeyed. Then came the Pathet Lao in my country and Pol Pot in Cambodia, and they murdered half the population." She shrugged. "By then the Americans were tired of Southeast Asia and Vietnam. But the killing did not stop. There is always talk about reparations for the six million Jews killed in Europe. Huge funds were collected for the victims at the World Trade Center. No one seems concerned about my father and mother or the millions of Cambodians who were killed." She gave him a wan smile. "I know Americans do not always care about the suffering in the jungles and the rice fields—places far from the TV cameras—but things may have been different if the good guys had come."

Steven regarded her. She seldom spoke out like this, yet he knew she was telling the truth. He leaned forward with his forearms on his knees, and Lon sensed in him a measure of resignation. "Making a difference will be dangerous. And perhaps costly. It will not bring about slaughter as you knew it in Southeast Asia," he managed, "but people will die, perhaps innocent people. And once I begin this, there will be no turning back; I'll have to see it through."

"Is there no other way?" she asked. He shook his head in resignation. "Then tell me this, my husband, why does it have to be you? Is this what you want?"

She was not belligerent or antagonistic, but she did need to understand why it had to be him. She knew her husband was a special man with special talents. And as always, she spoke from the heart. All she wanted to know was why he, or why he and this very rich stranger, had to do this alone.

Steven shrugged. "I don't know," he said simply. "It would seem that a country like ours, so rich and so powerful and so secure, could find the means—and the moral authority—to act decisively. It's just not the way it is."

"So to protect the freedom and the lives of others, you and Mr. Simpson must act alone?" Like most naturalized American citizens, Lon was very knowledgeable about liberty and freedom. Fagan again shrugged. "So, as I understand it, the work that you will do, you won't worry too much about politics or the law or individual rights, will you?"

Steven smiled weakly. Lon had a way of going right to

the core of the matter, cutting through all the ambiguities. She might have, he thought, even added morality to the list of things he didn't have to worry about. But it wasn't necessary. He already had.

They were silent for a very long time, then Lon continued. "America is a very strange and wonderful land, and not all of it is good or as it should be. Yet I think it is very important for the world to have a nation like America. America makes all other nations behave just a little better. Evil people, like terrorists and outlaws, will never be able to have it their own way as long as there is a place like America. Yet if America cannot stop these bad people, then you must. If you and Mr. Simpson can do something to stop evil things in the world, what choice do you have?"

She placed a hand on his thigh, and he turned to look at her. Her large eyes were clear and firm, and only a little sad. Yet she was very composed and serene. Lon was a Buddhist and an Asian, and that allowed her a perspective few Occidentals understand. She saw life in terms of cycles of suffering, and believed that the travails of this life help one to prepare for the ordeals of the next. And like most Buddhists, she was something of a fatalist. She felt that much of life is preordained and the path you travel is your destiny. One could only meet one's fate with dignity and a pure spirit.

Steven Fagan loved and cherished his wife very much, and while he respected her faith, he did not share it. He couldn't; he was a covert operator and a paramilitary specialist. For him, life was a series of events and outcomes that could be influenced and, more importantly, manipulated. People are free to choose, he believed, but with skill and understanding, many of those choices can be orchestrated and exploited. This conviction did not make him a candidate for a strong religious belief, but it did make him keenly aware of the responsibility that went along with his trade. The ability to change the course of lives and nations was normally the province of political and religious leaders. That he could also do this, without their consent or even their knowledge, made Steven Fagan a very cautious and humble man. He was neither a zealot, nor was he ambitious; he was simply a professional, and he fully understood the reach of his power.

He took her hand and squeezed it. They rose together, then slowly made their way back through the woods to their car, and he drove them home.

Later that evening the phone rang, and Lon answered on the second ring. She placed a hand over the mouthpiece and held it out.

"It's your friend, Joe."

Steven gave her a steady look and took the handset. She started to leave, but he placed a restraining hand on her shoulder, then dropped his arm to her waist to hold her there with him.

"Good evening, sir." He listened for a moment, then smiled. "Yes, of course, good evening, Joe."

He was silent for several minutes and listened while Simpson spoke. Then Steven responded, "No, I don't really need to speak to my wife; we've already talked about it." Lon ran her index finger gently along the tunnel of his spine in the lower portion of his back. Steven looked down directly into her eyes.

"If you are prepared to move ahead with this, then so am I—so are we."

Thursday, September 5,
Khalabad, Iran

The sun hung just above the rugged outline of the Kuh-e Hazaran range. The jagged horizon separated the desert of the broad central Iranian plain from the royal blue northwest sky. A small enclave of stone huts and sod stables clung to a shallow valley plateau bounded by rolling, barren hills. The little village was not unlike dozens of others in this part of central Iran, eking out a meager subsistence from farming and goatherding. Most of the residents in this village were either very old, very young, or men for whom this was only a temporary residence. There were few amenities, although some of the dwellings had recently obtained portable generators. The villagers were a mixture of mountain tribes—Central Asian nomads who had intermarried for generations so that ethnic differences were no longer distinguishable. But clan divisions were everything. This particular village was a little more prosperous than most because the few men who were there were accomplished smugglers. It was also a village at peace, because they were under the control of a village chief who was a strict fundamentalist. They were eight hundred miles and close to a century in time from Tehran. Punishments as prescribed by the Koran were interpreted literally. In recent memory, there had been only one incident of thievery in the village, which resulted in the amputation of a hand. There was one accusation of adultery last year, but the evidence was inconclusive. Otherwise, the woman would have been stoned to death.

The village of Khalabad was served by a single gravel road and a network of footpaths that led into the mountains that bordered the central plateau and finally to the

Dasht Lut wilderness and the Afghan border. The regional town of Kerman lay sixty-five miles to the north, some three hours by jeep on unimproved roads. Thanks to the miracle of cellular technology and encryption, there was secure telephone contact with the outside world. Still, there was no way one could drive to Khalabad without first traveling through Kerman and several other villages along the way. This was a distinct advantage for some of the residents of Khalabad.

Life here differed little from that in other mountain villages across central Iran, Afghanistan, and Pakistan; the men sat in small groups, smoking and drinking coffee, while heavily veiled women worked. Morning and evening prayers were strictly observed. Progressive changes brought about in other parts of Iran had yet to make their way to this village. But in Khalabad there was a small, freshly built stone compound at the edge of the main cluster of dwellings, and the occupants moved about at strange times. Sometimes they came out in twos and threes, usually midmorning but sometimes not until mid- or even late afternoon. At night or during the infrequent cloudy days, they seemed to move about freely. Most in the village thought this odd, but they asked no questions, for the strangers who occasionally came to Khalabad were men of power and influence. They were also under the protection of a regional sect that controlled who could and could not come to this village. The caretakers of the new compound never left the village, but the others came and went, often leaving for months at a time. Usually they traveled by jeep, but not always. These outsiders treated everyone in Khalabad with courtesy and respect, but the villagers treated the newcomers with some deference, for it was evident that they were hard and dangerous men. And the village of Khalabad produced some of the toughest mountain fighters in the world. When the Soviets invaded Afghanistan and jihad was declared, many of them left to fight the invaders. Not all of them came back, at least not immediately, but most did eventually return. More than a few were killed when the American-backed Northern Alliance swept in from the Uzbek border during the second Afghan invasion.

A short man in traditional robes stepped to the door of the compound and peered out. He turned back to one of those who waited at a discreet distance.

"Is it safe to go out?" he asked one of the others.

"Yes," one of them replied as he consulted a notebook. "There is nothing above us for a while, and we will be safe until nightfall."

He nodded thoughtfully. "Very well. I would like to go for a short walk. Ask Khalib if he would like to accompany me."

"I will tell him, Abu Dokhan."

There was an immediate bustle of activity. The robed man waited patiently by the door as four men armed with Kalashnikov rifles filed past him. They lowered their heads briefly in deference as they passed him and made their way outside. Moments later, another man stepped to the door—the same man who had met Moshe Abramin that first day at the café in Lahore. He no longer wore the garb of a cleric but the clothes of an al Qaeda mountain fighter. His coarse, thick beard and hairline circled a lean face, leathered by years of altitude and harsh weather. He was a severe man by any measure, but it was his pale blue, semi-opaque eyes that made him appear dangerous.

"You wished to see me, Dokhan?" His Arabic was quite good, though it was not his native language. He deferred to the man who waited by the door, but not with the subservience shown by the others. He had fought the Russians and the Americans, and was a man who would bow to no one.

"Yes, Khalib. Will you take a walk with me?" The smaller man's speech carried a Lebanese accent, one from the streets of Beirut.

"Of course, Dokhan."

Abu Dokhan was only one of Imad Mugniyah's noms de guerre. In Arabic it literally meant "father of smoke," for he was known as one who could disappear into thin air, like a puff of smoke. It was also a sign of respect, and one that Imad Mugniyah allowed, as it served his purpose. In other areas he was called by other names, which he thought might help to confuse the Western intelligence services. That it was a title of respect meant little to him personally, as Mugniyah was a man without ego or presumption. This had earned him another name–the Anti–bin Laden. Like bin Laden, Mugniyah was a man with an agenda, and while his alliance with al Qaeda was a marriage of convenience, he did not really care for the tall, outspoken Saudi. Yet he bore bin Laden no grudge. In fact, he rather missed him. While bin Laden was on the scene, it had taken a great deal of pressure off Mugniyah. But the sheik had brought the might of the West down on himself and his al Qaeda followers, and now that he was no longer in evidence, there were that many more hounds chasing Mugniyah and his Hezbollah organization.

Imad Mugniyah was born on the streets of Lebanon and educated in French parochial schools. He was in secondary school when Beirut ceased to be the Paris of the Middle East and dissolved into civil war. When the Druze militia killed his parents and younger sister, he became a street fighter and joined the ranks of the Hezbollah, the Party of God. Mugniyah killed his first Christian when he was fifteen. It wasn't until two years later that he killed his first Jew. The Hezbollah quickly learned what the French nuns had known for some time; Mugniyah was intelligent and very resourceful. By the age of twenty-five he had risen through the ranks to head the Hezbollah security apparatus. Mugniyah personally planned and supervised the attack on the Marine barracks in Beirut in 1983, the hijacking of TWA Flight 847, the bombings of the Israeli embassy and a Jewish community center in Argentina, and a long string of kidnaps and killings. He was part of the Lebanese Shiite power structure, and while he observed the teaching of the Koran, he did this more for his followers than for his faith. He neither drank nor smoked, nor did he use or abuse women. When it was convenient, he observed morning and evening prayer, more to meditate than to pray; it cleared his head and soothed his spirit, allowing him to focus on his true calling. Imad Mugniyah, aka Abu Dokhan, was simply the most accomplished terrorist on the planet.

Long ago Mugniyah recognized that Iran, after the fall of the Shah, was perhaps the safest and most stable regime in the Middle East if you were a terrorist. He quickly established both funding and intelligence links with the government in Tehran. Mugniyah still moved throughout the region, but since 9/11, Lebanon and Syria had become increasingly dangerous for him. There was a price on his head: 25 million American dollars. That could buy a great deal of information in the backstreets and bazaars of Beirut and Damascus, or even Islamabad. He had recently found himself only a step ahead of the Mossad or the CIA. Even the British operatives from MI5 had had a go at him. And money was now a problem; several of his Hezbollah-sourced accounts had been diverted, and fewer international banks would accept their wire transfers. The Iranians still provided him with useful information and refuge, but they were now not so forthcoming with their funds. Even the Saudis were becoming unreliable in this regard. No matter, Mugniyah told himself. A new source of funding had just made itself available. He himself had few material needs, and while he did not like to think of himself as a terrorist for hire, it did not hurt to be paid to do God's work. But if he were to continue his fight against the Jews, then they must have money. It was this need for money that had brought him here.

The two men stepped from the door and into the dying sunshine. It was dry and cool, with a light wind that spawned an occasional dust devil along the hard-packed dirt road. Mugniyah was shorter than his companion, and physically unimposing by comparison. His deep brown beard was only now showing some streaks of gray at the temple, and his brown eyes were deceptively soft. He lifted a shawl from his shoulders and draped it across his head as if to shield his features from those close by. Abu Dokhan had a fetish for anonymity, and it had served him well in his chosen profession. He and Khalib began to walk slowly away from the village along a well-trodden goat path. Mostly, the way was wide enough for both of them to pass, but when it wasn't, Khalib allowed Mugniyah to precede him. Forty meters to the front and rear, two armed men kept their pace and distance, searching the barren landscape for something out of place. These were Khalib's men, and they knew how to look for trouble. The other two armed men kept watch on either flank, also at a distance. At a bend in the path, Mugniyah paused to admire the view, then turned to his companion.

"Magnificent, is it not? Too bad that we are only free to enjoy this beauty during certain hours of the day."

Khalib looked skyward. "True, Dokhan, but the American spy satellites and reconnaissance drones do serve to remind us of the constant presence of our enemies, even in this remote place where we are given sanctuary." Both men were aware that the Americans maintained satellite coverage of most of Iran. They had to assume that Khalabad was one of them. Both also knew that though they were five hundred miles from the shores of the Arabian Sea, they were still in range of refueled American special operations helicopters.

They were quiet for some time before Mugniyah continued.

"We are losing ground, Khalib. My Hezbollah faction in Lebanon and your al Qaeda forces in Afghanistan. But I commend you on your careful planning. Most of your networks inside Pakistan are still intact. And your vision for a stay-behind presence anticipated the fall of the Taliban. Yet many rulers of nations that should be supporting our struggle are bowing to Western pressure. They fear the Americans and their technology. Leaders of our movement are in exile, and some of our most committed fighters are dead or in prison." He tugged at his beard. "Too many of our traditional allies see the power of the Americans as too formidable. Or they are more interested in settling old grudges than uniting with us against the Israelis—or the moderate Arabs. I was not in favor of bin Laden's attack on America; I would have been content to let them continue in decadence and ignorance. But that cannot be undone." Mugniyah was making an effort to keep the sarcasm from his voice. Khalib had been one of bin Laden's most trusted lieutenants. "Osama's great victory brought them here in force, and we must now deal with them. We are now in need of a great victory to force the Americans to leave. No matter what the consequences, we must break this hold the Americans have on us. If they are allowed to build this pipeline, then they will be able to dominate the flow of oil and the geography of the entire region. And you, Khalib, will never be able to go home again."

Khalib knew all this, but still he listened carefully. Mugniyah was a man to be treated with much respect. He had gone to Lahore at great personal risk to meet with this Pakistani nuclear scientist. Khalib, because of his secret al Qaeda organization in Pakistan, had arranged the meeting. Now he, Khalib, had crossed Pakistan at little personal risk but at great inconvenience to meet with Mugniyah in Iran. Movement in Pakistan, especially in the cities, was dangerous because of the Pakistani secret police. It was dangerous in the remote areas, even here in Iran, because of American technology. But this little village was safe as any he had known in Pakistan or Afghanistan during the last few years.

Somehow, Mugniyah had known of this wide-eyed Pakistani scientist, and of his willingness to do what was asked of him. *How did Dokhan know this? What else does he know?* Khalib knew that this Lebanese had good contacts in Iran and throughout the Middle East, and his reputation for cunning and courage were legendary. Khalib had guessed that the meeting in Lahore had something to do with the Trans-Afghan Pipeline the Americans were planning to build. After the meeting, he knew that it had to do with this scientist's access to nuclear materials and the vaults where the Pakistanis stored their nuclear weapons. Yet, he remained skeptical—very skeptical. It all seemed too improbable. One thing he did know; if and when it came to the operational planning, his knowledge of Afghanistan would be invaluable. When it came to the execution phase, his participation would be essential.

"Khalib, my al Qaeda friend," Mugniyah said quietly, "we must make this plan work. Osama brought the Americans here to our doorstep. Now we must act boldly, or they will never leave. What did you think of our wide-eyed young scientist?"

"You mean Abramin?"

"Yes, do you think we can trust him?"

Khalib did not reply immediately. He ran his pale eyes slowly along the ridge of these strange mountains. They were barely foothills when compared to his beloved Hindu Kush. After a moment's reflection, he turned to Mugniyah.

"I trust no one but God, Dokhan. And so far you have given me no reason not to trust you. Moshe Abramin? He is a true believer, and I do not think he would willingly betray us. But he is an academic and not a worldly person. He is capable of making mistakes that would betray us and not be aware that he is doing so."

"Do you feel he is indiscreet?"

"Not necessarily, Dokhan, but when the light in a man's soul burns bright, it often blinds him. And there is the matter of his associates. They are without doubt a dedicated group and capable of this mission, unless they have been penetrated. But like our friend Moshe, their intellect may overshadow their common sense. Still, if your plan is to succeed, we cannot do this without them." Khalib was silent for a moment, then added, "So your plan calls for a nuclear weapon?"

"Yes," Mugniyah replied, "the plan most definitely calls for a nuclear weapon. We will need two."

The reach of Mugniyah's connections and the wealth of his backers had long ago made a nuclear weapon available to the cause. But buying a nuclear weapon was a little like buying street drugs; it was hard to know exactly what you received for the price. With the fall of the Soviet Union and the economic collapse of Russia, tactical nuclear weapons had become available on the black market. They were expensive, but they were available. Even so, nuclear weapons were not like hand grenades, even the tactical weapons. They had a finite shelf life, and required costly maintenance and skilled technicians to keep them functional. The components of a nuclear weapon degraded—not so much the nuclear cores but the high-explosive components and wiring assemblies that made them function. And there were all manner of nuclear weapons. An implosion fission device, like the one Moshe Abramin had helped develop for Pakistan, was quite primitive. Only recently had the Pakistanis been able to create a weapon of suitable size for use on one of their intermediate-range rockets, a development viewed with much alarm by the Indians. But if Abramin and his small band of fundamentalists could steal two bombs, and they could be spirited out of Pakistan, then the essential criteria for a high-order nuclear explosion were in place—the bomb and those who knew how to detonate it.

For the next few minutes neither man spoke. "We have no choice," Khalib said softly. "We must trust Moshe Abramin and his people, up to a point, if we are to be successful. Nonetheless, it is a dangerous business. The objectives of your organization and mine are different, but we will both be served if we can succeed in getting the Americans out of the region."

Mugniyah nodded in acknowledgment. "And you, Khalib. I will need you to follow him and see that he does not compromise us. If he is able to remove the weapons from Kahuta, you must be there to make sure he can get them safely out of the area. And once that is done, we must throw the wolves off our trail until we are ready to strike. Can you do this?"

Khalib nodded. "As I said, Dokhan, we serve different constituents, but we have the same enemy. Yes, I will help you, but first I must know all the details of your plan."

The two men continued along the footpath, guarded by their flankers with automatic weapons.

Tuesday, September 17,
the island of Hawaii

"It is not unlike the foothills in the Plaine des Jarres," Lon said, "only cooler and a little more open. And here, there is only one big mountain. It appears that there is less rain here than along the coast."

Steven Fagan nodded. He too remembered the Plaine des Jarres, the broad highland plain in central Laos, and it sent a chill through him. It was there that his Hmong and the Lao nationalists had been defeated by the North Vietnamese. More than two NVA divisions were required to beat them, Steven reflected grimly, but it had spelled the beginning of the end for CIA-backed irregulars and a free Laos. No, this is entirely different; this bears no resemblance to those dark days in Laos, he told himself. Steven shook away his memories and pulled himself into the jeep behind the wheel. Lon climbed back in alongside him, and they continued along a well-maintained gravel road that twisted up the side of Mauna Kea.

The land had once belonged to the Parker Ranch before Joe Simpson purchased it almost twenty years ago. Most of it was steep and unsuitable for grazing, and too remote for residential use except for the most reclusive individuals. A single road led up from the lower valley and along the northwest slope of the big mountain. There were a few clearings, but most of the land was thick with scrub trees and hackthorn bush. An occasional stand of eucalyptus or tangleberry trees gave some relief from the ravines and shallow draws that cut down from the higher elevations. The property, some twenty thousand acres, was bordered on the east by a portion of the Parker Ranch and on the west by a treacherous, inhospitable lava flow. Above them to the south rose the upper reaches of Mauna Kea—all federal land. Below them was more Simpson property that was leased to the Parker consortium for grazing, although due to the poor quality of the land, there were few animals on it. It was largely rugged, isolated, semiarid terrain—not the most hospitable land at all. Yet it was perfect for what Steven Fagan had in mind.

As the road snaked up through the central portion of the property, they passed through the four-thousand-foot level and came to a large clearing. Here, two small bulldozers were busy filling and leveling the terrain. On the Big Island, a source of crushed rock and lava was never more than a few feet beneath the surface. On one side of the clearing, stacks of lumber and building materials waited under heavy canvas tarps. A single structure stood alone while workers air-nailed wooden siding on the frame and moved sheets of metal roofing into place. Another crew busied themselves with the foundation platform of a second building. None of the workers paid the slightest attention to the jeep that came to a stop a short distance away.

"They seem to be working very fast," Lon observed. "Are they Hawaiian?"

"Indonesian construction workers under contract from a company in Singapore. They will work fourteen hours a day, seven days a week, to complete the camp. The company that hired them will be paid a substantial bonus to finish this work in three weeks. When they are finished, the crews will then be driven from here directly to the Kona airport." He took a sheaf of blueprints and rolled them across the hood of the jeep. "This area will hold the barracks, galley and eating facility, classrooms, a small armory, an obstacle course, a recreation complex, and"—he pointed to the far side of the clearing—"a helicopter landing pad." He traced a finger over the map to where the contour lines were very dense. "South of here, backing up to the steeper elevations, we are building the firing ranges and mountain training areas. Crews are working there right now." He rerolled the plans and glanced about with a critical eye. "Hard to believe that it'll all be finished within thirty days. What's even more amazing is that we started only a week ago." But then, he reflected to himself, he had a very generous budget to make it happen.

Lon slowly surveyed the area and spotted a small group of tents in the shade of a eucalyptus grove at the edge of the clearing. "So you will also live here?"

He gave her a coy smile. "I'll show you my quarters in a little while. Let's take a look at the rest of the facility. I want to see how the construction on the ranges is coming."

Later that day, Steven drove them down the mountain and into the little town of Waimea, a cross between a picturesque Hawaiian village and a cow town in western Montana. They paused to stroll through a craft fair at a small shopping center near town. Lon was impressed by much of the artwork. Then they treated themselves to some shaved ice and drove on through the small business district.

Outside the village, Steven took a narrow, paved road whose flanks were riotous with windmill jasmine and Hawaiian wedding flower. Soon the blacktop gave way to crushed lava. He swung the jeep into a circular pea-gravel drive that served a neat, freshly painted white cottage. The drive, front yard, and cottage were shaded by several huge banyan trees. It was a dated structure built well off the ground, with latticework skirting its post-and-pillar foundation. A short flight of wooden stairs led to the generous sitting porch. The grounds were spacious and well tended. A healthy stand of tough island grass covered the rich clay right up to the mature flower beds that ringed the house. Blue sky flowering vine climbed the trellis by the porch. It was a scene from a tropical vacation brochure.

"Whose house is this? Someone you know?"

He grinned. "This is our home—our second home. It's where I will stay when I'm not at the site or traveling. It's where you can stay any time you like." He watched her take in the house and the grounds. "Of course, that assumes that you can take some time from Larkspur and your civic duties there to spend time here with me."

Without a word she got out and began to explore, first the grounds, then the house. He was waiting on the porch when she finished, seated comfortably in a generous wicker chair. She took a seat next to him, reached over, and took his hand.

"It's lovely; thank you, my husband. And even if it were only a barracks like you are building on the mountain, I would want to be here with you." Neither spoke for a few minutes, enjoying the bird sounds and the aroma of the late afternoon. "It's so perfect; how did you find it? When did you find the time to furnish it so well? It is exactly what I would have chosen."

"I didn't do any of those things." He frowned slightly. "My employer did this. He said it was here for us, or that we could find something different. Do you want something different?"

"No, my husband."

He again grinned. "Neither do I." Yet it bothered him slightly that Joe Simpson had been so accurate in finding the perfect place for them and furnishing it exactly to their tastes.

• • •

The next evening, Steven sat at a quiet table just off the bar area of the Kona Surf Hotel. Lon was in Waimea, settling into the new home. It was still early, and the bulk of the evening crowd would not arrive for another hour or so. Scattered across the dining area were a few tourists, dressed in T-shirts, shorts, and fanny packs. Some of them glowed pink from a day in the sun. Most were camped around fruit-colored drinks in chimney glasses, adorned with flowers and long straws. Steven looked more like a local in his cotton slacks and tasteful aloha shirt. He was already starting to think of himself as a local. The town of Kailua was a bustling tourist town. The largest town on the Kona coast, it had a near-mainland variety of shopping and dining, if not mainland prices. Steven sat with a tall glass of tonic, enjoying the warm afternoon and reading a thick file. He attracted little attention; people with his background seemed to blend in easily and naturally almost anywhere.

He glanced at his watch. The man he was meeting would just now be landing at the Kona airport. It would take him at least thirty minutes to deplane and take a taxi to the hotel—perhaps a few minutes more if he dropped his bags by the room ahead of their meeting. This was the last of the three meetings Steven had scheduled this week. From the file in front of him, it appeared to be the most promising. Steven was looking for a reliable man with an extensive special-operations background and current experience. There was no shortage of candidates, for the U.S. military trains large numbers of them and deploys them regularly. Thanks to the Freedom of Information Act and Steven's CIA contacts, the initial screening had gone rapidly, and Steven needed to move prudently but quickly. The trick was now to find the right one, and that could take some time.

Two days ago he had interviewed a former Army Special Forces major who was a veteran of the Gulf War, Kosovo, and Afghanistan. He had all the tickets and solid language skills, but Steven had not taken to him. He came across as rigid and inflexible—too military. And there was a touch of bravado that Steven didn't care for. The CIA had been burned on more than one occasion by hiring retired military types with inflated egos. Paramilitary work, even in support of a direct-action mission, required cool judgment, and often an inconspicuous presence.

Steven had thoroughly read Garrett Walker's file last night and wanted to review it prior to their meeting. His military record was impeccable; he had the right balance of leadership and operational experience. He was retired from the Navy on medical grounds because he couldn't pass a diving physical. Fagan didn't need divers; he needed men on the ground who could think and lead. Walker's short tenure as a civilian combat-shooting instructor was as impressive as his military record. Steven had tucked the file in his briefcase and was thinking about this when Garrett Walker appeared.

"Excuse me, are you Gary Bethke?"

Steven rose and offered his hand. "Yes, and you must be Garrett Walker. It's nice to meet you, Garrett, and thank you for coming. Please, have a seat. Would you like something to drink?"

"Yes, thank you." Garrett sat and turned to the waiter who had followed him to the table. "Could you please bring me a glass of iced tea?"

"Did you have a good flight?"

"It was long, but the connections were excellent, and I travel light. The accommodations are very nice, thank you."

Steven appraised him quickly. Garrett Walker was a confident, self-assured man, but very polite. He wore a freshly pressed long-sleeved dress shirt, tan cotton slacks, and sensible walking shoes. As information in the file suggested, he looked very fit. If he were curious about this meeting or the sketchy nature of the employment circular Steven had sent him, he gave no indication. Steven had not needed a résumé, for his file was very comprehensive, yet he asked for one. What Garrett had sent him was straightforward and accurate.

"Have you been to the Big Island before?"

"Several years ago. There's a military recreational facility near Kilauea Crater, not far from the Volcanoes National Park. I came over with some friends to do some mountaineering. Good country—rough country. And the diving around Kealakeku Bay is excellent."

The waiter arrived with Garrett's tea and brought Steven another club soda. After he left them, Steven turned to Garrett. "I'm sure you're curious as to why I brought you here and what kind of work we may be doing on this project."

Garrett gave him an easy grin. "I certainly am. An airplane ticket to Hawaii, per diem, and a nice hotel room. Who do I have to kill?"

Steven observed him closely. The easy grin was still there, but his eyes said, Let's get the cards on the table.

"No one just yet," Steven replied, still watching him. "But before we get to the specifics, let me say that I represent an organization that will contract for a certain range of security services—activities that may be considered interventionist in nature. None of this activity, other than the training of personnel, will be conducted within the United States. The work will be paramilitary in nature and perhaps dangerous. Of course there is a great deal more you need to know, but first I will ask you to sign an agreement of confidentiality." Steven smiled honestly. "I'm not sure how this agreement would stand up in a court of law, but the attorneys who drew up this document charged us a pretty hefty fee. Basically, Garrett, I want you to have a fair read on the kind of work we do, and what you will be doing if you become an employee. If there is no interest on your part, or ours, then we'd like you not to talk about it. For now and until you sign this, I can tell you no more, other than we are not the Mafia, and we are not the United States government."

Since he arrived at the hotel, Garrett had done what he could to study this man. He had immediately checked his carry-on bag with the concierge, then carefully approached the bar. Garrett watched Steven for a full ten minutes before he approached the table. He saw him put the thick file into the briefcase and concluded that this stranger probably knew a great deal about him. When he introduced himself, all his antennae were up. Yet he found this quiet, poised man strangely likable. He was affable, yet Garrett sensed he was a professional and highly intelligent. And no hint of bravado. Garrett had interviewed with several security consultants and military subcontractors. They were either bureaucrats who talked in terms of customer relations and billing rates, or macho ex-military types. This man was different. Garrett read the document, signed it, and pushed it across the table. Steven glanced at the signature and set it to one side.

"Thank you. I am the chief executive officer for Guardian Systems International. I'm currently its only permanent employee, but all that will change in the very near future. GSI is a privately owned firm incorporated in the state of Hawaii. Ostensibly we are in the business of providing trained security personnel and armed guards worldwide. We plan to do that, but the full range of our services will be a little more extensive." Steven paused to measure him. "Garrett, have you ever heard of a company called Executive Outcomes?"

Garrett furrowed his brow. "South African, right?" Steven nodded. "Mercenary work?"

Steven ignored the question and plunged ahead. "In 1995, Sierra Leone was another African catastrophe. Tens of thousands of civilians were killed or mutilated by street gangs operating loosely under the banners of competing warlords. There seemed to be no end to the chaos. After the debacle in Somalia in 1993, we essentially stood on the sidelines in Africa, where we have chosen to remain. Executive Actions was hired by the government of Sierra Leone to stop the slaughter. For a fraction of the cost of a western military expedition, Executive Outcomes restored order and stopped the killing. As you probably would expect, their rules of engagement were a little more liberal than those of a western military force or UN peacekeepers. They were able to do this with less than two hundred men. Executive Outcomes is no longer in business, but there is a British-based firm called Sandline that performs much the same function, usually on a consulting basis but not always. There are a few American players, but most of the firms are South African or European.

"I believe there are conditions when an armed contract force is the best and only solution. This especially applies in the early stages of a crisis or when the target is a limited number of people and covert in nature. The force we wish to employ could be only a few people or a company-size element—perhaps larger, if the need arises and we can control it. We feel that in certain phases of a dangerous and volatile situation, a direct-action strike force could prevent escalation. Generally speaking, our business at GSI will be the precise and surgical application of force by a team or teams of highly trained specialists. The current war on terror only confirms our belief in this concept. Perhaps a quick action by a surgical force can prevent a larger-scale military deployment. And force may not always be called for. We intend to practice a number of disciplines, including a broad range of covert action."

"Ah, forgive my interruption, but from what little I know of mercenary work, it has never been a commercially successful enterprise unless it had the backing of a government. Or more specifically in Africa, a lean on the mining revenues that the civil disturbance threatened. In the old days, Mike Hoare and Robert Denard tried a few ventures on their own, but they came to no end. Does GSI have government backing?"

"It does not. In fact, the for-profit appearance of the company is largely for public consumption. Guardian Systems is in fact a subsidiary of a well-endowed nonprofit organization."

Garrett regarded his companion dubiously. "You mean . . . some sort of a philanthropic mercenary force?"

Steven smiled. "I know this sounds far-fetched, but that's not far from the truth. Let me start at the beginning and tell you how this all came about, where we are now, and what we envision for the future."

For the next several hours, Steven told Garrett of his plans and the work completed to date. For the most part, he was accurate and forthcoming, but at no time did he mention names or exact locations. After dinner, they walked along the inner harbor breakwater. The evening was mild, and a light offshore breeze carried a sweet scent of hibiscus and jasmine down to them from the hills above Kailua. Garrett asked an occasional question, but for the most part he listened. Steven carefully skirted the nature or origin of the project's funding, saying only that it was more than adequate. Just after nine, they found a comfortable bench at the end of the promenade on the city dock near the Hilton Hotel.

"That's really about all I can tell you at this juncture, Garrett. From what I know about you and what you've told me, you seem like an individual we would like to have with us on this project. By that I mean, if you're still interested, I'd like to show you our facility and training camp tomorrow."

Garrett hid his surprise that this man was ready to hire him and that there was some sort of a training facility on Hawaii. He regarded this quiet, unassuming man.

"Your organization sounds interesting, and yes, I'd like to learn more. But tell me something about yourself."

Steven rubbed his hands together and smiled to himself. "There's not a lot to tell really. I did my time in Southeast Asia with the 5th Special Forces Group. Spent a good deal of time in Laos. After the war, I found work at the CIA as a paramilitary officer and covert-actions specialist. Since leaving the Agency I've worked as a consultant for corporate security and executive protection. For the last five months, I've been involved with this project." He hesitated, then continued. "It took me a while to get my arms around this venture—and to understand its complexity and the scope of the operation. I'm sure you'll also need some time to digest it. It's a bold venture and not without a whole range of potential risks. But I think a great deal of good can come of it. Those of us involved will be very well paid, but I'm not in it for the money. I consider it a challenging and worthy venture. In short, I believe in it."

Garrett did not answer immediately. "For the most part, I agree. An intervention force that can act quickly and decisively can do a lot of good. But there's also potential for abuse. Who determines just where and when to commit this force? What constitutes a crisis? Is it economic or humanitarian, or can it also be political? Just what is the decision-making process? Who makes the decision, executive and operationally, whether it's a go or a no-go? And why? This may not be a commercial enterprise, but we're still talking about people's lives. This is not some Frederick Forsyth novel."

Steven smiled to himself, recalling Forsyth's fine book, *The Dogs of War*. Garrett Walker had just passed a very important test. "Excellent questions. As in all corporations, there will be a board of directors, and any executive action will have to be endorsed by that board. Nothing will happen without the approval of our board. Board members are selected for character, integrity, and proven history of patriotism and public service." Steven paused to frame his words. "Look at it this way. I will function as the chief executive officer. You, or someone like you, will serve as chief operating officer. In place of a chief financial officer, we will have an intelligence specialist or mission planner. The three of us will have to agree not only that a mission or operation is feasible, but that it is in keeping with"—Steven paused, again searching for the right words—"the moral charter of our organization. In short, you will not be asked to do anything that violates your personal ethics. An undertaking has to be doable, and it has to have merit."

Garrett considered this a moment and quickly came to a decision. "What time tomorrow do you want to get started?"

4

Garrett made a practice of using his time on airplanes to good advantage. A long flight or a flight delay was an opportunity to get something done—something that required concentration or was difficult to weave into the fabric of his daily routine. And since he had joined Guardian Systems International, his daily routine had recently become exceptionally busy. Occasionally he encountered seat mates who required the attentions of their fellow passengers to pass the time. Those that loved to talk found Garrett a disappointment. He was always polite, but he kept to himself and his own agenda. He was in such deep concentration that the flight attendant had to squeeze him on the arm.

"Excuse me, sir," she said in her singsong English, "we are preparing for landing, and you must turn off your machine."

"*Kap khun,*" Garrett replied with a smile and a gentle nod of his head.

She flashed him a shy smile, bowed over steepled fingers in the Thai way, and moved on up the aisle. Garrett pulled the earphones to his lap and adjusted his seat belt. The Singapore Air 737 yawed and bucked gently as it carefully felt its way through the clouds in search of the Kathmandu airport.

Garrett closed his eyes and played the last portion of the tape back in his mind. Again he marveled at the recurring patterns and similarities of the Nepalese language and of the dialect to which he had been listening, Gurkhali. When he asked Steven Fagan where he had found a set of instructional tapes on Gurkhali, Fagan had simply shrugged. Then, with a smile, he admitted that he still had friends in low places. Asian languages were difficult for westerners because they seldom were able to recognize the subtle repetitions and patterns. Garrett Walker was quite intelligent, but since childhood he had struggled with a learning disability. Garrett was a twin. His brother, Brandon, was equally bright, but he had no learning disorders. So Garrett had listened very carefully in class, and at night his brother explained everything to him. Just as some people have a photographic memory for reading, Garrett developed a photographic ear. Sound and the spoken word became his primary sensory input. With time and maturity, he developed adequate reading and writing skills, but he still listened carefully. Because of this ability to listen and catalog sounds, he was able to quickly master the conversational skills of a new language.

"How did you know she was Thai?"

"I beg your pardon."

"The flight attendant," said the woman next to him. "How did you know she was Thai?"

"Chinese are taller, and Malays are broader," Garrett replied. Then he smiled. "I heard her speaking to one of the other attendants when I visited the lavatory," he admitted.

"Are you coming to Nepal on business or pleasure, Mr., ah—?"

"Walker. Garrett Walker," he replied, trying to be polite but not wanting to be drawn into a conversation about his work.

THE MERCENARY OPTION 165

She was a stocky woman who dressed like a student, but seemed a little dated for an undergraduate. There was a fanny pack perched on her stomach and a small knapsack stuffed under the seat in front of her. Garrett grimaced—probably some ecotourist coming to bring the green gospel to the uninformed. Americans, who had never known want or hunger, often took issue with how other cultures used and sometimes squandered their resources.

"Actually, this is a pleasure trip," Garrett replied. "I've never been to Nepal, and I wanted to do some hiking."

"Oh, how fun," she said, warming to the conversation. "I'm taking a class about Far Eastern religions. I can't wait to see some of the temples."

"Then you came to see the monkeys?" he said, lifting an eyebrow.

"You mean they have monkeys in the temples?"

"Not in them, on them." She gave him a puzzled expression. "The carvings of monkeys on the fascia of the temples," he continued, "hundreds of them, copulating with each other." Her mouth opened, but nothing came out. "Truly," Garrett continued, "it's one of their most cherished art forms. They're quite ornate and decorative."

"You're kidding me."

"No, I'm not. Some of them are quite creative, actually—that is, if you're into monkeys screwing." He lowered his voice. "And I mean in every imaginable position, and then some. You'll see when you visit the temples."

The plane touched down and taxied to the small terminal. Garrett recovered his briefcase from under the seat and pulled a small grip from the overhead. He left his seat mate pondering her visit to the Nepalese capital.

He caught a taxi from the airport to the center of town and the bus terminal. There was biweekly air service to his destination, but the next plane out was not for two days. Garrett decided to take the bus. The ride from Kathmandu to Pokhara was not unlike one in rural Central America. There were extended families, chickens, a few peacocks, and a goat aboard. The rack on top of the coach was crammed with luggage, household wares, and furniture, along with two adventuresome boys. It should have been a six-hour road trip but took close to eleven hours, as the bus stopped often. The driver and most of the passengers had relatives along the way, so politeness and adherence to local customs dictated the schedule. For Garrett, the time passed quickly, and he was a little disappointed when the trip was finally over. He was the only westerner on the bus. Garrett readily absorbed other cultures, much as he did languages. While he was often reserved and private among his own countrymen, he was the opposite as a stranger in a strange land. Soon into the journey, he was drinking curdled milk from a goatskin with a child on his lap. Once the Nepalese learned this handsome American could speak broken Gurkhali, he was immediately drawn into their midst. Garrett was not only able to improve his vocabulary and the subtle inflections of the language, but subconsciously he began to copy the gestures and mannerisms of those around him. It would have taken a serious language student, with a native-speaking instructor, a full semester to make as much progress as Garrett Walker did on this long bus ride. As he left the depot and made his way into town, he even walked differently; he no longer moved like an American with long confident strides. Now he took smaller, measured steps, and his head was slightly bowed, shoulders forward. He was less threatening in his movements, and he had assumed a more open, polite expression—all without conscious effort on his part.

Pokhara was a small city, and Garrett had little trouble finding his hotel. That he could ask for and take directions in Gurkhali delighted those he met along the way. Most thought he was British or at least Canadian. His hotel room was clean and basic. Though it was late, he managed to find a café open and ordered something unknown to him on the menu, but whose name he pronounced fairly well. Then he lingered over coffee, talking to the proprietor and his wife until it would have been rude for him to remain any longer.

His meeting with Bijay Gurung had been scheduled for ten o'clock in the morning. Garrett passed on his usual morning run to walk about Pokhara, absorbing the feel of the old city and stopping periodically to talk with shopkeepers. He had thought of trying to observe Bijay Gurung prior to the meeting, as he had done when he first met Steven Fagan, alias Gary Bethke. But Garrett had read a great deal about this famous Gurkha fighter. Gurung might be difficult to secretly watch, especially on his own ground. He was something of a national hero, and others might not respond well to a stranger observing him from the shadows. Additionally, Garrett's research on the man suggested that little could be gained from such a venture. Gurkhas were generally straightforward fighters—simple men with few of the soldierly vices found in Western military services. Gurung himself was reportedly intelligent, refined, and temperate, and unlike many retired Gurkhas he was not given to regaling youngsters about his military prowess. And Gurung's military prowess, Garrett had learned, was considerable. The man was a legend among the Gurkhas, and even more impressive, was held in high esteem by the British and Australian Special Air Services. Garrett was anxious to meet him.

Garrett stepped quietly into the cafe and recognized Gurung instantly from his photos. He smiled to himself. There was something about a true warrior—a certain quiet self-confidence that said this man was a professional soldier. That he was not in uniform was of no consequence; Garrett knew at a glance that he was a man to be reckoned with. Walking over to Gurung's table, he paused at a respectful distance, held his hands along his trouser seams, and bowed slightly, formally.

"My name is Garrett Walker. Is there room at your table for a weary traveler?" he said politely. He did not raise his eyes to meet Gurung's, for that would have been presumptuous and very Western.

Bijay Gurung watched the American walk in. He was tall, as were most Americans, but he carried himself like an Asian and did not seem out of place. When the owner glanced in Bijay's direction in response to his inquiry, the man lowered his head courteously and quietly thanked him—very un-Western. This American, who had traveled halfway around the world to see Bijay, appeared to be different from others who had sought him out. He moved with an ease and a sense of purpose, yet he gave no impression of arrogance. And he addressed Bijay in Gurkhali, very rare indeed for an American. Bijay could tell that he was new to the language, but his inflection, which is often difficult for the Western tongue, was near perfect.

"I would be honored to share my table with you," Bijay replied, then, switching to English, which due to his Sandhurst mentors carried the precision and nasal quality of an English public school, "and pleased if you were to join me."

Garrett slid into the chair across from Bijay and murmured his thanks. Then for the first time he looked into the man's face. Garrett was immediately taken by the rich, nut-brown quality of Bijay's skin—tough yet smooth. He knew Bijay was forty-one, at least according to his British Army service record. But many Gurkha boys lied about their age in order to serve in the Brigade of Gurkhas as soon as possible. Many others simply did not know how old they were. Since Gurung was tall for a hill tribesman, he may have done just that. But he looked as if he could

have been in his late twenties—or his mid-fifties. Gurung's eyes were dark liquid pools of intensity, firm but
not judgmental. Garrett held his eyes for an instant and
made a decision.

"While it is an honor to meet you, Bijay Gurung, it is
also painful to find a capable warrior here and not in garrison seeing to his men. This must be a terrible burden for
your spirit."

Bijay regarded him coldly. The words could be taken as
an insult, or at the very least a challenge, but they were
said with a certain respect and sincerity. And there was
something about this man's manner that said he understood about the exile of a soldier. There was also an economy of movement and assurance that said he had seen
danger and that he had led men in combat. Americans
were seldom regarded as warriors in the fashion that
Gurkhas considered themselves warriors; Americans were
from a wealthy nation and conducted war with technology. Yet Bijay's finely tuned instincts told him this man
was possibly a warrior very much in his own tradition.

"How can you be so sure of this, my tall American
friend?" He was silent for a moment, studying the man
across the table. Garrett said nothing. "You may have read
something of me, or been told something of me by the
British. But how can you presume to know the condition
of my spirit?"

"I know, Bijay Gurung. Believe me, I know." Garrett
stared at Bijay, and his eyes softened. "Because," he added
softly, "I have walked in your shoes."

Bijay did not know whether or not to believe him, but
he was not one to quickly judge others. He did sense this
bold American was a man to be treated with respect.

"Very well. You seem to know about me, but I know
nothing about you. Perhaps you should tell me something
of yourself."

"Thank you, Bijay Gurung. You honor me with your request. May we have tea together?"

Moments later, the tea service arrived, and Garrett waited patiently while Bijay attended to measuring the tea and pouring the scalding water over the dark leaves.

For the next hour, Garrett talked in quiet measured tones. He spoke in English, but occasionally used a phrase in Gurkhali. He told Bijay of his eighteen-year career as a Navy SEAL and of the unusual number of times he had been in combat. Talk of combat operations and the killing of men flows naturally between men of action. Garrett noticed that Bijay seemed to lean forward when he talked about his tour with the Australian Special Air Service. Like all Gurkhas, Bijay was an infantryman. Small, elite units like the SAS hold a special fascination for infantrymen. Garrett also knew service with an SAS unit was one of the things they had in common. For the most part, Garrett reviewed the highlights of his service career in a methodical, unemotional manner. But when he spoke of the condition that had forced him from active service, Bijay sensed a subtle change in the demeanor of the American. Was it, he thought, anger or sadness—or both?

"I will not go into the details, for they are unimportant," Garrett told him, "but I felt that I had not yet reached my full potential as a warrior."

Bijay felt the subtle measure of passion in these words, and he knew this quiet stranger still chafed at being separated from his unit. He was interested and somewhat impressed by Garrett's military experience. Now looking into his eyes, feeling his power, Bijay knew he was talking to a serious warrior—someone not unlike himself.

"I appealed the decision, but a medical reexamination found me unfit to return to an operational status. The United States military can be quite bureaucratic in that regard." Garrett paused to compose himself. Somehow, in the presence of this man, he had unconsciously allowed his guard to fall and his feelings to surface. He caught himself; this was not good, he quickly reflected, or was it? "I was totally unprepared to leave the Navy SEAL teams and the men of my unit." He pursed his lips and continued. "Of course, I would have been allowed to stay on in an administrative or training capacity, but I could not accept this. Or to be truthful, I chose not to. I believe there is a proper time to leave the company of other fighting men, and I was forced to go before my time. Tell me, Bijay Gurung, did you leave before it was your time?"

Bijay was quiet for several moments before he spoke. "Do you know why I no longer serve in the brigade?"

"I have heard some things," Garrett said with a shrug, "but I seldom attach value to what one man says of another, unless the speaker is someone who has proven himself to me." Garrett saw Bijay again hesitate, and he thought he saw a hint of a smile pass across his dark features.

"I served the Raj for almost twenty years. I asked not to serve in Brunei, as I felt the duty demeaning—the work of a palace guard and not a task worthy of a warrior. At the specific request of my colonel, I agreed to go. The battalion of the Royal Gurkha Rifles stationed there had earned a reputation for sloppiness and inattention to duty. They were, after all, a battalion of Gurkhas; they needed assistance, and I could not refuse. I had been there for about three months, serving as the command sergeant major. With the help of several of the senior sergeants, we began to bring the battalion into good order." He paused, choosing his words carefully. "Late one evening I made an unexpected tour of the garrison spaces and found a young Gurkha returning to the barracks. He told me that every few weeks he picked up a packet of 'dispatches' from a businessman outside the gate and delivered them to one of the subalterns. He was an inexperienced young man—

new to the battalion and quite naïve. I know the boy's family; his father and grandfather both served in the brigade. When he told me that he had been instructed not to report these deliveries to his platoon sergeant, I became suspicious.

"When the young man was directed to make another meeting, I went in his place. This businessman, when he saw it was I and not the young Gurkha, tried to pull a pistol from his jacket. I was ready for something like this. You know, Mr. Walker, they say that when a Gurkha unsheathes his *khukuri*, it cannot be returned to its scabbard until it has been bloodied." He smiled grimly at Garrett. "Of course, this is nonsense, but not on that particular night. I killed the man and called the guard. The packet contained drugs, and the so-called businessman was a distant relative of Haji Waddaulah, the Sultan of Brunei. Possession of drugs in Brunei is a capital offense, but it was widely known and accepted that some members of the royal family use drugs, especially the younger ones.

"There was quite a stir. I was taken into custody, but released pending further investigation. Charges were dropped on the testimony of the young Gurkha and the less-than-exemplary reputation of the dead businessman. But relations were strained between the sultan and his Gurkha battalion. When I confronted the subaltern, he denied everything. It came down to his word against that of my young Gurkha. This subaltern was not a Sandhurst man, but his father was a member of Parliament." A look of pure sadness passed over Bijay's features. "There was little they could do to me. I held the Victoria Cross, and to dishonor me would have invited too much disgrace on the Brigade of Gurkhas. The sultan demanded discipline, so they turned to the young Gurkha corporal. It was decided to separate him from the brigade—to send him home. Mr. Walker, you cannot imagine the shame that follows a Gurkha who is separated from the brigade, the blight it brings to his family name. He cannot go home, he cannot even enlist in the Indian regiments; no other Gurkha will serve with him. He is essentially a nonperson—a dead man. I had no option but to resign in protest. In deference to my years of service, I was allowed to leave before my enlistment period had ended." Then his eyes sparked with a flash of anger. "And that I agreed not to speak publicly of this incident."

Garrett could see that he was in pain. "*Kaphar hunu bhanda mornu ramro*," he murmured. It was an old Gurkha proverb that means, "It is better to die than to be a coward." Bijay met his eyes and nodded solemnly.

Of course, Garrett had thoroughly researched the matter of Bijay's retirement from the Gurkhas. There were a number of stories in circulation about the departure of this famous Gurkha, but Garrett had never quite been able to make sense of them. Steven Fagan had given him a file that suggested something of a scandal, one that involved a relative of the sultan, but there had been few details. What Bijay had just told him made sense. And it was in keeping with what he knew about the man—that he took care of his men, and honor was everything to him.

"And where is your young Gurkha now?"

"He is working for a company in Kathmandu who finds work for former Gurkhas in corporate security. At my insistence, he was awarded an honorable discharge, and I have personally vouched for his character. He will find work, but it is not the same as serving with the brigade. This young warrior was done a terrible disservice, and for that I will always hold the British responsible." He was again quiet for a long moment, then looked directly at Garrett. "Mr. Walker, from what you have told me, you also seem to be a man who has been wronged by your service—separated from your men and your work.

Yet I sense that you have found something to take its place." He smiled easily. "Could this be why you have traveled all the way from America to see me?"

Garrett returned his smile. "My first name is Garrett, and I would be honored if you would call me by that name. Warrant Officer Gurung, I believe only a fool thinks he can take back an insult or regain something that cannot be retrieved. My time with the Navy SEALs was good for me, and I treasure my memories. I was blessed. That I had to leave before I felt it was my time to go—well, I've made my peace with that. But yes, I have found something else—work that is important and requires the professional skill and discipline of a soldier. And it is work that I believe to be necessary and honorable."

"Would this work be dangerous?"

Garrett smiled again, broadly this time. "Would I be here talking with you if it were not?"

"*Gurkhali ayo*," Bijay replied. This traditional battle cry meant, "The Gurkhas are upon you."

Bijay Gurung and Garrett sat and talked through another pot of tea. Garrett told him of the plan and of the recently completed facility in Hawaii. Garrett knew of the history and loyalty that Gurkhas had traditionally held for Great Britain. That's why Steven Fagan had structured the payroll, insurance benefits, and service pensions for the new force through the Bank of England. This satisfied Bijay; his bitterness was at the British, not the Bank of England. For centuries Gurkhas had come down from the hills to willingly serve the Crown so long as the pay, pension, and death benefits were paid promptly, most of it going back to their families in Nepal. Bijay was not too concerned with where this new force would be sent or the kind of soldiering involved, but he took a keen interest in the uniforms they would wear during their training.

Garrett spent another three days in Pokhara. On one of

them, Bijay took him on a long hike in the foothills of Annapurna, a trek that rambled over close to six thousand vertical feet. Bijay was impressed; first, that the lanky American had the stamina of a Sherpa, and second, that his Gurkhali seemed to improve daily. They traveled back to Kathmandu by air and collected an ex-Gurkha corporal before catching a flight to Singapore, then continuing east to the Big Island of Hawaii.

Monday, November 11,
Kahuta, Pakistan

The A. Q. Khan Research Laboratory at Kahuta was located some thirty miles southwest of Islamabad and was one of the most carefully guarded facilities in Pakistan, perhaps on the subcontinent. It was here that the Pakistanis had developed their bomb. The research complex at Kahuta also housed their guided missile production and test facility. All that the government of India and the rest of the Central Asian nations feared from a nuclear-armed Pakistan emanated from this research complex. In May 1998 Pakistan detonated an atomic bomb and became a nuclear power. That it was a crude, first-generation fission device was of no concern. The Muslim world hailed this development as the Islamic bomb. When the Pakistanis, with the help of the Chinese and the North Koreans, developed the Ghauri II and the Shaheen II surface-to-surface missiles, the Indians now faced a Muslim adversary with nuclear weapons and the ability to deliver them with little or no warning. With this gambit, the Pakistanis essentially put in check the overwhelming conventional superiority of the Indian ground forces. A serious move by the Indian army in Kashmir could now provoke much more than an artillery barrage across the Line of Control that now divided the contested province and the two nations.

While most of the Pakistani arsenal is the product of highly enriched uranium from the massive gas-centrifuge equipment at Kahuta, the Pakistanis also developed a parallel plutonium weapons program. The plutonium production reactor at Kushab and the plutonium extraction plant at Chasma had provided enough material for ten weapons, about a third of the nation's growing nuclear capability. While plutonium is more difficult and dangerous to handle, the bombs are lighter and smaller. All of India's nuclear weapons were plutonium munitions. The reactor at Kushab was also used to irradiate lithium 6 to produce tritium for an enhanced-yield plutonium weapon. This tritium boost is a very tricky technology. The Pakistanis had yet to master it, but it would just be a matter of time until they did. They had been at it for some time.

After the Indians exploded their bomb in 1974, Pakistani President Benazir Bhutto encouraged Dr. Abdul Qadeer Khan to return to Pakistan from the Netherlands, where he had been working as a metallurgist. There he had worked for a European consortium that fabricated nuclear components for industrial and military uses. Bhutto gave him the task and the resources to develop the Pakistani bomb. Dr. Khan, an urban, aristocratic, and highly educated man, brought a great deal of experience and intellect to the project, but Pakistan was, and still is, a developing nation. It was a daunting challenge. One of the most serious obstacles he faced was the lack of engineering talent—talent to develop the reactor processes and facilities to make the plutonium and highly enriched uranium they would need. Knowing it would take time, Dr. Khan began sending bright and promising young men to America to attend the finest universities. One of the brightest and most promising was Moshe Abramin. He and others like him had worked tirelessly at the laboratory complex named for Dr. Khan. The fire that ignited their intellectual souls was religious conviction; there had to be an Islamic bomb to confront the Hindu bomb. But two things conspired to disillusion Moshe. One was the consumptive Western lifestyle of Abdul Khan. He was as arrogant as an upper-caste Hindu and as ostentatious as an American. The other was the support given by President Pervez Musharraf to the Americans in their war against the Taliban. Young men like Moshe Abramin thrived on religious passion, and the "Islamic" freedom fighters who fought the Russians and now the Americans had captured his imagination. When Americans prevailed in Afghanistan, idealistic young men like Moshe Abramin felt humiliated. And he was not alone. Early one afternoon, he and three other young scientist-engineers met in one of the laboratory bays.

"We have rehearsed this many times, but let us go over it one more time. The time has come, and may Allah grant us the courage to carry out our duties. With the help of our freedom-fighting brothers, we have a good plan. Now we must act. Much depends on us; we cannot fail."

The three men quietly shared glances among themselves, each with fear in his eyes. Had Moshe not been there to urge them forward, one or all of them would surely shrink from the task before them. But they were in his power, and they could feel his intensity.

"By our hand and our daring, we will put the wrath of God in the hands of the servants of God, and strike a blow that will send the infidels reeling back across the sea. They will not dare to oppose us once we have such power. The Great Satan who has so long plagued our lands will leave for good, and the people of God will be free to live and worship as God intended. Now, let us go over the plan a final time."

Glancing around to ensure that they were alone in the lab, Moshe carefully unrolled a set of design specifications for one of the centrifuge banks. Inside on a separate sheet of paper were two pencil drawings. One was of the nuclear core storage vault and the other was of the conventional explosive holding facility. The Pakistani bombs were fission devices, primitive by the thermonuclear standards of the United States and Russia but still very nasty little atomic bombs. While the current regime in Islamabad did more than a little saber-rattling with their nuclear status, they were very careful in safeguarding their nuclear arsenal. The weapons were unconstituted; that is, the warheads and the rockets were not mated, so there was no possibility of an unintended nuclear launch. Furthermore, the two primary functioning components, the nuclear core, or pit, and the nonnuclear high-explosive wrapper, or HEX, were stored separately. The fissionable material, cast in spheres of plutonium or highly enriched uranium, was kept in one part of the complex, and the carefully milled explosive hemispheres, which caused the precise implosion to create a nuclear event, were stored elsewhere. The mating of two explosive hemispheres to a nuclear core and the proper alignment of the firing harness to bring about a high-order nuclear detonation was but a formality for a nuclear engineer trained in such procedures. Moshe was such an engineer. He rolled out the two drawings onto one of the drafting tables. The three others gathered around him.

"Mirza, have you rechecked your clearances for entry to the atomic explosive storage vault?" Mirza Riaz was a slight man with rich chestnut-colored skin, oily black hair that clung to his scalp in ringlets, and a wisp of a mustache. He was Moshe's age, and they had studied at MIT together. Moshe trusted him and felt he had the nerve to carry off his part of the plan.

"All is in order; see for yourself." He proffered the clearance credentials hung on a lanyard around his neck.

On a sturdy, reinforced lab cart with pneumatic tires

were two oscilloscopes with an assortment of wires and probes attached. Clipped to the cart were the authorizations for Mirza to conduct continuity checks on the explosive components. The O-scopes were metal shells that contained plaster facsimiles of the real explosive wrappers. Moshe inspected his credentials and the cart.

"Excellent. When you are passed through to the storage facility, you will go about making your checks, just as you have done before. When you get to U-17 and P-18 storage areas here"—he pointed at the drawing—"you will be at the farthest limit of the television coverage. These are the HEX assemblies we must have. You, Naser, will stand here with your hands in your lab coat to shield Mirza while he makes the exchange. Move slowly and deliberately, just as you normally would in conducting these routine tests, and you should have no problems. Understood?"

Mirza nodded, but Naser stood and simply stared at the paper. "He understands, do you not, my large friend?" Mirza said. Naser was a big man, running to fat. He jumped slightly and mumbled something to the affirmative as Mirza gave him a sharp jab in the ribs with his elbow. Moshe gave him a long look and turned back to the second drawing.

"And do not forget the other components stored there as well," Moshe continued. "These are not under direct surveillance and should be no problem. You can collect them on the way out.

"Allama and I are scheduled to weigh ten of the nuclear pits and record their temperatures. In some respects, our job will be easier. There are TV monitors in the core storage vaults, but none are trained on the end of the vault where we will be weighing the spheres. There is, however, a viewing area on the upper level, and anyone watching from there can clearly observe us. We will have ten chances to switch two of the pits if we are to succeed. Are

you ready, Allama?" Allama was a lab assistant and worshiped Moshe as much as he did Allah. He nodded enthu-
siastically. Moshe made a show of checking his watch,
then looked at each man in turn. "Is everyone ready?" He
waited while each man looked him in the eye and said
that he was prepared to begin. "Then let us be about
God's work. Remember, you are scientists and engineers.
Conduct yourselves with assurance and confidence as you
go about your duties. Then move quickly when it is time
to do what must be done. *Allahu Akbar.*"

"*Allahu Akbar,*" they intoned and followed Moshe out
the door. Mirza was the last to leave, pushing his cart.

Later that afternoon, the four men were admitted to
the secure storage areas. They moved in pairs because of
the mandatory two-man rule. All of them padded about
in shoe-socks and white showerlike caps. Mirza and Naser
began to check the explosive components, moving their
instrumentation cart from one pair of hemispheres to the
next. Nasser read the checklists while Mirza poked and
prodded the wiring assemblies that surrounded the
molded HEX components. With each move, they connected their wire wrist straps to components they were
testing to prevent sparking from static electricity. Mirza
passed a stream of phony data to his hulking assistant.
Nasar duly noted the information on his clipboard. When
they reached U-17, Mirza tugged at his hair cap and
snatched a look behind him. They were alone save for the
black lens peering out from the white box in the corner of
the storage area.

"Okay, Naser, here we go. Move a little to your left and
start with the checklist." Naser just stood there, unmov-
ing. A single droplet of sweat fell from his nose to the clipboard he held. "Now," Mirza hissed with an emphatic tug
on his sleeve. Naser moved to his left.

Without incident, Mirza was able to exchange the HEX

components for the plaster duplicates. When they were finished with all their tests, they were able to remove two beryllium neutron reflectors and two neutron generators and spirit them from the HEX storage area in their lab cart.

Across the research complex, Moshe pushed and Allama pulled the scales through the security doors and into the vault where the nuclear materials were stored. It took them several minutes to level and test the scales that would weigh the material down to a fraction of a milligram. Once the scales were calibrated and in place, they began to take the nuclear pits in their storage containers from their storage cubicles and shuttle them to the scales. Once at the scales, they carefully removed the cantaloupe-sized spheres from their case and gently placed them on the scale. There was no actual radiation hazard, but both men were double-gloved in deference to the toxic material.

"Eleven point six, two, seven, one, one, three kilograms," Moshe said, adjusting the balance as they weighed the first pit.

Allama repeated the figure, entered it on his chart, and noted the reading on the temperature probe.

"Are we clear?" Moshe murmured.

Allama glanced up and saw two technicians standing at the viewing port above them. They were engrossed in conversation and paying them no particular attention.

"N–no," Allama reported. "We are under observation."

The two moved on. After weighing the sixth sphere, Moshe glanced upward and saw the two men still standing at the window, still talking. They continued, but after weighing the seventh pit, a sphere of plutonium, he returned it to the container waiting next to the scale. His instructions had been to obtain one pit of highly enriched uranium and a second of plutonium. Moshe removed an identical container from the compartment under the scale and handed it to Allama. He gasped and almost dropped it.

"Return it to the storage cubicle," Moshe ordered with measured firmness as he took the weighed pit and container next to the scale and with shaking hands placed it in the compartment below. A quick glance told him that the two men were more interested in their conversation than the work being done in the vault.

As they weighed the eighth pit, the two men left the viewing port, and a sphere of highly enriched uranium found its way into the compartment. Moshe and Allama finished their task and removed the scale from the vault, another routine of testing complete.

The following morning, two wooden boxes marked "Electronic Test Equipment, handle with extreme care" left the A. Q. Khan Research Laboratory for a calibration lab in Islamabad. When the crates arrived, two men in robes stood behind the dry-mouthed proprietor as he signed for the consignment. The two men carried the wooden crates through the facility to an old Toyota pickup truck waiting behind the building. At the A. Q. Khan Laboratory in the explosive storage area, four plaster hemispheres rested in the U-17 and P-18 containers alongside the authentic demolitions in other numbered containers. Across the grounds in the nuclear materials storage vaults, two hollow lead spheres waited with their nuclear lookalikes for the call to action.

Early Thursday morning, November 14, Villefranche

It was well after midnight when Pavel Zelinkow arrived back at the villa. He had shed his tuxedo jacket, and the bow tie ends draped down the front of his pleated shirt. Dominique, carrying a glass of seltzer in one hand and her shoes in the other, had wandered down the hall toward the bedroom. He stepped into the office. There were several voice mails on his secure line. Even so, they were in coded phrases. He listened to the last one and then quickly tapped the playback function key.

"Good evening, Mr. Dumas. This is a reminder that the cartridges for your printer have been shipped from the manufacturer and that the empty cartridges you sent us have been returned to the factory. Let us know how we may be of further service."

Zelinkow smiled, turned off the antitampering devices, and clipped on his computer. He then began to bring up his e-mail files. On confirming that the materials to configure two nuclear weapons had been successfully removed from Kahuta and were in hidden in Islamabad, he sent a cable to Riyadh. On the agreed-upon transfer of more funds, he would put the next phase of the plan in motion.

Zelinkow went to the sideboard and splashed a dollop of tawny port into a cut-crystal tumbler. Returning to the desk, he took a cautious sip and reflected on the project. There was a great deal of uncertainty ahead, but a major component of the plan, his plan, was now in place. Now it would be up to Mugniyah and Khalib to carry it off, with his help of course. Imad Mugniyah and Khalib Beniid; the elusive terror master and the mountain fighter. They were both, Zelinkow admitted, the very best in the world at their chosen professions. That was all to the good, and he would need them both if his bold plan were to succeed. And why shouldn't it? he thought. *Am I not the very best in the world at my profession?* He considered this a moment with detached, unemotional objectivity. Then he returned to the bar to pour a measure of port in a second tumbler and set off in search of Dominique.

Saturday, November 16,
central Afghanistan

David Wilson stood on a gentle rise and reviewed the desolation around him. The surveyor's markers they had placed only a few days ago had been carried off, but that did little to affect the project. Their track through this trackless wilderness was governed by satellite imagery and GPS fixes. The colored stakes had been there to help his engineers and planners get their visual bearings. What did bother him were the land mines that had to be found and disposed of along the route. And even more bothersome was the fact that some of the mines had been placed there only a few days ago. He had asked the army to send out patrols ahead of them to deal with this development, but this had not been done. It had been an issue of some debate. Finally, he was forced to agree with the colonel that it was probably just as easy to neutralize them as they moved across the wasteland. So far, they were all antipersonnel mines. An armored D-9 Cat simply cut an eight-inch-deep swath along the route, exploding any ordnance in its path. And the patrols were needed to secure the camp and the completed sections of the pipeline.

"Can you believe that anyone would want to live here, let alone fight for it?" the man at his elbow shouted above the turbine whine.

"It's what makes them such a hard lot. Pity the poor guys in uniform. After we go, they get to stay and guard it."

A man in sunglasses and a baseball cap approached. "We're ready when you are."

Wilson nodded and led the small group of men back to the helo that was turning a short distance away. Once aboard and strapped in, Wilson signaled to the pilot, and they lifted off in a cloud of dun-colored dust. They quickly spiraled up to twenty-five hundred feet. None of the helos had experienced ground fire, but it was prudent to stay at a safe altitude. Ten miles from the moving construction site they called Site South, he could see the dust cloud from the activity on the ground. Scrapers, haulers, concrete trucks, and cranes all buzzed about the area. To the north a solid dark line marked the completed section of the pipeline. At the other end of this line, another crew worked at Site North to take the pipeline north toward the Turkmen border. The work was moving rapidly on both ends. The technology was basically the same as with the Alaskan Pipeline, and many of the old-timers working in Afghanistan had spent time on the North Slope as young roustabouts. For the most part, the crew chiefs and skilled technicians were American. Most of the seven hundred "internationals" were Americans, but there was a liberal sprinkling of Brits and Aussies. Three hundred carefully selected Pakistanis and Afghans made up the rest. It was a hardy, professional crew.

As a young engineer, Dave Wilson had helped build the Alaskan Pipeline and had been called from retirement to build this one. He and Trish had been retired to a small resort town in Idaho. They were into skiing and fly fishing, and Dave had begun to dabble in local politics. He was recently elected mayor of Sun Valley. Then Unocal had come to him and made him a good offer. He had made what he felt was a ridiculous counter, and they had accepted. Central Afghanistan was not central Idaho, but he had to admit that he loved it—or at least, he loved the engineering challenge. The terrain and environmental factors were less formidable than those they had to deal with in Alaska, and there were no labor unions to contend with. There were, however, the remnants of the al Qaeda and Taliban forces, but those were not his problems. That was for the Army to deal with. Well, almost.

Several nights ago they had been mortared, but no one in the camp was injured. He had not heard the *krump* of mortar rounds since the days when he was dug in with his Marine platoon near Khe Sanh. However, this had been the only attack on the camp. The attacker's position had quickly been calculated by radar cuts on the incoming rounds. A Hellfire missile from an orbiting Predator drone had made short work of the mortar team. They found the baseplate, part of the tube, a few sandals, and a few body parts. All were left undisturbed for their al Qaeda brethren to see. Wilson thought of the sensors, active minefields, and passive listening devices along the completed pipeline corridor, and he shuddered. It was suicide to approach within two hundred meters of the completed pipeline, and nearly as lethal, as the mortar crew had found out, to use standoff weapons. There would be men to guard the completed pipeline, but most of the sentry duty would fall to sensors and robotic firing devices. Sensors and the robots were always alert, and they never slept.

When the helicopter set down at the site, Trish was waiting for him. Part of the ridiculous counteroffer he had given to Unocal was that Trish be hired onto the project at an equally obscene salary. Actually, he mused, she was probably more valuable to the project than was he. He only ramrodded the crews; she managed the administrative side of Site South.

"You know, I get really nervous when you're flying around out there," she said as they walked back to the trailer. She handed him a clipboard with a fat sheaf of messages and material requests.

"I like to know what is ahead of us and get a feel for the territory. You didn't seem to mind when I flew around when we were on the Slope." He quickly thumbed through the paperwork; she had already highlighted and circled items for his attention.

"They didn't shoot at us up there," Trish replied. "In Alaska we only had to contend with polar bears, grizzlies, and an occasional rampaging moose. I feel a lot better with you on the ground."

The site was a beehive of activity as six-foot-diameter sections of pipe were hoisted into place and welded to the preceding section. Ahead along the route, the concrete and steel cradles made their way ahead of the pipe-section cylinders. A steady stream of trucks brought material and fresh pipe sections up from Karachi along a recently constructed, unimproved highway they called I-5. I-5 served Site South and continued north along the pipeline corridor to resupply Site North. Once or twice a day, convoys of trucks escorted by an armed escort of Humvees rolled in or through the site. The pipeline consumed vast quantities of material. Wilson and Site South were making better progress than their counterparts to the north, but then he didn't have to contend with the mountains of northern Afghanistan.

"I get the feeling that you're having fun," Trish said when they got back to their trailer. It served as their office and home on the project, and was an oasis from the dust and the noise.

Dave smiled. "You weren't ready for full-time retirement, and neither was I."

"Oh, I don't know. I kind of thought you liked the leisure life." She pulled a plate of cold cuts from the small refrigerator and began to make sandwiches in the small galley-alcove. "Tennis and golf in the summer. A little fishing. Skiing in the winter." She smiled wryly. "And however will the city council get along without you?"

"They'll simply have to squabble among themselves until I get back," Dave said as he grabbed her and pulled her onto his lap, "just like they always do." She was on the short side of sixty, and he was just on the long side. They were fit, a little gray, sunburned, and full of life. And they both knew how to live on the trail.

"We can do all that shit when we get old. Hell, we got a pipeline to build. What could be better?" She smiled at him and rubbed a smudge off the side of his cheek. Then he said on a more serious note, "I have to fly up to Site North for a meeting tomorrow."

She frowned. "Can't they come here?"

He shook his head. "They came here last time; my turn to go."

She sighed. "You know I won't rest easy until you're back. You're not staying overnight, are you?" It was a good question. Site North had experienced a rocket and a mortar attack.

"I'll be back at sunset. Okay?"

"Okay."

"Happy?"

She looked out the window, through the dust film to the rocky, desolate plain that stretched as far as the eye could see. Then back at Dave. She pulled his yellow Caterpillar baseball cap off and ruffled his thinning hair.

"I've asked you not to wear this in the house, and yes"—she smiled—"I'm very happy."

Sunday evening, November 17, Oahu

Joseph Simpson rose when Steven Fagan walked into the Palm Terrace at Turtle Bay. Simpson had been in Honolulu for a fund-raiser and had asked Fagan to join him on Oahu for an evening. Steven had taken a flight over

from the Big Island that afternoon and caught the limo
out to the big hotel complex on the north shore of the
island. Simpson had visited the site on Kona, but only
once. Both had agreed that for security purposes, the
project would be better served if Simpson had little physical contact with the site or the Big Island.

"Steven, it's good to see you. Come, sit down."

It was early evening, and the gentle swishing of the
palms could just be heard over the distant boom of the famous North Shore surf break. There were tile floors, can-
dlelit tables with crisp linen and elegant settings, and an
abundance of flowering plants. The tasteful and serene
surrounding seemed at odds with the enterprise that
brought them together. Both were dressed in light slacks
and patterned shirts. Steven wore a brimmed straw hat
that he removed as soon as he reached the table, which was
situated in a private alcove.

"Thank you, sir. It's good to see you again as well."

They both ordered iced tea and Simpson a plate of
caviar. Simpson asked politely about Lon and the home in
Waimea, and Steven drew Simpson out about the recent
work of the Joseph Simpson Jr. Foundation. They talked
about the administration's growing problems in Iraq and
about the pipeline in Afghanistan.

"Well," Simpson began after the drinks and caviar were
served and the waiter withdrew, "if the project goes as well
as you look, things are coming along just fine. Your reports would seem to confirm just that. I'd say congratulations are in order." He raised his glass, as did Steven, and
they both drank to the toast.

"We've a long way to go, but I have to admit that we
are ahead of schedule, and the 'lads' as Garrett calls them,
are doing quite well. We've been training for a little over a
month and have our full complement now—a total of
twenty-eight Gurkhas. All of them are professional sol-

diers, so it not so surprising that they have come together as a unit so quickly."

"So they are happy with their new quarters and their new situation?"

"Very much so," Steven answered, "but then you would have to experience a British Army garrison posting to understand why they are so pleased to be with GSI. Yet it's more than that. Bijay Gurung has selected only the finest Gurkhas for us. They are splendid men in all respects, in the barracks and in the field. By their normal standards, they are being very well paid, but pay for a Gurkha, as I've come to learn, is secondary. Bijay has an immense hold over them. I have never seen men in or out of uniform respect someone as much as they do Bijay Gurung. Nor have I seen men so willingly respond to such a rigorous training program. Garrett has them working around the clock. The physical regime is like nothing I've ever seen. Three days ago, they walked under full pack to the top of Mauna Kea. They soldiered up 10,000 feet to a 14,000-foot summit. But then Garrett and Bijay train right alongside the younger men. And those two—well, I've seen some hard men in my travels, but they are in a class by themselves. And I've been privileged to serve with some very seasoned military professionals, both in and out of the service. I have never seen the likes of these two. They and the lads simply have the right stuff."

"Any problems?"

"Not really." Steven continued, "However, I know Garrett would like to see them shoot a little better. Oh, they could qualify as expert in any Western military outfit, but Garrett has some very demanding combat-shooting standards. They are improving, and Garrett has set up some interesting and challenging instinctive-fire courses." A smile came to Steven's tanned features. "If they do not maintain a certain average on the marksmen courses and the combat-shooting drills, he makes them wear their *khukuris* under their blouses. He could never ask a Gurkha to remove his *khukuri*, but to display it on his belt, he must shoot well. Any evening you go into the barracks, you will find Gurkhas practicing magazine quick-changes or dry-firing their rifles. God help whomever they face, because we have a magnificent fighting force in the making."

"You seem to put a great deal of stock into what Bijay and Garrett have been able to accomplish. So you believe that if we put the Gurkhas in the field against a determined foe, they will prevail?"

"In the field, without a doubt," Steven replied. "But this is a small unit in transition. Gurkhas are light infantry. They were all trained by the British in light-infantry tactics—fire and maneuver, direct assault, operations in support of a main-force army. Garrett and Bijay are training them to fight as a special operations force. This involves long-range patrolling, strategic reconnaissance, the use of special demolitions, developing sniper teams, and the like." Steven smiled. "One of the most difficult things we've had to do is to get them to let their hair grow. Many of them have no beards to speak of, and they are uncomfortable with long hair. We also make them train in a range of tribal and ethnic garb, but they are much more comfortable in uniforms. You go into the barracks or the mess hall on any evening, and they are all wearing their uniforms. They love to be in uniform, and they absolutely hate turbans. But that said, they are coming along better than we expected."

"Have weapons and ammunition been a problem?" Simpson asked.

"The permits we have obtained are in keeping with that of any law-enforcement training school. The amounts of ammunition are probably greater than that used by the entire Hawaiian state police force, but no one has raised a question. What weapons we were unable to obtain through legal channels come from arms dealers prepared to look the other way if we can pay a premium. For the most part we are using the standard special-operations weapon, the M-4 rifle with the Picatinny Rail System. This system can handle a number of sighting modifications and night-vision optics. It's a small rifle, perfect for the Gurkhas. The sniper rifles are commercial competition-grade weapons, much better than military issue. As for explosives, our priming charges, firing assemblies, and time delays are standard military demolitions. We have limited ourselves to quarter-pound blocks of C-4 so as not to attract attention. If we ever formalize an understanding with the U.S. Navy, it would be nice to get the lads over to Kahoolawe for some tactical demolitions work. We do most of the weapons training at the camp. We also have teams scheduled to train at the John Shaw School in Memphis and at Blackwater in North Carolina. These civilian shooting schools are, in Garrett's opinion, the best in the world. They have what are called kill houses where they train for urban battle. These schools train federal and local law enforcement organizations as well as private security firms, and their facilities are first-rate." Steven paused to frame his words. "Garrett has the men broken into four squads, or teams, of seven. By traveling to these various training sites, they get used to traveling and moving as a small group on commercial airlines. He also wants to put them in as many different shooting situations as possible. So he will be accompanying them on these training trips, a squad or two at a time."

"Excuse me," Simpson interrupted, "but why don't we have a—what did you call it—a kill house at our camp?"

"Well, there are only two companies in the nation with the expertise to construct these facilities, and they are very expensive. Each room has to be fitted with antiballistic sheeting, and to make it effective, the walls have to be movable to configure the rooms for different kinds of training scenarios. Like I said, it can be expensive."

Simpson simply said, "If cost is the only objection, then have one built. What else?"

Steven knew price was no object, but he had run black operations on a budget for so long he found it hard to spend money freely. He pulled a wheelbook from his rear trouser pocket and flipped through a few pages, then began to brief Simpson on camp activity. Most of the needed equipment—field gear, GPSs, night optics, laser gun sights—was available on the open market. The radios they would need for training on Hawaii and forward deployed in an operational posture were among the most expensive items. And they would have to rent satellite time. Steven had hired a retired Navy chief storekeeper to tend to the day-to-day needs of the camp. He was going to hire a cook for the galley, but the Gurkhas preferred to do their own cooking. Bijay and Garrett normally ate with them, and on occasion so did he, but more often than not, Lon had dinner waiting for him when he got home. As the operation expanded, they would be needing a cook, but that was in the future. Right now, the camp operated with the storekeeper, local contract labor, Bijay, Garrett, and Steven.

"It won't be too long until we can declare ourselves open for business. It's probably not too early to begin assembling an operations staff and some support personnel. At a minimum we will need an operations planner who can double as a security officer, a communications specialist, and an air operations/resupply type. I will also need someone who can falsify documents and travel overseas for advance work. I have just the man in mind. Garrett also has a list of names from which to select the others. For now, I'd like to have one or the other of us at the camp or nearby in the islands. That will free the other to travel as needed to conduct interviews. We need to get started on this as soon as we can. These people have to be trained as well and integrated with the operators. My question for you, sir, is about our air assets?"

Simpson rolled a cracker basted with caviar into his mouth and munched silently for a moment. "I can have an extended-range Gulfstream G550 here from L.A. within six hours of when you say it's needed. I could keep it at the Kona airport from time to time if we need to be in a high state of readiness, but it would be a little conspicuous if it were there for an extended period of time. We have a number of these planes, and while they are not troop transports, they can move small numbers of people and equipment very fast and very efficiently."

That was a $50 million aircraft, Steven mused, and I was concerned over the price of an expensive shooting facility.

"The foundation owns six modified C-130 transports," Simpson continued, "and we've tried to recruit crews from the First Special Operations Wing at Hurlburt Field in Florida. The word is out that we pay top dollar for experienced ex-military combat pilots. And it makes sense. We've been shot at more than once delivering food and medicine in Africa. We keep them based in Germany. Considering the humanitarian work we do, the U.S. Air Force has given us basing privileges at Ramstein Air Base in Frankfurt. We also have ten, soon to be twelve, H-60 helicopters. As with the C-130s, they have most of the modifications associated with military special-operations aircraft. They are scattered about because of range restrictions, and we keep them on the move a great deal—Africa, India, Malaysia, for the most part. Again, we've had no problem finding capable ex-military pilots. The extensive electronics and extra fuel

tanks on our aircraft have raised a few eyebrows among
our pilots, but for the most part, they're glad to be flying
well-equipped and well-maintained equipment. From
what I'm told, a few of them suspect that there may be
more to the job than flying humanitarian missions, but
that doesn't seem to bother them. At some point in time,
you or your staff will have to brief them about what may
be a special mission, one in which they will be carrying
something other than food. I'll leave that to you and
Garrett." He paused, rubbing his hands together. "This is
all very exciting, and I'd love to make another visit
sometime, but it may be best if I stay away for a while.
Too many people know me, and I'd like to protect our
cover story for as long as possible. Speaking of cover, are
we doing any of that?"

"Guardian Systems International is brokering Gurkhas
for private security work around the world, and through
Bijay's contacts, we get the best of the best. And since
Gurkhas are almost a commodity when it comes to loyalty and service, no one has questioned that the Gurkhas
we broker are from Nepal or Singapore rather than the
ones we train on the Big Island. Still, it helps our cover of
training men for corporate security work and executive
protection. We have a retired Gurkha sergeant major in
Kathmandu on the payroll who looks after our interests
there. From that standpoint, it looks like GSI will turn a
modest profit in its first year of operation." Steven
paused a moment before continuing. "As you know, I've
had some experience running secret organizations. We
have the best of all worlds here, providing a real product
while actually doing something different. If someone
looks a little closer at us, we have a fallback position; we
provide executive protection services and paramilitary
training cadres to foreign governments. This works well,
as it is a venture where discretion and secrecy are part of

normal business practice. And there are competitors like Global Options and O'Gara Security Services. But a good government investigator, or even the commercial competition, can cut through all this. They can find out about you if they're persistent. It will take them some time to peel back the onion, but they can do it. I can build a firewall on most commercial inquiries, but not a dedicated federal investigator. Somewhere along the line, it may be in our interest to let someone in the government, at some level, know what we're up to." Steven shrugged. "It may never happen, but I'd like not to leave it up to chance. We perhaps don't have to think about this right now, but somewhere down the line we should."

"So what are you saying, exactly?"

"I'm saying we should consider how our government may react if they learn of our venture. And we should do this before we employ this force we're training. We are not asking for funding, sanction, or approval, but if we have a contact, some communications with someone at a high level, then they can kill any official investigation before it gets started. There is also the matter of black support, and even a quid pro quo. An exchange at some level with Washington on what our government may feel needs to be done, but cannot do, might be very helpful."

Simpson was silent for some time. "Let me give that some thought. I will naturally consult you on any measures along this line, but I see what you're getting at—fair enough?"

"Fair enough, sir." Steven still found it difficult to call him Joe, and Simpson had grown weary of reminding him.

"And now," Simpson continued, "I understand that they have some very fine ahi here. Shall we indulge?"

Steven nodded, and they took up their menus for study.

Monday evening, November 18,
Manzai, Pakistan

Manzai was little more than a poor agriculture village in
northwestern Pakistan. At least, that's what it seemed—a
village whose only visible means of income were substance
farmers who lived in the area. Like so many who lived in the
foothills of the Sulaiman Range, the people of Manzai
made their living in a number of ways—smuggling, ban-
ditry, and even an occasional slave. There was still a market
for slaves, usually young boys, even in the twenty-first century. And now that the Taliban had been effectively removed from Afghanistan, the opium trade was booming. It
was a poor community where revenue was dear and services without question, cheap. They were sixty miles from
the Afghan border and three hundred miles by car from the
capital. Those in Islamabad and the Punjab couldn't care
less what the people here did. And those who lived in and
around Manzai couldn't care less about the government in
Islamabad. They could be roused by Hindus in Kashmir
and by infidels in Afghanistan, but the laws passed in Islamabad or the influence of the central government existed
in name only. Tribal and ethnic considerations were all that
mattered. The men of the village, whose fathers and grand-
fathers had fought for a Muslim nation, still talked about
the days when the Raj ruled India and they were a part of
Hindustan. In 1947 Pakistan had become an independent
state. That the provinces of Punjab and Bengal were cut in
half, and Kashmir still in dispute, was proof of the injustice
of the West and the treachery of the Indians. If that were
not enough, in 1972 East Pakistan became Bangladesh, further example of manipulation by the Indians and the West.
Because of this, no recent government in Islamabad had
been able to stay in power without external threats to the

nation. Kashmir was a Muslim point of honor. Only the Indian troops massed along the Line of Control in Kashmir had allowed the Musharraf government a free hand to help the Americans in Afghanistan. In Manzai, contempt for Americans was only slightly less than that for Hindus.

Per their instructions, Moshe Abramin and Mirza Riaz had driven the Toyota pickup from Kahuta to Manzai. The truck had magically appeared in front of Moshe's apartment only the previous evening. The keys, truck papers, and a thick wad of 500-rupee notes were in the glove box. The truck was battered, and there was a long crack in the windshield, but the tires were new and the engine ran perfectly. Moshe and Mirza's personal documents afforded them the highest security clearance and complete freedom of movement. Any army or ISI roadblock they encountered leaving the capital would pass them through, without questions or inspection, with these credentials. As it was, they were stopped only once, and passed through the checkpoint with a wave of a sergeant's hand. It had taken them almost eleven hours to make the drive. The road as far as Peshawar was paved, but when they turned south toward Kohat, they were dodging oxcarts in the dust rooster tails from other trucks like their own. When they arrived in Manzai late in the day, Moshe and Mirza no longer looked like laboratory engineers but dirty young men in a pickup trying to make some money. In the back, they had a crate of shoes, some shovels and picks, a bushel of oranges, and several new TVs, still in their boxes. All would be welcome in the marketplace in Manzai. They also had the components for two nuclear weapons nestled in a box of blankets and bound with duct tape. Along with the main nuclear and explosive components were the neutron generators and beryllium reflectors necessary to stimulate the nuclear reaction. It was all there, save for the weapon outer casings, waiting assembly into fully functioning nuclear bombs. They came to a crossroads that was the center of town. As instructed, Moshe parked near a café on the road that led from Manzai to Daraban and waited. Within ten minutes, a man in tattered trousers and a sweater approached. He appraised the truck and turned to the driver.

"From the looks of your vehicle, it seems that you have traveled far. Perhaps you should come inside for some refreshments. And do not worry about your truck or its contents. They will not be harmed." Moshe and Mirza got out and followed Khalib into the café. Once they were seated at a table in the corner, the proprietor brought them tea. "It appears you have done well," he continued. "Let us first get you something to eat, then you can tell me about your journey."

The small café served an excellent fare of lamb and vegetables. Moshe and Mirza were ravenous, and both accepted an additional portion. The food revived them considerably, but Moshe's spirit was boosted more by the manner in which Khalib treated him. He was not deferential, but there was a courtesy and a respect that had not been there before. When they had finished, more tea was served and Khalib poured.

"Now, tell me what you have brought us and exactly how you came by it," Khalib said. There was now a firmness to his voice. "Spare no detail; I need to know everything."

Moshe recounted the taking of the weapon components and the successful replacement of the fake materials. On the latter, Khalib questioned him closely, as he had been instructed to do by Imad Mugniyah. Moshe was impressed by Khalib's knowledge of the bomb components and the security arrangements that would attend them. Moshe made it clear that they were able to bring away from Kahuta the nuclear and nonnuclear components for two weapons, one plutonium bomb and one uranium bomb.

"And of the other two who helped you?"

"They are back at work, as we shall be in a few days. We are on authorized holiday leave from the laboratory."

"How long do you think the deception will last?"

"Anything is possible—there could be a random inspection or a military exercise where the components are mated and fitted to a warhead at any time. But there are no maintenance requirements or system checks scheduled for several weeks."

Khalib was silent for several moments. "Do you believe that what we are doing is right and just?" he asked Moshe.

"It is God's will," Moshe blurted.

"And you?" he said to Mirza.

"Without doubt. God is with us!"

"Brothers," he replied, "you have done well. You both have acted courageously, and your names will be repeated with honor among all true believers when we achieve the final victory. Humble servants like myself stand in your shadow. I salute you." He lowered his head as a measure of respect. Both Moshe and Mirza were stunned that a warrior of such presence would defer to them in this way.

"Tonight you will rest, and tomorrow you will return to Islamabad. I want you to return to your work as if nothing has happened. There are hundreds of scientists and technicians at Kahuta who have access to the weapons, and when the two bombs are found missing, many beside yourselves will come under suspicion. Trust me when I tell you that we have in place a plan that will throw blame away from you. My instructions are that you are to be protected at all costs. Again, by your courage and daring, you have helped to strike a blow that will be talked of for generations." Moshe and Mirza sat there in flattered silence.

"In the not-too-distance future, you will be called to join us. Be ready. Then you will live with us and become acknowledged freedom fighters in the service of God."

Both of the young scientists nodded vigorously.

Khalib made sure that they had comfortable accommodations and an excellent meal before their return journey. Only the oranges and a single TV remained in the truck. Khalib saw to it that the weapons were moved with great care, for they had to travel the length of Pakistan and into Iran. Their trek was slow, as agents of the ISI were everywhere. For the most part, Khalib and his precious cargo traveled through sympathetic territory, but among the border tribes, everything was for sale. Ten days later, they crossed into Iran. Well inside Iran, they were met by two Ford Explorers and driven to Khalabad. There the two weapons were securely stored under the control of Imad Mugniyah; their absence had yet to be discovered at Kahuta. Moshe Abramin and his three co-conspirators had had an anxious time of it, but with each passing day of routine at the lab, they began to breathe a little easier. On Monday, November 25, fourteen days from the date of the theft, none of the four would report for work. An investigation was quickly mounted, but all had disappeared without a trace. Three days later a wrecked van was found in Kashmir, not far from the Line of Control. Inside were two bodies later identified as employees missing from the A. Q. Khan Research Lab. The other two were never found. In the residences of three of the four, propaganda and leaflets were found that advocated the forceful recovery of Kashmir. The subsequent inventory of nuclear weapons at the facility produced some startling results. The unthinkable had happened, and the trail appeared to lead toward the heavily armed border between India and Pakistan in the contested province of Kashmir.

Wednesday, November 20,
the Big Island, Hawaii

Garrett Walker stepped up to the firing line. Downrange
some fifteen meters were eight pie-plate-sized targets
perched on a stand. Five meters to his left, Duhan stood
facing his eight targets. Both of them had M-4 rifles held at
the ready. Both of them were totally focused on the eight
targets. For Garrett, nothing else existed; not the soft breeze
blowing up from the ocean, not the twenty-seven Gurkhas
murmuring quietly behind him, and not the very accomplished shooter standing next to him. Just the targets.

"Standby . . . targets!" Bijay called in his proper British
accent.

Garrett brought his M-4 rifle up to a firing position
and looked over the top of his sights.

BANG, ping! BANG, ping! BANG, BANG, ping! BANG,
ping!

It took him five shots to clear the first four targets. He
was aware by some sixth sense that Duhan had cleared his
four with only four shots. Garrett safed his M-4 and swung
it down to his side, and as if with the same motion drew the
Glock 9mm pistol from the holster on his hip. Garrett was
up to a firing position a fraction of a second behind Duhan.

BANG, BANG, ping, ping!

Or that's what it sounded like. He had fired two rounds
almost before his first round got to his first target. Both
metal plates fell back as one. Now there were only two targets remaining. Garrett knew his competitor was better
than he with an M-4, but he was not yet as proficient with
the pistol, nor in the transition between weapons. He was
very good, but not quite in Garrett's league. In one
smooth motion, Garrett dropped the hammer to safe the
Glock, reholstered it, and reshouldered his M-4. He knew
he could not miss if he were to win.

BANG, ping! BANG, ping!

He brought his rifle down just a fraction ahead of Duhan. Behind him, there was a roar of approval from the Gurkhas watching the contest. They were clearly pulling for their fellow Gurkha, but all applauded the closeness of the duel. Garrett turned and bowed respectfully to his shooting partner. Duhan returned the gesture.

"You have come a long way in such a short time, Corporal. I am afraid that this old warrior may soon take instruction from you."

"You are too kind, Subadar. I was privileged to make a contest of it." Again, he lowered his head.

"Thank you," Garrett replied. "But you are clearly superior with the rifle. Pistols," he made a depreciating gesture, "are for policemen and the parade ground. The rifle is the weapon of the true fighting man."

"Again, Subadar, you are too kind."

The Gurkhas had given him the name of Subadar, which was their term for a British officer, specifically a British captain. It was also a title of respect. Bijay also called Garrett by that name, although when the two of them were alone, Garrett asked him to use his first name. In the company of the men, Garrett addressed Bijay as Sergeant Major, which was the American army equivalent of his rank in the Brigade of Gurkhas. The shooting contest had been a single-elimination event, something the Gurkhas had not experienced before, but they quickly warmed to the competition. Bijay considered this a good thing, though he himself was eliminated in the second round. Within the Navy SEAL teams, everything was competitive—winners and losers. SEAL culture was driven by competition. Gurkhas had a keen sense of duty that drove them to excel in their professional duties, but they were not competitive by nature—unless, of course, the contest was combat. So Garrett used head-to-head competition

judiciously. Yet this had been a good drill. Garrett knew
that very soon he would lose one of these infrequent
shooting contests, and that in itself would be a good thing
for this tough little band of soldiers. Garrett was accepting
the shy congratulations from the other Gurkhas when
he saw Steven Fagan roll up in his jeep. He motioned to
Garrett, and Garrett politely excused himself from the
group.

"Did you win?"

"This time, but I doubt it will happen again. These
guys are good and getting better every day. And they get a
lot more practice than I do."

Steven smiled and handed him a folder. "I managed to
find that operations planner you told me about. I set up a
meeting for day after tomorrow at the Honolulu airport—two o'clock in the afternoon. I plan to make the
meeting, but I thought you might want to fly over with
me. Can you take a day away from training?"

Garrett considered this. "Let's see, we have two jumps
scheduled for tomorrow, one in the afternoon and a night
drop, both equipment jumps. I may be a little short on
sleep, but yes, I think I'd like to be there." As he thumbed
through the folder, his tanned features creased in a smile.
"This operations planner is something else—a real piece
of work. You're in for a treat."

Friday, November 22,
Honolulu International Airport

Janet Brisco, Lieutenant Colonel, USAF (ret.), waited in a
comfortable armchair in the United Airlines Red Carpet
Room. She read the *Washington Post* while sipping on a
Starbucks Double Americano Grande. What she really
wanted was a cigarette, but the only places you could
smoke in an airport these days were those glass enclosures

that made you feel like you were in some county lockup waiting for the start of visiting hours. She swapped out the *Post* for the *New York Times*, pausing to once again consider why she was here. She had received the call only a week ago. Mr. Edwards was most polite in asking if she could fly to Honolulu to interview for a position for which she was uniquely qualified and that came with a generous compensation package. She would be paid a thousand dollars a day for her time during the interview process, and all expenses. The offer came with a first-class St. Louis–Honolulu round-trip ticket. This Mr. Edwards had rightly guessed that she was content but not really happy teaching international relations at Washington University in St. Louis. The day before yesterday, she had agreed to come.

"Colonel Brisco?" She looked up. "My name is Steven Edwards, and I believe you and my associate, Garrett Walker, have met. We appreciate your making the trip out from the mainland."

She rose and offered her hand. Janet Brisco was a tall, striking black woman of indeterminate age, but she looked much younger than her forty-two years. She was fire and ice—a blend of grace and a certain competitive, in-your-face aggression. She was unknown to other travelers in the lounge, but many felt she was an actress or a model—someone they should have known. When she traveled, she was often treated as a celebrity, which she carried off with the appropriate level of condescension and impatient courtesy.

"Pleased to meet you, Mr. Edwards." Then she turned to Garrett, smiling warmly. "Nice to see you again, Garrett. And due to the sketchy information concerning this meeting, I guess I'm not surprised to find you here. Or at least, someone like you." The smile faded, and she continued in a softer tone. "I was sorry to learn of your brother's death,

Garrett. I understand his actions more than justified his
Navy Cross. He was one of our best."

Few people, and indeed few women, could refer to a
Navy SEAL killed in action as one of ours, but Janet
Brisco could. She had earned the reputation in the tight-
knit special-operations community as the best operations
planner in the business. Most of her twenty-year Air Force
career had been spent in special operations. Because she
was so highly valued as a mission planner, she had not
been afforded the command opportunities that would
have led to her promotion to full-bird colonel. This had
rankled her because she was much more capable than
most colonels in the Air Force, and she had aspired to
command. But the Air Force had its reasons. One of those
was that she would have made a lousy commanding officer, just as she had been, in her words, a lousy wife. Like
many highly intelligent people, she could be short with
those not as gifted as herself, and that group included almost all of those serving in the U.S. Air Force, the U.S.
Special Operations Command, and the capable but unfortunate man she had married. She was gifted but often intolerant. Still, she might have stayed on for the love of the
job if not the service, but for her family. Her grand-
mother, who had raised her in East St. Louis and had encouraged her to accept the appointment to the Air Force
Academy, was ninety-one. Granny Brisco was still going
strong, but she was dependent on her granddaughter.
Janet's son, Aaron, now a teenager and the most important thing in her life, was rapidly becoming a man. He was
the only good thing to come from her brief marriage. And
then there was her extended family; she was their pride—
respected and admired. The Brisco clan was a large and
contentious brood. Her appearance at a parent-teacher
conference, an awards banquet, or a parole hearing was
impressive and effective. This "duty," she realized, was her

tour of command, one where she could be much more influential than in the Air Force. Still, she missed the business. Nothing she had ever done matched the intellectual
challenge and rush she got from the fast-paced life-and-
death event that was an unfolding special operation. Her
decisions were often as important and as critical as those
of a mission commander on the ground.

"So," she began after they were seated, "who are we
going to kidnap or which government are we going to
topple?" Her smile was radiant and genuine, but also said
Let's get down to business. In that respect, she was much
like Garrett Walker. She was also very comfortable in the
company of warriors. She had met Garrett on two occasions, once when he was going into harm's way under her
guidance and once when he was detailed to help her with
the planning of a special-operations mission in Serbia
when Milosevic was in power. His presence meant something interesting was in the works. She knew nothing of
this Steven Edwards, but she had learned long ago that
polite, observant men who take a moment to think before
they speak are to be taken seriously. Men often stared at
her, and Fagan was no exception. He had not taken his
eyes off her, but there was nothing suggestive or sexist in
his appraisal. Garrett watched all this in fascination. He
had wondered how Steven Fagan, aka Steven Edwards,
would handle her, and how she would react to what Garrett had come to call "the Fagan treatment." He assumed
that Fagan would try to overcome this strong woman with
gentleness, and he was right. After a long moment, Steven
began in a soft voice.

"Ms. Brisco, I want to give you some background on a
project that we have underway." Again, another pause.
Among Steven Fagan's many talents was to know exactly
how much information someone needed, and when. All
his instincts told him that candor was called for—to put

his cards on the table, faceup. "I should first ask you to sign a nondisclosure document or at the very least, talk in the hypothetical. But I am not going to insult you with innuendo or insinuation. Your past service and your professional credentials make that unnecessary. In short, I know a great deal about you, and you know nothing about me—about us—and our current undertaking. Let's fix that. First of all, my name is Steven Fagan, not Steven Edwards. In our recruiting process, and our business, we often elect not to use our real names. I am going to tell you what we have done to this point and what we plan for the future. Then Garrett and I will answer any and all of your questions. When we finish, and if what we have said kindles your interest, we can discuss your role in this venture at that time. If you have no interest, then we will just thank you for taking the time to talk with us. I do, however, ask that you treat what I am about to tell you as sensitive information. Is that reasonable?"

Fagan folded his hands and regarded her with an open, straightforward expression. He asked this with the same tone and respect one might ask a dinner companion for permission to select a wine for the meal.

"Mr. Fagan," she said with just a hint of a smile, "you have indeed piqued my curiosity." With a quick glance at Garrett, "Please continue."

Fagan told her the whole story, save for the involvement of Joseph Simpson and the source of funds. Garrett excused himself partway through Steven's presentation and returned with a tray of coffee and scones. Steven abruptly reached a conclusion, and stared at his hands before turning back to Janet Brisco.

"That's about it. I again want to assure you that as yet we have no official or unofficial link to the U.S. government. That may change, although any connection will certainly have to be plausibly deniable. Still interested?"

Now it was Janet Brisco's turn to be silent. It was no small matter, she later reflected, that she was very comfortable sitting with these two men. This seldom happened to her. Finally, she took a long look at Garrett and turned to Steven.

"Of course I'm interested. Who in my position, with my background, wouldn't be? Since you know a great deal about me, I can only assume that you are aware of my family situation and my roots in St. Louis."

"I am," Steven replied, "and at the risk of appearing intrusive, we would like to take that into consideration. We want you to be continually in touch with the project, but this may not require your full-time presence at the site. Please also understand that there will be times when your presence will be required twenty-four hours a day for an extended period of time. But there will be significant periods of time you can work from St. Louis. We are prepared to install a secure, interactive communications suite with an enhanced video teleconferencing capability in your home. Any travel, for whatever duration, here or to an advanced site, will include first-class accommodations. Should your son wish to join you here for a semester, I'm sure the Punahou School in Honolulu would be delighted to have him as a student." Again, the pause and the politeness. "With apologies for an invasion of your privacy, I also understand that you have responsibilities for an extended family. We have yet to discuss fees, but I have taken the matter up with my employer. We are all paid well at GSI, but your compensation would allow for a foundation, a family trust if you will, for the education of your extended family. The trust would be discreet, irrevocable, and you would be the sole trustee."

Brisco whistled softly. "You guys are pretty well dialed in, aren't you?"

"We are; it's our business," Steven said evenly, "and once again, forgive me if I have presumed too much."

"Can I have some time to think about this?"

"Absolutely." Steven glanced at his watch. "There is a flight leaving for the mainland within the hour if you need to get back. Or there is a suite reserved for you at the Royal Hawaiian if you'd like to stay over. And not to press the issue, Garrett and I would love to treat you to an early dinner before we fly back to Kona this evening—no business, just a good meal. We get our share of barracks fare, and it would be a treat for us." Steven could have said this with absolute sincerity if he didn't mean it, but he did.

Brisco chuckled. "You fellows are too much. I think I'll take you up on that."

Garrett walked her to the curb of the airport, hailed a cab, and handed her in.

"You sure do get around, sailor," she said, looking up at him.

"I do my best," he replied with a broad smile.

"Still wish you were back in the teams?"

"Not anymore. See you tonight, Janet."

After an early dinner, Steven gave Janet Brisco a cell phone equipped with a very efficient scrambler chip. "Use this," he told her, "for any questions that you may have or for points on which you need clarification. One way or another, we want your decision to be an informed one." Two days later she called, but he was unavailable. Her voice mail simply said, "I want to join the team." On Monday of the following week, right after Thanksgiving, she was on site on the Big Island and ready to go to work.

5

Armand Grummell sat in his office, deep in thought. On his credenza adjoining the desk were five reports, neatly arranged in a row. They were standard intelligence reports. The five reports were cause for concern but not alarm. All were raw data that might make a desk officer sit up and take notice, or even personally run it by his section chief. His division head would take notice, but then Near East Division had a great deal of information that needed to be noted, mostly concerning Iraq. Each of these five reports had been handled in the proper fashion and had resulted in a tickler file being opened. Each had generated ongoing reporting requirements and requests for more information. Yet collectively, the five reports, when read and digested by an experienced analyst with a feel for the Middle East, were cause for some anxiety. A number of things in the Middle East and Central Asia these days made people in the intelligence business anxious. And while Near East Division was not yet particularly alarmed, Elizabeth Johnstone was. Long ago, Armand Grummell had learned to take serious note whenever Elizabeth Johnstone became alarmed. He never let on to any of her superiors that he held the instincts of this particular analyst in such high regard; they would have massaged her product and perhaps cost him the benefit of her skill and intuition. It was she who had taken the five reports and arrived at a rather dramatic conclusion only a few days ago. She had not seen the recent message that had just landed on his desk. Could they be related, Grummell wondered? One thing was certain; if they were related, it spelled the worst kind of trouble.

The message that he had just been handed, by itself, was one of the most dangerous pieces of paper he had ever held. The Deputy Director of Operations had brought it to him straightaway. It had been sent as a flash priority message. Because of its importance and precedence, a copy had simultaneously gone to the White House. Grummell had immediately asked for a video teleconference with his Chief of Station in Islamabad and the case officer who obtained the information that generated the message. Grummell was not surprised when the ambassador asked to sit in on the meeting. Most ambassadors and even most COSs do not like a case officer to be present at a conference that includes the Director of Central Intelligence and his DDO. But Grummell insisted, as he wanted the person closest to the source on hand, and that would be the field officer who gathered the information. This particular case officer handled an agent inside the A. Q. Khan Laboratory in Kahuta. The Pakistani Ambassador, a very cool and savvy individual, had not objected to Grummell's request that he not contact the State Department until they, and the White House, had time to further evaluate the matter. In a matter of fifteen minutes, Grummell and his DDO were sitting in the CIA operation center, and the three men in Islamabad were sitting in "the bubble," a clear plastic room suspended in one of the embassy office spaces. It was the only room that was considered bug-free and totally secure. After listening to the COS and carefully questioning the case officer, Grummell and the others quickly came to the same conclusion. The report was confirmed as accurate; Pakistan had lost two nuclear weapons from the storage vaults at Kahuta. Four scientists had gone missing, and two of them had just been found dead in Kashmir. Grummell immediately excused himself, leaving the others to conclude the meeting. He was on his way south on the George Washington Parkway from Langley to the White House when his personal phone began to purr.

"Yes, sir," he answered, knowing perfectly well who would be calling. Grummell's secretary had phoned the President's chief of staff to say that he was on his way.

"Armand, what do you make of this? Can it be true?"

"We grade this information to be double-A. It has been checked by a second source and verified. Naturally, we have not gone to my counterpart in the ISI about this, nor have they come to us. It is a very ticklish situation." Then, sensing Bill St. Claire's next question, "I have asked our ambassador in Islamabad not to report this just yet, so as far as I know, State is still in the dark. I thought it might be helpful if we talked first." What Grummell was saying, in effect, was that he did not want the information coming in through channels. It was the President's call to bring Jim Powers into this. After all, the message had gone to the White House as well. Grummell felt certain that Powers would be there when he arrived. He hoped so. He did not particularly like to keep the State Department in the dark, but there were too many leaks at State. Secretary of State James Powers was another matter.

Powers was indeed in the Oval Office when he arrived, as was Secretary of Defense Anthony Barbata. All the better, Grummell thought. Grummell made his report, which added little but a measure of validity to what the White House had received from Islamabad. The discussion centered around the missing weapons, their size and configuration, and the indications that they may be headed for the Line of Control in Kashmir. Finally they reached a consensus, if not an agreement. The President would contact neither General Musharraf nor Prime Minister Vajpayee—for now. He would place a personal call to Musharraf in the near future, pending future developments and additional information, but in any case, no later than forty-eight hours from now. They would all meet again in twenty-four hours for further deliberations. In the meantime, a number of organizations within CIA, NRO, Defense, and State would quietly be tasked with additional duties and to seek additional information. And President St. Claire wanted his Ambassador to the United Nations to read into the problem. Other than that, all would be handled very quietly and very low-key. Oddly enough, not once was the pending confrontation with Iraq brought into the discussion nor did they talk about the President's growing frustration with UN weapons inspectors. Only after the others had left did Armand Grummell ask his President for a moment alone. Then he briefed him on the other five reports, and what that might mean in light of these new developments.

After his meeting at the Oval Office, Grummell returned to Langley. He gave instruction to his DDO and retired to his study with all the reports. He read them again while seated in his favorite chair near the settee in the corner of the room. He then sent for Elizabeth Johnstone. It was after working hours, but she was still in her cubicle, expecting his call. She knocked softly and stepped into the room, closing the door quietly behind her.

"Thank you for staying late, Elizabeth. I appreciate it. Sit down, please." After she had taken a leather armchair opposite him, he recovered his seat. "That was some very fine work you did on the movements of our Lebanese friend, tracking his travel in and out of Pakistan."

Elizabeth Johnstone was in her late fifties, and by any measure a handsome woman. She was intelligent, intuitive, possessing a tenacious work ethic, and like many capable analysts at the CIA, Mormon. Her husband of thirty-five years had been found slumped over his desk at the Bethesda–Chevy Chase Savings and Loan, the victim of a massive stroke. That was two years ago. Elizabeth had taken two weeks away from work to bury her husband and settle his affairs. Then she was back at headquarters, accepting condolences from coworkers and processing yet more raw intelligence data. Sometimes late on a Saturday night, while he listened to a Sinatra recording, Grummell found himself thinking about Elizabeth Johnstone. He would catch himself smiling and feeling more than a little foolish. Marvelous woman, he would admit, simply marvelous. Then he would turn the music lower and force himself back to the biography he would invariably be reading. Grummell himself was a widower and spent what little nonwork time he afforded himself alone.

Grummell touched the intercom and asked one of the attendants to bring Johnstone some tea. Only then did he hand her the flash message on the missing nuclear weapons. After a few moments she said, "This is not good . . . not good at all." She read on, tugging demurely on one earlobe. Finally she looked up. Her pleasant features registered concern but not surprise. "It would seem that Imad Mugniyah may have a hand in this. I can think of no other reason for him to be in that region for that long. And if he has the bombs, the question is, what is he going to do with them?"

Elizabeth Johnstone had put together a series of agent contacts, cell-phone intercepts, and NRO data that suggested Mugniyah had been keeping himself in central Iran and most probably had gone into Pakistan. Like most terrorists, Mugniyah would be on the move, probably not far from the city of Kerman, but in one or more of the smaller villages nearby. Kerman was a city of just under 400,000 on the western edge of the Dasht Lut, a vast high-plains desert. Kerman was the largest city on the vast central plateau of Iran. Khalib Beniid, a known bin Laden associate, had also been in Pakistan and was seen in Lahore. Beniid was simply known as Khalib. Like Mugniyah, he was featured on the FBI top-terrorist hit list, and he enjoyed a charismatic reputation in Afghanistan and Pakistan. All the Western intelligence services were on the lookout for him. Then there was rumor of a meeting of sorts between East and West—Middle East and Central Asia. Hezbollah and al Qaeda had little in common; the former was typically educated, urbane, and sophisticated, the latter tribal and uncivilized. Johnstone's reports suggested that these two senior leaders had met and that any meeting of these two organizations was highly unusual. Her deductions followed that such a meeting would most probably be for a specific reason, and that reason would most certainly not be in the best interest of the United States or its allies.

They sat in companionable silence for some time before Grummell intruded. "What do you think Mugniyah is going to do with his bombs, Elizabeth?"

She took her time before replying. "Given that Hezbollah's chief interests are in the Middle East, not Central Asia, one would think he would take them back to Lebanon, not to Kashmir. He could try to use them against Haifa or Tel Aviv, but that seems unlikely. The Israeli response would be overwhelming and devastating. Or he could simply declare Hezbollah a nuclear power, but that too is unlikely. As Saddam is learning, nuclear weapons are as much a liability as a source of power." She paused a moment before continuing. "For the first time in quite a while, Hezbollah is short of funds. They need capital. I think there may be a chance that Imad did this for the money."

"But why would he go to Khalib and al Qaeda? As you said, they are not a fit."

Elizabeth picked up the document on the missing weapons and reread it. Then she set it on the low table between her and the DCI, and was very still. Armand Grummell scarcely breathed. She was all instinct and intuition. For Elizabeth Johnstone, it was like seeing at night. To see a dimly lit object, you had to look just away from it. The rods and cones of her mind's eye also worked like that. She looked slightly away from the facts in an effort to see past them. Suddenly, she knew she had it, but she said nothing. For the next several minutes, she turned it over in her mind, approaching it from different directions to see if her conclusions were sound. All those years of experience, all that reading and that highly disciplined intellect—it all converged on the problem. She rummaged through the filing cabinets of her mind, pulling a fact here, an agent report there. There could be no certainties, but there was no other logical explanation.

"The other two engineers from the A.Q. Khan facility have yet to be found—is that correct, sir?"

"That is correct," Grummell answered.

"Then I believe they are going to attack the pipeline. Mugniyah is involved because it is a sophisticated operation, one that needs the cooperation of the mullahs in Tehran, or at least for them to look the other way. And Iran does not want this pipeline to be built, unless it's from the Caspian across Iran to the Persian Gulf. If Mugniyah is involved, it's the pipeline. My guess is the weapons are in Iran, or soon will be, and they will be taken to Afghanistan or back into Pakistan and detonated on or near the pipeline. "

"And not taken to the Middle East to serve the interests

of Hezbollah in Lebanon?" The DCI asked. He did not disbelieve Elizabeth, but he wanted to hear her reasoning. He would be asked that question by the President.

"I don't think so. Lebanon and Hezbollah's base is twenty-five hundred miles west. Let's say Mugniyah is in this for himself—for Hezbollah. He hasn't a prayer of getting those weapons out of Pakistan without al Qaeda help, and al Qaeda would not take this kind of risk just for Hezbollah. Then Mugniyah would have to take them across Iran and Iraq, or across Saudi Arabia, to get them even close to Israel. It would be a long shot, and what does it get him? The Mossad would run him to ground before he got close. And if he did succeed in getting one of those bombs into Israel, would he have the skill to detonate it? Nuclear weapons are not hand grenades. None of it adds up."

"How about the van found in Kashmir? Is it possible that the two weapons went that direction?"

"I doubt it. I've read the files on the four engineers who were involved. Only the two they have yet to account for have the knowledge to assemble a weapon. My guess is that he and his friend—and they were friends—are still with the bombs. The van was a false trail. And again, if Mugniyah and Khalib Beniid are together on this, then it must have something to do with our presence in Afghanistan. Mugniyah is smart, and Iran is something of a safe haven for him. It makes sense that he would have enlisted someone like Khalib to help him get the bombs out of Pakistan."

"If it's the pipeline, why not take them over the border right into Afghanistan?" Grummell knew the answer, but he wanted to hear Elizabeth confirm it.

"Too much U.S. presence there. We've been chasing al Qaeda across the Afghan-Pakistani border for several years now. Khalib has good contacts in Pakistan, and he can move easily in the western provinces, but it is not a safe haven for him. It's not an area from which he could stage an operation back into Afghanistan. I believe he will take the weapons west and south, and across the Pakistani-Iranian border. He probably already has. I believe they will stage an operation from Iran into Afghanistan against the pipeline."

"And who is paying for this?" Grummell asked. Again, he knew the answer.

"Saudi Arabia," she replied without hesitation. "They have the most to lose if the pipeline is completed. They could not go directly to al Qaeda for this kind of an operation; al Qaeda simply does not have the expertise to pull it off." She was not cold, but she began to get goose bumps on her arms, which meant she sensed something was amiss. "To be honest, this even seems a little beyond the capabilities of Imad Mugniyah. It's not the kind of plan he would hatch. I wonder, could someone else be involved? The Saudis would spare no expense to see construction on the pipeline halted and the blame passed along to al Qaeda or some other state sponsor." She gave Grummell a concerned look. "I wish there was another avenue from which I could approach this matter and come to a different conclusion, but right now, the facts suggest we have a nuclear threat directed at American interests in Afghanistan."

She waited while Grummell was lost in thought. He had missed it totally; all of them had. They had been too quick to jump on the India-Pakistan issue. In his heart, Grummell felt she was right, but he was looking for a plausible alternative. There simply was none. He knew this would mean another trip to the White House; there was also no way around that. But first, he had another meeting.

"Thank you, Elizabeth. As usual, your insight and your counsel have proved most valuable. I'd like you to stay with this, if you don't mind. Let me know if your section chief has a problem with that. Ask him to shift your normal workload to someone else. I want you on this full-time. Let me know immediately if you learn anything that supports or invalidates your theory. I think you're right, but I'd like nothing better than for you to prove yourself wrong."

"So would I, sir."

Grummell accompanied her to the door, through his office, and into the reception area. There was a secretary at the desk, even at this late hour. Whenever Armand Grummell was working, which was about eighteen hours a day, there was a secretary on duty and available to him.

On the way out they met Jim Watson, waiting in the outer office. He rose to his feet.

"Jim, this is Elizabeth Johnstone from the Near East desk. Elizabeth, Jim Watson. Have you two met?"

"I haven't had the pleasure," Watson said, "but I've read your product. It's always first-rate. A pleasure to meet you, Elizabeth."

"It's a pleasure to meet you as well, Mr. Watson." Then, turning to Grummell, "Thank you for your time, sir. Good night."

They watched her leave, then Grummell looked at his watch. He motioned for Watson to follow him into the office. When he reached the study, Grummell asked for coffee to be sent up. After it arrived, the DCI took a bottle of bourbon from the side bar.

"Join me?"

"Yes, sir."

Grummell poured the coffee, then splashed a measure of the amber liquid into each of their cups. He handed one to Watson, and they sat down.

"Jim, there's trouble brewing. Big trouble."

"I sensed that, sir, but nothing official has come across my desk."

"Some months back you came to me after a rather interesting meeting with Ambassador Joe Simpson. You came to me directly, not going through channels and not informing the DDO."

"That's right, sir." Jim Watson had thought long and hard about taking his concerns directly to Grummell. He had made a few discreet inquiries that were enough to convince him that the Ambassador was doing some very questionable things. He finally decided to seek a private interview with the DCI. Such a meeting was unusual but not entirely unprecedented. After all, he was Deputy DDO and former COS of Moscow Station. Watson half-expected Armand Grummell to know about it, as he and Simpson, while not close friends, knew each other quite well. Grummell was totally surprised.

"And, in as much as the Agency has no charter to monitor American citizens, I asked you to quietly do what you could to stay abreast of what the good ambassador was up to." Grummell again glanced at his watch. "Your reports to date have been most interesting. I wonder if you'd take just a moment and bring me current on the situation."

An hour later, Armand Grummell was again headed south on the George Washington Parkway for the White House.

Wednesday night, December 11, the Big Island, Hawaii

Five miles from the town of Naalehu, two white minivans with the GSI logo painted on the side waited on the side of a crushed-lava road. The windows were darkened, and except for an impressive array of small whip antennas, the vehicles looked commercial and benign. On closer inspection, the vans were four-wheel-drive vehicles and had robust suspension. Along the bodywork there were several electrical outlets, which attracted little or no attention unless they were in use. Tonight they were in use. The two vans were connected with a thick umbilical and there was a portable dish antenna erected near one of the vans. It was a curious mating of two vehicles out on a deserted road, but there was not a soul within miles to witness the event. They were actually just inside the boundaries of the old Pacific Range Missile Facility at Ka Lae. It was still a government reservation, but seldom used. They had permission to be there, sort of.

Several weeks ago, Steven Fagan had hired Bill Owens. For the better part of the last two decades, Owens had been the go-to guy in the documents section of the DDS&T— the Deputy Director for Science and Technology at the CIA. The DDO did the spying, but the espionage was often made possible by the technicians at DDS&T. Like all bureaucracies, CIA had passed Bill Owens over for promotion one too many times. Their logic was impeccable; Owens was a technician, albeit a very good one—a master forger, but he hadn't the people skills nor the temperament to be a manager. So he had maxed out his pay grade and had taken early retirement. Steven had found him at his small home in McLean, Virginia. Bill's wife had left him years ago, run off with some lowlife in the Agency's Domestic Collection Division. The last he had heard from her, she was living in Chicago with the snake. Steven had found him at home, drinking too much and feeling sorry for himself. He was spending a little time volunteering at the Smithsonian in the document archival department, but he was not doing well. Steven knew Owens was a man who cared little for money. For that matter, he could print it if he needed some, and it would pass for the real thing. In fact, he had done that very thing in several non-U.S. currencies. But he was clearly ready to go back to work. Steven had only partially described the documents laboratory he was having built at the site when Owens interrupted him to say he would go. Hence, the two vans had documents that gave them permission to be on government property and to be conducting seismic studies on this part of the Big Island.

The vans were nearly identical and packed with electronic and communications equipment. They were designed to operate in tandem or independently. Inside one van, Janet Brisco and Bill Owens sat in captains' chairs at their consoles. This was the smoking van, and both Brisco and Owens had cigarettes going. They were an odd couple, this tall, striking black woman seated next to this rumpled, anemic-looking little man. Owens looked like Don Knotts with a bad haircut and a muskratlike wisp of a mustache. He immediately attached himself to Brisco like an orphaned gosling, and she didn't seem to mind. They worked well together. This was their second "exercise," and Brisco was breaking him in on operational planning and the critical watch-standing duties that would take place when there was a team in the field. They sat in sociable silence and watched their screens.

The second van held Steven Fagan and Dodds LeMaster, a technical genius who had helped build the communications suite at the U.S. Special Operations Command. He also consulted on the Mission Support Center designed by the Navy to provide real-time intelligence and communications support for their deployed SEALs. Garrett had met him in San Diego when he was working with the SEALs. With the more-than-generous budget from GSI, LeMaster had been able to create a mini mission-support center in the two vans in short order. With the very latest in satellite communications technology and miniaturization, they had the capabilities in their little vans to do what the military did in their brick-and-mortar command centers. Along one side of each van were four flat plasma screens for visual displays. Both

Fagan and LeMaster wore wireless headsets. On their displays they could see almost any place in the world from satellite feeds that GSI paid for or that LeMaster pirated. Optical, infrared, and thermal images could be viewed independently or superimposed for composite resolution. The communications were sophisticated and secure. Neither of the vans seemed overcrowded; that was the marvel of miniaturization and high-speed processors. The visual presentation could be shifted and adjusted with the touch of a finger to the screen. They could transmit or receive coded audio signals from "friendly" forces and eavesdrop on most civilian and military channels. What they were doing this night on the deserted lava flow near the southernmost point of the United States, they could do anywhere in the world. But tonight they were here physically because they were the target as well as the mission controllers.

Outside the vans, a half dozen men walked a loose perimeter to provide security. The vans were in no danger, but the sentries were part of the exercise.

"Hallo, luv. There we go," reported LeMaster. LeMaster was not only a genius and a supergeek, but a cyber warrior; he loved all things military. He had come to the United States from Cambridge, where he taught physics and robotics. For close to a decade he made himself available to defense contractors who provided cutting-edge technologies to the military. He didn't really have to work; the royalties and license fees from his video war games provided him more than enough to live on. But he was also a patriot with a finely tuned sense of right and wrong, and a keen sense of history. He worshiped Winston Churchill, Margaret Thatcher, and the United States, in that order. Several years ago Garrett had met him on a simulation range he had designed, one of those shoot-at-the-projected-image trainers. Garrett had been immediately taken with his ingenuity and his strong feelings about the threat terrorism posed to the Western democracies. Steven Fagan's assessment was much the same when he met LeMaster. They hired him on the spot.

LeMaster moved a joystick on his console to adjust a pip on his map display and increased the magnification. Eight thermal dots seemed to float across the screen.

"Let's see if the other lads are about."

He electronically drew back to a smaller scale and quickly found another seven warm images. He zoomed in and watched them as they seemed to float like soap bubbles across the screen. Then, one by one, they stopped.

"On the ground?" Fagan asked.

"Looks like it, sir." LeMaster responded.

Steven Fagan nodded and smiled to himself. He could not keep LeMaster from calling him sir. The one thing Fagan could offer Dodds LeMaster that the U.S. military had not was the opportunity to operate the equipment he built and participate in operations. LeMaster now felt he had joined a fighting service and that Fagan was his commanding officer.

"Eagle One down," came the report on their headphones.

"Eagle Two down," a different voice added.

Garrett Walker and Bijay Gurung, each with a squad of Gurkhas, had just jumped from two separate GSI helicopters. They were to rally independently, patrol in, and attack their target simultaneously. There was no moon, and the stars were partially obscured by a high layer of clouds. Tonight, as for most training exercises, half the Gurkhas trained while the other half supported the training logistically, as well as providing opposition forces. Tomorrow night, they would be back out here, and tonight's support crew would be parachuting in. A night parachute and an assault on a fixed target was not a difficult nor a particularly challenging exercise for Garrett and his Gurkhas. But it kept them sharp. It was more an exercise for the mission planners and controllers in the vans.

"Eagle One is moving," LeMaster reported. He shifted the cursor and increased magnification, "and so is Eagle Two. You want to take it, Billy?"

"Got it, Dodds," Owens said. In the next van, he keyed the tactical frequency and keyed his headset. "Okay, Eagles, this is Home Plate, check in, please."

There was a two-second delay, then, "One here," followed by, "Two here."

For training purposes the signal was taken on an uplink and sent halfway around the world and back, even though sender and receiver were only a few miles apart. Through the slight time delay and the scrambler, it was just possible to discern Garrett's flat-toned voice and Bijay's cultured British accent. At twelve thousand feet, a Predator drone orbited the southernmost tip of the Big Island of Hawaii. With the advent of Global Hawk, the Predators had become a second-line platform, but still a highly capable one. They had any number of commercial security and surveillance applications. GSI had recently bought four of them from General Atomics at $25 million a copy and put them into service. This drone had been launched from a private airstrip on Oahu and flown southeast to Hawaii. There it was handed off to Dodds LeMaster, and now to Bill Owens. The end user did not need takeoff and landing skills; it was a video game—cursors and touch-sensitive plasma displays.

"Okay, One, you have a deep ravine in front of you," Owens said. "Come left to a heading of one-six-zero for fifty meters, and you should find a path across."

"Understood. One, clear."

"Two, stop where you are."

"Two stopped." Even the distance delay did little to mask Bijay's precise diction.

"There is a sentry at ten o'clock from your direction of travel and another at eleven thirty."

"This is Two, wait, out." After a few moments, "This is Two. We have them."

"Recommend that you turn left of track to box around them, fifty meters a side on the box."

"Understood. Two clear."

The drones and their infrastructure were expensive, too expensive for any hope for them to be commercially viable. But then, they didn't have to pencil out. Much like the Gurkhas in Kathmandu that GSI contracted out for physical security work, the drones were being contracted out for corporate security work. The Department of Energy and Nuclear Regulatory Commission had even contacted them about patrolling remote nuclear-waste-material storage sites. How could they refuse? GSI had ordered several more drones, and the ones in inventory were being modified under Dodds LeMaster's guidance to extend their utility, and in some cases, their lethality. Should the need arise, they could fly a long way and stay on station a long time. Since GSI considered them expendable in mission-critical situations, they could fly and perform their surveillance duties until they ran out of fuel. For that contingency, LeMaster had installed a self-destruct feature.

"They got us, we're lit up." said Janet Brisco, looking at a digital readout of one of her displays. Both teams had painted the vans with lasers. "You want to call them in?"

Steven thought for a minute. "Not yet; it's still early. Let's pass control to them and let them play for a while." Brisco nodded to Owens.

"Eagle One, this is Home Plate. Stand by to take control."

"Understood," Garrett replied. "Wait one, out."

In a dark, black-rock gully some two hundred yards from the vans, a Gurkha pulled a notebook computer from his backpack and clipped it on. While the computer booted up, he unfolded a small, omnidirectional antenna and connected it to the notebook. A hand squeezed his shoulder, and the Gurkha spoke into his headset.

"One is ready."

"You have it, One."

With the arrow buttons in place of a joystick, the Gurkha began to manipulate the cameras and sensors of the Predator. To get a better perspective, he shifted the drone's orbit slightly to the east and ordered it down two thousand feet. He looked back over his shoulder, and a broad smile cut his blackened features. Garrett Walker grinned back at his Gurkha and again squeezed his shoulder. The notebook and the display were identical to the video-game mockups LeMaster had put in the Gurkhas' barracks. In addition to their nightly dry-firing drills, they each had to take a turn on the Predator simulator. And since it was a game, the Gurkhas quickly became very good at it.

Two hours later the two parked vans were joined by three more. These were passenger vehicles. The Predator was on its way back to Oahu. Garrett, Bijay, and the Gurkhas who had parachuted in with them milled about the vehicles. They moved like ghosts, bathed in the interior lighting from the vans. All were dressed in black Nomex, one-piece suits with a full kit of combat and field gear. They had been in the field for only a few hours, but they could have remained for days. Each of their lightweight Kevlar helmets carried a night-vision optic, swung to one side now that they were not in use. Janet Brisco passed out mugs of strong tea to the Gurkhas, who accepted them shyly and murmured their thanks. She stooped to hand them out, but she still towered over them. Garrett and Bijay conducted a quick debriefing for the men, as did Janet Brisco for the van crews. Tactically, either Garrett or Bijay would be in charge. Operationally, Janet Brisco made the calls. Steven Fagan was speaking with one of the Gurkha sergeants when his cell phone began to purr. He took a moment to politely excuse himself, as Gurkha custom demanded, and stepped away.

"Fagan . . . I see . . . Understood." He listened for several moments, then consulted his watch. "We will be there and standing by. Understood . . . Good-bye."

Garrett Walker watched the exchange and the thoughtful, intense look on Steven's face. Fagan made two quick phone calls, then motioned for Garrett to join him.

"I've recalled one of the helicopters to come back for us. That was Joe; it looks like we might have some work. There is an extended-range Gulfstream inbound from Honolulu to the Kona Airport that will take us to Nellis Air Force Base in Nevada."

"Nellis!" Garrett exclaimed.

Steven nodded solemnly. "Normally, I would not like us both on the mainland at the same time, but this may have to be an exception. And I think we better take Janet with us. It seems that it's time for that. The helicopter will be here in ten minutes. You know what to do."

Garrett nodded. He called Bijay over, bowed politely, and then fell into deep conversation. Steven sought out Brisco.

Thursday afternoon, December 12, Villefranche

Pavel Zelinkow sat at his computer and verified the transfer of funds. He had received the first payment of $15 million once the weapons were removed from Kahuta. The second $15 million was paid when the two bombs were safely in Khalabad and in the hands of Imad Mugniyah. *Thirty million American dollars.* It was enough, he thought. Why not quit now? He paused and sat back from the terminal to consider this. There was a glass of Bordeaux on his desk, and he took a cautious sip. Zelinkow had always felt that he could disappear at will and no one would find him. To disappear did not mean that he would have to leave his home and go into hiding. He existed only through a number of false identities and a series of electronic communication links and banking relationships, all coded. No, for him to disappear meant only that he would have to cut and cauterize the ties to his work. Zelinkow was not foolish enough to think he would be impossible to track, but it would be very, very difficult. It would take, he thought, someone of his skill, and there were not too many of those around. But then who would want to try? The terrorists would simply take the weapons and sell them or use them on a target of their own choosing. And Mugniyah was being paid handsomely on his end—the same as himself. The Saudis could scream for his head, but to whom? The few in the royal family who knew what was planned hadn't the talent to find him, and they would be too busy covering their own tracks. And what were a few million to them? Then there was Amir Sahabi, the Iranian sheik. Zelinkow smiled. The Iranian sheik, indeed! He was smart, but what could he do without offending his royal patrons in Riyadh? No, thought Zelinkow, I could walk away from this; the question is, *do I want to*?

The final increment, another $20 million that he would receive when the bomb was detonated, was a consideration. There were always a few more orchestras and museums that could use his help; he could upgrade his status from benefactor to patron of the arts. Certainly he and Dominique would never have to suffer another performance from the orchestra seats or drive themselves to an event. The misfortunes of the stock market had forced a number of previous wealthy collectors to put their cellars up for sale, and there were some exquisite wines to be found at a bargain—if you had the disposable funds. The money was a consideration. Yet, he admitted, it was more than that.

Zelinkow had learned his craft under Vladimir Putin, and had tasted the greatness of the old Soviet Union. In those days the KGB was a feared and powerful organization. Putin had survived, but dedicated professionals like himself had been released with little or nothing for their years of dedication and hard work. A KGB officer was a man superbly trained to become a criminal; Zelinkow knew this and accepted it. But there was also honor. Crime was one thing, but to prey on the Russian people, as Putin and his inner circle had done, was more than criminal. It was traitorous. Mr. Putin now held power in Moscow and was thought to be respectable. With the exception of their differences in Iraq, he and the American president were fast friends. This pipeline could not have been built without Russian cooperation. The concessions the Americans would have to grant Putin would most certainly enhance his power and his wealth. And then, there were the Americans.

The Americans, with their wealth and their technology, had driven the Soviet Union under. They outspent us, Zelinkow admitted, and we were crushed by the weight of our military expenditures, trying to keep up with the West. The old system was not the best, but there was pride and there was order. Now the Putin and the Russian mafiosi were sucking the life from Russia, just as the arms race with America had done to the Soviet Union. At least under the Communists, the arts and the rich cultural tradition that were the soul of Russia had been respected, if not encouraged. With the move to a market economy, art and the theater were now commodities, left to fend for themselves without government help. One only had to look at what the Bolshoi once was and what it had become to know that things were not what they had been.

No, Zelinkow thought, I will do this. For the money, of course. But I owe Putin and the Americans one. One more, then I will cut my ties to the secret life and quietly make my exit. One last curtain call to set the record straight.

He took a measured sip from the glass at his elbow, then turned back to the terminal. First he had to deal with his recent fee. It was a question of how to move the money. He could move it about in smaller sums, ones that would be less noticeable to the network of corresponding banks. The funds came and went in a nanosecond, leaving only a transfer fee and a coded electronic signature in their wake. But the smaller amounts meant more transactions, more electronic events. The banks he dealt with were religious about their security, and indeed, their very existence depended upon it. But in the wake of 9/11, the Americans had shown a great deal of ingenuity in prying into the affairs of banks. The spy games between the investigators and those who did not want to be investigated was now played at a very elevated level. The alternative to multiple transfers of small amounts was a single transfer, from one bank to another. From a single financial institution who played the security game like Kasparov played chess, to another with the same high standards. These banks had a great many clients with much more money than Zelinkow and just as much to lose if their financial dealings were brought to light. Zelinkow made the single transfer.

With that decision behind him, he turned to issues that concerned Imad Mugniyah. What a unique and extraordinary man, Zelinkow thought as he reviewed the file. Mugniyah was yet another reason not to prematurely abandon the venture; Mugniyah was his financial partner. He was not only intelligent and methodical, he had the same passion for anonymity as did Zelinkow. It was no wonder that he had lasted this long in the business. Mugniyah had the coded phone and the encrypted e-mail capability that were all that a modern terrorist needed. Zelinkow and Mugniyah had done business for years. They had met only once in person, and had spoken on the phone less than a half dozen times. They never left voice mails. When they did speak, after the encryption and switching, the spoken word was almost robotic and lacking any human feeling. Mugniyah was, Zelinkow reflected, the perfect business associate.

Zelinkow busied himself for the next few hours, sending e-mails, making arrangements for services, and authorizing funds for those services. He could have false documents prepared by a master forger and securely sent to an undisclosed location and with no attribution to himself. He could do this as easily as most people could call Domino's and order a pizza for home delivery. It was part of his profession. He was almost finished when the intercom on his desk purred.

"Yes, *chérie?*"

"You said to call you at five," she said sweetly. "It's a few minutes past."

"Ah, thank you. I was just finishing and will be along in a few moments. *Ciao.*"

He finished and went through the ordered protocol to put his security measures in place. He showered and dressed carefully, and joined Dominique on the veranda. A simple, elegant dinner arrangement for two had been made at a small table positioned to best capture the evening sun on the Mediterranean. A selection of hors d'oeuvres and a sterling bottle of chilled pinot grigio waited on a side table. She had not told him what dish she had prepared and waited in the kitchen. Yet the mere thought of a culinary surprise by Dominique set his mouth watering. She too had been working this afternoon, and she was not unskilled in the kitchen. Rachmaninoff's Piano Concerto no. 3 gently mingled with the rich scent of jasmine and lilac. The sun had just passed over the crest of the coastal range. Any afternoon chill would be held off by the retained warmth of the stone patio. Zelinkow was attired in a white long-sleeved, pleated dinner shirt, white slacks, and woven leather loafers. Dominique wore a flowered silk ankle-length shift with a single strand of pearls and an orchid in her dark hair. They were both plump, scrubbed, and radiant. She poured two glasses of wine and handed him one with a fetching smile. They touched crystal, and turned wordlessly to admire the view.

Thursday evening, December 12, Washington, D.C.

A black limousine slid silently to the curb in front of Morton's, and a tall man in a topcoat standing well away from the restaurant entrance stepped to the curb. A young man in a tailored suit leaped from the front passenger seat and opened the rear door for him. The tall gentleman slid into the dark interior; no lights came on with the opening of the doors. The young man quickly regained his seat, and the long sedan eased from the curb and into the traffic. The process took less than five seconds. In L.A., such an occurrence would have indicated a celebrity; in St. Petersburg, the Mafia; in Zurich or Bonn, a banker. The same event in London might have been someone of peerage. In Washington it was the signature of wealth and power. Tonight, with this particular limo silently pulling away from an exclusive Georgetown restaurant, it was wealth, power, and a great deal of uncertainty.

"Good evening, Joseph," an older gentleman said,

offering his hand to his new passenger. "Thank you for flying down and agreeing to see me like this. How are you?"

"Very well, Armand. It's good to see you again. I hope you are well."

Joseph Simpson and Armand Grummell were men who understood the need to be polite at a cocktail party or a function of state as their duties required, but not in a private setting like this—unless they really meant it. They had known one another for years; how could they not? Grummell had been the DCI when Simpson was the Ambassador to Russia, and while it could not be said that they were close friends, there was a respect and consideration between them that flows naturally between men of ability and character. They exchanged pleasantries while the limo fought its way free of the congestion and onto the Key Bridge. The big car plunged into Roslyn before circling south in search of the George Washington Parkway. Grummell touched a button, and the partition behind the front seat hissed up into position. They were now in a soundproof cocoon in the generous rear compartment. Grummell decanted a glass of mineral water and offered it to Simpson, then poured one for himself.

"Again, it was good of you to come. I hope my phone call this morning didn't create any, ah, difficulties for you."

Simpson paused to frame his answer. "No, not really. It was a call that sooner or later, myself or one of my people was going to have to make to someone like you." Simpson smiled. "Perhaps not so soon and perhaps not at your level. We wanted to first build our organization and test our operational readiness. That has been done, and we are now conducting exercises to refine our capabilities and to train our planning and supervisory personnel." Simpson sat silently a moment before continuing. "Armand, in order to save time, perhaps you should tell me what you know about Guardian Systems International. Along with that, I would like to know, if it is not too much to ask, who else in your organization and the government knows about us?"

They were like schoolboys in the lavatory. If they were going to compare the size of their penises, they were both going to have to pull their pants down.

Grummell nodded and smiled. "Jim Watson contacted me after the two of you talked some nine months ago. He told me of your request that he tell no one about it, but Jim is a patriot. I asked him to do what he could, short of initiating any sort of an investigation, to see what you were up to. Basically, I think I have a fair idea of the composition and nature of your organization. It's certainly more than just a corporate security venture. I can only guess at its capabilities and what you have in mind for it. I was hoping you could elaborate on those points. As for who knows, until yesterday, only Jim and myself. But yesterday I briefed the President. I don't have to tell you that these are uncharted waters, for all of us. I told you that we had a crisis in the making, one that could seriously damage our national interests. It's of such a magnitude that we can't afford to ignore any option, even those which technically do not exist. In short"—Grummell chuckled mirthlessly—"we're trying to figure what the hell to do about it. It's serious, and we can rule nothing out. Your organization may even be able to help us. Are your people airborne?"

Simpson nodded. "They are."

Early that morning, Simpson had received a call in Boston from CIA headquarters in Langley to set up a secure line with the DCI. Armand Grummell had come on the line and asked for this meeting. He also asked if it would be possible for the key personnel of his Kona-based operation to come to the mainland for consultation. Grummell further said it was a matter of some importance and that time was of the essence. He had said no more, nor did he have to. Simpson was given a contact number at Nellis Air Force Base near Las Vegas and telephoned Steven Fagan to put things in motion. Steven had taken the call on the Big Island at one o'clock in the morning there.

"Then could I ask that you provide me with a very brief overview of your current posture and capabilities?"

"I assume you are versed on the general corporate structure and composition of Guardian Systems?" Grummell nodded. "Our Hawaii facility operates under that corporate umbrella and is now home to a group we call the Intervention Force, or IFOR for short. IFOR currently is made up of native Gurkha infantry trained in classic special operations and paramilitary disciplines." Simpson spoke for close to fifteen minutes, and Grummell listened without interruption. "We may not be capable of throwing Saddam out of Iraq," Simpson concluded, "or even help to disarm him, but our organization may be suitable for smaller, emerging crises."

Then both were silent for several minutes before the DCI cleared his throat. "Perhaps we might just have one for you. I told you earlier this morning that we were faced with a unique and dangerous situation, and on that basis alone you took the initiative to put your organization, your IFOR, as you call it, on alert. For that I would like to thank you again. Perhaps it's time for me to describe what we have just learned and the nature of our concern. This has nothing to do with Iraq, but although we've begun to move forces into the area, we can do nothing until this is settled." He took out a map of Central Asia and attached it to two alligator clips on the privacy partition. "We know that two nuclear weapons have been removed from the A. Q. Khan facility at Kahuta here"—he pointed to the facility in northern

Pakistan—"and are probably somewhere in central Iran. We think we know whose hands they are in, and we believe one or both of these weapons will be used to sabotage the Trans-Afghan Pipeline." Grummell paused to let this sink in. He watched Simpson, but his features were impassive.

"Go on," he said simply, and Grummell did. He held nothing back, save for any information that related to the sources that had produced the intelligence. He would not reveal those contacts, even to the President.

"So what do you require from us?" Simpson said at length.

"We'd like you read into the problem as the situation develops, and as appropriate, prepare options or a course of action to recover the weapons."

"And punish those responsible?"

"Perhaps," Grummell replied, "but later, if it comes to that. We need to get this genie back into the bottle. That is our first priority."

Simpson nodded. "How do you want to handle this?"

"I've sent Jim Watson to meet your people at Nellis. He will read them into the problem. He has a technician with him who will provide you with equipment for a secure and very closely held data feed from my headquarters. Any requests you may have for information, imagery, or anything else can be made via that link. It is a sterilized, coded link with no attribution. Which brings me to our relationship. We have been thrown together, if you will, by this crisis. The use of your IFOR at this stage is only a contingency— a possibility and no more. No matter what happens, the President and I personally want to thank you for responding to our call. For our part, we will do everything possible to protect your security and your anonymity. Past that, and going forward, well"—he smiled—"that is a new kettle of fish, I suppose."

"I suppose," Simpson replied with an easy smile.

There was nothing more to say; neither wanted to speculate about the future. They rode in companionable silence. "Where can I drop you?" Grummell asked finally.

"The Watergate would be fine."

Grummell pressed the intercom. "The Watergate, please."

The big limo held the speed limit back up the Parkway and took the Memorial Bridge across the Potomac back into town.

"Jim Watson will have instructions for communication and liaison. I have left the details to him to work out with your people." He handed Simpson a card with a number written on it. No name. "This is my secure line. Let me know if these arrangements, or any others he may propose, are not acceptable."

Simpson took the card and slipped it into his shirt pocket. "Thank you, Armand, for your candor and the professional way in which you are handling this. No doubt we'll talk further as events unfold."

The limousine coasted to a stop in front of the Watergate Apartments. The doorman would have come to the car, but the man in front was too quick for him.

"Good night, Joseph, and thank you again."

"You're quite welcome. Good night, Armand."

Simpson turned and walked away without a backward glance. The limo retrieved its man and pulled away. Not once had either man mentioned the need for security or discretion. They were, after all, men of ability and character.

Friday, December 13, Nellis Air Force Base, Las Vegas

The Gulfstream lightly kissed the tarmac and began its rollout. It was a delicate bird, gleaming and white, with blue striping and a modest GSI logo blocked on its tail. The tower gave the pilot his instructions, and he taxied to a piece of hardstand well away from the hangar area. It was approaching late afternoon, and the temperature was well over a hundred degrees. They parked next to another Gulfstream, also gleaming white, but this one was unmarked. Once the door was opened, Steven Fagan descended the stairs and walked around the nose of his aircraft.

"Hello, Steven."

"Hello, sir. Good to see you again."

"And you," Jim Watson replied. "It's pretty hot out here. My place or yours?"

Steven surveyed the unmarked military jet. "How about our place? Just a guess on my part, but I'll bet our bar is a lot better stocked than yours."

As they made their way up the boarding steps, a fuel bowser and an auxiliary power unit crossed the tarmac to service the aircraft. Once inside, Steven introduced Watson to Garrett and Janet. The Gulfstream was richly appointed, with light gray tucked-leather seating and burgundy carpeting. There was a lounge forward, but the rear of the aircraft was configured with a small oval conference table served by four comfortable, high-backed chairs. Behind the drawn curtains were four large oval windows on either side of the fuselage. It was an elegant flying conference facility. The attendant took their drink orders, then retired to the cockpit area with the pilots.

"As I understand," Watson began, "you as yet have no knowledge of the events that have brought us here, correct?"

"That's right," Steven answered for all of them.

"Well then, I had better fill you in." Watson, Steven, and Garrett all had iced tea before them. Janet Brisco settled for a tall mug of coffee. "First of all, I represent Armand Grummell, who is acting as a personal representative of the President. In short, I carry no official portfolio for my agency or my government, but you all know who I work for. I am here to brief you concerned citizens about a very serious problem that has just surfaced. I have been directed to tell you everything I know about this problem. I am then to establish communication links with you so as to keep you updated on the situation and to provide any information you may require. Okay so far?" Heads nodded. "Before I get started, let me share with you what knowledge the Director and I have of your organization thus far. Following my conversation with your principal some months back, I took the issue to Mr. Grummell." There was no hint of apology in his voice. "He directed me to keep an eye on you within the boundaries of casual inquiry. So I did. I'm sure there is much we don't know, but let's just say that we understand you have developed a certain paramilitary capability and that your reasons are not inconsistent with the national interest, fair enough?" Again, heads nodded. "So I am going to tell you about our problem. The President and Mr. Grummell feel you may be able to help us with it, or at least provide us with a response option we don't currently have. When I've finished, you can tell me more about what you are doing on Hawaii, or not. Fair enough?" He paused before continuing. "Okay, let me tell you what has happened and why it scares the hell out of us."

When he finished, Garrett Walker whistled softly and rose. "I think I'll get myself something stronger than iced tea. Anyone else?"

"What I really want is a cigarette," Janet Brisco replied, "but I'll settle for some gin on the rocks."

"So what do you want from us?" Steven asked Watson.

"For now, study the problem. If you think your force can come up with a plan to bring about a resolution to the issue, I will pass it along for consideration. We think, but as yet we have no hard evidence, that the bombs are in Iran. Going into Iran is a big step for us, almost impossible given the emerging crisis with Iraq. It would be strange if Tehran had no knowledge of Mugniyah's whereabouts, but whether they know what he's up to or not is anybody's guess."

Janet tapped the ice cubes in her drink with her ring finger and placed the tip of it thoughtfully in her mouth. Both Steven and Garrett looked at her; she was the planner. "We have our own resources," she told Watson, "but we are not the United States intelligence community. If we need something?"

"My instructions are to give you whatever information you request, quietly and securely. We will be directing a great deal of time and energy to this situation. Our only constraint is that we don't, at this time, want to alarm our allies or read about it in the papers. Anything we learn we will pass along. We will also respond as best we can to any requests you have for information."

"What about the military?" Garrett asked.

"What do you mean?" Watson replied.

"Any military response to this would normally come from the U.S. Special Operations Command. I know the security procedures and isolation protocols that would accompany such a mission tasking, and they're pretty good. But if word gets to these bomb stealers that there is a special operations in the works, it will make everyone's job that much harder. We have to assume that they will be watching for indicators. We have a lot of ship and aircraft movements in the Persian Gulf due to the business with Iraq. But military activity in the northern Arabian Sea or the Gulf of Oman could tip them off."

Watson pursed his lips. "This is a little out of my area, but I can only think that somewhere along the line, we will have to look at military and special-operations options. To my knowledge, this has not yet happened. Will it happen? Probably. This is very serious business, and I can't help but think the President will use every means within his power to resolve this threat. But I will pass it along that we must handle any prepositioning of assets with care." He took out a small notebook and made an entry. "Let's get back to my charter and what I can do for you. You will have the full resources of the CIA, the DIA, the NRO, and the Homeland Security Department available to you. If you want, I will request the information, collect it, sanitize it, and send it along to you. Everything will be passed along through a corporate shell organization so there is no risk of attribution. I understand that you have Dodds LeMaster on your team, is that right?"

"We do," answered Steven.

"Good. That makes it easier. I have a technician on the other aircraft who could brief you, but I don't think that will be necessary. I have two small suitcases of equipment for you to take back with you. I'm not a tech, but as I understand it, one case contains some special modems and interface equipment that will make data transfer quicker and more secure. If there's a problem"—he handed them a card—"just have LeMaster give us a call." He smiled. "More probably, if my comm techs have a problem, I should have them call LeMaster." He opened his hands on the table to signal he was finished.

"That's it?" Steven said with a half smile.

"That's it—for now." Then Watson turned serious. "If it comes to an actual mission tasking, and you move on this, we could possibly provide some operational support. But then, given the nature of your organization, I can't presume or promise anything. I can only guess there will be limited assistance as long as it can be provided with total deniability. With that said, good luck."

Watson shook hands with Garrett and Janet, and

Steven ushered him to the boarding stairs and down to the tarmac. They walked slowly to Watson's Gulfstream.

"Is it this hot in Hawaii?"

"Not this bad, but it can get warm. Thank you for coming, sir, and for your candor."

"Don't mention it. Who knows; we may be working together on this one." Watson took what looked like two aluminum camera cases from a man and passed them to Steven. He took them without comment. "One of the cases has the special modems and encryption equipment. The other has nuclear metering devices. They are designed to detect low-level alpha and gamma emissions. We got them from the Nuclear Emergency Search Teams, or NESTs. I've been told not to expect too much from them, but if the weapons are not in their metal casings, they can detect trace products from the decay of the nuclear cores. If you or LeMaster have any questions about the equipment, I will have a cleared and witting nuclear expert available to answer any questions.

"And one more thing," Watson continued. He was now talking to a fellow intelligence professional, a colleague, and his whole demeanor seemed to change. He became conspiratorial; once again, they were spies. "I don't see any problems with information and data transfer. If it comes to operational and tactical support, well, I think you and I can work through that. From my end there will be no bullshit. A straight yes, we can, or no, we can't." Steven acknowledged this. "But security is and always will be a problem. Armand will have to take this to Tad Coleson at the Bureau." Steven gave him a blank stare. "I know what you're thinking, but it's not like the old days, at least not quite. Coleson and Armand have a good understanding. Nine-eleven has made all the empire builders a little more accommodating. We feel that if we don't tell the Bureau, there's a fair chance they will find out about you somewhere along the line. Everyone's out looking for terrorists, and you do have a pretty suspicious operation. Armand feels that if we bring Coleson in and let him provide the liaison, then we will have put the FBI in check. They are also in a position to head off other agencies that may come nosing around. There is always a risk with the FBI, but I think it's reasonable." He gave Steven a furtive grin. "And some of them, only a few, mind you, are a lot smarter than they used to be."

Steven pretended to be lost in thought, but it was for appearance's sake. He had long ago felt that their venture stood its best chance of continued secrecy if "a few at the top" were made witting to the project. There were no guarantees, but this was exactly the outcome he had hoped for.

"It's the best we can do, I suppose." He offered Watson his hand. "Have a safe flight, sir."

Watson was about to ask him to dispense with the "sir," but he stopped short. Chances were that they would never meet again in person—certainly not like this. Meetings like this were bad for security.

"You too, Steven. Take care of yourself."

They both reboarded their corporate jets, two nondescript men who, for their personal appearance, could as well have been returning to the parking lot for their economy rental cars. The Gulfstreams were cleared to taxi, and the GSI aircraft led its government counterpart to the active runway. One lifted off and continued west; the other turned back to the east. Inside the eastbound jet, Jim Watson relaxed in the air-conditioned coolness. He accepted a martini from the uniformed flight attendant and placed a call to Armand Grummell. Fagan's chariot was a little nicer than his own, he reflected as he looked around the Air Force VIP aircraft, but not by much.

"Sir, could I get you something to eat?" the young airman asked. Watson was still waiting for his call to go through. Suddenly he realized he was very hungry.

"I think so," he replied. "What do you have?"

As they approached the California coast, the three passengers on the westbound Gulfstream looked around at each other. There were pleased and somewhat puzzled expressions on their faces. There were a lot of unanswered questions, but their project and their vision for an intervention force had just received a major validation. Janet Brisco could not wait to get back to LeMaster, Bill Owens, and her planning software. Garrett Walker needed to be with Bijay Gurung. The small phone in Steven's shirt pocket chirped softly. He unfolded it and put it to his ear.

"Yes, sir. . . . Yes, sir. . . . I don't think so. . . . For now, Ambassador, I believe things are going as well as can be expected."

Saturday morning, December 14, Tehran

The Airbus A320-300 touched down at Mehrabad Airport a few minutes late, which passed for a miraculous on-time arrival for an Air France flight to the Middle East. Neither the connecting cultures nor the carrier seemed to put much stock in their posted flight times. The gaping mouth of the boarding appendage found the side of the fuselage, and the passenger compartment began to disgorge into the terminal complex. Pavel Zelinkow had boarded the flight in Paris and took his seat in the first-class compartment. This fit his cover, which was that of a naturalized French citizen who had done well for himself in the import/export business. This cover was bolstered by the exorbitant amount of taxes he paid into the French treasury. He had accepted French citizenship—paid for it, actually—for two reasons. The French culture was to his liking, and no one outside of France took a Frenchman too seriously. They were—well, they were simply French. Zelinkow took his time gathering himself together to delay leaving his seat so as to enter the terminal among the mass of the exiting passengers.

"How long will you be staying, *Monsieur* Junot?" a uniformed official asked.

"Only a few days," he replied in halting Farsi as he handed over his passport to the official at the counter. He spoke it much better than he let on, but it was not one of his best languages.

"And your business in Tehran?"

"I will be sampling some of your olive oils for export to France. Some of them are exquisite, you know." He kissed his fingertips and rolled his eyes as he thought a Frenchman might do in expressing a sensual pleasure of the palate. The official looked at him and shrugged, stamped his passport, and handed it back to him.

"You may proceed, *monsieur*," and he turned to the next in line.

Zelinkow had only carry-on luggage. After careful inspection by a second official, he was passed through. He caught a taxi in front of the terminal. It was a fifteen-year-old Citroën that, in its prime, may have served the same purpose on the streets of Paris. As they pulled away from the airport, he casually glanced around for surveillance but could detect none. For a man in his business, Tehran was as safe as any major city in the world, but he was still on his guard. Over the years, in keeping with his training and profession, his business practices involved cutouts, third-party relationships, coded identities, and unwitting surrogates. This was one of the few times when he would conduct a personal meeting in which the other party knew his real identity. It would be, he reminded himself, the last one. It was a risk, and personal risk, while it involved danger, was a sign of poor tradecraft. On the other hand, he actually looked forward to this meeting. The man with whom he had an appointment was the most compelling individual he had encountered in his professional career. Zelinkow had met him only once before, in Damascus about four years ago. This would surely be the last time they saw one another.

The drive to the city center was a ten-mile, one-hour trek. He had checked into one of the better hotels and surrendered his passport at the desk. Later that evening, after taking a meal in his room, there was a light tapping at his door. He opened it just a crack. A swarthy Arab face looked at him a moment, nodded, and stepped back from the door. He turned and, without a word, walked back down the hall. Zelinkow made a point of darkening the room, leaving on only a single lamp. He knew his visitor was much more comfortable in dim light.

Ten minutes later there came a second tapping. Zelinkow opened the door, and there stood Imad Mugniyah. They embraced, and Zelinkow waved him into the room.

"Pavel, my friend, you look well."

"Thank you. And you are just as I remembered you."

Mugniyah was simply being kind. Zelinkow had a softer, more indulged appearance than he remembered, as did many in the West who enjoyed good fortune. But Zelinkow spoke the truth. The Lebanese had not changed, but the life of a terrorist, especially one of the caliber of Imad Mugniyah, keeps a man sharp and fit. Zelinkow led him to a table set with bottled water and a plate of dates, hummus, and fresh bread. The man who had first knocked followed Mugniyah inside and stood quietly by the door.

"Very well done, my friend," Zelinkow said in his best

Arabic. "You now have within your power the means to do great harm to the West. Very well done, indeed."

"It was a good plan, and the people you found to bring the weapons out managed to accomplish their task. I do not mind saying that I doubted them, but they performed well. And the money was transferred exactly as you said it would be. Now we will begin the long journey back to Afghanistan."

"Do you anticipate any difficulties?"

Mugniyah was silent for a moment. "This is Khalib's job, and for that I do not believe we could have chosen better. He is a very determined and capable man, and I have every reason to believe he will succeed. Have the bombs been found missing yet? I have heard nothing."

"Nor have I," Zelinkow replied. "But we must assume they have and that the Americans will also soon be aware that they are missing. Hopefully, the van and the scientists you had taken to Kashmir will lead them in that direction, at least for a while."

While Zelinkow refilled their water glasses, Mugniyah studied the man across the table. He had a great deal of respect for the capabilities of this Russian, and his planning to date had been impeccable. They now had in their possession two nuclear weapons. He himself was here because his cause needed money, and he knew Zelinkow was here solely for personal profit. They both needed money, but for very different reasons. Silently, he wondered, and not for the first time, why men could do what they did for personal gain. He wanted to believe that perhaps this former KGB man still bore allegiance to communism. Mugniyah had little regard for communist ideology, but he did understand commitment and loyalty. Why would men set such terrible forces upon one another simply for money? Surely this must do damage to a man's spirit. He knew he lacked understanding on this issue, yet he was curious. He also knew Zelinkow did not ask for this meeting simply to discuss their motives for this terrible business.

"If I may, Pavel, I have two questions for you."

"By all means," Zelinkow said, making an open gesture with his hands.

"First of all, what did Osama hope to gain by his attacks on the United States? You advised him. What did he really want to accomplish?" This was as close as Mugniyah would come to asking more directly why he had helped bin Laden.

Zelinkow eyed him carefully. This was an important question, perhaps even a dangerous one. If Mugniyah, or Mugniyah and the Iranians, had a different agenda then the one he had contracted for, then he had made a grave tactical error coming here. And that error would surely cost him his life. He knew his answer must have the ring of truth, but also be in keeping with what the man wanted to hear. It was difficult to fathom the thinking of men like Imad Mugniyah and Osama bin Laden—Hezbollah and al Qaeda. The two factions were like the Americans and the Soviet Union confronting Hitler, in league with each other so long as they had a common enemy.

"The plan succeeded beyond anyone's expectations. It was as much the inattention of the Americans as the skill of Mohammed Atta and the vision of Osama. Nonetheless, it was never about the Americans, not directly. Osama wanted to prove that he and his fundamentalists were worthy to lead Islam in the struggle against the Western powers. The attack had everything to do with uniting the Muslim nations under his leadership." Zelinkow hesitated before continuing, choosing his words very carefully. "I helped him with this, as you and very few others know. I am a soldier of fortune. But I was not unhappy to advance Osama's cause. We in the Soviet Union failed. They beat us; better said, we beat ourselves. Our system and our leaders became corrupt, and the West crushed us. Perhaps they will not beat you. Perhaps if we are successful in this venture, they will abandon their efforts here and end their support for Israel. A victory here could have them believe that their presence in this part of the world simply comes at too high a price. The Americans beat us because they outspent us. The currency of your struggle must be in lives, not dollars. The Americans have many dollars, but they do not suffer well the loss of life."

Mugniyah smiled, which gave no indication of what he was thinking. Perhaps he sensed Zelinkow's anxiety, and the smile was in grudging admiration for his little speech. Finally, he nodded slowly.

"And the second question; you had us steal two atomic bombs. What do you want me to do with the second bomb?"

Zelinkow tried not to show his relief. "As you said, Khalib has a very difficult task ahead of him. I came here to talk with you about an alternate plan. In the West they have a saying, 'belt and suspenders.' Are you familiar with it?" Mugniyah nodded. "And on the subject of Osama," Zelinkow continued, "since the audiotapes recently aired to the world indicate that Osama was not killed at Tora Bora and buried in an unmarked grave, might the success of this next blow against the Great Satan also be one of his doing?"

Again, Mugniyah nodded, and almost smiled.

Late Friday evening, December 13,
The Big Island, Hawaii

A Guardian Systems van was waiting for them when they deplaned at the Kona airport. Their Gulfstream touched down within minutes of the arrival of the Airbus that brought Pavel Zelinkow to Tehran. The three weary travelers quickly filed their declaration forms with the agricultural representative and piled into the van. Bill Owens was driving, and Dodds LeMaster was with him. It was a warm evening, so they took the Mamalahoa Highway back toward Waimea. Fagan and Janet Brisco had given some specific instructions to both while they were airborne, and Owens and LeMaster had much to report. Garrett had sent word for the Gurkhas to begin to assemble their gear. The planners, he knew, had a great deal of work ahead of them, but his men must be ready to move on a moment's notice. Time permitting, there would be a detailed plan, extensive briefings, and time to rehearse. But as Garrett knew all too well, special operations did not always go according to form. More than once he had had only the time to quickly sketch the plan in the dirt at some remote landing strip before he and his men climbed aboard the insertion helo. When the van pulled into the compound, Bijay was waiting for them.

"*Gurkhali ayo!*" he said quietly when they were out of earshot of the others. His voice was charged with excitement, and there was a wild gleam in his eye that Garrett had not seen before. It was the prospect of action. That it was an unknown enemy for an ambiguous reason did not seem to be a factor. Garrett had once tried to draw Bijay out regarding the need to tell the men why they were training to fight or that their enemy would be evil men.

"It does not matter," Bijay had told him. "They fight for you, they fight for me, they fight for each other. You are a good man; they are good men. If it is *your* enemy, then that is reason enough for us to fight. Why does there have to be more?"

Bijay collected himself and bowed slightly. "I have made tea, Subadar. Would you care to join me?"

"I would be honored, Sergeant Major," Garrett replied, inclining his head.

He followed Bijay into the barracks while the others headed for the operational center.

The next day the camp was busy. Bijay and his Gurkhas were up early putting their operational gear in order and cleaning their weapons, not that they were in need of it. Bijay had told them that they were to be ready to mount out for combat operations within an hour's notice. Once they had their personal equipment staged and ready, they set about preparing various loadings of ammunition and supporting arms. Then there were the radios, the rations, the rockets, parachutes, rappeling and fast-rope rigs, and a host of other essential items that might or might not be needed in a special operation or a long stay in the field. And to the consternation of the Gurkhas, they readied their turbans and hill-tribesmen garb. They might well have to pass for the clansmen of some warlord. Once the gear was readied and staged, they were permitted to return to their normal training duties in the local area. That's the way it would be until they mounted out or stood down from the alert. They would wait, but they would not be idle.

Janet Brisco and Dodds LeMaster were also up early. They were busy downloading satellite imagery and available intelligence reports on central Iran. There was a great deal of arid and rugged territory in the central plateau. It was almost certain that they had traveled overland and that they would again travel by ground if and when they headed toward the TAP. It was Brisco's job to find out how, where, and when they would move. She also had to make certain assumptions about where they might strike. It was doubtful that the terrorists would have the capability to deliver the weapon by any other means than by physically carrying it to the site. This would mean, reasoned Brisco, that they would attack a finished section of the pipeline or take the weapon and bury it ahead of the advancing construction crews. Given the security measures that were in place on the finished pipeline, it seemed likely that they would plant it like a mine. Should it be unearthed and exploded like a conventional land mine, so much the better. What Janet and her planners needed was to find the weapon well before it got near the TAP. If they managed to get through the wastes of Dasht Lut or into the border areas near Sistan, their task would be immeasurably more difficult.

By late that afternoon, Brisco and her crew knew what they had and what they needed. LeMaster e-mailed a coded request for specific imagery and high-resolution photography and sent it along to the server address given to Steven by Jim Watson. The equipment they brought back with them from Nellis set up a dedicated, high-speed link from their operations center on Hawaii, through a shell company in Rockville, Maryland, to a special communications cell in Langley. Requests for information would be routed through this link to Watson's office to serve this nameless intelligence customer. It was not normal procedure, but it had been done before. Bill Owens was busy in his photo lab creating documents for an Iranian Republican Guard reconnaissance platoon and Iranian national ID cards, should they be necessary. But he felt their best chance for deception on the ground would be as an oil survey crew. Garrett, whose French was only slightly better than his Farsi, would pose as a Dutch mining engineer in the employ of the Eramet Group, a French mining consortium. If they had to go into central Iran, some of the Gurkhas would pose as members of the survey crew; the others as an Iranian Army detachment sent along as security. This cover would not stand up along the coast in the oil fields between the Shatt al Arab and the Strait of Hormuz, but out in the eastern deserts, well, maybe—for a while. But first they would have to know where the bombs were. And then they would need to know when they were on the move.

Brisco desperately wanted to know the disposition of the Iranian military, especially around Kerman. Were they on any kind of alert? Mugniyah could not be there without the knowledge of the Ministry of Intelligence and Security, but what about the military? Surely the local military commander had to be told that there were foreigners in the area that must not be disturbed. The MIS and the army were not so paranoid as their counterparts in Iraq, yet they did not readily share information. In any closed society, information is power and closely guarded. But central Iran up to the border regions was something of a no-man's land. Many of the "Arabs" that fought the Russians in Afghanistan and later joined al Qaeda came from poor villages in central Iran. And Iran had become a sanctuary for al Qaeda irregulars who fled Afghanistan. There was a four-hundred-mile border between Iran and Afghanistan, rugged, inhospitable, and largely controlled by clans who recognized no border but those established by their clan chieftains, and enforced by arms. If the IFOR could get on the ground in character and close to their target, then with some bravado, bribe money, and a little luck, they might just be able to get the job done. If. There were a lot of ifs.

Steven Fagan was at his desk early the following day. He had thoroughly read and reread the intelligence summary Jim Watson had left them. This summary gave him two names to work with: Imad Mugniyah and Khalib Beniid. He had been on the phone most of the morning, and was waiting for another call to be put through when Janet Brisco tapped at his door. Steven motioned for her to come in. Just as she took a seat near his desk, the speaker on his phone crackled.

"I'll put you through to Mr. Beck now, sir."

"Thank you," Steven replied. There was clicking as the connection was made. "Hello, Gerhardt, this is William Reasoner calling."

"Who?"

"Reasoner, William Reasoner," Fagan said, speaking louder.

"William . . . Reasoner?"

"That's right. Look, Gerhardt, I understand it's late there, but I have something that is rather important. Are you still there?"

"Yes, but . . . but I don't know about this. I . . . I—"

"Now listen, Gerhardt. We've kept our end of the bargain pretty well, and it's time for you do us a favor."

"Well, I don't know, I—"

Fagan again cut him off, and there was a hardness to his voice that Brisco had never heard before. "Now you listen to me, Gerhardt, and listen closely. I have your personal fax number, and I am going to fax you a list of names and a list of corresponding banks you deal with. You will check the names for numbered accounts and give me a detailed history if any of those numbered accounts have wired funds in or out during the last thirty days. Do you understand me?"

"Well, I suppose perhaps I could try to—"

"You will not try; you will do exactly as I have requested. I don't want to have to remind you of the details of our arrangement. And your information had better be accurate, because as you know, we have ways to check on it. Is that also understood?"

"Yes, William, I understand. I will call you—"

"No, Gerhardt, I will call you. Wait there for my fax and look for my call back to you this time tomorrow."

"Yes, William, I will do as you say. I will expect your

call. Good-bye." There was an audible sigh as he broke the connection.

Brisco waited while Steven tapped the international phone number into the fax machine. It sucked the paper through in a matter of seconds, but it would take several minutes to make the connection, synchronize the coded ciphers on the other end, and send the fax. She watched him with an expression of open admiration.

"Damn, you can be a mean little son of a bitch when you want to be. Who was on the list of names?"

"Every alias Imad Mugniyah and Khalib Beniid have ever used, plus a list of wealthy patrons of terror who have the means to finance an operation like this. Most of them are Saudi or Kuwaiti. We might get a break."

"So who was that Gerhardt dude you just put the spurs to?"

"A Swiss banker. He was an asset several years ago, but at Langley we were finally asked to seek only voluntary and official cooperation from the international banking community. I recently learned that Gerhardt had got himself in a little financial trouble on the tables in Monte Carlo, and I was able to help him out. Now he has to help us out. He has the access, and there is very little chance of him being caught. He has a very senior position."

"Why, hell, he's a banker. Couldn't he just make himself a loan?"

"Well." Steven smiled. "It would have had to be a seven-figure loan, and then there's the matter of an extramarital affair."

"Caught ole Gerhardt with his girlfriend, huh?"

"Well . . . it was not quite a girlfriend."

Janet Brisco began to cackle. "You bad, Steven Fagan. A very, very bad man. What happens if he goes to the cops?"

"Well, about all he can tell them is that he is being

blackmailed by some guy named Reasoner from the CIA."

Brisco cackled again. "You're not bad, you're evil. Got any more of those calls to make? Maybe I could help. I'd love to get spy-mean with some dude on the phone."

"Ah, Janet, I think you better leave that to me. How's the planning coming?"

"Just waiting for your pal Watson to get back to us with some imagery and some troop dispositions. That's one big area. We have to find a way to cut it down." She got up to leave. "Let me know if you want me to do some of that heavy talk for you."

"I'll keep it in mind," Steven said. He smiled after her, knowing she was only kidding him. Or was she?

Steven made two more calls to bankers—one in the Caymans and one in Singapore. He reached both on secure commercial connections, which were quite standard in major international banks. One of his contacts he had to outright threaten, and the other seemed to almost welcome the call. A short time later he had fax confirmations back from both of them.

Monday, December 23,
Khalabad, Iran

"So you want to take only one of the scientists with you?"

"One will be sufficient, Dokhan," Khalib replied to Mugniyah. "Since we will be taking only one weapon, we need only one scientist. Abramin has been training one of my people who is a capable technician. He was a medical student before he became a mountain fighter. But since we cannot complete the final assembly until we are across the mountains and into Afghanistan, we will need him with us."

Mugniyah did not want to appear to tell Khalib his business, but he had gone to great lengths to bring Moshe

Abramin and his associate here to assemble the weapons. It made sense to load the gun before you left for the fight, and the assembly of a nuclear weapon was not something one would normally do in field conditions. Khalib sensed his apprehension.

"Crossing the desert in Iran will not be pleasant, but it will be relatively easy. Once we cross the border into Afghanistan, we will have to travel through the mountains by foot and pack train. The weapon is heavy, more so now that we have the bomb casing to deal with." One of the heavy components of the bombs had been their steel casings. They were not a design-critical element but would have been cumbersome to steal, so they were constructed by a metal fabricator in Kerman. "So," Khalib continued, "my bomb will have to remain disassembled if the animals are to carry it. We will have to complete the assembly when we are close to our objective. Travel in Afghanistan is very dangerous if you are in a vehicle. A few men with a string of animals are commonplace and not so interesting to the Americans."

"So it is Abramin you want to take along?"

"Yes. He is the better technician. Since I will have the uranium weapon, it must function properly. Perhaps it would have been better had we been able to acquire two plutonium bombs."

Mugniyah nodded. "Perhaps. But I am given to understand that the uranium bomb is of a more proven design."

Both men were terrorists. They knew the plutonium bomb could be a dangerous weapon even if the conventional explosives failed to achieve a high-order nuclear detonation. Highly enriched uranium was deadly as well, if not on quite the same scale as plutonium. The scattering of radioactive material, as the Iraqis had found out in Kurdistan, was of limited use in an open, sparsely populated area, but in an urban environment, the "dirty bomb" could create serious long-term medical problems for those exposed and render sizable portions of a city unusable for years. So Khalib would take the uranium bomb to the plains of Afghanistan, where there were few inhabitants but for the American pipeline crews. Pavel Zelinkow had given Mugniyah other instructions for the plutonium bomb.

"It is good that there are two bombs, two targets, and two of us to deliver them." Khalib assumed that there was a second target. If he resented the fact that Mugniyah did not share with him the target of the second weapon, he did not show it. He was a professional terrorist and was not offended by information denied him for matters of security.

"When you have completed your mission, Khalib Beniid, where will you go?"

"I do not know. Perhaps Kabul, for if we are successful, the city will surely be a welcome place for Islamic fighters. Perhaps Osama, if he is able, will come from hiding and return to the capital. But I have learned to never underestimate the Americans. It may be that I will remain a fugitive in the mountains, sometimes in Afghanistan, sometimes in Pakistan. Or perhaps the names of these countries or the lines drawn between them by Mountbatten, or some other British lord, will no longer be a distinction."

Mugniyah studied this wily mountain fighter. He was one of the few non-Arab native Afghans who had fought with al Qaeda. He was one of the few who was, in every sense of the word, a patriot. Khalib had fought the Russians, the Northern Alliance, and then the Americans. But would any of those who had been raised in that harsh land ever be able to put away their guns? What was there for them? Khalib would, Mugniyah sensed, continue with the struggle. If it ended, he would find a new one. Mugniyah almost envied him, to fight for the sake of fighting.

And if one ever settled down, there would always be someone who felt he was more deserving of the worthless piece of dirt on which you lived than you were. So you could then fight over the worthless piece of dirt. That was Afghanistan and the Afghans.

As for bin Laden, Mugniyah was not so sure that Khalib was speaking about the man or the myth. Khalib had been among the inner circle of the Taliban and close to the al Qaeda leader. If anyone were to know whether bin Laden were truly alive, he would. Yet, while he spoke of the tall Saudi sheik in reverent tones, there was a hint of sarcasm in his voice—or was there? Mugniyah had been at the game long enough to usually know when a man was lying and when he wasn't. But he had also been around long enough to know when it didn't matter.

"And you, Abu Dokhan, what will you do when you have taken your bomb to its proper place?" Khalib asked this evenly and with no emotion in his voice.

"I will return to Lebanon and the struggle there. What we do here will have an impact in the Middle East, but who knows in what way? Here you will only have to deal with the Americans. There, I will have to deal with the Americans and the Israelis."

Khalib spat but held his gaze. "Are they not the same?"

"Not entirely, my friend. How soon will you leave?"

"Perhaps a week. The scientists have some modifications to make to the bombs. And yourself, Dokhan?"

"Not long after you."

Tuesday, 24 December, the Big Island, Hawaii

Steven Fagan was hurrying to finish in the office so he could get down the mountain to see Lon, and get some sleep. It was, after all, Christmas Eve, yet he did feel a touch of guilt that he would be the only one who spent Christmas with his family. Well, almost the only one. Janet Brisco's son was flying into Waimea tomorrow, and she would be able to have dinner with him—unless something broke. He had not slept the night before and had only managed a short nap on the flights from Kona to Nellis. There had been too much to think about on the flight back and much to do once they arrived. After his call to his banking contacts, he reviewed each request for imagery and analysis they had sent along to Jim Watson at Langley. It was frighteningly similar to what he had done when he was a case officer—back when he was on the "inside." Yet he could see this was far more secure than sending his message traffic through the embassy code clerks and communicators. Fagan could only guess how Watson was set up on the other end, perhaps just himself. Most likely, Watson could personally take the information requests and redirect them from his office to the imagery and analysis teams. The data Watson received back could be encoded and transmitted from his office in Langley back to Fagan on the Big Island. The notion that the resources of the entire intelligence community could be made available to him with only two or three people at the CIA in the loop was well beyond Steven's experience only a few years ago.

"Got a minute, boss?"

"Sure, Garrett. C'mon in."

Garrett had a bottle of Jose Cuervo in one hand and two shot glasses in the other. "How about it, Steven? A drop of holiday cactus juice for the road."

Steven hesitated, then smiled and accepted one of the glasses. Garrett splashed some of the amber liquid in Fagan's glass, then charged his own.

"Here's to the lads," Garrett offered.

"The lads," Steven replied, and they both sipped at

their drinks. "How're things on your end?" he continued. "You ready to go?"

"We've done about all we can," Garrett said as he slid into a chair opposite Steven's desk, "until we can put a finer point on exactly where we may be going. I have only two Farsi speakers and four who can probably make themselves understood in Pashtun. Three, including Bijay, speak Arabic, but it's modern standard Arabic, and that's a limiting factor. We can go in as a mining survey crew, Iranian regular army, or as irregular mountain fighters. Unless we can find them in Iran and get near them on the ground, it's going to be hard. My guess is they will be in vehicles while in Iran, but once they get across the border and into the mountains, there are any number of ways they could travel. We could be in the mountain passes searching pack animals."

Steven nodded. He had been a Special Forces trooper in his day. There was a certain excitement about preparing men for possible combat and the prospect of a ground action. He was a "staffie" now, a controller and part of the support cadre. Still, he knew and envied the camaraderie only found in the barracks with the men.

"We've asked Langley for every kind of coverage and electronic analysis imaginable for central Iran. At our urging, they've asked to put up a Global Star drone in Iranian airspace, but that's a national security issue. It'll also depend on whether it can be done without tipping our hand. If you have to take a team in there, we don't want to give them any advance warning. In that regard, the buildup for a possible ground action in Iraq may serve as a smoke screen."

Garrett nodded. "A lot's changed in the last twenty-four hours. What do you think, Steven? Are we going in the right direction with this?"

It was a complex question, and Steven turned it over

carefully in his mind before answering. "I believe so. There are a lot of agencies out there looking for terrorists and illegal drugs. Our cover was pretty solid, but a good investigator could have made us and caused problems. Now that the FBI will be in on the deal, they can probably head off any official inquiries. Somewhere along the line, an official connection had to be made. The fact that an operation may be close on the heels of that connection may not be totally in our favor. I would have liked to have run some comm drills with them on a tactical level before we had to do it for real."

Garrett shrugged. "We got LeMaster, and LeMaster will always be able to talk to us. They will just have to talk to him."

"I suppose," Steven replied. "But it's nice to have that real-time download from the source or the platform. And that usually takes some practice. We'll see." He knocked back the last of his tequila. "I need to get some sleep; you look like you could use some yourself. I'll be at home. Call me if anything comes up." Steven followed Garrett out of the office. Steven headed for his jeep and swung inside. It was an island rig with a roll cage and a Bimini top.

"Garrett, one more thing." Garrett turned. "There is a liaison officer from the Bureau that's been read into the project and will be the official link between us and the government. I got a heads-up that he will be here day after tomorrow. I should have a name and contact instructions before he arrives." Steven started the jeep. "And hey—"

"Hey what?"

"Merry Christmas."

Garrett smiled and headed for the operations building. The mission planners would be working in shifts around the clock now. No holiday for them. They would do that until the IFOR was tasked with the mission, or some military special operations unit was sent in. Garrett could close his eyes and see a map of southeastern Iran, Pakistan, and western Afghanistan. *Where are those guys?* He thought about seeking out Janet Brisco for a nightcap, but thought better of it. The last thing he wanted to do was trade shots with that lady. He was tired, and sleep was the logical and best course of action. He could be called at any time to mount out, and then there would be little or no time for sleep.

6

**Friday, December 27,
the Big Island, Hawaii**

Janet Brisco sat at her desk, studying the latest satellite coverage from central Iran and the routes leading to the border reaches of Afghanistan. She had put her son on the plane late Christmas Day and had been at her desk ever since. There was now a pile of cigarettes in the ashtray on the desk and several empty coffee cups. She still didn't know for sure, but she was developing rough idea of where the bombs were. Once she could confirm it, they could do some serious planning. There was a gentle rapping on the door.

"Come!" she yelled, using the interruption to absent-mindedly light yet another cigarette. Steven had installed exhaust fans in the ceiling over her desk that quietly removed the smoke from her corner of the operations building. Her eyes never left the scope as she scrolled from hut to hut in yet another village near Kerman. So intense was her concentration that she failed to notice the Gurkha who appeared at her elbow.

"I thought you might like a cup of tea, miss."

She wheeled on him, then her expression immediately softened.

"Why, thank you, Prakash. That is very nice of you. Can you stay and visit for a few minutes?"

"Thank you, miss, but please, I must return to my duties. We must continue to prepare."

"Another time then. Thank you for the tea."

"Yes, another time. And you are most welcome, miss."

He bowed over steepled fingers and backed away from the desk toward the door. Brisco smiled after him. Owens and LeMaster exchanged knowing glances, but said nothing. A Gurkha might interrupt Brisco or even take a few minutes of her time, but that privilege did not extend to them. Since she, Garrett, and Steven had last returned to the island, she had done nothing but work, plan, fume, bark orders, and make demands. She drafted e-mails, made phone calls, checked and double-checked equipment and information, and spent hour upon hour on the photographic table going over satellite imagery. At any time, day or night, she could be found hunched over her stereoscope, comparing the current satellite pass to the previous one. And she never slept. Owens and LeMaster both lived in fear of incurring her wrath. Steven treated her like a lioness with cubs, while Garrett avoided her altogether. She was nasty and mean to all who came near her, save for the Gurkhas.

The Gurkhas almost worshiped Bijay Gurung and held Garrett nearly in the same regard, but they reserved a special awe and fascination for Janet Brisco. It was as if she were royalty—some Amazon warrior queen. From the beginning, they treated her with a special deference. Each morning one of them crept into her office with a cup of tea. At first she accepted it out of courtesy and with carefully concealed irritation. Then she came to relish the tea and their company. She would nearly always take time from what she was doing to speak with them. Neither LeMaster nor Owens quite understood the relationship, nor what they talked about. But they were happy and animated conversations, and seemed to have a soothing effect on her. Occasionally they would ask her to walk with them, and four or five of the Gurkhas would be seen escorting her along one of the trails near the camp. She was a full head taller than them and sometimes would walk with an arm casually around one of their shoulders in a maternal gesture. Garrett took to referring to these outings as Snow Not-so-White and the Dwarf Squad. When he asked Bijay about it, the older Gurkha simply shrugged.

"It is beyond my experience," he replied, "but I do not think it is a bad thing."

A plan had been forming in Brisco's mind, and she had been staging assets and aircraft in order to get IFOR into position for an operation. She, Steven, and Bill Owens talked at length about cover stories and documentation. But there was only so much any of them could do until they had a better idea of where the weapons might be and exactly how they might travel. To move too soon could tip their hand and send their quarry to ground. But good intelligence is often perishable. If they didn't get themselves prepositioned and ready to strike, then they would have no chance to act if and when they did get an intelligence break. It was all on Janet Brisco's shoulders. Steven Fagan would make the final decision, and Garrett would be in charge once they got to the ground, but she had to make it happen. It was for her to say, "This is our target, and this is how we are going to do it." Of course Garrett and Bijay would work with her on the final operational and tactical details of the mission. But it was her call; she would say, "We go here and we go now." If they received mission tasking.

Janet Brisco had been planning and coordinating special operations since well before the Gulf War. For close to thirteen of her twenty years at the U.S. Special Operations Command, she was the go-to planner when there was a dangerous or difficult mission in the works. A succession of four-star commanders, on learning that their forces might have to go into harm's way, had invariably turned to their chief staff officers and quietly said, "Let's get Brisco read into this one." Whenever she walked into an operations center, staff officers and senior planners braced themselves for a rough go of it—and with good reason. They knew she would be demanding, tenacious, and intolerant of anything less than a total commitment to the mission. Few really *liked* Lieutenant Colonel Janet Brisco, but no one questioned her competence or that when she was called in on an operation, it was because they wanted the first team on the job.

"Hey, boss," said Bill Owens as he watched a file downloading from a feed routed by Langley directly to them from their station in Bahrain, "we got something coming in you're going to want to—"

"I'm on it, Bill," she replied, the excitement taking the normal bite out of her voice. "Dodds, get this information into overlays and have them ready for comparison with our composite of the area."

"Right-o," replied Dodds obediently.

Unable to confirm her theories, Brisco had pressed Jim Watson for some drone coverage of the area. The Predators were good, but they were vulnerable; they had a maximum ceiling of twenty-five thousand feet. The Global Hawk could fly at sixty thousand feet, which made them *almost* invisible on radar, and *almost* was touchy business in Iranian airspace. It had taken an authorization from the President to overfly Iran. Some ten hours earlier, a Global Hawk had been launched from the USS *Carl Vinson* and vectored into the area. As the crow flies, it would have been a six-hundred-mile journey, but sophisticated drones don't fly like crows. It had taken the Global Star ten hours to find the soft spots in the Iranian air search radars and slip into the area. With something close to that for the trip home, the drone had about ten hours on station. Brisco and her planners had no need to control the Global Star on this mission. The aircraft had been sent in with a series of GPS coordinates and instructions to photograph the area from high altitude. Twenty minutes ago, they had asked the drone's controllers to shoot a specific set of coordinates from a specific angle. While they waited, Owens took the drone imagery, converted it to semitransparencies, and overlaid the data on their composites. The existing imagery had been culled from both government and commercial sources. Satellite imagery had reached a point where it was a commodity. Often, information they needed could be obtained by wiring funds to a numbered account—sometimes it belonged to a commercial entity, sometimes to an official of a foreign government. A near-unlimited source of funds could produce some amazing results. Just then, another imagery document appeared on the screen. She studied it a few moments, then turned to LeMaster. He grinned and nodded

"We got 'em. We got 'em cold." Then she punched the intercom. "Steven! Steven, you there!"

"Right here, Janet. What's up?"

"Steven, we got the bastards."

Moments later, Steven bolted into the operations building. Garrett was right behind him. Janet was ready for them as they joined her around the lighted photo-interpretation table. Owens and LeMaster crowded in.

"Okay, the folks at Langley first put our friend Imad and his new pal Khalib somewhere near Kerman in central Iran some three months ago, right? We assume that they had something to do with the missing weapons. Mugniyah probably doesn't care, and Khalib and al Qaeda would gain little by a nuclear exchange between Pakistan and India. Except for the van and the dead scientists, we found nothing in Kashmir. So we focused our search around Kerman and the routes there." She pulled out a section of overhead photography. "The bombs were taken maybe six weeks ago, headed for Iran, we think. A little more than four weeks ago, we have two Ford Explorers making their way south through Pakistan, not far from the Afghan border." She circled the two small dark rectangles on the imagery with a dry-erase marker, and pulled another sheet across it. "Then we see them again in Iran on the way to Gazak, the main highway up to Kerman. Got to be the same two Explorers. How many black Ford SUVs traveling together are there out there?" Another sheet. "Here we see them on a layby after they had turned off the main road past Bam, in all probability heading somewhere near Kerman. This is some of Dodds's work. Pretty good, huh?" They were looking at a grainy tire print in the sand. "Nothing that would stand up in court from a crime scene, but you can see that it's a—what, Dodds, a twelve-inch tread print made by a fairly new tire." LeMaster nodded his affirmative at the assessment. "And a very expensive tire, probably a top-of-the-line Bridgestone. We got lucky with this—clear desert air, good elevation—about as good as a satellite can do. Other vehicle print is identical, like someone went out and bought a pair of new four-by-fours with the same equipment at the same time. Who does that, besides some dot-com yuppie couple?

"Then we don't see them again. Where are they? Probably holed up in some remote village, but we don't know for sure. Given the roads in the area, we're looking for two needles in a twenty-four-hundred-square-mile haystack. We gotta get closer, but that's a big area even for overheads. So Dodds suggests we look for garages and warehouses where two big vehicles could be hidden. The Global Hawk did it. Look at this."

Brisco laid a photo enlargement on the table that was not more than forty-five minutes old. One was a near-vertical shot that showed two sets of wide tire prints tracking across the sand and into a small garage just outside of the town of Baghin, just forty miles west of Kerman and some fifteen miles north of a village called Khalabad.

"Khalabad is very primitive and a known refuge for al Qaeda. That would fit."

"So how do we know they're still at this garage?" Garrett asked.

She tossed down a second enlargement, like she was filling an inside straight with a hole card. It was still warm from the document copier. "We pulled the drone out a ways for a quartering shot at the garage for a more depressed angle. Fortunately, it's a hot day in Iran, and the garage door was open. See that headlight and section of grille." She smiled. "It's a Ford. If the bombs are there, that's one of the vehicles that brought them there. My guess is that the bombs are in those buildings. If not, they probably aren't far away."

"Well done, Madam Planner," Steven replied. "Very well done. And now?"

"And now I recommend that we launch to the primary staging area. From there, if we're still in the game, we can consider a direct-action mission on those two vehicles. If they move before we get there, we have to track them. Since we think we know where they're going, it shouldn't be hard. The only chance to do this quietly is to catch them in a remote area, and if the central Iranian plateau is anything, it is remote. Then it's decision time. The President will have a tough call to make. Do we send in an SOF element, a Tomahawk missile, or Garrett and friends? But we can't wait for him to make up his mind; we have to assume it will be us. I want the IFOR airborne as soon as possible."

Janet and Steven immediately set their contingency plan in motion. While Bijay prepared the Gurkhas to leave the compound, Garrett was tearing along the coast road about thirty miles an hour over the speed limit. Strapped into the passenger seat was a very apprehensive Bill Owens. Things were coming together quickly. Garrett really didn't have time for this, but right now, he had the least to do. Fortunately the road to the airport from Waimea was an excellent two-lane highway across deserted lava beds. For the most part, it was straight as an arrow and sparsely patrolled. It was like speeding across Wyoming.

Owens now needed to be closer to the potential forward staging areas to ensure that everything was in order before the rest of them arrived. Garrett had reluctantly volunteered to meet the FBI liaison officer assigned as IFOR's official contact, as well as get Owens to his flight. The imagery and operational intelligence data would still come through Jim Watson, but any requirements IFOR might have that involved the military or some government agency would be handled by this, this—Garrett pulled a scrap of paper from his shirt pocket—this J.D. Bechtel. Garrett had only a name and a flight number. Contact instructions had been passed through Langley. The meeting was originally to have taken place in Honolulu, but as time was becoming critical on their end, Bechtel had agreed to come to Kona. There was a small open-air bar at the little Kona airport. Garrett figured he could brief the guy, set up a contact plan, and have him back on the next Hawaiian Air shuttle back to Oahu. Government liaison, he admitted, was a necessary evil, yet it could prove to be an asset if this guy knew his stuff. He found himself wishing for an experienced CIA hand rather than someone from the Bureau. In any case, he wished he was back with the lads, and Steven were here to meet the federal agent.

"Thanks for the flight to the airport," Owens said, mopping his brow. "See you in a few days."

"Take care, Bill," Garrett replied as Owens ran off to the civilian air terminal. A GSI Gulfstream was waiting for him.

Garrett walked around to the commercial arrivals gate, getting there just as the passengers were deplaning. Feeling a little foolish, he waited by the security exit door with the hotel limo drivers and tour guides, holding a little paddle-sign that read, "GSI." As a SEAL he had worked with Bureau agents on occasion. He generally found them too bureaucratic and sometimes too aggressive—SWAT team wannabes. He did like and respect the agents on the Hostage Rescue Team, but then why shouldn't he? There was a liberal sprinkling of special-operations guys on the HRT. Suddenly he was taken by an odd feeling. Then, for no apparent reason, the hair on the back of his neck went up. A moment later he saw her.

"You can take the paddle down now, sailor," she said. "And close your mouth. Jeez, I thought you'd at least have a couple of those flowered leis for me."

"Judy, what the hell are you doing here?"

"Shhh. The name is J. D. Bechtel, or Ms. Bechtel, if you like. Gawd, I just love this spy stuff. And we finally get to work together. I'm stoked. I'll bet you're excited too, or you will be, once you calm down a bit."

"I need a drink," Garrett said feebly.

"Sounds great," she replied, slipping a hand through his arm. "You can brief me in the bar. Gotta be one around here someplace. I want something pastel with two long straws and a little umbrella in it."

Saturday, December 28, the White House

The issue that the IFOR planning team discussed over the latest imagery was now being considered by four very serious men. They were in one of the informal conference rooms in the West Wing, seated in overstuffed chairs around a low coffee table. Three of them were dressed in slacks and polo shirts, looking more like duffers at the nineteenth hole than the power structure of the United States of America. Only one, Armand Grummell, looked like someone for whom a round of golf might be a frivolous undertaking; he wore an oxford-cloth shirt with an open collar and a blazer. He was of the old school, a man for whom the absence of a jacket meant that you were about to mow the lawn or change the oil in your car. Oddly enough, while he did consider golf a silly pastime, he had been the only serious athlete of the group. He was drafted by the Boston Red Sox out of high school, and had played a summer of triple-A baseball. He was a serious big-league infield prospect until called away to the war in Korea. Now his only connection to the game, or any sport for that matter, was talking baseball with George Will, something they did on occasion over an informal dinner—both wearing bow ties and herringbone jackets.

The President turned to James Powers. "So there it is, Jim. If it's your problem, how do you solve it?"

Powers, like the others, was all too aware of the missing weapons and now their probable location. He and his department were also heavily engaged in diplomatic wrangling about the use of force in Iraq. Now he had to turn his attention to Iran. Powers and his colleagues at State had worked hard to improve relations with Iran, and were encouraged by their progress to date. It was not likely to become the next Turkey any time soon, but they were making headway. Now this.

"I don't have any good answers for this one," the Secretary of State replied. "We have no indication that Tehran has any knowledge, but then the Ministry of Intelligence and Security may be operating without the knowledge of the mullahs. I doubt that Mugniyah would be in the country without the knowledge of the MIS. My guess is that President Khatami is clean on this one, not that it would matter a great deal. I spoke with their foreign minister, Kamal Khaffazi, this morning again about Iraq. He gave no indications that something was amiss, but he's a pretty cool customer. If we go to them with this, I can almost guarantee a flat denial. Iran would like nothing better than for us to disarm Iraq and take Pakistan's nukes away from them. And they have no interest in seeing that we succeed with the pipeline. At best they will plead ignorance; at worst, we will have just made Iran a nuclear power."

"Tony."

The Secretary of Defense pursed his lips and began. "I've had the Special Operations Command working on this since we learned of it. I have two platoons of Navy SEALs and an Amphibious Ready Group quietly moving into the northern Arabian Sea. They are scheduled to transit the Strait of Hormuz tonight and will be in the Gulf by midday tomorrow. The Persian Gulf is not the best place geographically to launch into central Iran, but with the buildup for Iraq, I don't think anyone will notice. We also have a contingent of Rangers and Special Forces standing by in Afghanistan. I recommend the SF if it's to be a small action; Rangers if it's to be company-sized assault or larger. If the intelligence is good, they'll get the job done. The SEALs can handle this mission as well. But any way you cut it, it will be an invasion. There is a chance we can get in and out undetected, but I can't promise that. This is a mission our special operators have trained hard for. There are some very capable and dedicated young men waiting for the green light. Or"—Barbata turned his palms face up—"we can simply bomb the shit out of them, and there are any number of ways we can do that. We can probably get a Tomahawk in there at night without anyone seeing it coming over the beach. Or if you want a smaller munition, a Hellfire missile from a drone, but either way, there's going to be a smoking hole in the ground, and if the bombs are there, it will be very radioactive, perhaps dangerously so."

"I'd like to keep this as quiet as possible," the President said. "Is there any covert way to get in there and bring those bombs out?"

Barbata expelled a long breath. "Possibly. It would have to be a small, surgical special-operations strike, in and out in a single night." St. Claire nodded. "There's a chance, but as I said, we would have to stage out of Afghanistan or from a carrier. The electronic order of battle for their coastline and along the central plateau is not too difficult, but it would not be without risks. We're a lot better than we were back in 1980 when we failed in Desert One, and this is a much easier target than the embassy hostages outside of Tehran. But then, the Iranians are a little better now as well."

The legacy of Desert One was on everybody's mind. It was a tactical blunder and a foreign policy disaster. And it was the last time American troops were on Iranian soil. Oddly enough, that failed mission had led to the creation of the U.S. Special Operations Command, the very forces that would go in on the ground to recover the two nukes.

"It's doable," Barbata continued, "but we'll need some time to brief the teams and do the final planning. If something goes wrong, the comparison to Desert One will be obvious to the international community. And let's face it, it could damage the coalition we've built to go into Iraq. We can probably get in and out in a single night, but everything would have to go perfectly. And it may be hard to hide the fact that we were there."

The President paused for a long moment before speaking, turning to Armand Grummell as he did.

"There is another option, one that was not available to us until a few weeks ago. I'm at a loss to tell you exactly how it came about, so I'll let Armand do that. Armand?"

Armand Grummell appeared slightly taken aback. This was not the case. Although the President had given him no advanced warning, he fully expected to be called on to do this.

"There is a force in place that is prepared to take action in this matter, on the ground, with little or no attribution to the United States government. It is, for want of a better term, a mercenary force, composed of foreign nationals and trained in special-operations disciplines." Grummell went on to provide a very sketchy outline of the IFOR, carefully omitting any reference to its location, source of funding, or founder. "I am being purposefully oblique about the details, but I can assure you that this is not some corporate shell set up by my agency or one of our contractors. Also—and you may find this difficult to believe, so I will ask you to take it on faith from myself and the Commander in Chief—this capability, if you will, comes at no cost, monetarily or politically."

There was a moment of silence before both Powers and Barbata spoke at once.

"You mean there is some kind of a philanthropist out there providing counterterrorist services?" managed Powers.

"And they can conduct long-range, direct-action covert missions?" added Barbata.

"You are both correct," Grummell replied. "Unconventional as it may sound, it is an option worth considering."

"Special operations are not child's play," Barbata said. "How do we know they handle a mission of this complexity?"

"I'm given to understand they have recruited the very best," Grummell replied, "from your special-operations components as well as from my agency."

"But if we know where the bombs are headed," said Jim Powers, "why not let them cross into Afghanistan? We have the resources there and a mandate to conduct military operations." Powers was desperately looking for a way for any military action to occur someplace other than on Iranian soil.

"And if it is to be a special operation," Barbata persisted, "wherever it is, we have our own guys; we know with some certainty what they can and cannot do. And they can do a lot. Those men have worked long and hard to be ready for this. If it's to be a ground action, they deserve the chance to go in; they've earned it."

Grummell sighed and cleared his throat. This, he knew from past experience, was the kind of debate President St. Claire wanted; it would form the basis for his final decision.

"All that you say is true, gentlemen, but a few considerations would seem to favor action by a third party. First of all, the border area between Iran and Afghanistan is a warren of smuggling trails and secret mountain passes. It carries the highest volume of illegal opium in the world. Now that it is infested with al Qaeda and the remnants of the Taliban, it is doubly dangerous. Close to three thousand Iranian Republican Guards, or Pasdaran, have been killed along that border in the last ten years, and they have yet to blunt the transhipment of drugs. Our nuclear terrorist will be hard to find in there, and harder still coming into the plains east of the Afghan border." He was speaking patiently, as if he were lecturing undergraduates. "Secondly, we must consider our target. The best chance for a nonnuclear event is to surprise them and recover the weapons. But we must never forget that these are nuclear weapons in the hands of dangerous men—fanatical perhaps, but very disciplined and capable. There is always the chance that they would detonate the weapon if our surprise is not complete or the force not overwhelming. If we were to have a nuclear event and a number of Americans were involved, they would be vaporized in the blast. These men have families; how will we explain it to them? There are also the supporting military elements and units who will know that we sent those men on the mission. Denial would be risky and even shameful. And the Iranians will probably claim that it was our weapon that was detonated, especially if our people are involved." He was silent a moment, but what they were all thinking had to be articulated. "Our best chance of catching them is in Iran, and our best chance of minimizing collateral damage is to catch them in the open wasteland of the central Iranian plateau, well west of the Afghan border. If there is a nuclear event, what is lost and what is gained? The pipeline is safe, and we, along with the rest of the world, will demand an explanation of why stolen Pakistani weapons were detonated in Iran." He did not have to articulate that we could take this position only if no American military personnel were involved. Again, a silence held them in check until Grummell continued in a soft voice. "Our choice of action will be neither easy nor pleasant. I ask only that you consider all the factors."

Grummell lowered his head as if to signify he had finished. He was polishing his glasses in a firm, deliberate manner. This was not lost on the President, nor the Secretaries of State and Defense.

Monday afternoon, December 30, Baghin, Iran

Khalib and Mugniyah pulled through the open door and into the repair bay. The owner of the garage had been paid to empty his facility and make himself available to house and service only two vehicles. He was paid in cash more than he would see in a year of patching up old Toyotas and Peugeots. Khalib leapt from the big Mercedes sedan in which he was riding, not bothering to close the car door.

"Why is that door open?" he demanded.

"It is hot, and the fumes, we have no way of—"

"Put it down immediately." His tone of voice brooked no reply. The garage owner hurried to close the roll-up door.

Mollified, Khalib walked around the vehicles and nodded his approval. They would do. The Explorers had been rumpled with crowbars and sledges and painted—one tan and the other a dull white. Metal roof racks with wooden slats had been fitted to each vehicle, and there were extra gas cans and spare tires lashed in place. A few hours on the road, and they would look much the same as other vehicles forced to exist in a harsh, remote area and drive exclusively on unimproved roads. But for the purpose at hand, both vehicles were in perfect mechanical condition.

On one side of the garage, a half dozen very dangerous-looking men squatted in a circle, several of them with AK-47 assault rifles across their laps. They were dressed in what might have passed for Pashtun tribal garb, or for that matter, that of any number of clans that lived along the Iranian-Afghan border. These were hard men whose lives were bound by clan loyalty and violence. The prospect of killing Russians or Uzbeks or Americans was only a little more appealing than killing someone from a rival tribe. They gave their allegiance freely and fiercely to the head of their clan, and that man was Khalib. They cared for nothing else, save for their weapons or perhaps their sons, if they had them and if they were still alive. There were table and chairs nearby, but these men had little use for furniture. On the other side of the garage, as if to be as far away from the fierce tribesmen as possible, Moshe Abramin and Mirza Riaz waited in a little alcove. The preparation of the vehicles for extended desert travel and the presence of these fierce fighting men had curbed their zeal. Khalib had continued to treat them with respect, but it was now clear to them that they were captives as well as participants in this venture. Khalib conferred with the owner of the garage and with his men before addressing Moshe and Mirza.

"It will be dark in a few hours, and we will leave. Our struggle asks many things of us, and I am going to ask one more of you. Our plans call for the two weapons to travel separately. It would be a tragedy if, after all your courage and sacrifice, our plans came to nothing because we failed to do all in our power to ensure success. The Americans will be looking for us, if they are not yet doing so. By sending the bombs on two separate routes, we double our chances to strike a blow for our cause. Do you understand this?"

The hard look in Khalib's eyes conveyed equal measures of resolve and deadly firmness. They could do nothing but agree with him.

"And because the two weapons will travel by separate routes, I must ask that the two of you also travel separately, one of you with each bomb. Will you do this?" Again they could do nothing but concur. To both of these academics, it was becoming clear that their fate was in the hands of this fierce and charismatic Afghan.

"Excellent. I would expect nothing less from two warriors who have served God so nobly and with such dedication. Were the materials you requested satisfactory?"

"Yes, Khalib." Moshe replied. When they had met in Lahore, Moshe had given Khalib a list of tools and electrical components they would need to make timing and command detonation devices for the bombs, as the specifications to have the steel casings fabricated. The weapons, crude as they were, were designed for missile warheads. A small radar in the nose cone of the rocket was programmed to send an electrical impulse to the weapon when the warhead reached a certain altitude on its descent trajectory. At the prescribed altitude, the weapon would detonate. Moshe had asked for the materials he would need to build electronic initiators for the weapons. They were not complicated—a simple digital clock mechanism and a battery that together would deliver the proper electronic pulse at some future time, or on command. But they had to be compatible with the electrical components of the bombs' conventional explosives. Moshe also had to bypass the safety devices that had been designed into the weapons' components.

"And were you able to mate the timing devices to the explosives?"

"It has been done. All that remains is to marry the explosive and nuclear components, along with the neutron catalysts. The weapons will then be ready for detonation. The timer is a simple device. Once the triggers are activated, the timing mechanism is no more difficult to set than an alarm clock."

"Excellent. Then I want you to prepare one of the weapons for final detonation—all that is required except for the setting of the clock."

"M-may I ask why only one?"

"Of course," Khalib replied. He spoke to them as equals—fellow conspirators. Khalib Beniid was a skilled and compelling man, a natural leader whom men willingly followed, whether they were mountain fighters or urban engineers. "One of your bombs will travel by car to the target, so it can be assembled here, driven to its destination, and set in place. The second weapon will travel by car only so far, then it will have to be loaded on pack animals for a journey through the mountains. Only at the end of our mountain trek can you complete the final assembly."

Moshe nodded. He had told Khalib that the completed bombs would be far more delicate than the separate components, if for no other reason than that they had only the containers for the subassemblies—the containers they were in when they were taken from Kahuta. And there was also the weight factor. A single weapon weighed close to two hundred kilos—well over four hundred pounds. The separate components would travel much better unassembled.

"So which weapon do you want us to assemble?"

"The plutonium bomb."

That evening, just after dark, the two Ford Explorers left the garage with Khalib, Moshe, and the six mountain tribesmen, headed for Kerman. By sunrise the next day they were well clear of the city and headed northwest toward the Dasht Lut wilderness area and the Afghan border. They traveled on the main roads, but whenever possible skirted towns and villages, sometimes carefully working their way through the sand-covered wasteland. They made slow but steady progress and traveled mainly at night.

The sedan, a dated Mercedes S430, did not leave the garage until the following evening. In the trunk, swathed in many layers of foam cushioning material, was a fully assembled plutonium-fueled atomic bomb. There were four men in the vehicle. A driver and a bodyguard in front kept a careful eye on the road, while Imad Mugniyah and a senior MIS officer rode in the back. They took the main highway southwest that led to the Pakistan-Iranian border. The Mercedes was some fifty miles southwest when a raging fire swept through the garage, burning it to the foundation. Two corpses were later found in the rubble, charred beyond recognition. An investigation soon revealed that one of them was most probably the owner of the garage. The second was no one they could identify from the immediate area. He was probably, a local resident offered, one of the mysterious group of men who occupied the garage before it was destroyed.

Early Tuesday morning, December 31,
Honolulu

United Flight 907, direct service from Honolulu to Singapore, was a full flight. No one paid attention to Garrett Walker or Bijay Gurung as they boarded. Nor did anyone seem to notice a quiet group of men who boarded in twos and threes behind them, dressed in blue Nike jogging suits, most with rumpled gear bags over their shoulders as carry-on baggage. Two of them had net bags holding a half dozen soccer balls. They were a Burmese soccer club returning to Rangoon after a tournament in the States. There were another ten or so with them, dressed like students and tourists. A 747 headed for Singapore had enough Asian diversity to easily swallow twenty-eight men who, but for the way they dressed, looked like members of the same extended family. And those who were dressed alike had a reason to do so. They easily melded into the tide of Malays and Indonesians on board. Flight 907 left Hawaii Tuesday morning and touched down at Paya Lebar Airport outside Singapore on Wednesday afternoon, January 1. Several white vans were waiting for the team and their bags. Another two vans collected the tourist-student contingent and followed along. They didn't have far to go. The vans made their way to a rented general aviation hangar with a Gulfstream parked inside, a white aircraft with no windows and "The Joseph Simpson Jr. Foundation" neatly blocked on the tail. As soon as they arrived, the Gurkhas set to it with a will, unloading their operational gear and weapons from the corporate jet. They were an exceedingly happy group, like a throng of school children on a zoo outing. There was the prospect of going to war.

Singapore is a semi-police state, and the official religion is commerce. Drugs are prohibited under penalty of death, and firearms are not far behind. The hangar space was under lease by the Joseph Simpson Jr. Foundation and had served as a transshipment point for foodstuffs and medical supplies. A great many much-needed relief shipments for Central Asia and West Africa had gone through this hangar. Given the active involvement of the foundation, it was a busy facility. There was no reason to think that this was not just another high-priority shipment of generators for Bangladesh or water-purification equipment for Tanzania. Yet the men worked as quickly; the sooner they were on their way, the better. Janet Brisco stood at the boarding hatch with a clipboard. She, Steven, and Dodds LeMaster had made the trip in the Gulfstream with the equipment and weapons—Hawaii to Ponepe to Singapore. Garrett approached Steven, and they shook hands warmly.

"Any problems?"

"Just the airline food," Garrett replied. "How about yourself?"

"Just Janet fidgeting. We lost communications for about twenty minutes over New Guinea, and I thought she was going to go up and choke one of the pilots. The pilots were also keeping a close eye on their fuel state. The last jump was over four thousand miles, and we were at maximum gross weight."

"Any changes?"

"Nothing. Langley has promised to let us know the minute those SUVs are on the move. They've pulled the drones out, but the satellite coverage is quite good and getting better. This has the very highest priority, and more than a few birds have been reorbited to keep the area under surveillance. We'll know within the half hour if those Explorers are on the road. Still no word as to the military options, but I have a feeling we will get the nod on this one." Steven smiled. "They don't want any attribution in Iran, not with Iraq on the horizon. And they don't want another Desert One."

"Makes sense," Garrett replied. In many ways he felt sorry for the special-operations forces he knew would now be in play. Many of the individual operators he would know personally. More than a few he had trained for this very kind of mission. He himself had waited too many times with a platoon of SEALs in some remote location, locked and loaded—waiting for the call that never came. "How about Owens?"

Steven glanced at his watch. "He's in the air now and will be waiting for us on the other end. He says he has what he needs and he'll have it in place. Our bird should be here within the hour. If we're lucky, we'll be in position before those weapons are on the move. If not, we'll still be in good shape to take action. If we get the call."

"Things are happening fast," Garrett said. "Too fast, maybe?"

"We'll see," Steven replied.

Bijay approached and politely greeted Steven. "Everything arrived in good order and we are ready in all respects." Bijay and the other Gurkhas were now dressed in tan trousers and matching open-collared shirts, but they moved with a little too much purpose to pass as aid workers. Parked in the rear of the hangar were two communications vans with mission support electronic suites, identical to the ones in Kona. They had been pre-positioned here for just such a contingency.

Garrett turned to Steven. "Everything ready on the other end."

"As far as I know," Steven said; then, with a smile, "Our federal liaison officer will be there to help with any problems that may arise."

"Oh, wonderful," Garrett replied.

Just after dark, a C-130J Lockheed Hercules landed and was given permission to taxi to the hangar. The Gulfstream had gone, but the 130 was much too large for the hangar. The aircraft crept up to the hangar doors, neatly pirouetted, and dropped her stern ramp. A forklift took the paletted gear quickly aboard, and the load master secured it to the deck with chains and nylon cargo nets. Then two white comm vans drove up the ramp and into the cargo bay of the big Hercules. Finally the Gurkhas filed aboard and sat in two rows along each side of the fuselage on canvas bench-seats. Steven sat at the wheel of the lead van, and Garrett joined him in the front passenger seat. Janet and Dodds LeMaster buckled themselves into the captain's chairs at the consoles in the rear of the van. After they reached cruise altitude, Garrett left the van, found Bijay, and strapped himself in beside him. The rough ride, the uncomfortable seats, noise, and the smell of hydraulic fluid brought back a flood of nostalgia and anticipation. In a few minutes he nodded off to sleep like the rest of the Gurkhas. The big aircraft was well under her rated payload of thirty-six thousand pounds and just under her three-thousand-mile range as they continued west to their destination.

Late Tuesday morning, December 31,
Air Force One

President Bill St. Claire sat in a padded leather armchair
on Air Force One, on his way to a fund-raising luncheon
in Chicago. He had almost canceled the appearance, given
the breaking crisis, but with a covert operation in the off-
ing, he was advised not to deviate from his planned itiner-
ary. He recalled that Jimmy Carter had done the same
thing on the eve of Desert One. The man who gave that
advice was seated across the low table from him, carefully
stirring his tea. He had slipped aboard the President's
plane unnoticed by the accompanying press pool.

"So they are on the move, and you feel the two
weapons are headed for Afghanistan?"

"I do. The two vehicles our friends from Hawaii tracked
into central Iran most certainly brought the weapons out of
Pakistan. We have them moving past Kerman and heading
toward the Afghan border, probably for a crossing somewhere west or southwest of Herat."

The President turned and looked down on the snow-
brushed cornfields of Ohio. "What do you recommend,
Armand?"

"I recommend we let Joe Simpson and his people have
a crack at this one."

"You think this is the best option?"

"I do. There is a great deal to recommend their involvement. I have been given a rough outline of their
plan, and it looks promising. They are our only covert option with non-attribution. The IFOR can be in position to
intercept the weapons as quickly as any of our special-
operations forces, and I think they have the best chance of
doing the job quietly."

The whole world was focused on Saddam and Iraq,
and their reluctant European allies. St. Claire could only

picture the headlines if word of this got out. It would certainly be a blessing for Saddam if attention were somehow diverted away from Iraq. "What's Barbata say?"

"He reluctantly agreed, although he was quick to point out that his Special Forces and SEALs are straining at their leashes. I feel that in releasing the IFOR, this also gives us a chance to better position our special-operations elements in the mountain passes should Khalib and his weapons make it across the border and into Afghanistan. We're talking nuclear weapons, and we have to use every available means to stop them."

"Then why not send in a Tomahawk and simply erase the two vans while we have them in the desert?"

"We need to do two things, Mr. President. We need to eliminate the weapons as a threat, and we need to account for the weapons. We need confirmation. Our sources in Pakistan, now official, tell us that the two missing weapons were of two different types, one a uranium weapon and the other a plutonium weapon. We know that the two engineers still missing from the Kahuta weapons facility could arm either weapon."

"Any idea why they took one of each?"

Armand Grummell gave an imperceptible shrug of his shoulders. "There's no way of knowing at this juncture. It may have been by design, or perhaps it was by chance when they removed the weapons from the storage area. Either way, both need to be found and recovered. There is no other alternative. If we simply destroy the two vehicles, we do neither. And there is one other thing we should consider."

"And that is?"

"The pipeline crews. Until those weapons are accounted for, it may be advisable to at least put them on some kind of security alert."

"Yes," the President replied, "but those bombs are a long way from Afghanistan and the pipeline."

"Sir, we think they are a long way from the pipeline, but we're not one-hundred percent sure. We have, however, been given good reason to believe that nuclear weapons are now targeted at Americans. It's something to consider."

Bill St. Claire thought about this. What his DCI was saying, though it had nothing to do with his primary duty of reporting intelligence to the executive branch, was, "God help you, Mr. President, if this thing gets out of hand and you knew American citizens were at risk." Bill St. Claire again stared out the window, but no answers were forthcoming in the farmlands of northern Ohio. After several minutes, he turned back to Armand Grummell.

"I'll have Tony deploy his special-operations people along the Afghan border as a contingency. For now, a heightened state of alert should be enough for the pipeline crews. Let's see what Simpson's folks can do." The President hesitated, then added, "Get this done, Armand. We'll not be free to take any action in Iraq until this is resolved."

Late Wednesday afternoon, January 1, 2003,
Diego Garcia

The C-130J set down just before sundown and taxied off to a deserted piece of hardstand served by two prefab plywood buildings. Waiting for them was another C-130J and two lone figures. The temperature was still over ninety degrees, and the southeast trade winds blew at a steady fifteen knots. Diego Garcia is a seventeen-square-mile speck of land located seven degrees south of the equator in the middle of the Indian Ocean. One of the fifty-two islands in the Chagos Archipelago, it is owned by Great Britain and populated by the American military. It is home to the fleet of maritime pre-positioned ships, stationed there to support a major conflict in the Middle

East and serve as a base for B-52 and B-1 bombers and their aerial tanker fleet. Diego Garcia is the base from which America is able to project its military might into the Middle East and South Asia. It is a busy place. There was enough military activity in and around the island atoll for a pair of unmarked C-130s parked at the end of a remote taxiway to go unnoticed.

As soon as the rear ramp was partially down, a file of Gurkhas began to drop to the tarmac and jog into one of the buildings. Others remained to unload the equipment pallets. Steven, Garrett, Dodds LeMaster, and Janet Brisco deplaned right after the Gurkhas. Janet led them from the aircraft. At this phase of the operation, she was clearly in charge. Judy Burks and Bill Owens waited at the edge of the hardstand.

"You got the word that we have the green light?" Janet said to Owens, not wasting time with pleasantries or waiting for a reply. "Are you ready in all respects?"

"The vehicles are aboard the aircraft, gassed up and ready to go. The clothing and gear you specified are waiting for the insertion team inside that building."

"The pilots?"

"They're in the other building, standing by for their mission briefing."

Brisco carried a fat leather briefcase in one hand and had a thick sheaf of maps in the other. "Steven and I will brief the pilots," she said to Garrett. "You and Bijay get your troops ready to go. We'll muster them under the wing of the ready aircraft. I want you away within the hour. Dodds, get the comm vans unloaded and set up. I want to be operational as soon as the team is airborne." Then, noticing Judy Burks for the first time, "And who in the hell are you?"

"Ah, Janet, this is Judy Burks. She is our government liaison," Garrett replied.

"Oh, right," Brisco replied dubiously. "Glad to meet you."

"Judy arranged for our flight clearances and the use of these buildings," Garrett continued. "She will also see that we get the support and privacy we need from the island commander, and that no one will ask questions about why we're here. If you need anything while you're here, Judy will see to it."

Brisco gave Garrett an uncertain look. "Okay, thanks. Judy, we'll talk later. Right now, I have a mission to launch. Let's move, people." With that, she strode off to brief the pilots for the operation. Steven Fagan almost had to jog to keep up with her.

"How about you, sailor?" Judy said after the others had left. "Is there anything you need?"

"Well, I'm sure there is, but we probably don't have enough time to properly attend to it. Maybe on the return trip."

"I assume I shouldn't ask where you're going. I know it's probably going to be dangerous. You have the same goofy look on your face as the little guys that piled off that airplane."

"You assume right."

"Well then, tell me about that Amazon you flew in with. Is she the boss?"

"She is for now, absolutely. We have a special-operations tasking, and she is the mission planner. She will also be our operational control while we're in the field. She won't make the tactical calls, but she will decide everything else. She's also the best. I want you to look after her, and if need be, to stay out of her way."

"Don't worry about that," Judy replied. "That's one intimidating lady."

Inside, twelve of the Gurkhas selected for the insertion team were changing clothes. A few were changing into the dress of mountain tribesmen, but most of them were donning military uniforms. Garrett joined them and quickly switched into tan slacks, desert boots, and a bush coat. A slouch hat completed the look. Bill Owens sat at a table with a file box and a checklist. Each Gurkha received money, a gold chain for barter, and an Iranian national identity card. There were military IDs for the soldiers, confirming them as draftees in the Islamic Iranian Ground Forces, commonly known as the Iranian Army. Garrett received a full set of documents identifying him as a Dutch mining engineer on contract with a French minerals exploration firm. There was man sitting by himself in the corner, dressed much like Garrett. He watched all this activity with a detached amusement. Garrett walked over to him.

"You must be our weapons expert."

The man rose and extended his hand. "Frederick Janos. Pleased to meet you, Mr. . . ."

Garrett looked at his passport with its current Iranian visa. "Raemacher. Hans Raemacher. Are you ready to go?"

Janos was a South African expatriate who had worked in that nation's uranium mining industry. He had consulted with a number of countries, not always legally, for the procurement of fissionable materials to construct nuclear weapons. He was known to have worked with the Israelis, and they had given a good opinion of him. Janos was a bomb expert for hire—a nuclear soldier of fortune; he would work for anyone for a fee. This job would be his last. He had reached an agreement with Steven Fagan that would make him wealthy enough to retire. His retirement was part of the contract. No one associated with IFOR wanted him traveling about with that much knowledge of their operations. Janos pointed to a kit bag and backpack next to his chair.

"Everything I need is in there," he replied. He had a perpetual smile and spoke with a British-Afrikaners accent. "You're not going to get me killed on this little venture, are you?"

"I'll try not to. It's a tough piece of work, but we have a good plan and a good crew."

"I should say. These wogs you have here are a rugged-looking lot."

Garrett's expression became cold. "They're much more than that, and if you ever refer to them as wogs again, you just may not live to enjoy that fat fee you're being paid. We clear on that?"

"Too right, mate. How soon do we leave?"

Garrett glanced at his watch. "Within the half hour."

In the next building, Janet Brisco was briefing the pilots. Both were veterans of the Air Force 1st Special Operations Wing, and both had flown missions similar to this when they were on active duty. They had been flying relief supplies into Somalia and the Sudan until just a few days ago. Steven Fagan had asked certain pilots flying for Joseph Simpson Jr. Foundation if they would be interested in work that involved flying something other than food and generators—work that had an element of danger but paid a great deal more. They had responded like bird dogs when you take a shotgun down from the gun rack. These were experienced special-operations pilots, and they loved a good challenge. One of them had once been briefed by Brisco when they were both in uniform, but he had the good sense not to bring it up. The mission would not be without risk, and they would earn their generous bonus. But in keeping with the breed, it was the prospect of a difficult mission that had them sitting in on this briefing.

"What if we go down?" one of the flyers asked.

"Standard escape-and-evasion procedures. The other C-130 will be standing by with an armed reaction team. The beacons in your survival radios will allow us to find you, and I can assure you that we will come. There are two extended-range H-60s headed for Herat on a humanitarian mission, and they will remain there on standby for combat search and rescue."

"And if we get picked up by the locals?"

"We'll try to buy you back. The official presence there is the Pasdaran, along with local constabulary. We have identified no regular army units along your flight path. There are, however, bandits and drug smugglers. If you can be bought, we'll buy you. If not, you can kiss your sorry ass good-bye." Both pilots and the three aircrewmen chuckled. "Your best way home is to keep those beacons active. Any more questions?" There were none. "Then let's get that bird in the air. We're wasting darkness. I want that aircraft in Afghan airspace before the sun comes up."

The aircrew filed out and boarded the plane. The pilots went straight to the cockpit; the aircraft had already been preflighted. Strapped to the deck of the big Hercules were four Russian UAZ-469 jeeps in Iranian army dress, loaded and fueled. The vehicles were there due to the foresight of Steven Fagan and the procuring genius of Bill Owens. While the pilots and crewmen made the final checks, the Gurkhas stood in formation under the wing, illuminated by halogen lights from the buildings and the afterglow of the sunset. There were an even dozen of them, not counting Bijay, eight attired as Iranian Army regulars, the other four, including Bijay, in baggy trousers, tattered shirts, and mountain headdresses. No element of the Islamic Iranian Ground Force would be moving in this region without guides and baggage handlers. Only a close inspection would reveal that the soldiers were much better armed than the average Iranian infantryman, and that the AK-47s of the irregulars were in pristine condition. Garrett and Bijay quickly and professionally inspected them, more for the men than their two leaders; it was a formality always observed before going into combat. When they were finished, Bijay called them to attention and saluted.

"*Gurkhali ayo!*" he called to them.

"*GURKHALI AYO!*" they roared. The twelve double-timed to the rear of the aircraft and filed aboard. The other Gurkhas watched them in envious silence. Janet Brisco stood to one side observing all this, then turned a fierce glare to Bijay and Garrett.

"You take care of my boys, hear me? If anything happens to them, you will answer to me personally."

Bijay inclined his head in a formal gesture, straightened, then boarded the C-130. If he felt any rancor that a mere woman should remind a British Gurkha warrant officer to take care of his men, he was careful not to let it show. Garrett saluted Brisco, giving her a broad grin, then turned and walked over to where Judy waited.

"If all goes well, I'll see you in a few days."

"And if it doesn't?"

He shrugged. "Well, then thanks for coming all this way to see me off."

"This is the first time I've ever seen a man off to war," she replied, taking his hand in both of hers. "And I don't really even know where you're going."

Garrett regarded her. "There's no real need for you to know. But you can be sure that it is important—very important."

"Guess there's not much to say, then. Take care of yourself. I'm very selfish; I want you back."

Suddenly he took her in his arms, just as the port outboard Allison AE2100D3 turbofan began to spool up. "Look, this is a hell of a way to start the new year, but I *will* be careful, and I *will* see you in a few days. And, if it means anything to you, this is the first time I've ever climbed on a mission bird knowing there was someone waiting who cared." He kissed her tenderly and stepped back, again smiling broadly. "You are a piece of work, Judy Burks."

"Gee, thanks. You say the sweetest things." He turned to go as she yelled over the building whine of the turbine, "And yes, it means a great deal to me!"

Garrett leaped up to the tail ramp, waved, and was gone. The ramp and tail cargo door ground shut with finality. The big Hercules began to taxi as soon as the fourth engine reached RPM. Janet and Judy watched as it turned for the main taxiway. The C-130's short-field takeoff and landing capabilities would not be needed on runways that catered to loaded B-52s. It paused briefly at the head of the active runway, then began to accelerate with a controlled turbine shriek. Less than halfway down the strip, the big bird lifted and banked gracefully toward the northwest and into the night.

"Think they'll be all right?"

"Huh? Oh, I think so." Brisco had been lost in thought. Already she had begun to turn over in her mind just a few of the dozens of details and considerations that would consume her waking hours until the mission was complete. "It's a clear objective, and we have a very workable plan. Those are a very capable group of guys—as good as any I've seen." Then she suddenly focused on Judy, as if seeing her for the first time. She immediately read the concern on her face. "I'll bet that man of yours didn't tell you what all this fuss was about, did he?"

"Well, no, he didn't."

"Men!" Brisco scoffed. She lit a cigarette and tossed the match to the tarmac in a dismissive gesture. "They can be so thickheaded. I need to get to my station. We can get a cup of coffee there, and I'll tell you all about it."

"Isn't all this classified?" Judy said as Janet put an arm around her and guided her toward one of the vans. Dodds LeMaster had the power cables in place, and he instinc-

tively knew that one of his first duties in an operational
environment would be to have a pot of strong black coffee
ready for Janet Brisco. "I mean," Judy continued as they
walked, "don't I have to have a need to know?"

"Honey," Brisco replied, "around here, I say what is
classified and what isn't, and I say what needs to be
known and by whom. And I just decided that you have a
need to know."

Wednesday evening, January 1, central Afghanistan

One of the necessities Trish Wilson had brought with her
from Sun Valley, Idaho, to central Afghanistan was a boot
scraper. It was a two-foot board with stiff-bristled brushes
screwed to the center portion of the board. The board was
held in place by standing on the board with one boot
while drawing the other through the bristles in such a way
that snow, mud, or dust would be removed from the bottom and sides of the boot. Dave Wilson never entered
their dwelling, wherever it was, without thoroughly scrap-
ing one boot, then the other. And in Afghanistan, boots
were never left outside because of scorpions. This scrap-
ing ritual invariably seemed to humor his wife. This
evening, she was not to be humored, no matter how clean
his boots were.

"You better take a look at this." There was concern in
her voice.

She handed him a clipboard with a sheaf of e-
messages. On the top one she had circled the subject line
with a yellow highlighter: SECURITY ALERT: LEVEL THREE.

Security was always a priority with the pipeline crews,
but there were various heightened levels of alert, and Level
Three was the lowest of them. It meant that additional
military patrols would be sent out, and that no personnel

should venture beyond the moving perimeter of the compound without an armed escort. This was the second such alert they had received since the project began. The first one was in response to the time they were mortared, but it came after the attack.

"It says something about the possibility of heightened al Qaeda activity in the area. What the hell do they mean by that?"

"Not really sure," Dave replied, "but I'll have a talk with the colonel and see if he knows anything more. Could be they picked up a cell-phone conversation that the booger-eaters are going to try something." In keeping with a U.S. State Department directive, Dave had had to ask his construction workers to refrain from referring to the locals as towel-heads and a host of other derogatory terms, so another term for them had come into use. They picked it up from their military security detachment. He gave a sigh; it had been a very long day, and he was looking forward to a cold drink and Trish's company. As on the North Slope, any use of alcohol on site was prohibited, so their cocktail hour now consisted of lemonade and cribbage. He moved toward the door.

"I better get my foremen and supervisors together and let them know about this. They're not going to be terribly happy, as it will slow the survey work ahead of the pipeline." He shrugged. "Guess that's why they pay us the big bucks."

Trish leaned up and kissed him. "I suppose I better get out our bug-out kits and make sure everything is in order."

"Probably not a bad idea." Level Three alert also meant that all personnel must be prepared to evacuate the camp with a one-hour notice. They could take forty pounds with them, no more. These were usually in the form of backpacks or duffels called bug-out kits—a day's rations, a change of clothes, important personal documents, and the like. "You do that. And while you're at it, you might want to consider dumping your hair dryer and adding a few more energy bars."

"Never happen," she replied, giving him a wink and a warm smile.

Wednesday night, January 1,
northern Arabian Sea

The C-130J designated as 275 Charlie had been painted a dun color, and the Joseph Simpson Jr. Foundation logo on the tail had been carefully sanded out. This aircraft was actually one of the foundation's MC-130J models, which meant it carried a suite of sophisticated electronic countermeasures equipment and had terrain-following navigational radars. It also had an in-flight refueling capability. The electronics alone doubled the price of the aircraft. Outwardly, there was little visual difference; it was something of a wolf in sheep's clothing. 275 Charlie crossed the Arabian Sea at cruise altitude on a course for Bahrain. Well before it made a landfall off the coast of Oman, shortly before midnight, it rendezvoused with a military KC-135 tanker and topped off. For all the crew of the 135 tanker knew, it was a special-operations bird on some sort of a training mission. After 275 Charlie broke away from the tanker, it headed for the Empty Quarter along the Omani-Saudi border. The aircraft then banked sharply to the north and dove for the deck, a terrifying ride down until they leveled out at two hundred feet. Several times during the flight, Garrett had gone forward and up to the flight deck to chat with the pilots and check on their progress. Now he was securely strapped into his seat. They cut the north coast of Oman midway between Muscat and Abu Dhabi. During the hundred or so miles over the Gulf

of Oman, 275 Charlie sniffed the coast of Iran for radar
emissions. Thanks to Jim Watson, the electronic order of
battle for that section of coast had been downloaded into
the plane's computers before they left Diego Garcia. 275
Charlie knew where it wanted to cross, but would use all
its capable sensors to look for any change in the coastal
radar coverage. They made a landfall between Jask and
Surak, continuing north for the Dasht Lut.

Just before crossing the coastline, the aircraft dropped
to an altitude of one hundred feet. The ride in back had
been relatively comfortable over the deserts of Oman and
the twenty-minute water crossing, but the mountains between the coast and the wastelands of the Dasht Lut made
for a very jerky ride. 275 Charlie did all the flying; no
pilot, even with the skill of those now at the controls and
with the updated avionics and heads-up displays of the J
model, could fly that much airplane that close to the
ground in this kind of terrain in the daytime, much less at
night. 275 Charlie's terrain-following radar and autopilot
did not care whether it was dark or not. To Garrett, Janos,
and the Gurkhas in the cargo bay, it felt like the aircraft
was all over the sky. The pilots up front had more perspective, since they could watch the oncoming ridges and
valleys with their night-vision optics and anticipate the
gyrations of the aircraft. Not so for those in back. Oddly
enough, it did not seem to bother the Gurkhas. The
wilder it became, the more they grinned, like children on
a carnival ride. Garrett had done this many times before,
but he did not particularly care for it. He almost lost it
when Janos threw up all over himself. It lasted for almost
an hour, then the aircraft steadied a bit over the broad
highlands of the central Iranian plateau. Garrett could feel
the transition when one of the pilots took the controls.

"Fifteen minutes from our primary insertion point,"
came the call from the cockpit over Garrett's headset. He

rogered back and signaled with ten fingers plus another five, and the Gurkhas all gave him a thumbs-up. The cargo bay was bathed in red light to protect their night vision. The troopers, strapped into the bulkhead seats, looked like two files of Martian insect larvae. Even in the red light, Janos was green. He sat there in his own filth, eyes closed, waiting for the ordeal to pass.

"Primary in five minutes."

"Roger, five minutes."

"Three minutes."

"Roger, three."

275 Charlie began to buck and yaw as the flaps and gear came down. They slowed to stall speed.

"Primary in sight . . . primary looks good; we're committed."

Garrett held one palm up and tapped it with his fist, indicating they would land on this pass. The Gurkhas checked and tightened their restraints. Seconds later 275 Charlie slammed down onto the dry lakebed, not unlike the Bonneville Salt Flats, but not nearly so smooth. The engines immediately reversed, and the big Hercules ground to a halt. The loadmaster lowered the ramp, and six Gurkhas, all with night-vision goggles, raced from the cargo bay and set up a loose perimeter around the aircraft. The others immediately began to unchain the vehicles. In less than five minutes the Russian jeeps were out onto the desert floor. One of them, with two Gurkhas aboard, raced around the aircraft and sped a half mile in front of it. This portion of the desert, or *kavir*, was mostly salt flat, but there were a few ravines. The reconnaissance made sure there were no obstacles. The Gurkhas in the jeep flashed an infrared beacon to signal the pilots that their takeoff path was clear.

"Two-Seven-Five ready to roll," came the pilot's voice over Garrett's intersquad radio. "You guys good to go?"

He looked to Bijay, who signaled that the men and vehicles were secure. Janos had been unceremoniously slung
into one of the jeeps and driven from the plane.

"Thanks for the lift, Two-Seven-Five. Have a safe trip
home."

"Roger and good luck to you. Two-Seven-Five clear."

The four Allison turbofans quickly spun up to full
power. Then, as the four six-bladed Dowty R391 pro-
pellers bit into the night air, the Hercules surged forward,
hurling a plume of dust and salt behind it. The big bird
gobbled up a thousand yards of dirt before it clawed its
way into the air and turned east for the Afghan border.
Less than ten minutes after the big 130 had touched
down, a dead silence again hung over the desert. For close
to thirty minutes the little force sat and listened. Then the
sound of engines cut the stillness, and the four-jeep convoy moved cautiously away from the insertion point.

They had landed on the edge of the Dasht Kavir or salt
desert, some fifty miles northwest of the oasis village of
Ferdows, a crossroads of sort between the Dasht Kavir
and the Dasht Lut. These deserts of the central Iranian
plateau are some of the harshest and most inhospitable
areas in the world. Much of them is still unexplored. Because of the chemical composition of the soil in this almost rainless area, the surface soils draw moisture from
the substrata and the atmosphere, giving certain areas the
composition of quicksand. Travel is extremely hazardous
and confined to the few roads across this treacherous
wilderness. The four jeeps kept an interval of thirty yards
between them, with stout nylon ropes binding the vehicles
together, like climbers working their way across a dangerous glacier. In the few hours of remaining darkness, they
managed to skirt Ferdows and gain the main road that
took them to the village of Juymand, some forty miles
northwest. Outside of Juymand, the jeeps lagered up,

pitched a ragged canvas shelter, and began to brew coffee. They were a mineral-exploration venture, and the soldiers were along to protect them from the bandits and drug traffickers. It made sense to hide in plain sight. One of the Gurkhas in tribal dress who spoke Farsi well went into the village to buy some tobacco. He casually let slip who they were and why they were in the area. As a measure of goodwill, he bought a small quantity of hashish. Later that morning, two Republican Guards from the Pasdaran and an official from the village came out for a visit. The Farsi speakers sat close to the fire while the others busied themselves elsewhere. One of them spoke French, and Garrett managed to convey that while they found ample deposits of chlorides, sulphates, and carbonates, the rugged terrain would make commercial exploitation difficult at best. He also allowed that he had never seen a more uninviting place, and that as soon as he was safely back in Tehran, he would be catching the first plane for Amsterdam. But first, they would rest here for the day before heading south into the Dasht Lut for more prospecting.

After the village delegation retired, the lead Gurkha radioman set up a small satellite antenna. Garrett quickly hooked up with Janet Brisco. The crew of 275 Charlie had reported them safely on the ground, and this was their first scheduled radio contact.

"Aloha, Home Plate," Garrett said, coming up on the encrypted link. "Desert Two, checking in."

"Cut the crap, First Base," Janet replied. All business, she was and not appreciative of his attempt at humor. The frequency-hopping and coding capabilities of their radio were such that they really didn't have to deal with call signs and prowords, but Janet Brisco and Garrett Walker had forty-five years of uniform time between them. Old habits die hard. "Your two bogies reached Deyhuk early this morning. As we expected, they are traveling only at night. We think they will stay there for the day and be back on the road this evening. That puts them about a hundred miles southwest of your posit. They may only try for Ferdows tonight, or they may push on to your location. Recommend that you move away from Juymand this afternoon and get into position. I don't want to take a chance on them getting past you."

Garrett was studying the map as he listened. West of Juymand there were no passable roads for the SUVs. To get to the Afghan border, their quarry would have to leave Juymand and travel either north or south before turning east for the border. They could not get past them, but it meant that Garrett would have to split his small force.

"Understood, Home Plate. We'll break camp just before sundown and set up on the north-south road. Keep us posted. I'll want to know what direction they take and when to expect them."

"We'll do our best, First Base. Let me know when your elements are in place and your grid coordinates."

"Will do, Home Plate. My regards to Steven and the federal agent. First Base, out."

"Good luck," Brisco replied. "Home Plate, out."

They sweltered under the awning, drank coffee, and swatted flies. One of the Gurkhas bought a goat, and they roasted it for most of the afternoon. The foul stench of singed hair and charred meat said that they were travelers who had made their peace with the desert. Just before sunset, they packed up and drove south away from Juymand. A trail of dust followed them into the Dasht Lut. After dark, Garrett, two of the jeeps, and six of the Gurkhas left the road, turning east. After they were well off the road, they began to work their way north, keeping well to the east of Juymand. Garrett knew exactly where he wanted to be, and with the help of his GPS, they arrived at that position just before midnight. He reported to

Janet Brisco that he was in position on the main road leading north from Juymand; Bijay checked in that he was in place on the road south. Now they would wait.

Thursday afternoon, January 2, Langley, Virginia

Armand Grummell had just had his morning briefing from Jim Watson. Janet Brisco kept Watson advised in general terms, a quid pro quo for the intelligence feed from Langley. He knew the IFOR element was safely on the ground and that the insertion aircraft had landed at Herat, refueled, and was on its way back to Diego Garcia. The two SUVs carrying the nuclear weapons had been seen leaving Deyhuk and heading northeast for Ferdows. They had left after dark, but IR satellite imagery confirmed that the two vehicles were on the move. If they kept to the main road and drove reasonably, they would be in Ferdows by midnight. They could stay there or continue on toward Juymand and beyond. From Juymand, there were two options; two small cities that could serve as staging areas for crossing into Afghanistan. Both Birjand and Torbat were under a hundred miles from the border, with access to numerous cross-border trade routes. These border areas were porous, with little or no monitoring by either government. There was some effort by the Pasdaran to interdict drugs coming in from Afghanistan, but they were no more successful than DEA agents along the southern border of the United States. Birjand, south of Juymand, was an ancient, multiethnic city of a hundred and thirty thousand. Torbat, to the north, was perhaps a third that size and half that of nearby Kashmar, but Torbat was known to be a haven for al Qaeda operatives and Arab expatriates who had served the Taliban. Birjand was a more direct route to the site of the pipeline crews, but Torbat enjoyed a robust flow of illegal border traffic, most of it heroin and most of it from the city of Herat. If Khalib and his bombs reached Juymand, they would go one way or the other. They would know soon enough; the orbiting satellites would tell them that. Armand Grummell had long ago learned not to fret about things over which he had no control. He had set this information aside for the moment to attend to a number of lesser but important issues that pertained to running the Central Intelligence Agency. The possible invasion of Iraq had all the intelligence agencies on a wartime footing. His intercom purred softly.

"Sir, Mrs. Johnstone is here to see you. Shall I say you're busy?"

Johnstone would not come directly to his office without first calling if she didn't have something urgent for him. He had asked her to come to him directly if her research surfaced something of importance.

"Send her right in," Grummell replied. It took him only a few seconds to clear his desk and his mind before rising to meet Elizabeth Johnstone. She slipped through the door carrying a large file.

"I'm sorry to bother you like this, sir, but I have some concerns about the location of those missing nuclear weapons."

Grummell held a chair for her, then returned to the swivel behind his desk. "Tell me about it."

She sat quietly for a moment, then cleared her throat. "I debated with myself about coming to you with this, because I have little hard evidence to support my suspicions. What I have here"—she indicated the file that she clutched as if it were a sick child—"is really only circumstantial data, a series of clues—satellite photos of a car, a big Mercedes, that showed itself too often in the areas near Khalabad and Baghin at odd times. We've just picked up some coded cell-phone activity that is typical of high-level Hezbollah activity. Then there have been some strange movements around MIS headquarters in Tehran. And, of course, the fire at that garage near Baghin. That kind of thing was out of character for Khalib. We have followed him for some time now. He is a man of the people; it's not like him to do something like that. It's just that . . ."

Suddenly she fell silent. Grummell rose quietly and walked around the desk. He eased himself into a chair next to her.

"It's just what?" he said gently. "Please, I want to hear it."

"It's just a feeling, really, that's all. But I've come to know Imad Mugniyah over the years. I think I understand something of how he thinks. It's not like him to give this job completely over to only one person, even someone as good as Khalib. Two bombs and one route to the target. That's not like Mugniyah. The cell-phone intercepts and the satellite imagery are not conclusive, but they support my suspicions. From the start, I've been uneasy with the idea that both weapons would take the wilderness route across Iran to Afghanistan. It never quite made sense to me. There is some logic that the two weapons were designated for the two pipeline crews, or even that both of them would be headed for a single crew. But I began to think about it—from the perspective of the Iranians. It would be a strange thing indeed if our old friend Yunisi at the MIS did not have a hand in this. There's bad blood between Iran and the Musharraf government, and we know Ali Yunisi is something of a fox." Yunisi was the head of the Iranian Ministry of Internal Security, and often operated without the knowledge of his government. "He would love nothing better than to cause a break between Pakistan and the United States, and to erode Pakistan's status as a nuclear power. A nuclear detonation in Afghanistan and perhaps a second one in Pakistan would do just that. With Pakistani nukes loose internally and externally, the International Atomic Energy Agency in Vienna would ask for full United Nations sanctions against Pakistan, and Congress would back such a measure. They would be branded a rogue, just like Saddam's Iraq. India could roll into Kashmir, and we will have little to say about it. My guess is that it would cause Pakistan to implode, and there would be a Taliban-like government to replace Musharraf. There's also the chance that we would no longer be able to restrain the nuclear forces of Pakistan and India. And Iran will sit on the sidelines and watch."

She sat back and demurely folded her arms. "At first it puzzled me that Yunisi did not extract one of the nuclear weapons as a tariff for allowing Khalib and Mugniyah to operate in Iran. But nuclear weapons can be a liability. They invite Western intervention."

Armand Grummell was thoughtfully polishing his glasses. "Secretly developing nuclear weapons and then presenting them to the world with a test explosion, as India and Pakistan did, is one thing. But to be involved in stealing one, well, that is something else altogether. It might invite a response such as the one we're contemplating in Iraq. Yunisi plays a little more thoughtful hand. Iran's involvement in this venture is completely deniable; they stop the pipeline and destabilize, perhaps even disarm, Pakistan." He was silent a moment before continuing. "So where do you think this other weapon may be headed?"

"My guess would be Karachi, or perhaps to the port that will serve as a terminus for the pipeline—possibly even along the supply route from Karachi that serves the construction crews. It's my understanding from our nuclear experts that the Pakistani uranium weapon represents the more rugged and stable of the two weapons that were taken. It is by far the most suitable for transport across a mountainous region toward the pipeline. The plutonium weapon is equally destructive if the detonation results in a nuclear explosion, but plutonium is a deadly contaminant. The amount of plutonium in that warhead, if atomized by conventional explosives in a nonnuclear event, would present an immense cleanup effort, not to mention the sickness and death of those exposed. In some ways, the nonnuclear effect of a plutonium weapon in an urban area could be more psychologically damaging than a nuclear blast." She shivered involuntarily. "This whole thing worries me deeply. I would like to be proven wrong, but my every instinct tells me that a second nuclear weapon is headed for southern Pakistan."

Grummell was silent for several moments. His job was to report specific intelligence to the executive branch of the government, and to other agencies and institutions as directed by the executive branch. It was not to make policy, nor was it to make executive decisions. But time was running out.

"Elizabeth, within the next few hours, we may just know if weapons are in central Iran headed for the Afghan border and how many. I want you to assume that there is a second weapon headed back into southern Pakistan. Find out where it is and where it may be going. And thank you for staying with this problem. You kept us from following a decoy once before, and it appears that you may be doing us that service again."

After he saw her to the door, Grummell walked quickly to his desk. For a moment, he thought about waiting for the IFOR team in Iran to report with a confirmation on the weapons. But only for a moment. He punched the intercom on his desk.

"Yes, sir?"

"Would you put through a call to the President on the secure line as soon as possible?"

"Right away, sir."

"Then I want to see the DDO, Jim Watson, the Near East Division Chief, and the senior Pakistan desk officer in my office immediately."

"Sir, I believe the DDO is over at the Pentagon at the moment."

"I see. Please, send word that I want him to drop what he is doing and return to Langley immediately."

Grummell knew that keeping his Deputy Director for Operations in the dark about IFOR had its risks, especially since his deputy, Jim Watson, knew everything. Well, so be it, Grummell said to himself. He had given his word, and that of the President, that the knowledge of IFOR would be restricted to those at the highest levels. He would honor that pledge. While he waited for his call to the President to go through, he sat deeply in thought. *What can we do to stop a rogue nuclear weapon that may be headed for southern Pakistan?*

Early Friday morning, January 3, central Iranian plain, north of Juymand

"You should be seeing them at any moment now."

"Understood, standby. . . . Okay, we got a thermal print . . . two of them, both very similar. Got to be them."

"Good luck, First Base. Call when it's done, break, Second Base, you copy this."

"I have a good copy, Home Plate." Even over the encrypted satellite link, Bijay Gurung's precise, measured speech was clearly discernible. "We are mounted and now moving to the First Base position. ETA about ninety minutes."

"Understand ninety minutes. Home Plate, clear."

Through the good offices of Jim Watson, one of the Predator drones being flown out of Qandahar on a routine surveillance of the completed pipeline had been handed off to Dodds LeMaster, who under the guise of a military special-operations ground unit controller, took the drone high over the Afghan border and about ninety miles into Iranian airspace. At night it had been an easy task to pick up two IR blooms on the road from Deyhuk to Ferdows. LeMaster was able to track the two vehicles through Ferdows to Juymand, and followed their progress when they turned north. The two Explorers had made good time, trying to get to Torbat before sunrise. That meant Garrett, or at least Garrett's Gurkhas, had drawn the lucky straw. With the terrorists headed their way, they would be most likely to whet the appetite of their *khukuris*.

Garrett put aside the thermal imaging device and slipped on his night-vision goggles. Then he took up his rifle and watched the two vehicles as they approached. He and his six Gurkhas waited for them on the far side of a shallow dry wash. The gravel road dipped into the wash from a flat plain and crawled back up a ten-percent grade to the flat. The Gurkhas were deployed in a shallow "V" ambush formation on either side of the road. There was little cover for them, save for the rise as the road rose out of the wash. There were three claymore mines tied to rocks and well camouflaged along the side of the road. Duhan was in charge of the demolition element. From his position on the top of the rise, he knew that when he saw the top of the first Explorer, it was just past the center of the kill zone. He waited a second to allow for the trailing vehicle to come into range.

"Ho!" he called loudly and squeezed the clacker that electrically fired the claymores.

At Duhan's call, Garrett and the other Gurkhas hugged sand and covered their eyes and ears. The explosion was deafening. Over two thousand steel, ball-bearing-like pellets shredded the two Explorers. A few of the men in the

Explorers may have known what hit them, but the others had no idea. About half of them were killed outright or mortally wounded by the claymores. The first vehicle slumped on four flat tires in a cloud of steam as the water from the vented radiator sprayed onto the hot engine. The Gurkhas were on their feet immediately, three men in each leg of the "V." They swept down either shoulder of the road, firing rhythmically into the passenger compartment of the lead vehicle. Garrett advanced with them at the apex of the shallow "V." Two Gurkhas stayed with the lead vehicle while Garrett and the other four advanced on the second vehicle.

The trailing Ford Explorer had not been damaged so severely as the first. The man in the front passenger seat was killed instantly and the driver mortally wounded. But their bodies shielded Khalib and Moshe Abramin, seated in the rear. The SUV stalled and rolled slowly back down the hill on two flat tires, then slewed off the shoulder of the road and tipped onto the passenger side. The four Gurkhas continued their assault, firing steadily, pausing only to change out the empty magazines in their M-4 rifles. They approached the Explorer from the underside and cautiously rounded the vehicle. Two of them closed on the battered passenger compartment while two of them swung wide so as to avoid being in a crossfire. The wounded driver managed to get his hand to his pistol and started firing wildly. The muzzle flashes were like large firecrackers in the night-vision goggles of the Gurkhas. The one closest to the driver went down, but the other sent a half dozen rounds into the now inert form at the wheel.

"Cease fire, cease fire," Garrett called in Gurkhali and leaped up on the side of the wounded vehicle. He kicked in the rear-door window, weapon ready to fire down into the rear passenger compartment. The man on the downside of the rear seat struggled, trying to pull a pistol from his belt, but the lifeless form of his companion now on top of him restricted his movements. Garrett instantly recognized Khalib. He pulled open the door and dropped onto the two men. Khalib had finally managed to shoulder the inert Moshe aside enough to get his hand to the butt of his pistol when a heavy boot pinned his forearm to the door of the car. His eyes followed the boot, up the man's leg and torso, then to his face. He was an American.

"I know you do not fear death, my friend," the man said in halting Arabic, "but it does not have to be now and in this way." Khalib had a good command of Arabic. His eyes narrowed, then he managed to spit on the man's boot before he fainted from his wounds.

They worked fast, as it would be dawn in a few hours.

"Okay, got him; go on to the next one." Janet Brisco glanced at a name and biographical readout on the adjacent monitor. "Christ, it's beginning to look like who's-who in the al Qaeda Mafia. That's good, hold that one a second. . . . Okay, next one."

One of the Gurkhas was moving from dead man to dead man with a digital camera while another held or turned his head so the camera could frame it. A thin transmission cord connected the camera to the radio on the Gurkha's back. The radio made a line-of-site connection to a satellite communications set in one of the jeeps. A datalink transmission to the GSI vans on Diego Garcia was almost instantaneous. Occasionally one of the Gurkhas would wipe the features with a rag so they would be more recognizable, but it wasn't necessary. The Viiasage face-recognition software could read and calibrate more than a 180 facial-recognition features in a nanosecond. Only one of the slain al Qaeda members was not in the database and not instantly identifiable.

"Hold it there," the cameraman heard on his earpiece and froze. "Great. That accounts for one of our nuclear scientists. Abramin will not be stealing any more nuclear weapons. All right, next one." The Gurkha cameraman stepped over to a man who had been laid out on a poncho liner with his head slightly elevated. He focused on the harsh, lined face. Janet Brisco almost jumped back when the eyes fluttered open.

"Well, well," she said to the cameraman, as well as to Steven Fagan and Dodds LeMaster, who hovered over her shoulder inside the comm van. "Looks like we have Khalib Beniid with a little life in him. You with us, First Base?"

"Right here, Home Plate," Garrett replied.

"Don't suppose he's been of any help to us."

"None at all. I know the type; he'll die without saying a word." Garrett stepped away from where Khalib lay. He would die soon anyway if he didn't get medical treatment; it might too late already. One of the Gurkhas gave him an injection that would relieve some of his suffering, but it also included a drug that would both stimulate and confuse him. "Second Base is twenty minutes away. Recommend we extract and have the second element do a follow-up operation. It might work and it might not. It shouldn't take more than a half hour in any case. Do we have the time?"

Janet looked up at Steven. He nodded. "Go ahead. Got a confirmation on the weapons yet?"

"Standby," Garrett replied and walked over to where Janos was carefully examining the two cases removed from one of the wrecked Explorers. He wore a miner's light bungeed to his forehead and carefully unpacked the encased nuclear materials. He moved deliberately, sniffing at the cases with a probe that registered low-level gamma emissions. Garrett had the detection equipment provided them by Jim Watson in one of their jeeps, but Janos preferred his own gear.

"I hate to rush a guy who's handling atomic bombs," Garrett said softly, "but we can't stay here much longer."

"About got it," Janos replied without looking up. "I'm ninety-nine percent sure, but let me get through this next seal . . . okay, got it." He sighed and slumped back onto his heels. "It's an HEU weapon, and it's still in pieces. It's completely harmless, so we can take it with us."

"You sure?"

Janos finally turned from the cases in front of him and peered at Garrett over half-moon reading glasses. "I was pretty sure it wasn't a plutonium weapon, but sometimes they're shielded in such a way as to fool you. But now I'm sure. It's a uranium weapon, and there is only one. It's not assembled, so there is no chance of detonation."

Garrett exhaled sharply. "You're positive there's only one?"

Janos nodded. "Me and the boys searched the vehicles thoroughly; this is it. I'll have it packed up and ready for travel in about five minutes." He pointed to a metal suitcase. "The timing device and explosive materials are in there. Bring that too?"

"Bring it all, and hurry." He stepped away from Janos and keyed his radio. "Home Plate, this is First Base. We have only one egg, confirmed; repeat one egg of the HEU variety, over."

There was a moment before Janet's voice came over his earpiece. "Understand one HEU egg. Your chariot will be to your posit in about seven mikes. You can pick him up on channel four."

"Roger channel four; thanks, Home Plate. First Base, out."

Garrett adjusted his radio to the proper frequency. "Boomer Lead, this is First Base, Over. How copy, over?"

"Lima Charlie, First Base. We're about ten clicks away from you and closing. We have a green deck?" Six miles out, two MH-60 Pavehawks hugged the floor of the Dasht Lut, heading for the ambush site.

"Wait one, Boomer."

Garrett quickly checked that the Gurkhas had completed their tasks and were ready to leave. Janos indicated he was finished. Duhan was with the Gurkha who had been wounded in the one-sided skirmish. He still had a 9mm round in his thigh, but could hobble with some assistance.

"Okay, Boomer, I want you to send in your trail bird to pick us up. Guide on my IR beacon. Repeat, trail bird only, over."

"Understand, one bird. You copy Boomer Trail?"

The second helo pilot's voice came on the net. "Boomer Trail, good copy. I'll be there in three mikes . . . I have your beacon. Standby, Trail out."

Just over the horizon, the lead Pavehawk peeled itself from the desert floor and banked away. The trail helo continued on at a hundred knots and fifty feet. The flight from Herat, some two hundred miles to the west, had taken them just under two hours. The lead MH-60 throttled back to ninety knots and began to trace a comfortable orbit over the sand. The second helo homed in on the flashing infrared blip. Both pilots wore night-vision goggles, one flying and the other searching the barren desert for any signs of trouble. The Pavehawk rocked back on its tail, bleeding away airspeed. When it had almost stopped, it pitched forward to a level hover and settled onto the desert floor. It sat there turning while a file of dusty figures made their way to the turning chopper. All carried a heavy pack, and one of them helped another who half ran, half hopped to the helo door. Suddenly the two Ford Explorers burst into flame. The corpses of the former occupants could be seen in the glare of the fire, scattered across the dry wash. Garrett walked over to where Khalib now lay, his head cushioned by a drop pad. He was a safe distance away from the burning vehicles. Awake now,

Khalib coldly regarded Garrett. There was no fear in his eyes, only pure hated.

"Pig!" Garrett said in Arabic. He then spat in Khalib's face and gave the wounded man a vicious kick in the ribs. Garrett turned on his heel and walked to the waiting helicopter. The pain almost took Khalib—almost, but the intense hatred for this tall, arrogant American kept him from passing out. Khalib glared after Garrett and watched as the helo dissolved in a cloud of dust and noise. They were gone, and he was finally alone, and the desert was quiet.

7

Amir Sahabi had been sitting in the comfortable anteroom for close to an hour. It was humiliating, to say the least, but he had no choice. He had come to the capital the night before so he could be first on his calendar and had arrived immediately after morning prayers. He had done what he could to quiet the fears of the extended royal family about this gamble, but they had grown increasingly anxious over the past few weeks. Although there was no direct connection, nor would there be, he felt sure the anxiety reached all the way to the crown prince. Now he had been summoned to one of the lesser palaces and made to wait. Sahabi glanced at his Rolex President—it had been more than an hour. Patience, he told himself. *You are dealing with rich, arrogant and not terribly smart people. And they are becoming nervous, which is sure to make them more difficult.*

"His Excellency will see you now."

Sahabi was escorted into a chamber that was used for audiences like this. It was certainly not one for receiving important guests, but above the tradesmen level.

"Amir, my friend, welcome. I am sorry to have kept you waiting, but the affairs of state sometimes dictate my schedule. My time is often not my own, I'm sorry to say. Please, sit. May I offer you tea?"

Prince Abdul Majid was a second cousin twice removed from the Crown Prince. If he were to have an official title, it would be akin to a special assistant to the National Security Adviser in the United States. It meant that the Crown Prince would have incomplete knowledge of the efforts to stop the American pipeline, but would have, at some point, endorsed the project. The Crown Prince, Sahabi reflected, was not as stupid as those who surrounded him. If things got out of hand, he would deny knowledge of the whole affair, not unlike President Reagan in the Iran-Contra affair. But the Crown Prince was informed to some degree, and he was worried, perhaps even agitated, or Sahabi would not have been cooling his heels in Majid's chambers.

"Thank you, Excellency, but I think not. You are looking well, Excellency. How is your health, and how are your sons?" They went through the exchange of pleasantries that protocol demanded before Majid came to the point.

"We have some concerns about the project you brought to us some months ago. We agreed in principle that the American pipeline is not in our interest and should somehow be discouraged. Since that time we have provided you with funds to see that the project does not succeed. But it goes forward, and the Americans seem to be making rapid progress. There are those in my government who wonder why we have provided these funds when we have seen no results. And, I might add, there are those who have expressed concern that our interest in seeing this project fail might be viewed by the Americans in a negative light. Due to their sizable military presence here, they are after all, guests in our kingdom."

What Majid said confirmed in Sahabi's mind that the royal family still wanted the TAP sabotaged, but they wanted no attribution. And the American military guests were something of a hot potato as the United States con-

templated military action in Iraq. The House of Saud was
very fragile, and the Saudi people did not hold their
monarchy in high regard. Yet here the royals were, asking
for some assurance that they were getting something for
their hundred-million-dollar investment. The royal family
was not without its sources. Had they somehow learned of
the missing Pakistani nuclear weapons? Had they made
the connection? And how much did the House of Saud
really want to know? Sahabi smiled to himself, but his features revealed nothing. If he could somehow confirm to
Majid, without saying as much, that nuclear weapons in
fact were in play, it would put an end to these summonses
to Riyadh and these little games. Yet there was no denying
that his role in this scheme was a very dangerous business.

"Excellency, we agreed I was to see if there was a way in
which the Americans could be encouraged to abandon
their efforts to bring Caspian oil to a port on the Arabian
Sea. I was given to understand that you wanted them to
permanently abandon this undertaking." He paused inten-
tionally, wanting Majid not to miss his meaning. "The
Americans have a very capable *conventional* military presence in Afghanistan, especially along the corridor of the
pipeline. So I retained a consultant who has developed a
plan that will stop the construction of the pipeline, and
deter further American interest in Central Asia. It is a bold
plan, but one that has the promise of humbling even the
military might of the United States. The position of the
House of Saud, which we both serve, is threatened by this
project. Bold measures are necessary, perhaps even measures that only a few years ago would have been, shall we say,
unthinkable. You have entrusted the solution to this problem to me. I can assure you that steps are being taken, dramatic steps if you will, to achieve our objectives."

While he was speaking, Sahabi carefully watched his
host. Majid stiffened noticeably and swallowed hard, as if

what he was hearing confirmed some preconception he held.

"If Your Excellency would like, I can expand on the measures that were taken." Sahabi did not have to add, "measures taken on behalf of the royal family." Majid demurred; he was not that stupid.

"That will not be necessary. But tell me, Amir, are these plans well under way?"

"Yes, Excellency."

"In such a way that this undertaking could not be recalled if it became desirable to do so?"

"That is correct, Excellency."

Majid rose to signal that the interview was over. They again exchanged routine pleasantries before Sahabi was shown from the room. Moments later he was in his chauffeured Rolls and headed back to Al Kharj. He kept an apartment and a mistress here in the capital. She was charming in the most exotic ways, and he was tempted to return to the apartment. Yet he felt the need to put distance between himself and Riyadh. He reflected on the meeting, how it might have gone differently had he so chosen. They knew, he was sure, that the nuclear weapons taken from Kahuta were involved, and now they knew that what had been set in motion could not be recalled. The Saudis, at least many of them, might be stupid, but they were also cunning. And they were past masters at playing off the fundamentalists in Saudi Arabia against the oil-hungry West. Majid had dismissed him with a strained cordiality. He had not said, "Keep us informed." They would, he knew, now be earnestly planning how they would proclaim their innocence if the plan succeeded or their ignorance if it failed. Sahabi smiled. It was not unexpected. The game they played was no less dangerous than his own. He settled back into the comfort of the Rolls as it whispered along the highway between Riyadh and Al Kharj.

Friday morning, January 3,
the central Iranian plain, north of Juymand

Bijay halted his two-vehicle convoy several hundred yards
from the two burning pyres that were visible just over the
next dry wash. Those would be the SUVs they had tracked
across central Iran. Moments earlier, they had felt the con-
cussion waves from two explosions. Those explosions would
be from the destruction of Garrett's two jeeps, parked well
away from the ambush site. They could later be identified
with some difficulty, but the shattered hulks of two Russian
vehicles, a few hundred yards from two burned-out Ford Explorers, would cause more curiosity than concern. There
was money in the opium trade, and those who engaged in it
were violent and territorial men, even those who lived
within the borders of the Islamic Republic of Iran. This
would not be an unusual scene to come upon.

Bijay and two others crept forward to observe the over-
turned, burning Explorer. They could see the bodies of
the dead strewn across the sand. Then he saw what he was
looking for—a single form, separate from the others, lying
on his side next to an outcrop of boulders. Bijay led two
of his men forward. All three were dressed in tattered
mountain-fighter garb, and their faces were unwashed
and caked with salt. Bijay approached Khalib cautiously,
his AK-47 held at the ready. Khalib's eyes fluttered open,
and he took in the three men. Two of them kept to the
shadows, but the taller one approached and squatted beside him.

"May God be with you, my brother," he said in broken
Arabic. "We heard explosions and gunfire, and saw the
fires from our camp. What manner of men would do this
to you?"

"Who are you?" Khalib managed. "Where do you come
from?"

"Does it matter?" Bijay replied, bringing a goatskin with water to Khalib's lips. "We travel in the service of God. We trust in Him and"—he patted the Kalashnikov—"in our rifles."

Bijay sat back on his heels and stared at Khalib, saying nothing. Khalib stared back. He was confused and suspicious, and in pain—nothing like before, but he was hurting. There were many in al Qaeda like this man, Khalib thought, Arabs who came to fight and to support the Taliban. Many of them had been chased from Afghanistan. They took sanctuary in Iran after the Americans took Kabul and now roamed the border areas of Afghanistan, Pakistan, and Iran. Some had returned to Saudi Arabia or Georgia or to Egypt, but not many. They were unwanted in their homelands, and most were stateless persons. Under the protection of the Taliban, they had been able to take what they wanted. Now they lived a seminomadic bandit life, giving their allegiance and their gun to some clan chief who treated them little better than guard dogs. As Khalib studied the man who squatted beside him, he saw the man's eyes suddenly widen.

"I know you, my brother. You are Khalib. I saw you in Kabul before the Taliban fled. You are a mighty clansman, a fighter of great reputation. How is it that you are here? What can we do to help you?"

"How . . . How many of you are there?"

"Perhaps a dozen. Our camp is several kilometers to the north. We are in the service of an Iranian dog in Kashmar. We help him to bring opium across the border."

"I must get word to someone," Khalib gasped, "and I must ask you to do this for me. It is most important. Will you help me, brother?"

"As God is my witness, I will do what you ask." Bijay was only mildly distressed at making such a promise to a dying man. As a Buddhist, there was room for many gods

in his continuum, so he at least had the comfort in knowing that he was offending only one of them.

"My belt, take my belt," Khalib rasped.

Bijay did as he was instructed. He easily found the
long, flapped compartment on the inside that held Iranian rials and Pakistani rupees.

"There is a paper," Khalib continued in a weak voice,
"and a number written on it."

Bijay unfolded the small, tightly folded note. A twelve-
digit international phone number was scribbled in pencil.
"I have it, my brother. It is a number. What would you
have me do?"

There was no cell-phone coverage in the Dasht Lut, even
if his cell phone survived the attack. Khalib knew this man
was his only hope to get word to the others. There would be
some consolation, some victory, in their knowing he had
failed. If the others were warned, perhaps they would not
fail with the second bomb. He was very tired now, and the
pain was becoming easier. Having lived the life of a mountain fighter, he had seen many men die. Now it was to be his
turn. *Will Allah reward me for the infidels I have slain? I will
soon find out.* He closed his eyes, and a vision of the American standing over him came into focus, the one who spat
on him and called him a pig. The image, seared into his
consciousness, gave him strength, and he willed himself to
hold on. He turned his head to see the man with the firm,
kind face still squatting nearby. The goatskin was once
again to his mouth, wetting his lips.

"You must call that number. Say . . . say exactly this.
'The hammer of God is not in place. The Americans have
taken the hammer of God. All is in your hands.' Do you
understand?"

"Yes, I understand. The hammer of God is not in place.
The Americans have taken the hammer of God. All is in
your hands."

"God be with you, brother. . . . God . . . be . . . with . . . you."

Bijay had to bend close to hear the last of his words. He said a short prayer for his soul, then felt for his pulse. It was weak but firm; he was a strong man. When the drug wore off, he would probably regain consciousness, and then he would be in a great deal of pain—until the end. Bijay pulled a pistol from under his robe, placed the muzzle under Khalib's ear, and fired. He replaced the weapon. In another short prayer, he asked Lord Buddha to look after this man in his next life—that Khalib's courage and strong spirit be made more polished and more pure than in his last. The other two Gurkhas had watched impassively from the shadows. Now they moved forward.

"Help me get him to the fire."

They took the corpse to the still burning Explorer and tossed him on the hulk. There was not enough flame left to consume Khalib's remains, but they would be charred beyond recognition. With a last look at the area, Bijay led the other two at a brisk trot back to the jeeps. Dawn was not far off, and they had to hurry.

"This is Second Base. We are on the way to your position," Bijay said into the transceiver. He was looking at the display of his handheld GPS. "We should be there in fifteen minutes."

"Understand fifteen minutes, Second Base." Garrett replied. "How did it go with our friend?"

"He was a very brave man, but in his confusion, he gave us a contact that may prove useful. Do you have a beacon in place?"

"There is a beacon on your bird. You should have it by now."

Bijay did what he could in the bouncing jeep to steady the IR binoculars. "I have you in sight. We will be there soon. Second Base, clear." In the cool, dry air, an infrared beacon could be seen a long way off. The two UAZ jeeps bounded across the desert hardpan toward the flashing light.

"Understood, Second Base. We will be standing by and turning. First Base, Out."

Bijay's two jeeps pulled to a stop not fifty yards from the two helos. The two MH-60s sat whining on the packed sand, rotor blades at a comfortable idle. Bijay led his men from the jeeps onto the helo with the active beacon. Then both birds began to spool up. First one, then the other lifted, hesitated, and began to accelerate low across the desert. In sequence, they banked to the east and headed for the Afghan border. A short time later, the silence of the Dasht Lut was again shattered as the explosive charges in the remaining two jeeps turned them into yet two more smoking hulks on the central Iranian plateau.

Late Thursday evening, January 2, the White House

"Thank you for the update, Armand. I can't say that I'm not disappointed, but you and your people are doing some terrific work. Please keep me informed."

President William St. Claire recradled the receiver to the private, secure phone that linked his office to Langley and his DCI. He checked his watch. It was almost midnight—midmorning the next day in Afghanistan. He was weary; they all were weary. Then he rose and began to pace the Oval Office, pausing occasionally to thrust his hands into his trouser pockets and stare out at the Rose Garden, bathed in security lighting. After two laps he halted abruptly behind his desk and leaned across it, arms stiff, head down.

"I'm open to suggestions, gentlemen, so feel free to speak up." James Powers and Tony Barbata had watched their President roam the office. "Here's how things stand," St. Claire continued. "We now *think* there is a nuclear weapon in the hands of the most notorious terrorist on the planet. As far as we can tell, he has taken this second bomb into a city that has a population of close to twelve million souls, but we're not sure. We also have reason to believe that his target is most probably"—he turned to retrieve a slip of paper from his blotter—"six hundred and thirty American civilians working on the southern site of the TAP. Plus, at any given time, there are as many as three hundred military personnel. That's a thousand Americans plus an assortment of foreign nationals and several hundred native workers." The President again began to pace. "Or he may take his bomb and go elsewhere. For all we really know, our most notorious terrorist on the planet is headed for Tel Aviv or Haifa or even New York." St. Claire slowly began to shake his head. "Hell, I don't know. Maybe I should have taken the chance and put a Tomahawk on them when they were holed up in Iran."

Barabata cleared his throat. "I don't think he'll get out of Karachi by sea. We have a naval task group in the northern Arabian Sea. We can commence MIO and LIO operations on your authorization."

The U.S. Navy had been engaged in MIO, or material interdiction operations, since the Gulf War, inspecting cargos at sea for contraband entering or leaving Iraq. Since the Taliban and their al Qaeda backers had largely been chased from Afghanistan, the Navy began LIO, leadership interdiction operations. Ships were routinely stopped on the high seas and searched by Marines or boarded clandestinely at night by Navy SEALs. The goal was to deny the al Qaeda leadership the ability to leave the area by sea. What the Secretary of Defense was proposing was that all oceangoing vessels leaving Karachi be searched. It was no small task; some fifteen hundred containers entered or left the port of Karachi each day. And it would put naval personnel at risk; this terrorist had a nuclear weapon.

"Do it," the President said. "Jim, what about the Paks—how much do we tell them?"

James Powers thought a moment before he replied. "At this juncture, I recommend we tell them everything. Karachi is by far the most populous city in Pakistan. The ISI is a very capable, if sometimes brutal, security service. If they can concentrate their efforts in Karachi and southern Pakistan, they may just be able to find him. But I wouldn't count on it; this guy Mugniyah is one elusive fellow. There's nothing more we can do. After all, it's not our bomb. What does Armand think?"

The President slumped into his chair and sighed. "He thinks there are three possibilities. One, of course, is Karachi. But to set off a nuclear weapon there would cause massive Muslim casualties. He thinks Mugniyah is probably too smart to do that. It would do him no good, and perhaps hurt his cause and that of Hezbollah. He feels that Mugniyah could also try to get the weapon to Pasni, on the coast. Pasni is to be the deepwater terminal for the TAP. Currently, the population of the town is about thirty thousand, but there is a large Pakistani military base there. And it was one of the bases where we staged aircraft and Marines for the initial operations into Afghanistan. It is a viable target, and if that is his intention, he's probably already there. Pasni is only a hundred and twenty-five miles from the Iranian border. But neither our satellites nor our surveillance aircraft have been able to find the car in which we think he is traveling." Bill St. Claire rose and again began to pace. "And there is always the TAP. We know the first weapon was headed there; why not the second? Based on our last overhead sighting, Mugniyah was headed for Karachi. The terrorists have learned that they now have to hide in cities. From Karachi, where there are undoubtedly secret al Qaeda cells, he can do any of the three things Armand suggested. Or try to get the weapon out and make Hezbollah nuclear-capable. We just don't know, yet we have to plan for every contingency. But to answer your question, Armand doesn't know—nobody knows."

Friday morning, January 3,
central Afghanistan

Lieutenant Colonel Tom Carswell was inspecting one of his patrols some fifteen miles east of Site South. He had been warned to increase his surveillance activity toward the south and west of the site. They were already on alert, and his men were working twelve on, twelve off as they shepherded the progress of the pipeline crews across the Afghan plain. Here in the Dasht Margow there were few inhabitants, but those few they did encounter had to be searched for weapons and warned away from the construction areas. There was a ten-mile exclusion zone along the pipeline corridor, but Afghans were not known for accepting restrictions on their movements from foreigners or a central government. The area was clearly marked, but they often found breaks in the six-foot chain-link fencing, and occasionally body parts from the detonation of a land mine. On those rare occasions, Carswell would observe the carnage and wonder about these Afghan hill people. If anyone should understand land mines, it was these people, and the minefields that guarded the pipeline were clearly marked. They were, he concluded, ignorant, illiterate, independent, defiant, or more probably, all of the above.

"Hey, Colonel," his driver called from his Humvee, "they want you on the radio."

Carswell was talking to the sergeant in charge of the patrol. Like Carswell, he was wearing desert-pattern battle dress, Kevlar helmet, goggles, and body armor. "Tell them I'll call 'em back," he shouted and turned back to his sergeant.

"No can do, sir. They say it's urgent, and they have to speak with you now."

Carswell returned to the Humvee and snatched the handset from his driver. "Carswell here. . . . Oh, yes, sir. . . . Understood, sir." He looked at his wristwatch. "It'll take us about thirty minutes to get back. We should be there by ten-hundred. . . . Right away, sir. We're leaving now." He returned the handset. "Saddle up, Corporal; we're headed back to the site." Then turning to his patrol leader, "Sergeant, we're now at Level Two alert. That means deadly force is authorized if you come across anything that you even remotely consider a threat. And I want you to double the frequency of your comm checks."

"Yes, sir," the sergeant replied and returned Carswell's salute.

Tom Carswell found Dave Wilson arguing with one of his foremen. They were across from each other over a section of plywood and two sawhorses. A roll of blueprints was held in place by rocks, and the debate concerned how many recent pipe welds had or had not been x-rayed.

"Aw, for Christ's sake, Dave, my guys have already done that! How many goddamn times do I have to tell you that?"

"Frank, you know the procedure, I know the procedure, and those welders sure as hell know the procedure. If it isn't logged in at the time of the inspection, it didn't happen. You weld it, you inspect it, and you x-ray it. And you record it—right then, not a few days later. It's in the contract. I know it'll cost you a few hours to x-ray them again, but that's the way it is."

"A few hours! Hell, more like the better part of a day."

"Excuse me," Carswell said. Wilson and the foreman had been glaring across the makeshift table so intently that Carswell's approach had gone unnoticed. "I hate to interrupt his conjugal visit, but we've got some bigger fish to fry. I just got the word that we're under a Level Two alert."

The weld X-rays were forgotten. "Jesus, Colonel. Do you know what this means?" exclaimed Wilson.

"All too well, Dave, but there's no way around it. The sooner you get your people mobilized, the sooner I can make my report."

Dave Wilson stood silent for a moment, hands on his hips, gazing skyward. A Level Two meant that all work stopped and that all construction personnel had to be ready to evacuate the site with ten minutes' notice. Wilson was wearing Levi's, a soiled T-shirt, and a white plastic hard hat. Only the black lettering on the front of the helmet, identifying him as "The Man," distinguished him from hundreds of other workers on Site South.

"Well, for crying out loud. Okay, Frank, get back to your crew and pass the word. Report to me at my trailer when you're ready." Frank snatched up the blueprints and strode off, mumbling a string of obscenities. "Where are you going to be, Tom?"

"Who knows," Carswell replied. "I'll be rounding up transport—probably best to get me on my radio. Sorry about this, Dave, but I agree with the higher-ups on this. Better to be safe than sorry."

"I know, Tom. Any idea what this is all about?"

"They haven't told me," Carswell replied. "Probably a piece of hard intelligence that says we are targeted. When I know, you'll know." He swung himself back into the

Humvee. "We'll talk soon. Let me know when the camp is ready to move."

Dave Wilson headed off in search of his various crew foremen. They worked in shifts, twenty-four hours a day, so many of them would be sleeping. Rather than get on the radio and put out a general alert, he wanted to talk personally with each one. It would take a few minutes longer initially, but it would save time in the long run. Men tended to grouse a little less if they were told in person. Strange thing, Wilson mused; the longer the project took, the more money he and others on the TAP crews would make. Yet anything that delayed the project angered them all. He grinned to himself; guess that's why I unretired and came back to work, he thought. It's all about getting the job done.

Dave had not enjoyed telling his foremen to drop what they were doing and get their people ready to leave. He dreaded telling Trish even more. But when he got back to the trailer, she was dressed in traveling attire, and their two bug-out kits were resting by the door.

"We may as well try to eat some of this," she said, peering into the small fridge, not bothering to look up. "It'll go to waste when they shut the power down. How about some tuna on rye?"

Late Friday morning, January 3,
Herat, Afghanistan

The airport at Herat still bore scars from the U.S. and British fighter-bomber attacks delivered the night of October 7, less than a month after 9/11 and just prior to the Northern Alliance push south. Since then, the control tower, eight-thousand-foot runway, and fuel depot had been rebuilt and made serviceable. Ariana Afghan Airlines, the national carrier, which boasted two Boeing

727s, maintained a single-flight scheduled service to Kabul on Mondays, Wednesdays, and Fridays. For the most part, the airport handled military traffic and non-scheduled flights from Karachi and Lahore. Over the last six months, traffic in and out of Herat had almost doubled as a result of support for Site North of the TAP. The two MH-60 helicopters that landed just after sunrise were not infrequent visitors to Herat, as was the nonmilitary C-130 that had landed the previous evening from Diego Garcia. This was the same MC-130 that took Garrett and company into the Dasht Lut, but now it was in civilian dress. All three aircraft now bore the markings and logo of the Joseph Simpson Jr. Foundation. The foundation had been active in delivering food and medical supplies to central and western Afghanistan. The flight crews seldom remained overnight, but they paid a premium for refueling services so were treated with respect by airport personnel. The MH-60s, like the MC-130, did their best to look like conventional civilian versions of the aircraft, but occasionally a curious military pilot would wander by and appraise the aircraft with a critical eye.

The Gurkhas left their rucksacks and weapons on the helos and got off the aircraft in twos and threes and made their way to the C-130. They were parked near one of the deserted general aviation buildings well away from the small terminal, and left to themselves. Inside the 130 was everything needed in the way of food, ammunition, and clothing to resupply the men coming out of the field. The sun was well up, but an auxiliary power unit kept the inside of the aircraft cool. There were also another half dozen Gurkhas, ready for duty as needed. On the flight deck, just behind the pilots' seats, where the flight engineer and navigator were stationed, Steven Fagan rose to greet Garrett Walker and Bijay Gurung. After a few polite words, Bijay excused himself to attend to his men. Garrett and Steven seated themselves in the comfortable flight-crew captain's chairs. The two pilots sat forward at the controls, talking quietly and allowing what privacy they could to the men behind them.

"Hot coffee?" Garrett nodded, and Steven poured him some from a carafe and freshened his own. "So tell me about it, and tell me again about the phone number that Bijay got from Khalib."

Garrett gave him a quick narrative of their insertion, their trek across the Dasht Lut, the engagement, and the successful extraction. "I thought for certain we'd find both weapons there, but we searched the two vehicles thoroughly. There was only one. Any ideas about where the other one is?"

"We think it may be in Karachi or somewhere nearby. There's a possibility that Mugniyah wanted one for his own purposes. The thought of him in possession of a nuclear weapon has them tied up in knots in Washington. The Pakistani security services and military forces are on full alert in and around Karachi. They will be out looking for Mugniyah, but they will be doing it quietly. The U.S. Navy will be checking any ship coming out of Karachi, but there are a lot of ways to move contraband in and out of Pakistan. Our best bet is that phone number Khalib gave to Bijay. I passed it along to Janet and Dodds. They're working up a plan of action. We should be hearing from them in the next few minutes. How's our wounded Gurkha?"

"He'll be okay. It was Padam, and he has a 9mm round that embedded in his thigh. One of the other Gurkhas cut it out during the helo flight here, if you can imagine that. He's sleeping it off now with a heavy dose of morphine and antibiotics. He told Bijay to wake him if there was another operation—said that he'd be ready for duty if needed."

"I have a GSI Gulfstream on the tarmac in Islamabad for contingencies. Want him medevaced?"

Garrett thought about it for a moment. The man's life was certainly not in danger; he knew enough about combat casualty care to know that. But it would send a message to the other Gurkhas that no expense would be spared when one of them got hurt.

"Not a bad idea. How long will it take?"

Steven took up a handset from the console and dialed a number. "We have a dedicated satellite channel for secure comm. . . . Yes, hello, Pinch Hitter, this is Base Runner. We need you at our location as soon as you can get here . . . within the hour as soon as you have takeoff clearance. Get back to me with an ETA when you're airborne and advise Home Plate. . . . Understood, Base Runner, out." Steven looked at Garrett and grinned, "Helluva way to fight a war, huh?"

A few moments later, the console speaker crackled, and Janet Brisco's voice came over clearly, as if she were in the next room.

"Base Runner, this is Home Plate. You there, Steven?"

"I hear you fine, Janet. I have Garrett here with me, and you're on the speaker phone. What do you have for us?" They were working with a secure, dedicated satellite link so with conscious effort, she abandoned the military-speak.

"Well, we may have a one-time shot at this guy. Dodds is right here; I'll let him tell you about his plan. Go ahead, Dodds."

"G'day, gentlemen. How's the weather where you are?"

"Hot and dry, but the air conditioning is working, thank God," Steven replied. "What do we do next?"

"I think we can pinpoint the location of the phone

number you have. Our preliminaries show that it belongs to an import-export company in Tehran. Probably an accommodation address or a shell corporation of the MIS. Is Bijay there with you?"

"We can get him," Garrett said. "Wait one." Garrett spun from his seat and dropped from the flight deck to the cargo area. Bijay was there with the other Gurkhas. They were cleaning their weapons and overhauling their field gear, preparing for battle. The two quickly returned to the flight deck.

"Okay, Dodds, we have Bijay here. Go ahead."

"Janet says this is for your ears only, so why don't you guys put on your headsets." There was a moment of scrambling while the three of them donned headsets. Each was fitted with a boom mic. Garrett and Steven were seated, while Bijay leaned over Garrett's shoulder.

"Everybody on?" Steven asked. Garrett and Bijay gave him a thumbs-up. "Go ahead, Dodds."

"Okay," LeMaster continued, "here's the deal. This number is a cell phone number that probably has a scrambler, but can take calls in the clear. If Bijay can call him and keep the connection open for a few minutes, we can track the exact location of that cell phone. We don't necessarily have to have the connection open, but we can be quicker and more precise if we can keep him talking. You okay with that, Bijay?"

"I understand. I believe I can do this, or at least I will do my best. After all, I have in fact been given a message of some importance from a dying man."

"How are you going to do this, Dodds?" Steven cut in. "And is this a real-time capability?"

"It will be real-time. A great deal of effort has gone into cell-phone locator technology. It's based worldwide on the twenty-four orbiting GPS satellites. The commercial application is called E-911, or enhanced-911, as a locator for

people in distress. But commercially this requires a special
chip and user permission due to privacy issues. The military and NSA research efforts have taken this to a level
where we can find any bloke with a cell phone if we know
roughly where to look. Cell coverage is the problem, so we
piggyback on the Iridium Global Star Network to extend
local coverage out into remote areas, in case this guy is not
in Karachi."

"We get the idea, Dodds," Steven interjected; Dodds
LeMaster could go on in great detail about technical issues. "Did you get help from our friends at Langley on
this?"

"I'm sure we would have, but there wasn't time,"
LeMaster replied. There was a hint of smugness in his
voice. "Since I know we'd have a lot of interagency bu-
reaucracy to deal with, I just hacked into the NSA system.
Janet says it'd be better to ask for forgiveness than for permission."

"Janet's right on this one. What do you want us to do?"

"I'm going to dial the number from here. The call will
go through a local exchange in Karachi. I am in the NSA
system right now. When the call goes through, we start the
tracking process. You ready, Bijay?"

"I am prepared. You may make the connection."

There was silence on the net save for the pulse tones of
LeMaster's dialing.

After three rings, a heavily accented voice came on the
line, speaking in English. "Yes."

"This number was given to me," Bijay began in halting
Arabic, "by a man in the desert. His name is, or was,
Khalib. Do you understand me?"

"What is it that you want?" the voice came back in fluent Arabic.

"One moment," Bijay replied, again searching for the
right words. "Ah, here I think. I was given a message for

you to hear. I am sorry. My speech is not good."

"Please go on," the voice said. There was the noise of machinery or an engine in the background. "I am listening."

"The man named Khalib is dead. He said I must communicate with you. Please, do you understand me?"

"I am listening," the voice intoned.

For the next three minutes, Bijay delivered Khalib's message in his halting accent, pausing often to ask if his listener understood his meaning. When he was finished, the other party broke the connection with no acknowledgment other than a terse *"Allahu Akbar."* There was an immediate outgoing call from the phone, but LeMaster was unable to monitor the call, as it was coded. He recorded it for future examination. He was, however, able to download an exact set of GPS coordinates. Dodds read them back to Steven and Garrett. There was a rustling of paper as they unfolded a map to reveal a wider coverage of central Afghanistan and southern Pakistan. Back on Diego Garcia, Dodds LeMaster and Janet Brisco were doing the same thing. Brisco was quicker than the others.

"Oh, my God; get those choppers turning!" she said over the net. "Get airborne. Get airborne now! Light combat load!"

Friday noon, January 3, central Afghanistan

"Okay, Colonel," Dave Wilson said into his Motorola transceiver. "All of my crew foremen have reported in. We're ready to move as soon as you give us the word. What now?"

"Now we wait, Dave," Carswell replied. "My patrols report no unusual activity. If I had to guess, I'd say it's a false alarm. We'll get the all-clear soon, and you can go back to work."

"And if we don't, then what? If it is the real thing, how are you going to get us out of here? We have more people than you have Humvees. You going to lead us across the desert on foot like Moses?"

"Very funny. The plan calls for a military escort for an evacuation. We have a supply convoy due in here in about an hour. If push comes to shove, they'll dump their load, and we'll truck you out of here. In the meantime, stand by to stand by."

"Thanks, Tom. Keep me posted. I'll be out roaming around the camp, checking on my people."

He turned to Trish, who was working a crossword puzzle at the table in the kitchen alcove.

"Want to take a walk around the camp?"

"Why not. Hey—what's a six-letter word that means 'To go forth from'?"

"How about 'exodus'?"

"Perfect!" She scribbled in the word, then rose from the table. "Let's go."

Early Friday afternoon, January 3, Herat

As the GSI Gulfstream was on its final approach into the Herat Airport, the two MH-60 Pavehawks lifted into the air and headed south. Each helo carried six passengers; Garrett, Janos, and four Gurkhas were on one bird, Bijay and five other Gurkhas on the other. After the wounded Gurkha was loaded onto the Gulfstream, both the MC-130 and the GSI jet left Herat. The Gulfstream headed for Diego Garcia and the Naval Medical Facility there. The 130 followed the Pavehawks south, but at a much higher altitude. With Steven Fagan aboard and the aircraft's ex-

tensive communications suite, they were well positioned
to serve as a command and control platform, and airborne relay.

Aboard the lead Pavehawk, Garrett Walker had his
hands full. His first problem was talking with Janet
Brisco. It would take a few minutes to extend their secure, dedicated satellite coverage along their new flight
path, but as soon as the 130 made altitude, Fagan was
able to establish a HF link to Diego Garcia. None of
them, especially Janet Brisco, wanted to rely on the HF
patch any longer than she had to. High-frequency trans-
missions were unreliable; satcom technology was cell-
phone technology—clear, secure, and if you could afford
a dedicated communications satellite channel, highly reliable. Garrett's second problem was Frederick Janos. After
they landed in Herat, Janos stated that he had fulfilled his
contract and that the job was over. Steven immediately
offered to double his fee to continue. He refused. Garrett
literally had to put him on the helicopter at gunpoint.

"Home Plate, you there?"

"Right here, First Base. Hear you five-by, how do you
hear me?"

"Lima Charlie. How are we going to go about this?"

They were transmitting in the clear, but time was
short, and there was nothing they could do about it. And
it was again Janet Brisco's game. She was the one who
would make the operational decisions. It would be up to
Garrett and Bijay for the tactical execution. It was a simple mission; find and recover a tactical nuclear weapon
before it was detonated by some lunatic.

"Okay, First Base. Our egg is somewhere on the resupply convoy, and the convoy is on the move. Thanks to
your lady-friend here we were able to bypass a lot of the
military chain of command, and I am in contact with the
officer in charge of the convoy escort detachment travel-

ing with the convoy. When we get secure comms, I will tell
him our problem is a conventional one, so I want everyone to play along with this. No sense making this any
more scary than it is. He has been given orders to cooper-
ate with us. Now, I estimate you will reach the convoy in
about thirty minutes. You getting all this, First Base?"

"I'm with you, Home Plate."

"Second Base, are you with us?"

"Yes, hello, I am here," said Bijay from the trail Pavehawk. "Can you hear me?"

"This is Home Plate, I hear you fine," Brisco quickly
cut in. "We now have our satcom channel in place. Shift to
the dedicated net and get back with me."

In less than a minute, each of them had checked in on
the secure satellite link. "All right, everyone," Brisco resumed. The relief was evident in her voice; secure communication was the lifeline of any special operation. "I
want you to listen closely. I will not have time to repeat
myself. We have to assume that this weapon is armed and
on a timed delay. We also have to assume that it can be
detonated on command. Therefore, we have to take the
weapon and whoever is with the weapon by surprise. This
means we may have only one shot at it. To do this, we
have to work together, and timing is everything. You guys
copy?"

"Steven, good copy," from the flight deck of the 130.

Both Garrett and Bijay rogered up from the two Pavehawks.

Early Friday morning, January 3,
the White House

It would be dawn on the Potomac in another hour. In the
White House Situation Room, the President was joined
by his Secretaries of State and Defense, his DCI, and his

National Security Adviser. They had immediately gathered here when they learned of the location of the second bomb. Rita Westinghouse was often excluded from what she called the Big Four, but she was with them today. The Situation Room was officially her turf. Westinghouse had a Ph.D. in systems analysis, as well as a masters in international affairs. She functioned more as a senior staffer, with little exposure to the public and the press. If she resented this nontraditional, behind-the-scenes role in the administration, she kept it to herself. In truth, she was content to bury herself in the inner workings and technical details of the NSA and leave the press conferences to others. At the direction of the President, she had kept a steady flow of selected information relating to the crisis coming to the Oval Office and the other three men present. She was included today because all the decisions had been made; now they would await the outcome together. No matter how this turned out, she would be a very busy lady for the next few weeks.

They sat around a large conference table, surrounded by military communications specialists and NSA staffers who worked at consoles on the periphery of the room. At William St. Claire's direction, the massive electronic intercept capability of several agencies had been brought to bear so those assembled could follow the course of events. Thanks to this electronic eavesdropping capability, now highly refined by the war on terrorism, they had tapped into Janet Brisco's control net. Perhaps the fate of the world did not hang in the balance, but the fate of his administration probably did. They would have been like a gathering of baseball fans in the 1930s listening to the World Series on the radio save for the large monitor at the end of the table. The picture was grainy, but it was in color. There was almost a three-second delay because of some dated transfer technologies, but the Global Hawk drone held focus on the lead vehicles in the convoy. It was like a long, dusty caterpillar crawling across the Afghan desert terrain known as the Dasht Margow. There were some enclosed vans for machinery and a refrigeration unit with food stores, but most of the convoy vehicles were lowboys with pipeline sections chained in place. Shepherding the convoy, like fighter escorts tending a formation of WWII bombers, were Humvees with mounted weapons. Most were open vehicles with goggled, helmeted figures looking not unlike Rommel's desert rats in North Africa. They had no idea that half a world away, their Commander in Chief and his closest advisers were watching their every move.

"How far are they from the TAP construction site?" James Powers asked no one in particular. The men were in shirtsleeves, and all but Armand Grummell had loosened their ties. Rita Westinghouse wore a tailored charcoal suit.

"About fifty-five miles," Barbata replied. "More to the point, some forty-five miles to where the bursting radius of that weapon will begin to take effect on those at the construction site. At the speed they're making, they will be at the site in an hour and a quarter."

"And there's no way to get those people out of there?"

"Not unless you want them to begin to trek across the desert on foot."

The group was quiet for a moment before the President spoke.

"So when do they reach the end of our response window?"

Again, Barbata answered. "Sir, we have about an hour to respond. Then we risk physical or radiological damage to the site."

As a contingency to avoid a possible nuclear event, and to protect those at Site South, the USS *Princeton* (CG-59) was stationed just over the horizon off the coast of Pakistan. Several of her Tomahawk land-attack cruise missiles were being fed a steady diet of updated coordinates of the moving convoy. If it became necessary, *Princeton* would launch three of those Tomahawks. The deadly missiles would overfly the length of the convoy and distribute hundreds of antipersonnel bomblets that would shred the unarmored vehicles, killing virtually everyone. The notion of killing some fifty contract drivers and close to eighty military personnel with friendly fire would have been unthinkable a few years ago, but 9/11 had changed all that. Surface-to-air missiles and armed fighter jets occasionally were put on alert around Washington, D.C., to shoot down airliners that might come under the control of terrorists. This contingency had the collective approval of the five seated around the table, but only one individual would make the decision to launch the Tomahawks. There was a special Delta Force strike element on the tarmac at Kandahar ready to respond, but it was decided to place no more lives at risk—at least no more lives that would have to be accounted for.

"Well, Armand," Bill St. Claire said with a forced jocularity, "I hope our little band of mercenaries can pull this off."

"So do I, Mr. President," Grummell replied as he burnished his spectacles. "So do I."

Friday Afternoon, January 3, central Afghanistan

Captain Grant Heber rode along in his command Humvee along the left flank of the convoy. This particular line of trucks was Convoy 127. It was open, desert hardpan, and the Hummer easily bounded over the flat, rolling terrain. When possible, he liked to drive on the flank; it gave him a better view of the convoy. Heber

took his job seriously, but he would much rather be
with an Army Ranger company chasing booger-eaters in
the mountains than playing nursemaid to this caravan.
The convoy road was well-worn, hard-packed gravel
that had been handling heavy trucks for just over six
months. The roadbed was firm but very dusty. Leading
his convoy was a five-ton N52A2 cargo truck with a reinforced suspension and twenty-five hundred pounds of
armor plating. Its duty was to serve as a vehicular mine
sweeper. They had not had a land mine incident in three
months, and the "armadillo," as the soldiers called it,
could protect the single driver against all antipersonnel
and most vehicle mines that the al Qaeda guerrillas
could muster. Still, they continued to try. The roadway
was clearly marked and fenced, but every three or four
weeks al Qaeda sappers tried to mine the road at night.
Motion sensors set up along the road would detect the
sappers. This led to an air burst from a five-hundred-
pound, air-dropped JDAM. The explosion did little to
the roadbed, but sent a lethal shock wave through anyone nearby. Heber himself had found two of the would-
be sappers alongside the road, stone dead but with little
evidence of physical trauma save for the dried blood
around their ears and mouth. It broke the monotony.
Convoy escort work, Heber admitted, was important
and relatively safe as duty in Afghanistan went, but it
was boring. Until today.

An hour ago he was boring holes in the desert, trying to
keep his mind off his next leave period. In ten days he
would be in Bangkok, soaking in a tub of cool water with
two Thai beauties catering to his every wish. Then a call
had come through from his battalion commander saying
that OPCON, or operational control, of his escort element
had been passed to a civilian agency, which Heber immediately took to be the CIA. The Colonel had given him

only a frequency that could be programmed into the sat-com radio on his Humvee. Moments later, a woman's voice came over his radio with unusual clarity. She identified herself only as "Control," and she was very businesslike.

"Listen carefully, Sheep Dog One-Two-Seven. We believe there is a bomb aboard one of your vehicles. We don't know which one. I have been tasked with finding and disarming it. Now, I'm going to give you some instruction, and I want them carried out to the letter, do you understand?"

"A bomb! How can you—"

"Break, One-Two-Seven, we don't have time for this. Again, I have some very simple and specific instructions for you. Lives are at risk, and that includes yours." The voice softened, but only a little. "Now, I'm going to need your trust and your help. If we work together on this, we can keep you and your men safe. But you have to work with me on this, okay?"

"Okay, Control, go ahead with your traffic." Then Janet Brisco told Captain Grant Heber exactly what she wanted him to do. For the next thirty minutes or so, he and his convoy rolled across the central Afghan plain as though nothing was amiss.

"Hey, Cap," his driver called over the engine noise of the Hummer, "you're sweating like a pig." His corporal at the wheel had a heavy New York accent. "You want I should switch on the AC?" Unlike the trucks in the convoy, the Humvee had no air conditioning.

"I want you to keep your fuckin' eyes on your drivin', and keep station on the middle of the convoy."

"Yes, sir," the driver replied with exaggerated formality. His captain was normally not so uptight.

After what seemed like an eternity, the radio speaker again came alive with a female voice. "Sheep Dog One-Two-Seven, this is Control, over."

Heber took up the handset to speak. "This is One-Two-Seven. Go ahead."

"This is Control. Are you ready to execute?"

"Sheep Dog One-Two-Seven, that's affirmative,"

"Okay, One-Two-Seven, standby, out."

Two minutes later Brisco was back on the radio to Heber. During the intervening time, she had updated Steven in the MC-130 circling overhead and the two Pavehawks just over the horizon.

"Sheep Dog One-Two-Seven, this is Control. Execute, execute, over."

"This is One-Two-Seven. Understand execute. One-Two-Seven, out."

Heber took up a Motorola transceiver. "In the sweeper, you there, Sweeney?"

Leading the resupply convoy, Corporal John Sweeney took his turn driving the heavily reinforced 6X6 armadillo. The duty was rotated among the convoy military escort with each man taking two hours of drive time in the armored lead vehicle. Corporal John Sweeney was from Little Rock, Arkansas. In spite of the elevated danger of driving the sweeper, John Sweeney actually looked forward to it. For two hours, he was the convoy leader. There was no dust, no following some vehicle in front of him, no bounding across the desert in a Humvee, just the unobstructed view of the broad Afghan plain from the high cab of the big five-ton truck.

"Yes, sir. Corporal Sweeney here."

"Okay, Sweeney," Heber said, "listen up. I want you to make like you're having a breakdown. Stop the truck, get out, climb up on the front bumper, and raise the hood."

"But, Captain, the truck's runnin' fine. Why would I want to do that?"

Heber sighed. Sweeney was a good trooper, but not the sharpest tool in the drawer. "Because you don't want to become Private Sweeney. Just do what I asked." Then Heber, with a flash of inspiration that illustrated why he had two bars on his collar and Sweeney had two chevrons on his sleeve, added, "It's a drill, Corporal—a test of convoy security." Every soldier understood drills.

"Yes, sir; I'm on it," Sweeney replied as he brought the big truck to a halt. "I'll get right under the hood and have a look-see."

Heber put down the Motorola and took up the radio handset for the convoy control circuit. "This is Sheep Dog One-Two-Seven to convoy. All vehicles halt. I repeat, all vehicles come to a complete stop. We have a breakdown with the sweeper. Stand by in convoy formation, and we will keep you advised when we can resume travel. Sheep Dog, out."

Heber directed his driver to head for the sweeper, then took up his satcom radio. "Control, this is Sheep Dog One-Two-Seven. Convoy is now halted, over."

"Thank you, One-Two-Seven. Stand by, and we'll let you know when you can resume travel. Control out." Janet Brisco shifted frequencies on her satcom set. "Steven, Garrett, Bijay; are you with me?" She breathed a sigh of relief as they all came up on the dedicated satcom frequency. There was no the time to repair a failed communications link.

Janet Brisco sat in her control station in the air-conditioned van in Diego Garcia. Her eyes flicked over the communications console like an experienced pilot sweeping his flight gauges. At a glance, she saw all was in order. Then she lit a cigarette and steadied down on the large flat-screen color display in front of her. She watched as the convoy stopped and a man driving the lead vehicle climbed from the cab and raised the hood of the large truck.

"You can come down a few thousand feet," she said to Dodds LeMaster, seated at the console next to her, "and move off a few miles; I want to see this from a lower angle." LeMaster deftly moved the Global Hawk drone away from the flank of the convoy and lost altitude. As he did, the cameras of the drone remain locked on the convoy. Judy Burks sat between and behind them, looking over their shoulders. Brisco adjusted the boom mic on her headset as she keyed the transmit button. Her concentration, Judy noted, was so intense it was scary. She reached forward without looking and clipped two toggle switches on her radio panel.

"All right, gentlemen, let's do this right and get that son of a bitch. I have convoy control on the net. You with us, One-Two-Seven?"

"Ah, yes, ma'am, Sheep Dog One-Two-Seven copies you five by, over."

"What's your name, son?"

"My name?"

"C'mon, we don't have all day; what's your first name?"

"Uh, it's Grant, ma'am."

"Okay, Grant, you're on the varsity team now. I want you to keep that convoy where it is for now. Pass the word along the line as you normally would when you experience a breakdown. Keep everything as normal as possible; just another glitch en route, okay?"

"Yes, ma'am."

Five miles in front of the convoy and a quarter mile off the road, the trail Pavehawk swooped in low and came to a hover near a dry wash. Bijay and five Gurkhas tumbled from the door, tucked and rolled, and made for cover as the helo banked away and headed north.

"This is Bijay; we're on the ground and standing by."

"Very well, I want silence on this net. Bijay, it's all yours, same drill as before. Ready?"

"I am ready," came the precise reply.

There was a rapid series of pulse tones as a speed dialer punched in the number. After the fifth ring there was an answer.

"Yes."

"Please, sir, I forgot a part of the message I was supposed to deliver. I must give you the rest of the message. Are you there, sir?"

"Do not call me again, ever."

"Please, sir, I must—" But the connection was broken.

Janet Brisco was right there. "Stand by, that may have been enough for a fix." She looked over to Dodds LeMaster, whose hands flew over the keyboard. His screen flickered once and came up with an overhead shot of the convoy. Then the computer took over and plotted the data. A grid superimposed itself on the convoy, and the machine gave a long chirp. A blinking cursor circled the fifth truck in the file, a lowboy semi trailer with three six-foot sections of pipe chained to the flatbed.

"We got him," Brisco said evenly, but her voice carried a trace of electricity. "Fifth vehicle in the file. That's truck number five, counting the one that's broken down."

"Understand truck five," Garrett replied.

"Truck number five in the convoy. We'll be waiting," said Bijay.

"Okay, Grant, this is Control. You still with us?"

"Yes, ma'am. What do you want me to do?"

"Your lead vehicle is fixed. Get that convoy moving, just as if you fixed a routine breakdown."

"Then what happens?" Heber asked. There was a measure of irritation in his voice. "What are you going to do to my convoy?"

"Just get it moving, Grant. Then take your station on

the left flank and keep that fifth truck well in front of you. I'll fill you in once you're on the move."

Heber acknowledged, but he was not happy. *First they tell me I got a bomb in one of my trucks, then some bitch named Control, who wants to call me by my first name, takes over my convoy and tells me to fake a breakdown. Now she tells me to saddle up and get moving. Christ, I wish I was back in a line Ranger company.*

"So what's th' word, Captain." Sweeney was sitting on the front fender of the sweeper truck, drinking from his canteen when Heber drove up. "Are we broke down, or are we fixed?"

"Get off your ass, Corporal. Get that hood down and get that thing moving."

"Yes, sir; right away, sir."

Corporal Sweeney dropped the hood of the truck, slipped back into his body armor, and climbed up into the driver's seat. The big turbo-diesel caught on the first try and belched a cloud of black smoke. A moment later, the armadillo was grinding along the convoy road and leading the supply procession north toward Site South.

The four gentlemen and one lady seated around a small conference table in the White House Situation Room listened to the voice traffic and watched the convoy stop on the Afghan plain, courtesy of the Global Hawk drone. Armand Grummell had been against this real-time following of events, more from considerations of deniability than of security. As Grummell patiently explained to the others, the problem would resolve itself favorably with the recovery of the second nuclear weapon, or there would be a nuclear incident. In the case of the former, nothing need be made public of the matter. In the case of the latter, the President would have to go before the

American people and tell them that it had finally happened; the nation had experienced a nuclear terrorist attack. His speech writer was already working on the verbiage, just in case. But only Rita Westinghouse agreed with Armand Grummell. That they were watching and listening to the drama unfold was due to plain old-fashioned curiosity.

"Hell," the President had fumed in the face of Grummell's objections, "if I'm going to have to deny something, I might as well know exactly what I'm going to disavow. Any way you cut it, it's my ass on the line."

So there was a viewing gallery for the events unfolding on the Afghan plain with Convoy 127. While the convoy was halted, William St. Claire turned to his DCI.

"Armand, how in the hell did they get that weapon on one of those trucks, anyway?"

"There are any number of ways. Details of the construction project are not my forte, but we had to come to some balance between security and economic pass-through to the host countries. There are Pakistanis and Afghans working on this as well as our American crews. We know that al Qaeda has some very deep roots in the fabric of the Pakistani and Afghan society. Evidently, someone managed to get that bomb mixed in with the supplies headed north. And we have to assume that this someone is with the bomb, escorting it en route. It's my understanding that we have long considered this a possibility; we just didn't think it would be a nuclear device."

"How about the guy with the bomb?" James Powers asked. "Could it be Mugniyah?"

"I seriously doubt it," Grummell replied. "This would be a job for one of his fanatical followers, but then we will soon see, will we not?" While the President had been talking with Grummell, he had missed the events that led to the convoy's resumed progress.

"What's this?" William St. Claire announced. He was on his feet, almost shouting. "The convoy is on the move again! What in the hell is going on?"

They all watched as the lead vehicle began to generate a trail of dust, and the other trucks followed in turn. Soon they were all again moving north along the convoy road toward Site South. The President whirled and pointed to one of the enlisted Air Force communications men.

"I want on that circuit. Make the connection." The tech sergeant simply stood gaping at his Commander in Chief. "Now, son; move!" The sergeant fled to his communications station.

"Ah, sir, I'm not so sure this is a good idea," said Tony Barbata.

"I quite agree," seconded Armand Grummell.

"It's to your console, Mr. President," the sergeant reported. He took orders only from the Commander in Chief.

St. Claire glared around the table. The anger and frustration on his face stifled any further attempt to dissuade him. With a measure of defiance he leaned forward and stabbed the button that activated his speaker phone.

"Control, this is POTUS; I say again, this POTUS. Why is that convoy again moving north?"

Everyone at the table knew what POTUS, or President of the United States, was thinking. If that convoy made good another ten miles, he would be forced to order the Tomahawk strike. In his mind, William St. Claire would rather have the terrorists set off their bomb than have to order those deaths himself. A nuclear event would consume everything. The submunitions from the Tomahawks would rake the convoy like a giant claw, and there would be no hiding from the grisly aftermath.

"Dammit, I want to know why—"

"Silence on the net!" came the strong voice of Janet

Brisco over the speaker. "Sir, I have no idea how you got on this circuit, but I must demand that you keep quiet. I have an operation to run and men at risk in the field. We have a shot at this, but you will have to stay off my circuit. I will tolerate no interference. Are we clear on that, sir?"

You could have heard a pin drop in the Situation Room. President St. Claire stared at the speaker phone for a long moment. Slowly, the rage drained from his face, replaced by resignation. He slumped back into his chair and dragged a hand across his mouth and chin, then turned back to the speaker phone.

"Very well. You do your job, and I'll do mine."

"Cheeky bloke, wouldn't you say?" observed Dodds LeMaster lightly. "I mean, who the hell does he think he is, anyway?"

Judy Burks recognized the President's voice and was incredulous, but said nothing, not wanting Janet Brisco's wrath turned her way. The three of them stared at the moving convoy. Dodds deftly held the Global Hawk drone in a lazy orbit to keep the convoy under surveillance. He also maintained an ongoing electronic surveillance of the area in case their target made or received any cell-phone calls.

"Dodds, I want a split-screen presentation. On one I want to see just the road and Bijay's location. On the other, give me the front of the convoy from the lead vehicle back to the target truck. Expand it if you can to include Grant Heber's command Hummer." Moments later, the large display in the comm van complied; half of the plasma screen showed the lead elements of the convoy and the other an uninhabited piece of desert. Brisco lit another cigarette with the butt of her old one.

"Bijay, Janet here. Can you see them?"

"This is Bijay. I see the dust plume, but can only make out the lead vehicle. It will be a few minutes until they are abreast of us. It is the fifth vehicle, correct."

"That is affirmative—truck number five in the column. Garrett, are you in position?"

"This is Garrett. We are coming around from the south now. Currently we are at fifteen hundred feet and will use the dust cloud from the convoy to mask our approach."

"Understood," Janet replied. "Are your people ready to go?"

"We'll be there, one way or another," Garrett promised. "Sergeant Major, give me a countdown as they approach your position."

"As you wish, Subadar," Bijay reported with a hint of humor in his voice. "The lead vehicle will be here in perhaps two minutes; the target vehicle thirty seconds after that. Good hunting, Subadar."

Garrett scrambled forward in the tight troop compartment of the MH-60 and wedged himself between the pilots. The trailing vehicle of the convoy was just under the nose of the helo. Garrett told the pilots what he wanted and when, and they both nodded. They were former special-operations pilots; they had done this many times before. Garrett returned to the others in the rear of the helo. The four Gurkhas crouched forward expectantly. Like Garrett, they were dressed for urban battle—tan Nomex coveralls, vests with ammunition pouches and grenades, and their M-4 rifles. Each had a 9mm Glock pistol strapped to his thigh, and all wore close-fitting body armor and Kevlar helmets. Garrett tapped three of the Gurkhas on the helmets.

"Do you have any questions?" They shook their heads.

"All right, get down fast and get into position as quickly as possible." All grinned with delight. The prospect of action clearly made them happy. No need, Garrett realized, for any words of encouragement or inspiration here. Then he turned to Janos, who sat apart with the fourth Gurkha. His name was Pun. He was humorless, for a Gurkha, and at a muscular six feet was the largest of the IFOR Gurkhas. Garrett put one hand on Pun's shoulder and the other on Janos's knee.

"Pun, after the helo lands, I want you to find me and bring this man with you. If he resists or refuses to come, I want you to shoot him."

"I understand, Subadar," Pun replied in a sober, matter-of-fact tone. "Do you want me to kill him?"

"Not with the first round. Shoot him here," he replied, tapping Janos's knee, "then drag him to me. If he is still making a fuss, put your second round here." Garrett stuck his finger in Janos's ear, causing him to wince and jerk away.

"You can't do that!" Janos cried.

"It will be as you say, Subadar," Pun replied evenly.

Garrett glanced down from the open helo door—not long now. They were a third of the way up from the rear of the convoy at three hundred feet. Due to the dust and the roar of the diesel engines, no one but Captain Grant Heber on the flank of the convoy knew they were there.

"Thirty seconds," Bijay reported.

Garrett keyed his transceiver and spoke into the boom mike coming down from his headset. "Understand, thirty seconds." Then to the others in the troop compartment, "Everyone ready?"

They all gave him a thumbs-up, all but Janos. Pun slung his M-4 and drew out his pistol. He pulled the slide, chambering a round, and put the weapon on safe, all in one fluid motion. Then he gave Janos a devilish grin.

• • •

Bijay and his five Gurkhas were in a skirmish line, lying
prone on the desert hardpan. They were four hundred
yards from the road, and with their tan coveralls and
chestnut-colored faces, all but invisible. They had moved to
a rise with a good view of the convoy. Fortunately, this area
had not yet been mined. Bijay watched the convoy through
a small pair of Zeiss binoculars. Beside him, Duhan lay
motionless, his cheek welded to the fiberglass stock of a
Winchester Magnum 300. The long barrel and thick,
pipelike suppressor was supported by a bipod. Camouflage
netting had been draped across shooter and rifle to destroy
their silhouette.

"On target?" Bijay said quietly in Gurkhali.

"On target," Duhan replied.

"Fire."

There was a sharp crack from the sonic boom as the
hundred-ninety-grain, boat-tailed match round raced
across the desert. The fifth truck in the column rolled to a
stop, its nose drooping from the flat front tire.

"Shot, over," said Bijay.

"Shot, out," Garrett replied, and the helo dropped suddenly.

The Pavehawk pilot, seeing the fifth truck in the file
skid to a stop, dove for it. Midway through its stoop, a
white cloud of steam erupted from the grill of the truck
as Duhan's second bullet tore through the truck's radiator. Neither the driver nor the man in the passenger seat
heard the shots. They felt the second one, but the metallic
thunk was quickly replaced by the overcast of steam that
filled the windshield. Instinctively, the Pakistani driver
turned off the engine and leaped from the cab. Only then
did he hear the beating rotor blades of the helicopter and
look up. The thick fast-ropes had already been thrown
from the helo, and the men were on them, racing earth-

ward like drops of oil sliding down a string. The first
Gurkha hit the ground, rolled once, and came up in a
shooting crouch barely twenty yards away. The driver
fumbled for a pistol in his belt. His effort earned him
three bullets, Mozambique style—two to the chest and
one to the head.

The man in the passenger seat sat confused, momentarily wondering what had happened to the truck. When
the driver killed the engine, he heard the beat of the helicopter and knew something was very wrong. He reached
into the side pocket of his jacket and withdrew a small
transmitter. There were two toggle switches on it, one
black and one red. He flipped the black one and was ex-
tending the small telescoping antenna from the housing
when he happened to glance out the window of the cab.
There he saw a tall man sighting over a small rifle. Then
he registered a vague *thunk* followed quickly by a burst of
white light, not unlike what had happened in the truck
cab a few moments before when the radiator exploded.
But the white light faded swiftly to darkness and the
darkness into eternity. He never felt the second bullet
that tore through his brain.

From the flank of the convoy, Captain Grant Heber
watched as events unfolded. It was over very quickly, but
he had been a Ranger long enough to know a superbly ex-
ecuted takedown when he saw one.

"Jesus, sir, did you see that?" his driver yelped. "That's
gotta be Delta Force!"

"Get over to that truck," Heber yelled back, "on the
double!"

When Heber and the Humvee arrived at the scene,
four small, efficient-looking soldiers were unchaining a
wooden crate with black lettering from the bed of the
lowboy. Then they took the heavy box by the four rope
carrying handles and shuffled it over to the helo that was

turning nearby. Heber looked from the dead man lying in the sand to the form with the shattered skull in the cab. Then he turned to the tall man in the black battle dress, obviously the only American in the attacking element.

"You did all this for a generator?" Heber said, knowing full well the single wooden box chained to the rear of the truck cab did not contain a generator, in spite of the inscription on the crate.

"Never know when you're going to need one out here," Garrett replied as he followed the Gurkhas to the helo. Heber almost had to run to keep up.

"You guys are Delta, right?"

"Something like that," Garrett replied. He held the small transmitter gingerly between thumb and forefinger, as if he was forced to handle a piece of excrement. The Gurkhas carefully slid the box into the troop compartment of the Pavehawk. Just outside the envelope of the rotors, Janos waited with Pun. Pun still held the pistol firmly in hand, leveled on him.

Heber motioned to Janos. "Is he one of the bad guys?"

"Naw," Garrett yelled over the whine of the turbine, "he's one of ours."

"Oh," Heber replied skeptically.

"You and me, Fred," Garrett said, turning to Jano, "we're going to take a little ride."

"And if I refuse?"

"Then I leave you here with him," Garrett said, motioning to Pun, "and he can handle it any way he likes." The burly Gurkha holstered his pistol and drew his *khukuri*. The gleaming blade flashed in the desert sun. Janos turned and boarded the waiting helo.

"I have men out there," Garrett said to Heber. "Keep your men in close to the convoy until they've left. And thanks. You did just fine."

"What'd I do?" Heber stammered.

"More than you know," Garrett replied, and followed Janos to the Pavehawk. The single crewman stood at the door of the helo, connected to the bird and his pilot by a communications cable. Garrett leaned close.

"This could be dangerous. Why don't you stay here with the others?" Garrett suggested.

"I go with my crew, sir. You ought to know that."

Garrett eyed him. Once a Specops guy, he mused, always a Specops guy. He leaped aboard and strapped himself in next to Janos. The crewman climbed in behind them as the Pavehawk began to crowd on power. It lifted gently, sandblasting those on the ground. As the helo banked toward the horizon, the four remaining Gurkhas, without a word, carefully made their way into the desert to join their waiting comrades. Moments later, the second Pavehawk came and collected Pun, Bijay, and the remaining Gurkhas. Heber watched them go, wondering what he was going to do with the broken-down truck and the two dead men, and just what he was going to tell his colonel in Karachi about all this.

Janet Brisco and Dodds LeMaster, like those in the Situation Room at the White House, held their breath as the bomb was loaded onto the Pavehawk and lifted away from the convoy. Only when they were at a safe distance did Brisco contact them, and then it was all business.

"Okay, Garrett, I've given the pilots a set of coordinates in the middle of nowhere." Thanks to the relay from the MC-130, Garrett received Brisco loud and clear on his personal transceiver. "You sure you want to do this? You could just dump it now and clear off."

"Good thought, but let's not leave any loose ends. We started this; let's finish it. How long until we get there?"

"I hold you about seven minutes out. Good luck."

The Pavehawk glided down to an isolated piece of wilderness and gently touched down. Garrett and the helo crewman hoisted the crate to the ground while Janos removed his backpack and a kit bag. Before the helo again lifted into the air, the crewman tossed Garrett a pint bottle of Jack Daniel's. Then Garrett and Janos watched the Pavehawk disappear over the horizon. The number of those at risk from terror had been reduced dramatically. It had gone from close to a thousand at Site South, to well over a hundred in the convoy, to the five souls aboard the Pavehawk. Now there were only two at risk. Acceptable levels from a strategic perspective, unless you were one of the two. Garrett and Janos looked at each other. There was not a breath of wind, nor a moving thing in sight. Garrett held his rifle in one hand and the bottle in the other.

"You know," Janos said, "you've been a real asshole during this whole ordeal. I ought to just set this thing off."

Garrett took the top off the bottle and tossed it away. Then he took a long pull. "Tell you what," he said. "You disarm that thing, and I'll save you a couple of swallows."

"A complete asshole," Janos replied as he began to remove tools and test equipment from his backpack. He handed Garrett a small crowbar. "Here, make yourself useful."

Soon the two of them began to carefully disassemble the crate around the bomb. Next, they removed the metal casing. The device itself was egg-shaped and surrounded by heavy wiring and metal conduit. It looked like a crude science-fair project. Janos carefully inspected the assembly, then began to probe the weapon with his metered equipment. The inspection lasted close to ten minutes. Garrett sat on a rock nearby, occasionally taking a pull at the bottle.

"You better hurry up," Garrett offered. "This bottle won't last much longer."

"Screw you, Yank," Janos intoned as he concentrated on his work.

Finally he removed a component from the assembly, cutting two wire leads in the process. Then, he sat back slowly and shook his head.

"Oh shit—oh dear," Janos said, eyes widening. "I blew it! The damn things going to blow in about thirty seconds, and there's not a blessed thing I can do about it." He leaned back from the weapon so Garrett could see an LED display on the device. It was counting down the seconds by tenths, like a basketball-game clock. He dropped his head in defeat. Then looking over to Garrett, "A drink, man, for God's sake."

Garrett numbly handed him the bottle. He tried to say something, but his mouth had gone dry. There was about four inches of whiskey remaining. Janos turned the bottle up and emptied it like he was draining a water cooler. The two of them then sat there staring at the display until it was a line of zeros. Suddenly there was a loud crash as Janos broke the empty bottle across the bomb casing. Garrett involuntarily flinched.

"Well, I'll be damned," Janos said with a knowing grin. "I guess the bloody thing was a dud. And after all that trouble we just went through."

"Janos," Garrett managed, "I don't know whether to kill you myself or give you over to that big Gurkha."

Janos reached into his backpack and pulled out a long, square bottle. He pulled the cork with his teeth and spit it into the sand. "Hang on there, mate," he said, offering the bottle to Garrett. "D'you think we might first have a drink and talk about it?"

In the comm van at Diego Garcia, they listened and watched. Dodds LeMaster followed the Pavehawk, surrendering altitude, which enabled the Global Hawk to keep up with the speeding helo. The lower orbit also gave them a great view of the drama and the two men. Per Steven's instruction, Garrett had left his radio in the open transmit mode. If the unthinkable happened, the voice and video would be needed to piece together events.

Judy Burks bit the hardest on the ruse of Janos. She was sure she was about to see the man she loved vaporized, given that vaporization could have been a visual event, as the electromagnetic pulse would have instantly fried the Global Hawk's electronics package. All she could do was stare at the monitor. Her hands were pressed to her face to keep from crying out, but she could not take her eyes from the screen. Her knees almost buckled when she saw Garrett accept the bottle from Janos and take a generous swig.

"Oh, my God!" she said in a barely audible voice. "I thought it was going to go off. I thought I was going to lose him!"

She slid down the side of the van's interior paneling, crouched on her heels, and began to weep softly.

Janet Brisco closed her eyes for ten seconds, then lit a cigarette. Her hand was shaking so much that she had to steady her lighter with both hands. Then she was right back into it.

"Boomer Lead, this is Home Plate. What is your state time?"

"This is Boomer Lead. I have about two and a half hours left, over?"

"Understood. Go back and retrieve our two friends and take them back north, over?"

"Boomer Lead, returning for two pax and then heading north, out."

Brisco shifted to another frequency. "You with me, Steven?"

"Right here, Janet." He too was all business, but there was a slight tremor in his voice that had not been there a few minutes ago. "After the pickup, tell Dodds to lock that drone into an orbit around the coordinates of that weapon. Then have him hand it back to the military controller. I'll let Langley know where it is and what it is. It's their worry now. Time to wrap this up and pretend that we were never there. We'll pick everyone up in Herat and get airborne as soon as we can."

"Understood," Brisco replied. "What can I do?"

"We'll be twelve hours getting back to Diego Garcia. We will need to stop in Karachi for fuel, but if you can get us a KC-135, that would save us a few hours and a fuel stop."

"I'll see what I can do. We'll have everything loaded and ready to go when you get here. I've already filed a flight plan for Singapore."

"Excellent. I'll check in when we're on the ground in Herat."

"Understood. Tell my boys I'm proud of them."

"Will do," Steven replied and signed off.

Dodds LeMaster handed off the Global Hawk drone to the controller in Qandahar, then pulled off his headset. He took a bottle from under his console, poured a generous dollop into a coffee cup, and handed it to Judy Burks. He then poured one for himself and handed the bottle to Brisco. She splashed some right into her cold coffee and raised her mug.

"To the lads," she offered.

"To the lads," Dodds and Judy echoed.

"And to your man," she said, touching Judy's mug, and they all drank again.

In the White House Situation Room, there was silence. Their audio feed ended abruptly after the woman directed the helo to recover the two men in the desert. They watched as the helo collected them, and then there was nothing but a slowly revolving, 360-degree presentation of the uncrated weapon and an empty wooden box. Finally President William St. Claire turned to one of the uniformed techs.

"Can you run that back, please—fast reverse?"

Immediately the monitor began to rapidly reverse the orbit. Helos flashed on and off the screen.

"Hold it right there. . . . No, back it up a bit . . . There. Now focus in on the hand of the guy nearest the crate . . . perfect. Just as I thought; they're drinking Bushmills." He turned to a waiting steward. "See if you can find a bottle of that, the older the better."

While they waited, a soldier came over and whispered something to Barbata. "Sir, an Air Force special weapons team has taken custody of the first weapon, and they are on their way by helicopter to retrieve the second. They should have it aboard within the hour."

St. Claire nodded. "So what do we do with them? Armand?"

"Perhaps we should hang onto them for a while and inspect them." For the last several minutes, Grummell had been steadily polishing his glasses. Now he put the glasses away, carefully folded his linen handkerchief, and replaced it in his front jacket pocket. Two corners peeked from the pocket like a pair of rabbit ears. "It would be good to assess the state of their technology, and," he added with a smile, "not unwise to let Musharraf and the Pakistanis stew about this for a few days. Then we can give them back."

The steward returned with a twenty-five-year-old bottle of Bushmills and five crystal tumblers. The President took the tray and poured out five neat shots.

"Gentlemen, madam, to those brave men and that one tough lady, whoever they are."

They drank in a companionable silence until it was broken by POTUS. "Now we can devote our time and energy to that bastard Saddam Hussein, you'll pardon the language, Rita."

"Of course, Mr. President," Westinghouse replied.

The MC-130 was not on the ground more than ten minutes and did not even shut down. They had enough fuel on board to cross Afghanistan, southern Pakistan, and get well out into the Indian Ocean before they needed a drink. Thanks to Janet Brisco and a grateful U.S. government, a KC-135 tanker would be waiting for them some three hundred miles west of Bombay. Once they reached cruise altitude, Garrett climbed up to the flight deck. There Steven extended him a warm welcome.

"Glad to have you back," he said as they shook hands. Steven eyed him critically. "You okay?" Garrett nodded. "I wasn't sure it was going to come together there for a while. And then that stunt with Janos." Steven's grin faded a bit. "You know, the White House hacked onto our audio and video link."

"How much did they see?"

"Everything, including the little drama with you and our South African friend. How is he, by the way?"

The plan had called for them to leave Janos in Herat and fly him commercially from there to Karachi and on to Rome. They wanted to be done with him as soon as possible. But between them, Garrett and Frederick Janos had killed a quart and a half of whiskey, with Janos getting the lion's share. When the Pavehawks landed in Herat, he could barely crawl. Steven decided to sober him up on the way to Diego Garcia and get him to the airport when they went back through Singapore.

"He's snoring like a wino on a park bench."

"Is he going to be a problem?" Steven asked. A covert operator was always looking ahead.

"No way. He saw what we do to people we consider a threat. Give him a bonus and tell him that all he has to do is keep his mouth shut. He does that, and he'll never see another Gurkha for the rest of his natural life. And speaking of Gurkhas, how's Padam?"

"They have him at the Naval Medical Facility on Diego Garcia. From what Janet says, they will have him ready to go, and we can take him with us."

"Guess that's it, then. All we have to do is get the lads home and the gear repositioned."

Steven hesitated a moment, then continued. "Well, the threat has been taken care of, but not the cause."

"Oh, really?" Garrett replied, his interest now fully aroused. If there were any lingering effects of the whiskey, they were suddenly gone.

"On the way up here, I checked my messages for any loose ends. There was a call from a banker in the Caymans who suddenly found it in his interest to commit a breach of bank confidentiality regulations. So we talked. There were several large transfers of money that involved one Imad Mugniyah. I was able to trace it to a corresponding bank in Bahrain, which led me to two other accounts; one was a payer, and the other was a payee. I think I know who and where."

"So what do we do?"

"I'm not sure, but whatever it is, it will be in-house. We'll not need to involve Langley on this one."

They were silent for several moments before Garrett spoke. "Is Janet still up on the net?"

Steven nodded and smiled. "She won't rest until all her boys have been safely returned to her bosom."

Garrett grinned and picked up the handset. "Home Plate, you still with us?"

"Right here, Garrett. How's the hangover?"

"Tolerable. You wouldn't have a federal agent handy, would you?"

"Right here, but don't clutter up my net for too long."

"Whatever you say, mother."

While Garrett soothed a very anxious Judy Burks, Steven Fagan put through a call to Joe Simpson. He was in San Francisco, speaking to a corporate gathering about the good works of the Joseph Simpson Jr. Foundation.

Epilogue

The morning after the recovery of the second bomb, David Wilson was walking through Site South. He was on his way to one of the huge diesel storage bladders they used to fuel the site construction vehicles. If they were to abandon the facility, he wanted them towed away from the camp in case one of the scavengers that never seemed to be too far away came into the camp after they had gone. Diesel oil was not that easy to burn, but the last thing he wanted to see was his camp torched with his own fuel. Using bulldozers, they had them hitched up and were just starting to drag them off when Colonel Carswell came roaring up in his Humvee. He was wearing battle dress, complete with flack jacket and helmet.

"What's up, Tom?" Wilson asked, turning away from the bladder drag.

"It's like I said," Carswell replied with a huge grin, "it was a false alarm. We're back to a Level Three alert, but my guess is that it too will be lifted in twenty-four hours."

Wilson smiled and shook his head. He led up a clenched fist to the lead dozer driver, then drew a finger across his throat to signal the bladders need not be moved. Then he spoke a few words into his Motorola transceiver. After getting a reply, he turned back to Carswell.

"What was the problem?"

Carswell shrugged. "Who knows? Might have something to do with that convoy that's still halted south of here. Maybe they intercepted a couple camels loaded with dynamite."

"Thanks, Tom. I better get with my foremen and get these crews back to work."

"Take care, Dave."

On the way back through the site, Dave Wilson stuck his head in to tell Trish that the alert status had been downgraded, but as he expected, she was already unpacking.

Exactly seven days after the recovery of the second nuclear weapon, Armand Grummell was seated quietly in his study at Langley, reading intelligence summaries and estimations. Most of his agency was paperless, and the reading was done on-line, on computer terminals. Computer management and distribution of intelligence were essential, and Grummell found the computer a useful tool, but only to screen his reading documents. So late each afternoon he scrolled through the series of reports, which represented a great deal of his agency's intelligence product—most of it now concerned with Iraq and weapons of mass destruction. He tagged those he wanted to revisit or spend some time with later. Then he hit a button, and a high-speed printer did the rest. He liked his reading formatted in Times New Roman font, size twelve print. Over the years he had come to know his analysts and production staff well. Some handled the English language effectively, and some didn't. Most presented the facts in a straightforward, antiseptic manner. Yet a few could, within the strict reporting format, craft the information so that it was actually fun to read. It was the difference between reading a piece by William Safire and one by Charles Krauthammer. Some writers just made it less of a chore.

Grummell worked through the stack of selected reports. Most he set aside; these would find their way to the shredder. Others, he scribbled a line or two across the top in red ink. These reports had raised a question for which he wanted clarification, or he found issue with the content. And there were those few, the ones that were both discerning and clever, to which he penned a compliment, or a simple "Well done, A. G." in blue ink. They would find their way back to the originator, by way of their superiors, to let them know the DCI personally approved of their work.

"Sir, Mrs. Johnstone is here to see you."

Grummell glanced at his watch; it was six-fifteen. She had no reason to be here this late, he mused. Grummell was from a generation that still found it curious that a woman could have the same passion for professional excellence as a man.

"Please ask her to come in." He was at the door to meet her when she came in. "Good afternoon, or I suppose I should say good evening, Elizabeth. Let me guess; this has to do with our old friend Imad Mugniyah." He seated her in one of the armchairs away from his desk and took a seat opposite her on the settee.

"Yes, sir, it does. You had asked me to find him and the second atomic weapon, but as we know, he was well ahead of us. The man that Mugniyah entrusted with the bomb was Youssef Amhaz. It seems he passed through Damascus on his way to Baghdad several weeks ago. From there we lost him, but it's certain he arrived in Karachi soon after Mugniyah. He was a low-level Hezbollah operative and a fanatic. He was chosen as the courier for the nuclear weapon—the ultimate suicide bomber. The driver of the truck was a Pakistani national with connections to al Qaeda.

"As for Mugniyah, he was in and out of Karachi before we knew it. We are quite certain that he is now back in

Lebanon, probably at a safe house in the Bakkah Valley. We've had some pretty intense satellite coverage of central Iran over the past few weeks. That big Mercedes was seen northwest of Kerman the day before the capture of the second bomb and on the outskirts of Tehran the day of the recovery. I think it's safe to conclude that the MIS got him out of Iran as quickly as possible. Then there's the matter of the bank transfers that Mr. Watson showed me. I don't know how he was able to come by that information, but it would seem that Mugniyah and Hezbollah are some fifty million dollars the richer for their part in this venture. I wonder what his benefactors think of paying him that much for a failed operation?"

"It's pocket change for them. It may cost the Royal Family some regional political capital, or serve as leverage in some of our future dealings with them, but who really knows? They are as arrogant as camels. Thank you for all your hard work during this crisis."

She smiled shyly. "It's my job. I just wish we could have caught Mugniyah. He is a bad one. Perhaps another time. I'll certainly continue to keep an eye on him."

"I know you will. Elizabeth, you've been putting in a lot of late evenings lately. You want to be careful about that, or you'll end up like me." They both smiled at this. Grummell hesitated, as if he were at a momentary loss for words, then plunged ahead, "There is this new Chinese restaurant over in Chevy Chase that I understand has some very decent Szechuan cuisine. I don't suppose you would care to join me for supper?"

Now it was she who was at a loss for words. "Why, sir, that would be delightful."

"Excellent. Give me about twenty minutes to wrap up here. Would it be convenient for you to meet me at the executive entrance at, say, seven-thirty?"

"Certainly. I'll see you there."

Grummell went back to his desk and took a few minutes to organize the stack of reports and his desk. Those with which he had finished were placed in his outbox; the others he set in a queue for tomorrow morning. There was a memo that he simply had to get out, but he made short work of it. He then pressed a button on his intercom.

"I'll be leaving in a few minutes. You can tell my driver that I'll not be needing him this evening. I'll drive myself."

"Very good, sir."

While he shrugged into his topcoat, he found himself smiling. And why not? he thought to himself. As he passed through the outer office, his secretary swore that she heard a familiar tune, skillfully whistled, but immediately dismissed the thought. Armand Grummell was not the kind of man who went about whistling, however accomplished he might be.

Special Agent Walter O'Hara walked quietly down the steep, winding lane. Close by his side was Chief Inspector Claude Dru. The lane emptied out onto a flat asphalt terrace that served a modest two-car garage. An iron gate, cradled in an ivy bower, led to a tier of flagstone steps and down to the main house. Several yards ahead of O'Hara and Dru, a file of dark figures slipped though the gate and fanned out around the door. O'Hara started to follow them, but Dru held him back.

"I am sorry, monsieur, but you know the rules. We wait here." There was a burst of static on the transceiver; Dru brought it to his mouth. "*Oui . . . Oui . . . Bon.*" Then to O'Hara, "The other units are in position. No one can leave the house. Now we shall see what we shall see, eh?" Then, suspecting what O'Hara was thinking, "You must understand that we are not inexperienced at this sort of thing."

"You mean like that takedown at the docks in Mar-
seilles last month," O'Hara said quietly, without taking his
eyes off the door. "Or the dragnet you threw around
Malaga to nab that mafioso who came in on his yacht." He
did not have to add that both were embarrassing failures.

Agent O'Hara was experiencing one of the most frus-
trating tours in his FBI career— liaison officer to the Gendarmerie Nationale. He couldn't carry a gun, and he
couldn't participate in an arrest, much less a forced entry
or a raid. The men making the assault, Les Unites d' Intervention, were not an incapable SWAT team, but neither
were they anything close to the FBI's Hostage Rescue
Team. Not a day went by that O'Hara didn't mutter the
line delivered by Gene Hackman, alias Popeye Doyle, in
French Connection II: "I'd rather be a lamppost in New
York than the president of France." From their position on
the landing just above the house, they heard the splinter-
ing crash when the door gave way as the assault element
made their entry. Moments later there was the sound of a
woman's scream, a shrill voice that was more of a yelp
than a scream, and then silence. After a short wait, Dru
was again on his radio.

"*Oui . . . Bon.*" Then to O'Hara, "We can go in now."

They quickly made their way into the home. There
were men now stationed both inside and out. The assault
leader motioned them to the bedroom. There, a terrified
woman lay in bed, clutching the bedclothes up around her
neck. Her eyes were wide with fear, and her long hair lay
scattered across the silk pillow. Dru sat on the edge of the
bed and began to question her in a consoling voice. After
a lengthy exchange, Dru turned to O'Hara.

"She says her companion left early this evening, saying
only that he would not be back until late." O'Hara understood the exchange completely, but since he spoke with
what his French counterpart considered an atrocious ac-

cent, Dru felt translation was necessary. "She says she doesn't understand why he is not back, nor does she know where he has gone."

She probably doesn't, thought O'Hara. "Claude, my friend, looks as if our man is gone, and that means he's gone for good. I doubt he will have told her anything of value, and we will find nothing here."

"Oh, I wouldn't be too sure of that. We will conduct a thorough search of the premises." Dru was now peering into the closet. There was a row of custom-tailored suits. "He seems to have left very quickly. Perhaps something will turn up."

On the hill well above his home, Pavel Zelinkow watched the drama unfold. Although he had always known this kind of thing could happen, he was still miffed with his informant at the Gendarmerie Nationale headquarters in Paris. She had given him only six hours' advance warning. Of course that left him plenty of time to attend to his personal security and to give the impression that he had left in haste. Zelinkow knew it would precipitate an immediate search for clues of his whereabouts.

All was quiet about the house, save for the two minivans that had just eased down the drive, showing only their parking lights. There were no obnoxious two-tone sirens or flashing blue lights, Zelinkow noted, which meant they had managed to keep the local constabulary out of it. There was a quarter moon up to provide soft lighting on the otherwise dark night. From the overlook, his home was a stunning structure, well placed in the gentle curve of the cliff. Before he took the property, he had studied it from every angle—even from this very spot. The builder had taken a great deal of care and effort to achieve a harmony between the construction and the sweep of the hillside. He had, Zelinkow reflected, been very happy there. He sighed with resignation and took out a small radio control unit, not unlike the one Garrett Walker had taken from Youssef Amhaz in western Afghanistan less than ten days before.

They will probably make the decision for me, Zelinkow thought, but we shall see. He visually showed a measure of relief when he saw them bring Dominique out. She was in one of his terry-cloth bathrobes. She held the lapels close around her throat with one hand while she tried to corral her flowing hair with the other. He was relieved on two accounts. One, he wanted her clear of the house, and two, he wanted to avoid casualties among the search teams. Without a moment's hesitation, he toggled the arming switch and pressed the button. A moment later, the first termite grenade in his office detonated, followed by a series of others in various parts of the house. Those inside could still escape serious injury, but only if they fled immediately. Zelinkow watched impassively as dark forms fled from every door. He rose and paused a moment for a last look at Dominique. He knew her well enough to know her state of mind; she would be confused and weeping softly. Yet she held her head high, trying to maintain her dignity. She knew nothing of his affairs, of course, but she was perceptive enough to know that their life together might end abruptly—if not perhaps this abruptly.

Zelinkow turned and walked to the waiting BMW sedan. He drove away, waiting until he was well away from the overlook before he clipped on the lights. The image of the burning home stayed with him for a time, as did the vision of Dominique, her classic features lit by the flames. He had cared for the home, and perhaps for the first time in a long time, he had grown fond of the woman.

Walter O'Hara sat in his Paris office the following morning, reviewing the events of the previous night. They were given precise and timely intelligence about a dangerous and important target. There was ample warning that the target may have connections within the French intelligence establishment, and would in all probability be very difficult to surprise. In short, they'd been given everything they needed.

"We had it all," O'Hara said aloud to no one in particular, "and the frogs still managed to fuck it up." For several minutes, he sat staring at the green STU-3 secure phone on his desk. He desperately tried to think of a way to put the call off, but there was no way around it; time to face the music. He was again thinking about Gene Hackman, aka Popeye Doyle, when he picked up the phone and dialed.

"Yes . . . Hello, this is Walter O'Hara in Paris, FBI liaison officer. I need to speak with Special Agent Judy Burks."

In quick succession, four forms dropped from the sky, tucked, and rolled. Instinctively each man began to gather in the shrouds from his parachute. The aircraft, a Pilatus Porter, identical to those under contract to Aramco, was already out of earshot. Each man quickly secured his parachute, cramming it into a dun-colored nylon stuff bag. They then camouflaged the bags with rocks and brush and moved from the area in a single file. The bags undoubtedly would be found later. If it was by scavengers, nothing would be heard from them again. If they came into the possession of the authorities, the equipment would be identified as Czech, the kind used by many elite European special-operations forces. In either case, there would be no attribution to IFOR. The four men were lightly armed and carried only small field packs. They moved easily across the dark, arid landscape at an easy trot. After fifteen minutes and two miles of travel, the leader signaled a halt. He dropped to one knee as the other three went to security positions in a loose perimeter around him. The leader consulted a small GPS for a moment, then adjusted the boom mic on his headset.

"I am at point alpha and all is in order, over." The leader's voice was calm and his diction incredibly precise.

"Roger, we copy point alpha. How do you hear us?"

"I hear you perfectly. Request permission to proceed."

"Wait one," Janet Brisco said. GSI had rented time on one of the commercial low-orbital satellites, and they were due for a close overhead pass within the next few minutes. The IR scan was quick and of low resolution, but that was not their primary consideration. Had there been any kind of alert by the Saudi air defense command, by the local police or the private security at the villa, the sensors on the low orbiter would have detected a heightened level of communications traffic. There was none.

"You're clean. Go ahead, but remember, slow and deliberate." This, she realized, was like telling a bird dog to follow his nose.

Another fifteen minutes took them to the perimeter of the villa. They came out of the desert near the rear gate to the compound and well away from normal approaches to the compound. There was a single sentry patrolling the back wall. He was smoking a cigarette and carried an AK-47 assault rifle slung loosely over his shoulder. His head was capped by a set of earphones, and his head bobbed to the beat of some Western rap tune. The leader merely nodded to one of his men, who then moved silently in the direction of the preoccupied sentry. It was like stealing from a blind beggar. The sentry caught a flash of something as the moonlight glanced from steel. The *khukuri* hissed as it made a tight arc, slicing cleanly through the desert night air and the man's neck. The sentry's head hit the ground a fraction of a second before his torso, connected only by the single black thread of the Sony CD Walkman. Moments later, all four were over the wall.

They made their way across the compound, expertly dodging all the surveillance cameras. Periodically, the last man in the file paused to set out mini video cams, then noiselessly hurried after the others. The leader took them at a fast walk, moving silently on Nike urban trekkers. They came to an ornate, eight-sided building away from the others in the compound. The main entrance was served by a columned portico. They set up for a forced entry, SWAT-style, and put out the final mini-cam.

"Ready to move," said the leader quietly in his boom mic. "Give me a status."

Janet Brisco's hands flew over the controls on her console. A lighted cigarette dangled from the side of her mouth. This time the GSI comm vans were parked inside a liquor-distribution warehouse. Although the consumption of alcohol was against holy law and a banned substance in most Arab countries, Bahrain was not one of them. A causeway connected Bahrain to the kingdom of Saudi Arabia, and a steady flow of Saudis made use of this connection to indulge in the Western pleasures forbidden them by the Koran and outlawed in their own country. Therefore, it was a very large warehouse. The two vans parked in the rear of the building largely went unnoticed, as did the small array of satellite antennas on the roof of the warehouse.

"Okay, let's see what is going on," Brisco replied, the cigarette bobbing as she spoke. One by one she flicked through the mini-cams. Each one sent a continuous feed to the dedicated satellite link serving the vans and Brisco's console; she had only to shift to one to the next. "Nothing on the perimeter, and no one has come to check the sentry." *Click*—"No one in the courtyard." *Click*—"The approaches to the main house are clear." *Click*—"And there is no one in sight along the porticos leading to the other outbuildings." The final cam was directed at the door. Bijay and Pun were on one side; two other Gurkhas were positioned on the other. "Okay, Bijay, you're clear to move. Good luck."

"Understood, clear. We are moving."

In the van, they watched as one of the Gurkhas quickly and quietly made short work of the deadbolt on the large wooden door. Then the file slipped through the entrance, closing the door behind them. No one spoke for close to thirty seconds, then Steven Fagan broke the tension.

"Well, how does it feel to be on this side of the special-operations equation?"

Garrett pulled a hand across his face. He was actually sweating in the air-conditioned van. "It's a hell of a lot harder being here than being there, I can tell you that."

"Maybe we'll get you back into the game next time."

"I can't wait," Garrett replied, unable to take his eyes from Brisco's screen.

Steven had been surprised when Garrett readily agreed that Bijay should lead the operation. While he knew Garrett desperately wanted to be a part of this, both of them knew that any combination of Gurkhas under Bijay's leadership could do the job. And Garrett represented potential attribution if they were caught. Yet it was more than that. Both Steven and Garrett knew it was necessary for the Gurkhas to go it alone with Bijay leading. Then they could begin to move Gurkhas like Pun and Duhan into leadership roles for future operations.

Inside, the four men moved unchallenged into the central chamber. Huge woven rugs littered the stone floor. Beyond a large sunken tub was an enormous circular bed. Bijay carefully pulled aside the silk sheers that hung loosely from the canopy frame. There were three forms in the bed. Bijay nodded, and the Gurkha behind him shot the two forms on either side of the large one in the middle. The capacitors discharged a massive burst of electricity into the two women; they did not awake, but the tensor units instantly turned their dreams into violent nightmares. They stirred uneasily. The man between them sat up, but was immediately pinned to the mattress with Pun's knees on his shoulders and his hand clamped over his mouth. Bijay watched while the two other Gurkhas held ethered gauze squares to the faces of the two young women; the nightmares went back to dreams. Pun too had his work to do. Before they left, Bijay held a mini-cam to the grisly scene.

"Is this acceptable for our purposes?"

In the van, Janet, Steven, and Garrett stared at the screen. They might have sat in stunned silence for some time had not Dodds LeMaster, seated at the console next to Janet, retched violently and bolted from the van through the rear door. Steven was the first to find his voice.

"That will do fine, Bijay." Then to Janet, "Get them out of there."

The four men withdrew much as they had come. A mini-cam alerted them to one of the few sentries who was walking his post with some semblance of duty, and they were able to avoid him. They slipped back over the wall, dragging the decapitated sentry several hundred yards into the desert. The four raiders cached their weapons in a dry wash, except for their sidearms, and made their way to one of the secondary roads. They were now dressed in shabby trousers, sandals, and an odd assortment of long-sleeved shirts, much like any number of stateless Asians who worked at menial tasks in Saudi Arabia. A small minivan drove slowly down a secondary road just outside of Al Kharj. It stopped as one of the Gurkhas stepped out to hail it. The others materialized from the desert and quickly piled in. Two hours later they were in Riyadh.

"Okay, Dodds," Janet Brisco called out from the back of the van, "get your butt back in here and do your job." A still-shaken Dodds LeMaster returned to his station and went to work.

Crown Prince Abdullah rose early at his palatial residence in Riyadh. His duties included making himself aware of domestic and international events. Like half the world, he relied on CNN to do much of the work for him. Five minutes into the news, the smiling, angelic face of Paula Zahn was abruptly replaced by something entirely different. A burst of static was followed by the scene in Amir Sahabi's harem chamber, barely an hour old. The two women dozed on either side of the Iranian, their ample breasts spilling over their ripe young nudity. They stirred fitfully during the thirty-second clip. Sahabi's head had been positioned on top of his crimson-streaked torso, his baleful, sightless eyes staring at the camera. Fifteen minutes later, a frantic call reached a shaken Abdul Majid from the office of the Crown Prince. He had only to turn on his own TV to view the same macabre scene.

Garrett Walker found Steven Fagan seated on a folding chair just outside the van. He pulled up a chair, and they sat in companionable silence for several minutes.

"I just got a call from Joe Simpson," Steven said at length. "He wanted me to be sure everyone, especially you and Bijay, understands what a great service you rendered to the nation."

"Speaking of Bijay," Garrett replied, "he and the others are on their way out through Qatar."

Steven simply nodded. The extraction of the team had gone as he had planned it.

"You know," Garrett continued with a grin, "it could just be that you've seen too many *Godfather* movies."

"Possibly," Steven replied. He tried to smile, but he was very weary—they all were. "But, y'know, Garrett, they watch our movies too; Hollywood is a part of their culture, and sometimes they lack the perspective to separate facts from American cultural fiction." He paused for several moments, and Garrett did not intrude. "This was not a nice thing that we just did, but it was necessary. It was a message we needed to send, and one they needed to hear. Word will get out. Now the terrorist cells and the governments that support terrorism know there is a new force out there, one that will act in the interest of the United States, but that plays by a whole different set of rules."

"Think it will make a difference?"

Steven took a while to answer. "Perhaps—maybe in the long run. Perhaps not. Either way, I think it unlikely that we will be unemployed anytime soon."

Visit
❖ Pocket Books ❖
online at

---

www.SimonSays.com

Keep up on the latest new
releases from your favorite
authors, as well as author
appearances, news, chats,
special offers and more.

SIMON & SCHUSTER
A VIACOM COMPANY
www.SimonSays.com

Pocket
Books